About the Authors

Susan Stephens is passionate about writing books set in fabulous locations where an outstanding man comes to grips with a cool, feisty woman. Susan's hobbies include travel, reading, theatre, long walks, playing the piano, and she loves hearing from readers at her website. www.susanstephens.com

Annie West has devoted her life to an intensive study of charismatic heroes who cause the best kind of trouble in the lives of their heroines. As a side-line, she researches locations for romance, from vibrant cities to desert encampments and fairytale castles. Annie lives in eastern Australia with her hero husband, between sandy beaches and gorgeous wine country. She finds writing the perfect excuse to postpone housework. To contact her or join her newsletter, visit www.annie-west.com

Anne Mather always wanted to write. For years she wrote only for her own pleasure, and it wasn't until her husband suggested that she ought to send one of her stories to a publisher that they put several publishers' names into a hat and pulled one out. Th__ __ as they say in history _____ ____ aggered by the result _____ @msn.com nd she w_____ er readers.

/494

000003090981

Latin Lovers

Latin Lovers:
Dusk 'til Dawn

SUSAN STEPHENS

ANNIE WEST

ANNE MATHER

MILLS & BOON

1st Floor, Watermarque Building,
Ringsend Road, Dublin 4, Ireland

LATIN LOVERS: DUSK 'TIL DAWN © 2021 Harlequin Books S.A.

The Untamed Argentinian © 2011 Susan Stephens
Damaso Claims His Heir © 2014 Annie West
Alejandro's Revenge © 2003 Anne Mather

ISBN: 978-0-263-30026-0

MIX
Paper from
responsible sources
FSC www.fsc.org   **FSC™ C007454**

This book is produced from independently certified FSC™ paper to ensure responsible forest management.

For more information visit: www.harpercollins.co.uk/green

Printed and bound in Spain
by CPI, Barcelona

THE UNTAMED ARGENTINIAN

SUSAN STEPHENS

CHAPTER ONE

'Do you mind if I join you?'

A shiver of recognition ran down Bella's back as the man with the husky Latin American voice lifted the latch on the stable door and walked in. There was only one man who could breeze through security in Her Majesty's backyard: the Guards' Polo Club in Windsor. Nero Caracas, known as the Assassin in polo circles, played off ten, the highest ranking a polo player could achieve, and enjoyed privileges around the world others could only dream of. Impossibly good-looking, Bella had seen Nero commanding the field of play, and had lusted after him like every other hot-blooded woman, but nothing could have prepared her to be this close to so much man.

'So this is Misty,' he said, running an experienced palm down the pony's shoulder. 'She looks smaller close up—'

'Appearances can be deceptive.' Racing to the defence of her favourite pony, Bella forced her hands to go on oiling the mare's dainty hooves. She'd lived close to animals for so long she was as acutely tuned in to danger as they were and, though the mare seemed calm, Bella was on red alert.

'The match starts soon—'

And? Bella thought, still polishing. As trainer and one of the coaches of the British team, she knew only too well when the match started. Surely it was Nero, as captain of the opposing team, who should be elsewhere?

Nero's reputation preceded him. He had obviously thought he could drop in and his smallest wish would be granted with one eye on the timetable for a match in which he would captain the Argentinian team. No such luck. The Assassin could yield to the Ice Maiden on this occasion. And he did, but with a warning glint in his eye. 'I need to speak to you about Misty,' he said, running another appreciative glance over her pony.

'This isn't the time,' Bella said coolly, realising only when their stares clashed that she was running the same type of assessing look over Nero—experience had nothing to do with it. Her points of reference were in her head. And all the better for staying there, she thought, having taken in Nero's dark tan, close-fitting white breeches, plain dark polo shirt, wayward curls catching on his ferocious black stubble, not to mention the leather boots hugging his hard-muscled calves. It was safer, certainly.

'As you wish,' he said.

When he dipped his head, one professional acknowledging another, she saw the steel of challenge in his eyes. Nero Caracas was hardly the most sensible enemy for a woman in Bella's precarious financial position to make. The recession had taken a deep bite out of her resources and the polo world was too small, too incestuous to take chances. You failed in the eyes of one, you failed in the eyes of everyone. But she wouldn't fail, Bella told herself firmly, straightening up to confront this god of the game. 'Is that everything?'

Nero's lips pressed down. 'No,' he said with a shake

of his head. 'I think Misty would benefit from being ridden by a man who really appreciates her—'

'I can assure you that the captain of the English team appreciates Misty—'

'But does he ride her in a way that brings Misty pleasure?'

Did Nero Caracas have to make everything sound like an invitation to bed?

She glanced at her watch.

'Do I make you nervous, Bella?'

She laughed. 'Certainly not—I'm merely concerned that you're leaving yourself dangerously short of time.'

'My timing is split second,' Nero assured her.

Was that humour in his eyes? As the rugged Argentinian caressed Misty's neck, Bella lost herself for a moment. All muscles and tough, virile appeal, Nero Caracas was quite a man. Another woman, another time—who knew what might come of this meeting? Bella thought wryly, dragging herself round.

'En garde,' Nero murmured when she came to stand between him and the dapple grey polo pony. 'I would like you on my side, Isabella, not working against me for the competition.'

Bella gave him an ironic look. 'I'm very happy where I am, thank you.'

'Maybe I can change your mind—'

'I wish you joy of that—'

'If that's a gauntlet, I should warn you, Bella, I always pick them up.'

Too much man—too close—too desperately disturbing...

Irritated by the fact that her highly strung mare had remained calm when Nero had entered the stable, Bella demanded sharply, 'Anything else?'

Sensation overload, she registered dizzily as Nero's long dark stare made her heart go crazy. Nero Caracas was ridiculously attractive and had more charisma than was good for any man. No woman wanted to be reduced to a primal mating state by an unreconstructed male. A woman wanted control—something Bella possessed in vast amounts…usually.

Nero raised his hands in mock surrender. 'Don't worry, I'm going. But I'll be back to see you, Misty,' he crooned to the unusually compliant mare.

Bella's eyes flashed fire. 'When I'm not here, Misty is protected by the most stringent security measures.'

'Which I'll be sure to bear in mind—' Nero's Latin shrug could easily be translated as *So what?*

No one would keep him out. Nero Caracas could do anything he wanted, buy anything he wanted. Chatter around the yard suggested the famous Argentinian wanted to buy Misty, the polo pony Bella had foolishly allowed herself to love.

'You've done well with Misty, Bella,' Nero observed as he paused by the stable door. 'She's in prime condition—'

'Because she's happy with me—'

Nero's head dipped in acknowledgement of this, but the sardonic smile on his lips suggested he had more to offer any horse than she did.

She was at risk of losing Misty. The thought struck Bella like a bombshell. There was always pressure—honour in the game that demanded the best players were given the best polo ponies to ride. Misty was the best, and only a fool would stand in the way of a rider like Nero Caracas and expect to keep the career she loved intact.

'Until the next time, Bella—'

I wouldn't count on it, Bella thought, tightening her lips. There would be no *next time.* Misty was all she had left of her late father's yard—her late father's honour. While Misty was on the field people still talked of Jack Wheeler as the best of trainers, and forgot for that moment that Bella's father had been a gambler who had lost everything he had ever worked for. 'Misty only runs for those she trusts.'

'Like any woman.' Nero's smile deepened, carving an attractive crease in the side of his face. Coming back to the pony, he ran an experienced hand down Misty's near foreleg. 'Good legs,' he commented as he straightened up.

And she felt hers tingling too. The look Nero gave her left Bella in no doubt that everything in the stable had been assessed. She was way out of her depth here. If only Nero would go and everything could return to normal. 'Enjoy the match,' she said numbly, conscious of the power he wielded in the game.

'You too, Bella—' There was both humour and challenge in his voice.

'Misty will outrun your Criolla ponies from the Pampas—'

'We'll see.' Nero shot her an amused glance. 'My Criollo are descendants of the Spanish war horses. Their power is second to none. Their loyalty? Unquestioned. Stamina?' His lips pressed down in the most attractive way. 'Unrivalled, Bella. And it goes without saying that combat is in their genes.'

And Nero's, Bella thought. She'd watched him play, and had marvelled at his speed and agility, his hand-to-eye coordination, uncanny intuition, and the eager way Nero's ponies responded to him. She had never thought she would feel those subtle powers working on her. 'May the best man win,' she said, tilting her chin at a defiant angle as she rested a protective hand on Misty's neck.

'I have no doubt that he will,' the undisputed king of the game informed her.

She had always felt safe in the stables, with the scent of clean hay in her nostrils and the warmth of an animal she could trust close by, but that safety had just been challenged by a man whose voice was like a smoky cellar, deep and evocative, though ultimately cold. Whatever game it was, she must never forget that Nero Caracas always played to win. 'Win or lose today, Misty is not for sale—'

'I've completed my examination, and I like what I see,' Nero remarked as if she hadn't spoken. 'Of course, Misty would need to pass the vet's exam,' he went on thoughtfully, 'but if she fulfils her promise today, as I'm sure she will, I'd like to make you an offer, Bella. Name your price.'

'There is no price, Señor Caracas.' She wasn't going to roll over just because Nero Caracas said she must. 'I don't need your money.'

Nero angled his head. He didn't need to say anything to echo the thoughts of everyone else in the polo world, all of whom knew that couldn't be true. 'You might not need my money, *chica*,' he said with a faint mocking edge to his voice, 'but you must need something. Everybody does…'

'Is that a threat?' Was she to lose everything she had worked for? A flash of panic speared through her as the dark master of the game stared her down. Why should Nero answer when he was the centre of the polo universe, around which everything else revolved? He had more money, more skill on the field and a better eye for the horse than any man alive. Why was she challenging him when Nero Caracas could dash her career against the wall with a flick of his wrist?

'Relax,' he murmured. 'You work too hard and worry too much, Bella. Polo?' The massive shoulders eased in a shrug. 'It's only a game.'

Only a game?

'I look forward to seeing Misty play.' The dark eyes stared deeper into her soul than they had any right to and then he was gone.

Bella let out a shuddering breath and slumped back against the cold stone wall. How could she fight him? But fight him she would if Nero pushed her, Bella determined as one of her grooms came in and, after a few covert sideways glances, asked if Bella was all right.

'I'm fine… Fine,' Bella confirmed, wishing she was back at home with her dogs and horses, where life was uncomplicated, and where the children she encouraged to visit her stable yard learned how to care for animals in a blissfully down-to-earth setting. Mess with Nero and she would lose all that.

'Shall I take Misty to the pony lines?'

The girl glanced towards the stable door as she spoke, and Bella guessed she must have passed the master of the game on his way out. Nero threw off an aura of power and danger, which had made the young girl anxious. 'Yes, take her,' she confirmed, 'but don't let her out of your sight for a moment.'

'I won't,' the girl promised. 'Come on, Misty,' she coaxed, taking hold of the reins.

'Actually, I've changed my mind—I'll come with you.' She had intended to check the other ponies first, but she could do that at the pony lines. Nero Caracas turning up unannounced had really shaken her. He had reminded her that her life was a house of cards that could collapse at any time and that Nero Caracas never paid anyone a visit without a purpose in mind.

She would just have to fight his fire with her ice, Bella concluded, shutting the stable door behind them. She had done it before and come through in one piece. There was still talk about how her father's gambling had destroyed his career, which was one reason she still had the Ice Maiden tag. Life had taught her to keep rigid control over her feelings at all times. And Misty was more than just a pony; the small mare was a symbol of Bella's determination to rebuild the family name. She had promised her father before he died that she would always keep Misty safe. So could she fight off this bid from Nero Caracas?

She had to. Nero might be every woman's dream with his blacksmith's shoulders, wicked eyes and piratical stubble, but she had a job to do.

'Good luck, Bella,' the stable hands chorused as she crossed the yard.

Lifting her hand in recognition of their support, she hurried on, afraid to let Misty out of her sight now.

'The Argentine team is looking good,' one of the grooms observed, keeping pace with her for a few steps. 'Especially Nero Caracas—he's been living up to his nickname in the last few matches. The Assassin has cut a swathe through the competition—'

'Great. Thank you.' She didn't need reminding that Nero inhabited a brutal world. He might feel at home here, and play the role of gentleman in the prince's backyard, but Nero lived in Argentina, where he bred and trained his ponies on an *estancia* the size of a country on the vast untamed reaches of the pampas.

The pampas.

This conjured up such fabulous images—terrifyingly wild and impossibly dangerous.

And the sooner he went back there, the sooner she could relax, Bella told herself firmly. They had reached the pony lines where the horses were tethered to wait their turn to enter the match. 'I'll never let you go,' she whispered, throwing her arms around Misty's firm grey neck. 'And I'd certainly never sell you on to some black-hearted savage like Nero Caracas. Why, I'd sooner—'

The images that conjured up had to stop there. Burying her face against Misty's warm hide, Bella tried and failed to blot out the image of her moaning with pleasure in Nero's arms. Daydreams were one thing, but she'd be sure to lock the stable door in future.

He never listened to gossip. He preferred to make up his own mind about people, places, animals, things—

And Isabella Wheeler.

The Ice Maiden's eyes had been wary and hostile to begin with, but not by the time he had left her. Why was Bella's luscious, long red hair cruelly contained beneath a net? It was preternaturally neat, but he had detected a wild streak beneath that icy veneer. He had seen enough ponies standing meekly in the corral, only to kick the daylights out of a groom if they weren't approached with respect. Control ruled Bella. She had earned the highest respect in equine circles, but still managed to remain an enigma, without a shred of gossip concerning her private life. How could she not present him with a challenge he found impossible to resist?

Mounting up, he gathered his reins and called his team around him for the pep talk. He was unusually wired and the men knew it. They stared at him warily whilst keeping a tight rein on their own restless mounts.

'No mercy,' he warned, 'but don't risk the horses. And take care of the grey the English captain will be riding. Depending on how the grey does today, I might want to buy her—'

Bella wouldn't sell her horse to him?

His determination to change that mounted as he remembered Bella would barely speak to him. The thought of unbuttoning that tightly laced exterior and seeing her eyes beg for pleasure instead of challenging him was all the encouragement he needed. He wanted her to relax for him. He wanted to discover who Bella Wheeler really was—

The light of challenge was so fierce in his eyes that his team, mistaking it for the fire of battle, wheeled away.

Bella would be different. Not easy, Nero thought as he took his helmet off to acknowledge the roar of the crowd when he galloped onto the field. Bella would not yield to him as easily as her pretty mare had. There was something else behind that composed stare. Fear. He wondered at it. She feared the loss of her pony—that he could understand, but there was something more. And there was another question: why did such a successful and attractive woman live the life of a celibate in what was a notoriously libidinous society?

Because Bella was different. She was an independent woman, and courageous. She had coped well with her father's disgrace, supporting Jack Wheeler to the bitter end and salvaging what she could of the business. But where a private life was concerned she seemed to have none, and planned to keep it that way, or why else would she dress so severely?

Bella was all business and no fun, Nero concluded, as if to show the slightest warmth or humour might put her at risk. Yet beneath that Ice Maiden façade he'd heard she was much loved by the children she invited to her stables. She could be useful to him. With that thought in mind, he replaced his helmet and lowered his face guard. Training his restless gaze on the stands he searched for Bella as he cantered up to start the match.

CHAPTER TWO

BELLA hated him. Nero Caracas had almost single-handedly annihilated the home team. Never mind that his three team-mates had played well, she held Nero directly responsible for trouncing the team whose ponies she had trained. She had one bittersweet moment when the prince, who was awarding the prizes that day, had named Misty pony of the match, but even that triumph was quickly smashed by the quick look Nero shot her—the look that said, *I'm having her. She's mine.* The look that had prompted Bella to flare back silently, *Over my dead body.*

Over your body, certainly, had been Nero's outrageously confident response, which he had laced with a wolfish grin. And now she was being forced into his company in the evening too. The prince had invited all the players and their trainers to dinner at the castle. It was not the type of invitation Bella could easily refuse. And why should she? The opportunity to eat dinner with the prince, to see round the royal castle—was she going to let Nero Caracas stand in the way of that? It was a signal from the prince himself that her father's yard was back in favour. Jack Wheeler's name would be spoken again with pride. And, realistically, her chance of being seated next to Nero was zero, Bella reassured

herself. Protocol was everything in royal circles and she
was sure to be seated with her team.

'I hope you don't mind that I put you next to me,' the
prince said, smiling warmly at Bella, 'and that you're
not sitting with your team…?'

'Of course not, Sir, it's an honour,' Bella replied graciously, trying not to care who was sitting across the
table from her on the other side of the prince. Or the fact
that Nero seemed unusually chummy with their royal
host.

'The captain of the winning team and the owner and
trainer of the pony of the match—it seemed an inevitable pairing to me,' the prince confided in his usual
laid-back manner.

'Indeed, Sir,' Bella agreed, coolly meeting Nero's
amused stare. What was going on?

'Your Royal Highness is, as ever, a most perceptive
man,' Nero drawled, raising one sweeping ebony brow
as he connected with Bella's narrow-eyed stare.

Bella Wheeler in a dinner gown. This was an image
he had toyed with on his way to the castle. He had
thought she might free her shiny auburn hair from its
cruel captivity and reveal the young body that lurked beneath her workmanlike clothes. Instead, she was trussed
up in a gown her grandmother would have approved of,
and her hair was more tightly dressed than he had ever
seen it. Did she have to make a statement every time
they met? If it went on like this, he fully expected her
to be wearing a sandwich board on the next occasion,
proclaiming: Look, Don't Touch.

'So, Bella,' the prince said, distracting him, 'I've been
hearing good things about you—and not just as far as

training polo ponies goes. I'm thinking more of your work with children,' he explained.

Bella blushed. She didn't like to make a song and dance about the work she undertook in her free time.

'Have you ever thought of expanding your scheme?' the prince pressed.

Bella noticed Nero appeared to be equally intent on her answer. 'My polo commitments don't allow for it, Sir—'

'But you do what you can, which is more than most people even attempt,' the prince went on. 'And I've been hearing some very good things about you—'

Bella answered this with a modest smile.

As the meal continued her tension relaxed. She was imagining things, Bella reassured herself. Nero sitting across the table had made her edgy. There was no plan afoot between Nero and the prince. Her royal host was always well briefed, and was not only genuinely interested in the people he met but was an excellent conversationalist. Her father had been invited to the castle in his heyday, but this was Bella's first time and she wasn't going to waste it fretting about the prince's fanciful seating plan that saw spinster-and-contented-with-her-lot Bella Wheeler seated across the table from the world's most desirable man. She could only hope Nero had got her message—*Butt out of my life, Caracas. You're not wanted here.*

But she did want him. She wanted Nero with an ache so bad she could only hope the prince, who was undoubtedly a man of the world, hadn't picked up on it. Nero was a force of nature, a man who could have any woman in the world. What if he suspected how she felt about him? How professional would Nero think her then?

He'd think her a naïve fool. And he wouldn't be that far out. Right now, she was feeling as if she'd been parachuted in from Little Town in Nowhere Land to a life of such pomp and privilege she had to pinch herself to prove she wasn't dreaming. Thank goodness she'd found a gown at the back of the wardrobe suitable for dinner—ten years out of date, but conservative, which was all that mattered. She didn't like to draw attention to herself, which was another reason she appeared cold.

She stiffened and held Nero's gaze as he looked at her for one long potent moment, then turned away when the prince began talking to him. It was an opportunity to soak everything in—all the life-sized oil paintings on the ruby silk walls. Stout kings and thin kings, with glittering swords and crowns bearing testament to their wealth and power. Happy women and sad women, wearing sumptuous gowns, some of whom were surrounded by strangely disaffected children staring off bleakly into an unknowable future. With a shiver, she dragged her gaze away and began to study the vaulted ceiling instead. On a ground of rich cobalt blue, this was lavishly decorated with rosy-cheeked cherubs and cotton wool clouds and, coming back down to earth again, there was more crystal and silver on a dinner table made magical by candlelight than she had ever seen before. There must have been fifty people sitting at the table with them, and it was longer than a bowling alley to accommodate that number. A mischievous smile played around her lips when the royal butler and his team of efficient footmen strode silently by—some wild child inside her wanted to dance a crazy quickstep after them down the jewel-coloured runners that marked out their transit through the hall.

She could act serene, but inside her there was a wild

child longing to get out. Nero was as relaxed in this setting as he was on the polo field. How elegant and confident he appeared, lounging back in his chair, chatting easily to the prince—as well he might. Rumour said Nero lived in considerable style on his *estancia* back home, where he ruled his estate like his own private fiefdom. And if he had been devastating in match clothes, he was off the scale tonight in a beautifully cut evening suit. The dark cloth moulded his powerful frame to perfection, while the crisp white shirt and steel-grey tie showed off his tan.

Damn! He was watching her. She turned her attention quickly to her plate. She was safer with her ponies than with all these men. Men were strong and could physically overwhelm her, and Nero Caracas was the strongest of them all. When you'd fought and lost as badly as she had, you never forgot—

Yet here she was, wrapping her lips around the tines of her fork as if she wanted him to look at her.

Must she court danger at every opportunity?

It must be the Nero effect. She was never so foolish, but just sitting across from him was enough to make her act differently—made her monitor how she held herself and how she ate. She had even taken to sipping her drink demurely!

Damn this to hell! She was a professional woman, not some impressionable teenager. Straightening up, she made a special effort to engage the prince in a topic of conversation which she knew he would appreciate, but even the prince seemed to be on Nero's side.

'I'm surprised you haven't made an offer for the pony of the match, Caracas,' the prince observed after a few minutes of conversation which had fallen well within the bounds of what Bella considered safe.

Bella tensed. Must everything come back to this?

'But I have,' Nero said mildly. 'I would love to own Misty, but Ms Wheeler seems to have her doubts—'

'Doubts?' The prince's eyebrows shot up as he turned to stare at Bella. 'Señor Caracas has an enviable *estancia* in Argentina, with the best living conditions for polo ponies I've seen anywhere in the world—'

'And still Ms Wheeler doubts me.' Nero's eyes were glinting with humour as he attempted to capture Bella's stony stare.

'You must reconsider, Ms Wheeler,' the prince insisted. 'Nero is the best rider in the world, and as such he should have access to the best ponies.'

Should he? By whose right?

Bella flashed a furious look across the table, only to be met by Nero's relaxed, sardonic stare. Her heart thundered—and not with anger. She could have coped with that more easily than this lust-fuelled desire to engage in combat with him. But the prince's message was unmistakable. If she was intransigent she would lose his favour and, as the prince was one of the foremost sponsors of the game, everything she had worked so hard to build could quickly turn to dust. 'Your Royal Highness.' She appeared to agree—even adding a meek dip of her head, but inside she was fuming. She would not be forced to sell her most cherished possession—and Nero Caracas could stop pulling the prince's strings. There must be a way out of this and she would find it.

But then Nero foiled her by mentioning a project close to her heart and now, it appeared, close to his. He planned to work with children who wouldn't normally have the opportunity to ride. She'd been doing that for years, and had seen the benefits first hand.

'I want them to experience the freedom of the pampas,' Nero was explaining to the prince, 'and discover what life is like on my *estancia* in Argentina.'

She would like to find out too, Bella thought wryly. But then her suspicions grew when it became clear that the prince and Nero had been in negotiations for some time over this proposed scheme—long enough for Nero to persuade the prince to be its patron.

'There are many similarities to your own work,' the prince observed, turning to include Bella in their discussion. 'Perhaps you remember, I mentioned the possibility of spreading your good work a little further earlier this evening?'

She'd been set up, Bella thought angrily, noting the spark of triumph in Nero's eyes. And since when was Argentina *a little further*? It was half a world away. She must have paled as the prince indicated that one of the hovering footmen should refill her water glass.

'Sir, I cannot think of leaving England—especially so close to Christmas.' She was clutching at straws— and had broken royal protocol by speaking to the prince before he invited her to do so, but the prince, sensing her distress, was at pains to make amends. 'But Christmas in Argentina is so beautiful and warm. I'm sure that your concerns in this country could be addressed, and Nero would ensure paid professionals were on hand to help you with the day-to-day running of the scheme in Argentina.'

Had this already been decided?

Bella had never found it so hard in her life to hold her tongue, but to interrupt the prince a second time would be an unforgivable breach of etiquette.

'I understand your concerns,' the prince assured her. 'There's so much paperwork when schemes such as this are set up, but I don't see you being involved in that. I see you taking more of a hands-on role, Bella—teaching the children to ride, and sharing your love of horses with them.'

'But, Sir—' Bella's eyes implored the prince to understand that she couldn't leave her yard. She worked every hour of every day to be the best. She even turned to Nero for help, but he merely raised a sardonic brow.

'There would be ample reward,' the prince said, as if this would make a difference.

Bella flinched with embarrassment. 'It isn't the money, Sir—'

'Pride is a great thing, Bella, but we all have to be practical,' the prince replied. 'Nero's gauchos have centuries of knowledge that working closely with horses has brought them, just as we do. There's nothing wrong with sharing that knowledge amongst friends, is there?' The prince stared at her intently.

What could she say without appearing mean-spirited? 'You're quite right, Sir,' she agreed, avoiding Nero's sardonic stare.

'And you could take Misty with you,' the prince added, warming to his theme. 'I'm sure Nero would have no objections?'

Was this a joke? Bella wondered as the two men exchanged a knowing glance. And now Nero's stare was heating her face, but she couldn't pretend the cash on offer wouldn't be useful—

So Nero had won.

Misty could only benefit by being ridden by the greatest polo player in the world, and riding high in the prince's approval meant the future of her stable yard was assured. 'This doesn't mean I would sell Misty to you,' she assured Nero.

As the prince exclaimed with disappointment on

Nero's behalf, Nero said smoothly, 'I don't think we need to worry about that yet.'

But some time she would need to worry, Bella interpreted, tensing even as the prince relaxed. She was up against the might of Nero Caracas with no one, not even the prince, to back her up. 'I couldn't leave my work here,' she said firmly.

The prince sat forward as Nero offered what must have sounded to him like a reassurance. 'I would send a team to take over what is already an established scheme,' Nero said with a relaxed shrug. 'They would handle all your outstanding commitments.'

Was she the only one who could see the glint of irony in Nero's eyes?

Apparently, Bella thought as the prince sighed with approval. 'We would be in this together, Bella,' the prince confirmed, tying the knot between them even tighter. 'All I'm asking from you is that you share your expertise in the setting up of a similar scheme in Argentina to the one you already run in England.'

How reasonable that sounded, Bella thought as the prince turned his kind-hearted gaze on her face. Nero might as well have hog-tied her and served her up on a silver platter. Had his penetrating stare also worked out that he scrambled her brain cells and made her stomach melt? Almost certainly, she thought as his ebony brow lifted.

'Well, what do you think, Bella?' the prince prompted gently.

'Could I have some time to think about this, Sir?'

His Royal Highness hesitated.

'Not too much time,' Nero cut in, apparently oblivious to the rules of royal etiquette when it came to getting his own way.

* * *

After dinner a recital was to be held in the Blue drawing room, with the chance for everyone to freshen up first.

Freshen up? Bella raged silently, checking her hair was still securely tied back in the gilt-framed mirror hanging on the wall of the unimaginably ornate restroom. After listening to the prince's well-intentioned suggestions on one side, and batting off Nero's sardonic sallies on the other, she felt like a tennis ball being swiped between the two, frayed a little around the edges, but still ready to bounce—right over Nero, preferably.

Conclusion?

Her carefully controlled life was rapidly spiralling out of control.

Taking one last look around at all the beautiful things in the restroom—dainty chairs with soft leaf-green covers and the comforting array of traditional organic scent bottles lined up on a crystal tray for visitors to sample—she had the strongest feeling that if Nero had anything to do with it, it would be some time before she would be making a return visit here.

In this same anxious mood she opened the door and managed to bump straight into him.

'Ill met by moonlight,' Nero murmured with amusement as Bella exclaimed with alarm.

Her breath echoed in the silence as she stared up at Nero's strong, tanned hand on the wall by her face. 'Excuse me, please—'

He didn't move.

'I said—'

'I heard what you said.'

'Then would you let me pass, please?' She would fight off the effects of that deceptively sleepy stare.

'What's your hurry, Bella?'

'We should be getting back to the recital...'

Nero hummed.

Bracing herself, she looked up. Moonlight was indeed bathing them both in a strange sapphire light as it poured in through one of the castle's many stained-glass windows. The effect was wonderful for Nero's dark skin and thick black hair—she guessed her own face was a watery blue and her red hair a strange shade of green. Heating up under Nero's amused scrutiny, she launched a counter-attack. 'What were you doing at dinner with the prince and all that talk of a scheme?'

'It wasn't talk, Bella—'

'And I suppose it wasn't a ruse to make me sell Misty to you, either?'

'The scheme will continue, with or without your help, Bella.'

In his severe formal clothes, in this most refined of settings, Nero Caracas looked like a dark angel and more dangerous than ever. 'You led the prince to think I might sell Misty—and that my compliance with the scheme was a given.'

Nero's lips pressed down in a most attractive way. 'There's no mystery,' he said with a shrug. 'I offered to pay whatever price you ask for the pony. I doubt you'll find anyone who will match my offer.'

Or match Nero's compelling aura, or his physical strength, Bella thought, fighting off the seductive effect. It was impossible to be this close to Nero Caracas without feeling something, she reasoned, willing her voice to remain steady. 'I told you once—and this is the last time—Misty isn't for sale.'

'And what if the prince wants to buy her?'

Stunned by the idea, Bella gasped.

'Don't tell me that thought hasn't occurred to you,'

Nero murmured in his lazy South American drawl. 'And if the prince does want your mare, how can you refuse him?' Nero gave her a moment to soak this up, before adding dryly, 'Perhaps I can save the situation for you.'

Bella's eyes narrowed. 'What would it cost me?'

'Oh, come now, Bella. You know Misty would be happier with me than the prince.'

Check. And mate. Nero had cut the legs from under her. Forget the threat he posed in the personal sense— polo ponies lived to play the game and Misty adored the high-powered cut and thrust of the international arena. It was common knowledge that the prince had practically retired from the game, which meant Misty would hardly be played at all, whereas as one of Nero's pampered ponies, Misty would get every opportunity to indulge the passion the small mare lived for.

'Having doubts?' Nero prompted, pouncing on her hesitation.

'None,' she lied. 'I only wish you had some scruples.'

Nero laughed. Throwing back his head, he revealed the long, firm column of his throat. 'Your innocence is touching, Bella.' Dipping his head, he stared her in the eyes to drive the point home. 'I have no scruples when it comes to the game.'

Which game?

In the heat of the moment, she grabbed his arm. 'Just keep the prince out of this.' Feeling the heat and muscle beneath her hand, she quickly released her grip. Inhaling sharply, she shook herself round. Nero was an experienced man. You didn't come up against him without getting burned. This was all a game to him and if she had any sense she'd put some much needed space between them…

Nero's hand slammed against the wall at the side of her face.

'Get out of my way,' Bella raged with shock, green eyes blazing.

'So I am right,' Nero murmured, standing back.

'Right about what?' she said angrily, thoroughly discomfited.

'There is fire beneath that ice of yours,' Nero murmured.

Bella inhaled sharply as Nero stroked back a strand of her hair that had escaped its stern captivity. 'You can stop congratulating yourself on your perception,' she said coldly. 'It doesn't seem to have helped you where Misty is concerned.'

Nero's mouth curved disconcertingly. 'You seem very sure of that, Bella.'

'I am.' Her voice was shaking, but in some strange way she was enjoying this. Nero made her feel alive. She should thank him for goading her.

'Temper, temper,' Nero murmured, reading her.

She stood aloof, but they were still so close she could feel his heat warming her, and his spicy scent invading her senses and making her dizzy. Nero was enjoying this too, Bella realised with a rush of concern and excitement mixed.

And have you chosen to overlook that small thing called consequences?

How she hated her inner voice for intruding at a time like this, but she couldn't ignore it. Her fighting spirit might have made a comeback, but her ability to trust a man still had a long way to go.

CHAPTER THREE

THE corridor was silent until the sound of doors closing made them both turn. 'Oh, dear,' Nero observed dryly, 'it appears we've missed the recital.'

'And what will the prince have to say about that?' Bella murmured defiantly.

Nero sighed in response but didn't look a bit repentant. 'It seems we're both in trouble.'

More than he could know, Bella thought, brewing up a storm.

Nero lounged back against the wall with footmen playing silent sentry as he waited for the music to end. The moment the doors were opened again, the prince summoned them both over.

She might as well give up now, Bella thought as the prince said how happy it made him to indulge a friend. She had just smiled her thanks when the prince made it clear that friend was Nero. 'As you know, I have agreed to be the patron of Nero's charity,' the prince confided in her, 'but as I have so many calls on my time I would like you, Bella, to represent me.'

'Me, Sir?' Of course she was surprised but, crucially, the prince had taken the decision about going to Argentina out of her hands.

'I can't think of anyone better qualified,' he continued.

'You are the best trainer I know, Bella. And when the polo season comes to an end, what better use of your time could there be than introducing more young people to the joys of riding? See what you can do over there, Bella—what you can both do,' the prince added, gazing at Bella and Nero in turn. 'Though I should warn you, Bella, that when you leave the northern hemisphere behind and experience the very different world you are going to, you might want to stay there. Passions run high on the pampas—isn't that so, Caracas?'

'Exactly so, Your Royal Highness.' Nero's amused gaze switched to Bella.

'I know you'll enjoy the teaching, Bella,' the prince continued, turning serious again. 'And if you would do this one thing for me, I would feel I was still there, in some way. I'm afraid I can't spare anyone from my own staff. But who knows the relationship between man and horse better than you?' he added persuasively. 'It will mean you spending quite some time in Argentina, Bella, but I feel certain you will enjoy that as much as I did.'

How could she refuse now?

By taking in the triumph in Nero's eyes, possibly? Bella thought tensely. Or the amused tug at the corner of his mouth? How she wished she could snatch some reason out of the air why she couldn't go, but she couldn't afford to risk offending the prince. There was no escape, she concluded. 'I would consider it a great honour to assist you in any way I can, Sir.'

'Excellent. I'm glad that's settled,' the prince said, beaming. 'And now... If you will both excuse me?'

'Of course.' At last she could look at Nero. His expression was exactly what she had expected. And she hoped hers left Nero in no doubt that she would do this, but only because the prince had asked her. Working as an adviser for Nero's charitable scheme was a privilege; she was too polite to even think of the word to describe working alongside a man who challenged every sensible boundary she had ever put in place.

'You'll be my guest, of course,' Nero explained, all business now his triumph was in the bag. 'Working and living on the pampas will be very different to anything you are used to here, but I am confident that in time you will grow to love it.'

In time? Bella swallowed deep. There were so many undertones to that apparently innocent statement she could only be glad the well-meaning prince hadn't stayed to hear them. 'I wouldn't be able to stay very long…'

'But long enough for the project to be established. The children need you, Bella.'

'As does my yard and my horses. I have my own scheme, Nero.'

He checked her at every turn. 'You'd break your word to the prince?'

'Had you already decided this plan between the two of you? Was my agreement to the prince's proposal merely a formality?'

Nero smiled faintly. 'You're so suspicious, Bella.'

'With good reason, I think,' she flashed.

'I will hold myself personally responsible for maintaining the high standards you have set at your yard in the UK. As I told both you and the prince, I will send my most trusted team to ensure you have nothing to worry about—financially, or otherwise.'

Was he serious? The systems she had set in place to take care of things should she be incapacitated by illness, or be taken out of the picture in some other way, would ensure the yard ran smoothly. If she chose to do this, it was Nero she was worried about, working in close proximity to him being the major problem. 'I have made enough money to keep everything ticking over nicely, thank you. I don't need any help from you!'

'Your reputation does you much credit, Bella,' Nero snapped. 'It seems you are your father's daughter, after all.'

Bella blenched. 'What's that supposed to mean?'

Nero's powerful shoulders eased in a shrug. 'You can't make a decision and stick to it.'

'How dare you—'

'How dare I speak the truth?' Nero's eyes drilled into her. 'If you break your word as easily as this, Bella Wheeler, I'm not sure I want you as part of my scheme.'

For a moment she didn't trust herself to speak. Nero had blatantly manipulated her, but if she lost her temper and blackened her father's memory even more she would never forgive herself. Taking a deep steadying breath, she buried her pride. 'You give me your word that my work in England wouldn't suffer?'

'I do,' Nero assured her in a clipped voice.

'And my visit to Argentina would be conditional on coming home as soon as the scheme is set up.'

'I can't imagine why I would want you to stay beyond that.'

Her heart beat with outrage. Nero really knew how to cut her with words, she realised, smiling prettily for the prince as Nero escorted her out of the royal presence.

'This is a win-win situation, Bella,' Nero insisted as they strolled across the room. 'I'm surprised you can't see it.'

'How do you reach that conclusion?'

'The prince secures you as his representative. My

project secures your experience. And you get to keep your pony.'

'In spite of your scare tactics, my ownership of Misty has never been in doubt. So what do you get out of it?' Bella demanded suspiciously.

'I get to keep Misty on my yard—and even ride her—if you will allow me to?'

Nero's tongue was firmly planted in his cheek, Bella suspected. And his face was close enough to make her lips tingle. 'Do you really need my permission?' she countered. And would she be able to resist seeing the world's best polo player mounted on the best pony? Nero's laughing eyes and the curve of his sensuous mouth reflected his confidence that this would be the case.

'Most important of all, Bella, the children benefit,' Nero said, turning serious.

And that was the one thing she couldn't argue with. 'Believe me, your project is the only reason I'm saying yes to Argentina.'

'But of course,' Nero agreed smoothly. 'What other reason could there be for a respectable woman to visit my *estancia*?'

'I can't imagine,' Bella said frostily, smiling her thanks as a royal footman opened the outer doors for them.

'And where will you go now?' Nero asked her as a driver brought his ink-black four-wheel-drive up to the foot of the steps for him.

'Back to the stables for one last check on the horses.'

'As I'm going there myself, why don't I give you a lift?'

'I prefer to walk, thank you.'

'In an evening dress?'

'It's a pleasant evening, and I need the fresh air.'

'Well, if you're sure?'

'I am.' Her mind was still whirling with the fact that she had agreed of her own free will to walk into the lion's den—and not here on familiar turf, but Argentina, and the wild, untamed pampas, where she would be staying on Nero's *estancia*. She needed some fresh air to come to terms with that alone—lots of it.

'Then good night,' Nero murmured, his eyes glittering with triumph. 'I'll see you tomorrow when we will firm up your travel arrangements.'

Life had suddenly become very interesting, Nero reflected as he gunned the engine and drove away from the castle. Word had it that Isabella Wheeler lived in an ivory tower whose walls had never been breached, but he'd caught flashes of internal fires raging out of control. She reminded him of one of his spirited mares. They took their time to trust and were always looking for trouble, but that was because they had lost the freedom of the pampas, something they would never forget. What had Bella Wheeler lost that caused her such torment? Rumour said there was some mystery surrounding her. He could confirm that. Bella said one thing and her eyes, the mirror of Bella's soul, said something different. She was lying by omission. She was hiding something big.

Bella's outwardly contained manner intrigued him almost as much as her unnaturally well-groomed appearance irritated him. It wasn't often he met a woman who had her own life, her own successful career and wasn't looking for anything material from him. Far from it, Nero reflected wryly. If he had to categorise Bella after getting to know her a little better, it would still be under the heading: Ice Maiden. He had never met a woman who went all out to make herself as unobtainable and as aloof as she could and, the irony was, Bella didn't realise what a desirable prize that made her. He'd seen the way men looked at her as they dreamed of loosening her tight-fitting breeches. He knew how he felt about her. And, judging by the way Bella responded to him, she wasn't exactly immune to him either.

He wanted her. She wanted him. There should have been a very easy solution, but there wasn't, and he was going to find out why.

When she had satisfied herself that everything at the stables was as it should be, Bella's thoughts turned to her grooms. Some of them were very young and she felt responsible for them. Hearing that a couple of the girls hadn't returned to the small bed and breakfast where Bella had rented them rooms, she set out to look for them. She knew exactly where they would be. After the match a large, luxurious nightclub had set up camp in a marquee in the grounds. It was *the* place to be, the girls had assured her. Bella had seen pictures on the news and could understand their excitement. The huge white tent was decorated like something out of *Arabian Nights* with exotic silken drapes in a variety of jewel colours and dramatic water features shooting plumes of glittering spray into the air. A dance floor had been erected in the middle of the tent and one of the top DJs had been booked to keep the excitement of the polo match alive until dawn.

She was only halfway across the field when the bass beat started pounding through her. She was really out of her comfort zone. Even before the prince's invitation, she had refused the young grooms' invitation to join them. She had made all sorts of excuses—she was too old, too boring—and had laughed when they had protested she was neither. It was never easy to mix business with pleasure, even had she wanted to, but like an old mother hen, she was determined to make sure her girls were safe tonight.

She was off to a good start, having the right credentials, apparently. A member of the security staff recognised her and showed her straight in through the VIP entrance. The noise was amazing and there was such a crowd it was a while before she spotted the girls, by which time she had been sucked deep into the throng and men were speaking to her, offering her drinks and wanting to dance with her. She was here for business purposes, she told them frostily, tilting her chin at a determined angle as she headed for the girls.

The heat was overwhelming inside the tent after the chill night air. What with the press of people, the noise, the screams of laughter, the relentless beat, the flash of chandeliers and the glittering, garish splendour of it all, it was no wonder she was disorientated to begin with. Shaking off the faint sense of danger approaching, she pressed on, determined not to leave until she knew the girls had arranged to get home safely.

'Bella!' they exclaimed the moment they caught sight of her.

Before she knew it, she was on the dance floor.

'Meet...'

She didn't hear the rest—there were too many names and far too many new faces. She smiled and jigged around a bit, trying to string a few steps together on a heavily overpopulated dance floor on which there was hardly room to move, let alone dance. And she felt silly in her strait-laced dinner gown amongst so many cool young girls.

'Are you sure you're all okay?' she asked, drawing one of them aside. 'Have you made plans for later, or shall I call a taxi for you?'

'My brother's here,' the girl explained, angling her chin towards a tall, good-looking youth. 'No worries, Bella. Woo-hoo! Enjoy yourself!' And, grabbing hold of Bella's wrist, the girl dragged her back onto the dance floor.

And why not? Bella reasoned, glancing round. Everyone was here for a good time, and one dance wouldn't hurt. She didn't want to be a killjoy, and there was such an air of celebration it felt great to be part of it. There was certainly nothing to be concerned about—even if that persistent prickle down her spine refused to go away.

'Come on—you can't go now. You've only just arrived,' the girls insisted, gathering round Bella, who was still glancing anxiously over her shoulder, hardly knowing what she was looking for. They formed a circle round her so she couldn't escape, which made her laugh, and soon she was dancing again and everyone was shooting their arms in the air. After some persuasion, Bella did too. It was fun. It felt good to let go. Her hair tumbled down and swung around her shoulders. She tossed it back, making no attempt to tidy herself for once. She was just happy to lose her inhibitions—happy to lose herself in the music, and the moment.

Until it all came crashing down.

So this was where Miss Bluestocking hung out when she wasn't preaching death to desire and all-natural female responses. Those responses were only curbed when he was around, it seemed. Her glorious hair was flying free, and was as spectacular as he had always imagined it would be, and she was dancing with all the abandon he had suspected she might possess—a fact that wasn't lost on the men around her, though Bella appeared to be oblivious to the interest she was arousing.

The crowd parted like the Red Sea as he strode up to her. He stopped in the centre of the dance floor in front of the one person oblivious to his approach. Currently gyrating with her eyes closed and her hands reaching for the sky, the so-called Ice Maiden was mouthing lyrics to the raunchy track and grinding her hips in time to the beat with extremely un-maidenly relish. 'What the hell are you doing here?' he rapped for the sheer pleasure of seeing the shock in her eyes.

'Nero!'

'Yes, Nero,' he confirmed. 'So this is why you refused my offer of a lift.'

She pretended not to understand him, and was pleasingly flushed and unsettled as she smoothed back her hair. He showed her no mercy. Instead, he tugged her into his arms.

'What are you doing?' she demanded, struggling to find her severe face as their bodies brushed and finally connected.

'Oh, I'm sorry,' he mocked as she let out a shocked breath. 'I didn't realise you had come here to lead a temperance rally. I thought you were dancing...'

She manoeuvred herself so their lower bodies were no longer touching. 'You don't understand—'

'Oh, I think I do,' Nero argued, drawing her close again as the uptempo track segued into a slower number. 'I understand things such as this very well.'

'I mean you don't understand me,' she said, going as stiff as a board. 'This isn't what it seems—'

'This is exactly what it seems,' he argued.

'I'm only here to...'

'Check out the ponies?' he reminded her in a deceptively mild tone.

'I'm here to check up on my girls,' Bella argued hotly. 'Not that it's any business of yours what I choose to do with my free time.'

'Not yet it isn't.'

Nero's powerful hands were on her arm and on her waist, making it hard to think straight. And he was radically changed. No more the suave aristocrat in an impeccably tailored suit, Nero had found time to change his clothes and in a tight-fitting top and well-worn jeans that sculpted his hard, toned muscles it was no wonder the crowds had parted for him. He looked like an invading warrior. His shoulders were massive. His biceps were ripped. His thick, inky-black hair tumbled over his brow, while his sharp black stubble seemed more piratical than ever, giving him the appearance of some brigand on a raid. Worse—he had caught her off guard, obliterating her carefully constructed image for the sake of one reckless dance.

'So why are you here?' she demanded, determined to turn the tables on him. 'Looking for entertainment, Nero?'

'I was looking for you,' he fired back. 'I expected to find you at the stables so we could discuss your travel plans for tomorrow. Imagine my surprise when one of the stable lads told me where you'd gone.' As one inky brow rose it coincided with a move that brought them into even closer contact. 'I wouldn't have missed this for the world,' he murmured as she gasped. 'Imagine my surprise at finding Miss Butter-Wouldn't-Melt in Sodom and Gomorrah.'

'I was dancing with my friends!'

Nero shot a glance around at the men staring open-mouthed at Bella. 'Really?' He guessed none of them had seen Bella Wheeler breaking free before. The flickering light played into his hands, giving everything a hellish glow. Flashing and reflecting off the glitter balls hanging from the ceiling, the coloured lights made the mass of dancing figures seem contorted as if they were taking part in some primitive orgiastic rite. This was as far removed from the hushed sanctuary of the stable yard as it was possible to imagine. 'I would never have guessed this was your scene,' he murmured, twisting the knife. 'I understood you preferred an innocent stroll in the clean night air.'

He loved the way she writhed in his arms. She even balled her tiny hand into a fist, but thought better of using it on him, and gradually, in spite of all her best efforts, the stiffness seeped out of her and she softened in his arms.

'That's better,' he commented as she responded to the persuasive beat.

'Don't think I'm dancing with you because I want to.'

'Of course you aren't,' he agreed, soothing her as they moved to the music. There were only two things a man and woman could do to a rhythm when they were as close as this, and dancing was step one.

She couldn't have been more humiliated. Of all the things to happen, Nero discovering her midbellow in the middle of a raunchy song… How often did she let herself go?

Try never.

And that cringing feeling she got when some man she didn't know touched her—where was that? Nero felt amazing, not that she was touching him unnecessarily.

And then the music quietened and faded, and she waited for him to release her...

Was he going to kiss her?

Nero was staring down as if he might. They were alone in the middle of a packed dance floor. Closing her eyes, she drew in a shaking breath. Nero dipped his head...

The wait went on too long.

'See you tomorrow, Bella.'

She was left standing in confusion. Nero had walked off. People were staring at her.

With as little fuss as possible, she left the floor, making sure she took a different route. He was playing games with her, and she had no one to blame but herself. She could have brought that encounter to an end at any time. Why on earth hadn't she?

CHAPTER FOUR

IT WAS dawn when Nero rang the next morning. Bella was already at the stables. It had nothing to do with a restless night; this was her usual routine. 'Yes?' she said coolly. Answering the phone was easier than facing him.

'Travel plans,' Nero said briskly in the same no-nonsense tone.

'I'm listening.' And with some relief, she realised. After last night, she wouldn't have been surprised if Nero had left the country without another word.

The conversation that followed never strayed from the point, with Nero doing most of the talking. Bella was a highly respected professional, but Nero was the owner of countless polo ponies as well as being a top international player, so their respective positions in the game put him firmly in the driving seat. 'You will travel with me to Argentina,' he informed her. 'The horses will follow later when I'm satisfied everything is ready for them.'

Before she could ask if she would have any part to play in this, Nero went on to say that he would wind down in Buenos Aires before travelling to his *estancia*, which would give Bella chance to recover from the flight.

What form would Nero's wind-down take? And how much did she hate herself for wondering if she would even see him in Buenos Aires? She was still brooding about it when she ate breakfast with a group of red-eyed grooms.

It was ridiculous to care. This was business, Bella told herself firmly as she paid the bill and checked out of the small bed and breakfast hotel where she and the grooms had been staying. And she could hardly ask Nero what his intentions were—unless she wanted to appear desperate, of course.

Nero had been all male disapproval last night, but a spark had flared between them. She had acted cool at the castle, only for him to discover her dancing the night away, apparently surrounded by men. He had chosen not to notice the girlfriends dancing with her. Nero hadn't seen anything beyond the heat of the night, the throb of the music and the fact that everyone but him was in the same abandoned state. Nero would keep his word and honour their business arrangement, but he wouldn't forget. That pride of his would never allow it.

As she walked up the steps of Nero's private jet, Bella felt she was leaving everything certain behind and entering a world far beyond the scope of her imagination. There was a uniformed flight attendant to show her round while Nero joined his copilot in the cockpit. Everything in the interior of the plane was of the best— thick cream carpets, pale leather armchairs, just like a topclass hotel. Señor Caracas had his own private suite, the attendant explained, but Bella could take her pick from any of the other four options on board. She was still reeling from this information when the attendant added that Señor Caracas would meet her for breakfast the next morning as this was an overnight flight, and that in the meantime if she needed anything at all she only had to call him.

Was Nero avoiding her? Thinking back to her wild abandonment the previous evening, Bella went hot with embarrassment. It was so unlike her to expose herself like that—to become the butt of speculation.

But she'd done nothing wrong, Bella told herself firmly. Meanwhile, she should enjoy this. Her bedroom was small, but beautifully fitted with polished wood and a comfortable-looking bed dressed with crisp white linen. Thanking the attendant as he put her small suitcase down on the soft wool carpet, she vowed to put last night behind her and start again. This was just a short and fascinating interlude, after which she would return to her old life and Nero would carry on with his as if they'd never met.

And on that prescription she spent a restless night, tossing and turning, and waking long before the steward had arranged to call her. Having showered and dressed neatly in jeans and a long-sleeved top, she went to find breakfast. Nero was already lounging at the table in the salon, also dressed casually, his damp hair suggesting he was fresh from the shower. He greeted her politely above the hum of the engines and put down his newspaper.

Beyond that…nothing.

Nero was aloof, but knowing, Bella thought, flashing him a covert glance as she gave her order to the hovering steward. He had perfected the art of saying nothing and conveying too much, she thought, feeling her cheeks blaze red. Nero knew she had wanted him the other night—knew she had expected him to kiss her. It hadn't changed his mind about their business arrangement, but it had changed Nero's manner towards her, giving him more the upper hand than ever. He had formed an opinion about her and, mistaken though that opinion was, she didn't feel like offering an explanation for having fun in her free time.

He stared at Bella thoughtfully. She was discreetly dressed with her hair scraped back from a make-up-less face. Did she think he was going to throw her to the floor and have his evil way with her? After the other night he'd got her message loud and clear, as if he needed a reminder. As if he was interested.

But he was interested, which gave him a problem. And the more Bella played him, the more interested he became.

Bella wasn't sure what to expect when the plane landed. She had thought plenty about their destination and had bought every travel guide going, though beyond describing the pampas she had learned nothing about Nero's ranch. She couldn't wait to see where he lived and realised it was a measure of the power Nero wielded, as well as the security surrounding him, that only wild speculation could be rooted out regarding the lifestyle of one of the world's most private men. The first surprise came when they landed. She hadn't really thought about the practicalities of leaving a private jet. It proved to be a real eye-opener. Her passport was checked on board and a sleek black saloon was waiting for them on the tarmac at the foot of the steps.

The first thing Bella noticed as she exited the aircraft was how beautifully warm it was after the chill of London. The sky was blue and as she walked down the steps the spicy scent of Argentina blotted out the sickly fumes of aviation fuel. Waving the chauffeur away, Nero opened the passenger door for her and as soon as she was comfortably settled inside he shut the door and walked round to the driver's side. The checkpoint at the exit might not have existed. The bar was quickly raised and they were waved on their way by a guard who saluted them as if they were royalty. Which, in many ways, Nero was, Bella reflected, shooting him a sideways glance. The king of polo was looking more than usually splendid this morning and, in spite of all her strongest warnings to self, she felt her senses roar. Dark and dangerous described Nero to a T and who didn't like to dabble their toes in danger from time to time…?

'Are you going to buckle your seat belt any time soon?'

Nero's voice was rough and husky and she nearly jumped out of her seat to be caught in the middle of some rather raunchy thoughts about him. She buckled up without reply and gave herself a telling off. Better she leave the danger to those sophisticated women—the 'stick chicks' as they were known in polo circles. Far better for someone like her to stay in the stables with the ponies, Bella concluded wryly.

They were soon speeding down the highway towards the city. It was impossible to relax in such a confined space with Nero sitting beside her. He broke the silence only once to explain that he had booked her into a hotel in the centre of Buenos Aires where she would have the chance to recover from the thirteen-hour flight.

'Thank you,' she said, falling silent again. Nero didn't want conversation, and she didn't have the first clue how to start one with him. Without their mutual interest in horses or the kindly prince to prompt her, she was lost.

Nero drove as he played polo, at speed and with

confidence, and there was enough testosterone bouncing round the small cabin of his high-powered car to drown in. If a man could increase his sex appeal just to taunt her, then that was exactly what Nero had done. The relentless march of his sharp black stubble had won the razor war and he looked every bit the tough, tanned lover, wearing jeans that clung to his hard-muscled thighs and sleeves rolled back on his casual shirt to expose his powerful forearms.

What would working for him be like? Bella wondered. Everything in Nero's life was his way or no way. It remained to be seen what would happen when he worked alongside a woman who felt exactly the same way about her ponies.

As they drove on through the unprepossessing outskirts of the city Bella's personal concerns shrank to nothing in the shadow of the shanty town stalking the highway. No wonder Nero wanted to share his good fortune with youngsters who had so little. What she was seeing now would make it easy to forget her personal feelings about Nero and throw everything she'd got behind his scheme.

'It's known as Villa 31,' he said, noticing her interest in the depressing sprawl. 'It's been here fifty years or more, and it's still growing. No point dwelling on it,' he added. 'We have to *do* something.'

Narrowing his eyes, Nero stared ahead as they sped past the chaotic urbanisation, but he was seeing a lot more than the road, Bella guessed.

It was late afternoon when they arrived in the centre of Buenos Aires, by which time shadows were falling over the graceful buildings. This was another side of the coin, Bella thought, as she peered out of the car window at the romantic soul of Argentina. No wonder Buenos

Aires was known as the Paris of South America, or that Nero was so proud of his homeland. The sun was still putting up a good fight and as it sank had turned the ancient stone a rosy pink, though as the day waned she thought Nero seemed to grow in force and intent like a creature of the night. It was as if this return to his homeland had stirred fresh passion in him, and as it swirled around them in the confined space of the car it infected Bella too. She had never felt so acutely aware, or so excited by the prospect of what lay ahead of her.

Nero had joined the heavy traffic on a grand twelve-lane boulevard with a soaring monument at the end of it. 'El Obelisco,' he explained, his glance sparking a lightning flash down Bella's spine. 'The tapering obelisk celebrates four hundred years of the founding of our capital city. There is so much beauty here,' he murmured, resting his stubble-shaded chin on one arm as he waited for the traffic to move. 'As you will learn, Bella,' he said, turning to lavish a longer look into her eyes, 'Argentina is a country of huge contrasts and monumental passions.'

The passion she already knew about, but the pride in Nero's voice made Bella envy his sense of belonging. She felt her body thrill at his attention, and it was all she could do to stop her imagination taking over. The most she could reasonably hope for, she told herself sensibly, was that this trip heralded a fresh start between them. If they could put their differences behind them she could experience something of the diversity of Argentina with Nero as her guide.

'Everything is on such a vast scale,' she commented, dragging her stare away from the huge phallic monument. It was a relief to let her gaze linger on what appeared to be a glorious fairy-tale chateau lifted straight out of some lush green valley in France.

'That's the French embassy,' Nero explained. 'It's a fantastic example of Belle Epoque architecture, don't you think?'

Bella nodded, relieved to be talking about something innocent after the way her thoughts had been turning.

'It was built in the golden age before the First World War when the world was still innocent,' Nero mused.

Bella turned to keep the magical building in sight. 'And yet it looks so right here—'

'Where nothing is innocent,' Nero murmured.

Silence hung between them for a while and then it became clear they were leaving the centre behind and entering an area with a uniquely quaint beat rather than a city atmosphere. 'I thought you might like the cobbled streets and Bohemian atmosphere...'

Was Nero teasing her? It was never easy to tell. Whatever his motive, it was clear he had booked the strait-laced Ice Maiden into one of the hottest areas of the city. The narrow streets were still crowded with pedestrians and there was a wide choice of clubs and bars and interesting little shops.

'I hope you approve, Bella?'

'I'm certainly intrigued.' She was longing to explore.

'Here we are.' Nero drew the vehicle to a halt outside a small chic boutique hotel. 'I chose this particular hotel because it's far enough away from the action for you to get some sleep, but close enough, should you wish to sample it,' he added with a touch of irony.

'I'll be far too busy sleeping,' she countered, turning away from Nero's mocking stare.

She was acutely aware of his strong hands on the

wheel and the determined jut of his chin. Nero was in control for now and she had to step up to the plate or go home, and she had no intention of going anywhere until her job was done. Nero might think he could control every woman as he controlled his polo ponies, but not this woman. And with that silent pep talk over Bella felt a lot more confident. 'Thank you for the lift.'

Leaning across, Nero stopped her opening the door, which was enough in itself to blank her mind of all her fragile resolutions. 'Allow me,' he said, staring into her eyes.

Oh, that long, confident Latin stare—when would she ever learn to deal with it? Bella wondered as Nero opened the door for her. She hadn't missed the ironic twist of his mouth. Nero thought she was easy meat and simply acting tough. He was right about one of those—she was acting. She was in a strange country with a man she hardly knew, and she felt vulnerable. Only when they reached Nero's *estancia* and she was working with her horses in a setting she understood would she be totally at ease again.

She stood for a moment on the cobbles in the warm gardenia-scented air. She just wanted to soak everything in. She could hear music playing in the distance. This was even better than the Buenos Aires she had dreamed about. And was that really a couple dancing in the street?

'Tango—the lifeblood of Buenos Aires,' Nero informed her in his deep, husky voice.

Bella's heart was beating off the scale—surely Nero must hear it? She hadn't even realised he'd come to stand so close beside her. Sensibly, she moved away. She had to keep all her wits about her on this trip. This was only page one of her Argentinian adventure, and the book promised to be as exciting and surprising as the country Nero called home.

CHAPTER FIVE

DETERMINED to maintain her cool, Bella fixed her gaze on the hotel entrance as she started up the steps. The polished wooden door had black wrought-iron decoration of a type that seemed to be fashionable in the area. Nero was definitely right about the area's appeal. The cobbled streets and colonial buildings, coupled with Bohemian chic *and* the tango, gave it an irresistible charm.

She gasped as Nero held her back.

'Don't you want to stay and watch the dancers for a moment?'

Night was closing fast and shadows elongated the dancing couple into lean, languorous shapes. They were dancing without inhibition—not for an audience, but for themselves. They were unaware that they had been captured in the spotlight of a street lamp in the middle of the city. Staring intently into each other's faces, the dancers inhabited their own erotic world of fierce stares and abrupt movements, finishing in sinuous reconciliation. The tango was the dance of love, Bella realised.

'There is a *milonga*, a neighbourhood dance hall where people go to dance tango—quite famous, actually—just across the street,' Nero explained, bringing Bella back down to earth again. 'That couple will almost certainly be practising for their performance tonight.'

'I'd love to see them dance,' Bella murmured, transfixed by their skill. The man was resting the woman over his arm so that her hair almost brushed the pavement, and the woman was slim and lithe, and dressed for a night of dancing such as Bella couldn't even begin to imagine—and had certainly never experienced.

And was never likely to, she told herself sensibly, but how she envied the woman her confidence and her style. She was wearing the highest stiletto heels and the sheerest black tights with a fine seam up the back, and her dress was the merest whisper of black silk that flicked and clung to her toned, tanned body. The man was taller, but he too was lean and strong. He guided and directed his partner in a way that seemed to have no answer to it until she snapped her legs around him, and that spoke of another truth—that a woman with the right sort of confidence could tame any man.

Right, Bella thought as she watched them, but not this woman, not me. And not this man, she reflected, stealing a glance at Nero. No wonder she was a stranger to this type of dancing. Pulling herself round, she turned to follow the porter into the hotel.

'Do you want to go there later?'

She stopped dead, completely dumbfounded by Nero's question. She felt a shiver of awareness streak down her back. She must have misheard him, surely? 'I'm sorry?' She turned to face him.

'Perhaps you're too tired to go out tonight?' Nero suggested dryly.

Nero was inviting her to join him at the tango club? The mocking challenge in his voice sent warning tingles down her spine. But wasn't this what she had wanted?

On the simplest level she longed to see something of Buenos Aires while she had the chance. Let's not even go near the complicated level, Bella concluded. But hadn't Nero said that tango was the lifeblood of the city? 'As long as I don't have to dance,' she said, feeling happy now she had put a condition on accepting his invitation.

'Don't worry,' he said dryly, 'I've seen you dance.'

A curl of excitement unfurled inside her as Nero met her stare. 'I'll pick you up at ten,' he said.

Now what had she done? Bella wondered as Nero got back into his car and roared away. One thing was sure; she was playing a far more sophisticated game than she was used to.

Up in her hotel room, with its state portrait of a very beautiful and glamorous Eva Peron smiling down, Bella's problems were mounting. She had packed three sets of riding gear for this trip, an unflattering old-fashioned swimming costume that covered up far more than it revealed, a matching cover-up, a pair of shorts, some work clothes, jeans, sneakers, boots, a pile of T-shirts, some serviceable underwear and a couple of sweaters. At the very last minute she had added a neat pencil skirt with a pair of chunky-heeled shoes, a tailored blouse and jacket, just in case she needed to attend a business meeting during her visit. Tango costume, it was not.

Though as she wouldn't be dancing...

She definitely wouldn't be dancing, Bella told herself firmly, remembering how it had felt to be held in Nero's arms at the polo party. And, as strictly speaking this was a business outing with her boss, the pencil skirt would be perfect. Tying her hair back neatly, she told her heart to stop behaving so erratically and, with a final check in the mirror, she drew a deep breath and left the room.

Nero was leaning against the wall at the foot of the stairs. Surrounded by an adoring crowd, he was signing autographs. Yet another reminder that she was out of her depth here. Thank goodness for her sensible business outfit. There was no danger she could be mistaken for one of Nero's girlfriends looking like this. In fact, she should be able to reach the front door without anyone noticing her—

'Bella?'

Wrong. Nero was at her elbow. Or, rather, she was at his. He was so much taller than she was. He was like a solid wall of muscle protecting her from his fans, all of whom seemed intent on getting a piece of him. But all he had to do was speak a few words in his own language and with a collective sigh of understanding the crowd fell back.

'What did you say to them?' Bella asked, impressed.

'I told them you were here so you could learn to dance—' Nero's powerful shoulders eased into a typical Latin shrug. 'I explained that you come from a place where dancing is practically unheard of, and that this is a mercy mission on my part. They understood completely.'

I bet they did, Bella thought. She tilted her chin as Nero held the door for her and walked past him with what she sincerely hoped was a businesslike expression on her face—in the manner of a woman whose intention was to do anything but dance her way into danger tonight.

The tango club was situated on the top floor of an old building. Vast and echoey, the white-flagged floors had turned grey with age and the tiled staircase was of the same vintage, but the people hadn't come to admire the architecture. They were being drawn upstairs by the heady pulse of music, which floated down from an open doorway on the upper landing.

Bella was soon to discover that the whole of the attic space had been transformed into a dance hall. The air was warm and sultry, and the room was lit by candlelight which gave it a golden shadowy hue. The scent of wax melting was added to the faint overlay of perfume and warm clean bodies—and something else…something heady and alluring, which Bella flatly refused to identify as emotion, let alone passion.

Wooden chairs surrounded tables covered with welcoming red-and-white cloths—though no one seemed to be eating as far as Bella could tell—they all were too intent on watching the tango demonstration. The room was packed and hushed. A couple was about to start. A table was quickly found for Bella and Nero, who murmured something in Spanish to a waiter before ushering her ahead of him. She was so drawn to the upcoming performance she almost stumbled—and would have done if Nero hadn't steadied her. 'Sit, Bella,' he prompted.

She sank down on the hard wooden chair, tingling from his touch. This next couple seemed to be the one everyone had been waiting for—and this wasn't the glitzy entertainment Bella had seen on TV back home, but something earthy and sensual, and unashamedly erotic. The moment the accordionist began to play she was drawn into another world. The couple on the dance floor held each other's gaze intently as they moved with feline languor to the steady beat of the music—though this could change in a heel tap into something fierce and aggressive. As the rhythm rose in a climactic wave Bella realised that these dramatic changes from slumbering passion to outright conflict and back again to soothing gestures were exactly what the spectators had come to see. There was no doubt the woman gave as good as she got—pushing her partner away with a blistering glare, only for him to snatch her back again.

This was how her life could be, Bella reflected whimsically, leaning her chin on the heel of her hand. Instead of safe and bland, she could change it in an instant to risk and danger and attack—

Nero returned her to reality with a jolt, asking her what she'd like to drink. 'Water, please.' She didn't trust herself with anything stronger.

How far out of her comfort zone was she now? Bella thought as the performance heated up. If there was one thing she had already learned in Argentina, it was that the tango was the vertical expression of horizontal desire, and she'd have preferred something a touch safer for her first outing with the boss.

Her boss...

It could be worse, she reflected dryly, taking him in. Nero had dressed for the evening in slim black trousers that complemented his incredible physique. His powerful shoulders tapered to his narrow waist, which was cinched by a leather belt. His shoes were black and highly polished, and his shirt was white and crisp—

And he was dressed for dancing, Bella realised with a sudden blaze of panic. Nero was an athlete—one of the world's top athletes. And the tango at this level couldn't be attempted by anyone who didn't enjoy peak fitness. 'Do you dance?' she said weakly as the crashing finale and riotous applause brought the display they'd been watching to a close.

'I love to dance,' Nero assured her, putting down his

glass of wine. 'I love anything where I have to use my body.'

She didn't doubt it, Bella thought, swallowing deep as one of the startlingly beautiful young girls in the club sashayed towards their table. How could she compete with this? Was that why Nero had brought her here? To humiliate her? Was this Nero's revenge for not allowing him to buy Misty?

She was clutching her glass so hard she would break it if she wasn't careful, Bella realised. Then some demon got into her and, throwing caution to the wind, she sprang to her feet. 'I'll dance,' she said wildly, only to find her voice blasting through a momentary silence.

People stared at her. The young girl stared at her. How ridiculous she must seem in her office clothes when everyone else around her was dressed…well, not for the office.

'Bella?'

Tall and imposing, Nero was holding out his hand to her. The music was thrumming with an almost irresistible beat. She did a quick inventory. Her skirt had a slit up the back and everything that should be covered was covered—

And she was nothing if not game. She hadn't come to Argentina to be pushed around, or to be pushed into the shadows. Adopting the typical haughty stare of a female tango dancer, she tilted her chin as a challenge to Nero to follow her to the dance floor.

'Are you sure about this?' he murmured.

The sexy sibilant syllables tickled her ear as she whispered back, 'Absolutely certain—'

She wasn't sure about anything—her own sanity was most in question. But she had excelled in Scottish country dancing at her all-girls school.

'In that case…'

Snatching her to him, Nero managed in the shadows of the dimly lit club to look more saturnine and menacing than he ever had. She tilted her chin a little higher to acknowledge the round of somewhat hesitant applause. 'You'd better lead,' she conceded.

'Oh, I'll lead,' Nero assured her.

'And take it slowly, please—'

'I will,' he promised, sounding amused.

And then her palm was flat against Nero's strong, warm hand and a whole universe of new feelings opened up to her. It would pass, Bella told herself confidently. She was only going to dance with him. What was the worst that could happen? She could make a fool of herself. Something told her that Nero would never allow that to happen. And for just once in her life she wanted to unselfconsciously do something she had watched and admired others do. 'I just have to make sure I don't tread on your feet,' she said awkwardly as they waited for the music to begin.

'Relax,' Nero murmured. 'Just imagine that you're a pony I am breaking in.'

What? 'I'd rather imagine I'm a woman and you're a man who is very kindly teaching me an unfamiliar dance.'

'Oh, I think you'll be familiar with this dance,' Nero murmured.

Bella gulped. She had to be the only person here who wasn't familiar with the dance of love. But how could she not respond to Nero's hand in the small of her back, or the insistent pressure of his thigh? He could be so subtle and so persuasive and, though she wasn't doing anything clever like flicking her leg through his, she was moving to the music. Nero's control of the dance was absolute, and yet his control was so light she could understand why his polo ponies were so responsive to him. Was it wrong to want a little more pressure? Was it really possible that Nero had such an incredible level of sensitivity, or such a sense of rhythm, and such an acute insight into what pleased her most?

'You dance well,' he said as a smattering of applause greeted their first experiment. 'You have a natural flair.'

Only thanks to him, she thought.

'And now let's try and put a little more passion into it. Look at me, Bella. Look at me as if you hate me.'

At least something was easy.

'That's good. Now soften a little…entice me…'

She could do that too—but not too much. A brush from Nero's body was like a lightning bolt to her system. No one was required to weld themselves to their teacher, Bella reassured herself. She would call upon her under-used acting skills instead. Raising a brow, she stared at Nero beneath her eyelashes. Lifting her ribcage, she adopted a more dramatic pose—a move that got her a little more applause.

'Easy,' Nero growled in her ear when she attempted to lead him. 'This is only your first lesson.'

'Then there will have to be many more,' she assured him, growing in confidence and feeling invincible as more couples joined them on the floor.

Perhaps the right word was invisible…

Whatever. She was beginning to think the ability to dance the tango was a prerequisite for living in Argentina. 'From what I've seen tonight, I'm going to need those lessons,' she admitted.

'You certainly will,' Nero agreed. 'And I'll be sure to find someone good to teach you.'

As Bella went stiff and pulled away Nero drew her back again, inch by steady inch. And, yes, she should put an end to this, but why, when Nero kept each move so slow and deliberate and she could easily follow him, and he never once made her feel that he was mocking her, or that he would step over the all-important boundary from stylised dancing into something more threatening and real? He always maintained a space between them and, though some people undoubtedly found tango as intoxicating as sex, she had realised it was the promise of sex rather than the act itself, and as a woman who didn't like admitting how inexperienced she was, that held enormous appeal. Unlike the frenzied bouncing in the marquee at the polo ground, this was dance as art.

Nero loosened his grip when the music faded and led Bella back to their table. 'You're full of surprises, Bella Wheeler,' he said, narrowing his eyes as he gave her a considering look. Raising his hand, he called the waiter over to bring them another drink.

'Just some more water, please.' She had more surprises locked away inside her than Nero could possibly guess at, and she was going to keep a clear head while she was in Argentina to make sure she kept it that way.

CHAPTER SIX

KEEPING a clear head guaranteed Bella an early night. Nero delivered her to the door of her hotel and, with a brisk nod, bid her good night. Put him out of your head, she told herself next morning. She was ready to explore.

The Sunday traffic was every bit as crazy as when she had arrived, but she welcomed the noise and bustle of a new day, thinking this was the most exhilarating introduction to a city as fascinating as Buenos Aires that she could possibly have. And she certainly wasn't going to sit in her hotel room wondering what Nero was doing. He had said he would call for her at eleven that morning to take her to his *estancia*. Where he was or what he did before then was Nero's business.

And she didn't care a jot.

Liar, Bella thought as she left the hotel. But she was determined to make the most of her short stay in one of the world's most vibrant and beautiful cities. This was just one of the places Nero called home, and she was curious to explore it. Buenos Aires was full of personality and charm, the staff in the hotel had assured her. Everywhere she went she would find *porteños*, as the residents of Buenos Aires were called, performing the tango on the streets. Crowds gathered, music played, and dancers dressed for the occasion would entertain you, they told her with a smile.

She didn't have to look far before she discovered a small square at the end of the street where an impromptu dance floor had been created simply by laying board down on the cobbles. The sun was warm, the sky was blue, the setting was exquisite and she joined the crowd to watch. Colourful gardens surrounded her and the central fountain in the tiny square provided a pleasant overlay to the music. A small white rococo church with steeples like plump figs added to the charm of the setting. She was really in South America now, Bella thought, feeling excited and rather cosmopolitan. Shading her eyes, she watched the dancers and soon she was lost in their skill, and in the music, and was hardly aware that someone had walked up behind her.

'How easy it would be to relieve you of this,' a husky male voice very close to her ear said disapprovingly.

'Nero!' Her heart lurched violently. So much for playing it cool. The heat of the dance was all around them—most of it in her cheeks when Nero held up the wallet he had taken from her handbag.

'Your handbag was open,' he explained. 'Lucky for you the hotel told me where I could find you. I hope you're packed and ready to leave?'

'Of course.' She was thrown immediately from carefree tourist into awkward sort-of-employee, and had to move quickly on from that mind-set to professional woman whose only purpose in being in Argentina was to do a worthwhile job for the prince of her country. She held out her hand for the wallet and Nero gave it to her. Stuffing it back into her shoulder bag, she fastened the catch securely. 'Do you make a habit of this?' she demanded.

'Do you make a habit of leaving your wits behind when you travel?' Nero countered.

They stared at each other. The dance between them had begun. Tango must be catching, Bella thought dryly. 'Shall we?' she said, keen to break eye contact.

'By all means.'

She turned for the hotel. That husky Argentine accent was the sexiest in the world, she decided as she led the way.

And she'd soon get used to Nero's voice and let it wash over her, Bella told herself firmly, quickening her step. But however prim she tried to act, Buenos Aires worked against her. There was too much passion here—too many dancers expressing their feelings on this Sunday morning, swirling, spinning, legs flicking, arms raised at acute angles—men in spats, women dropping as if into a dead faint in their partners' arms, only to revive so they could continue the fight. It was exhausting just watching them.

'Tango gets into your blood,' Nero commented when they reached the steps of Bella's hotel.

Then she must be sure not to let it get into her own blood, Bella thought. 'I'll just ask the porter for my suitcase. I left it ready in the lobby when I checked out.'

'Your case has already been taken to the airport.'

'The airport?' Bella's throat dried. Was Nero sending her home? Were her services no longer required?

'I take it you won't mind being my only passenger?' he demanded.

She must have looked at him blankly. 'In the jet,' he prompted.

'You'll be flying a jet to the *estancia*?' she confirmed.

'Yes. Is something wrong with that?'

'No, of course not.' Didn't everyone have a selection of private jets from which to choose?

The cockpit of Nero's executive jet was yet another confined space in which Bella was forced to sit too close to Nero. Of course, she could have sat in the back where there were comfortable leather seats, and entertainment as well as refreshments on tap, but she had given way to a childish urge to sit next to the pilot.

And taste a little of that danger she was growing so fond of?

She had always been fascinated by the concept of flight, Bella argued primly with her inner voice.

And fascinated by Nero.

Why pretend? She had an overriding desire to sit next to Nero.

He checked the buckles on her seat belt and helped her to fit the headphones securely. 'Okay?'

Her senses soared to answer him before she could. He smiled deep into her eyes. Nero saw everything, Bella realised, turning quickly to stare out of the window. By the time he had completed his pre-flight checks she could hardly breathe for arousal. He was totally in control, and his self-assurance filled her with confidence—and not just as to how well Nero would fly a jet.

'There's no need to be nervous,' he said, turning to look at her.

'I'm not nervous,' she protested, consciously relaxing her grip on the seat. Just sitting next to him was making her nervous. Going to Nero's *estancia*, where the only way out was by private plane, or goodness knew how long a road trip, was nothing short of insanity.

'Don't look so worried, Bella; I'll take care of you.'

That was what she was afraid of. 'The only thing

wrong with me,' she said as Nero lined up the jet for take-off, 'is that I like to be in control. Sitting in the copilot's seat doesn't suit me.'

'But it suits me very well,' Nero assured her, breaking off to acknowledge instructions from the control tower. Having been given the all-clear, he opened the throttle and released the brake and in seconds, or so it seemed, the small jet rocketed into the clear blue sky.

There was no turning back now, Bella thought as the jet soared through the first bank of cloud.

After a couple of hours the clouds parted to reveal a very different world from the towering skyscrapers and sprawling urbanisations of Buenos Aires. Nero's private airstrip was little more than a thin stripe of bleached earth on what seemed to be an endless carpet of green and russet and gold, stretching towards a horizon where misty mountains clawed at the cobalt sky with jagged fingers.

The Pampas. Bella's heart leapt with an intoxicating mixture of excitement and fear. The thought of riding here—of living here—with so much space, and so close to nature—

'Wait until you breathe the air,' Nero murmured.

Pollution-free and as heady as the most refined wine, Bella guessed.

'Here,' Nero told her as he banked the jet steeply. 'Take a look out of the side window and you'll see the *estancia*.'

Bella gasped as the g-force hit her.

'Nervous now?' Nero suggested with a wicked grin.

'Not at all,' Bella lied as the jet levelled off.

'You'll need steady nerves while you're working here. Life is tough on the pampas, Bella.'

'I'm not here for easy,' she told him frankly. 'I'm here to do the best job I can.' Her gaze turned to the hundreds of horses on the ground below.

'We had a lot of foals born this year.'

'Incredible,' Bella murmured. Everyone knew Nero was a wealthy man, but this was a polo establishment on an unimaginable scale.

'I'll fly you over the house before we land.'

Her stomach flipped as the plane dropped lower. The house Nero was referring to was an elegant colonial-style building the size of a small town, and now they were only a hundred feet or so above it she could see the long shaded verandas and a formal garden as vast as a park. There was even a polo field at one end of the cultivated grounds, with a stand and clubhouse, while in the central courtyard of the main building a fountain spurted diamond plumes into the air. Behind the house there was a glistening lake with a fabulous sandy beach and one—no, two swimming pools...

'One is for the horses,' Nero said when he saw her looking. 'We use it for treatment and for strengthening exercises, though we ride in the lake for preference—'

Bella exclaimed with pleasure, but then her usual common sense kicked in. What on earth had she been thinking when she had agreed to this? Nero's vast estate was like a country in its own right. She would be as isolated here as if she had been shipwrecked with him and they were stranded on a desert island with the ocean surrounding them. Unless she could find some way to ignore the electricity that constantly sparked between them, this could turn into a very tense and challenging stay.

Nero landed the jet skilfully with scarcely a bump. As he slowed to a halt and cut the engines Bella's concerns gave way to excitement. 'Oh, just look at that,' she exclaimed as she stared out across the miles of rolling grass. 'I can't wait to get out there and smell the air.'

'Feel the sun, and ride the horses,' Nero added with matching enthusiasm. 'It's beautiful, isn't it?'

When the door of the jet swung open Bella was greeted by a gust of warm, fragrant air. She was so excited she didn't even shrug off Nero's steadying hand when he helped her down the steps. There was always that small adjustment from sitting and floating to stepping out onto terra firma—add her eagerness to that and she was like a wild pony who, for that moment at least, was glad of Nero's reassuring presence. A wind had kicked up, blowing her hair about, and the ground was dusty and hard beneath her feet, but the warmth of her welcome was in no doubt at all.

'This is Ignacio,' Nero explained, introducing an elderly man standing by the utility vehicle waiting to take them to the ranch. 'My estate manager and right-hand man.'

Now she really was on the pampas, Bella thought, feeling a thrill of excitement as the elderly man stepped forward to shake her hand. She took in the slouched hat and red bandana, the voluminous trousers worn with leather chaps to protect the gaucho's legs from the constant friction of riding a horse. 'Welcome to Estancia Caracas,' he said in heavily accented English, bowing briefly over Bella's hand.

'*Buenas tardes*—good afternoon,' Bella replied, feeling more than welcome.

'We have heard many good things about your work with the English horses,' Ignacio added graciously.

'And battled the proof of it on the polo field,' Nero said as both men laughed.

'You're too kind. Your work with horses is second to none in Argentina.' Nero's estate manager had skin like beaten leather and was as wrinkled as a turtle, but his raisin-black eyes were full of kindness and warmth, and his handshake was firm. 'I'm so pleased to meet you, Ignacio. *Mucho gusto.*'

Ignacio grunted appreciatively at Bella's attempt to speak his language and said something in rapid Spanish to Nero that elicited a noncommittal hum.

Whether Nero was pleased or not by her clumsy effort, she had made one friend, Bella thought, judging by the warmth in the elderly gaucho's eyes as he invited her to sit in the vehicle for the short drive to the house.

She found everything thrilling, even the bumpy ride during which Ignacio pointed out the colourful ducks flying in arrow formation against the flawless blue sky, and then Nero spotted one of the giant hares native to the pampas as it bounced across the road. 'Look, Bella,' he said, grabbing hold of her arm in his excitement.

That touch was most thrilling of all, she thought, and the sights were pretty spectacular. And now Nero's powerful arm was resting across the seat in front of her. The only decoration he wore was a steel wristwatch that could probably tell their position in relation to the moon, but his sheer physical presence was what overwhelmed her.

'Good, huh?'

She jumped alert as he prompted her. 'Amazing,' she murmured, staring into his eyes. This time she had to force her stubborn gaze outside the vehicle.

They entered Estancia Caracas through an arched

entrance that reminded Bella of old cowboy films where the gates loomed large and impressive in what was otherwise a barren landscape. A long, well-groomed drive led the way to the sprawling hacienda—though this was a hacienda with a capital H—far larger and better kept than seemed humanly possible in such a wild and remote area, she decided as Ignacio turned into a cobbled courtyard the size of a football pitch.

'Wow,' Bella murmured. Nero's home was seriously fabulous.

They got out and she paused for a moment. The breeze was tickling the leaves on the eucalyptus trees and the only other sound was the distant whinnying of a horse. The courtyard was full of flowers—vivid cascades tumbling down the walls and draping in lush swags over the balconies. 'You must find it so hard to leave here,' she murmured.

'And so good to come back,' Nero agreed. 'Shall we?'

'Yes, of course.' The walls of the hacienda were painted in a muted shade of chalky terracotta, while the smooth cobbles beneath her feet were a deeper shade of golden red. Everything looked so warm and welcoming beneath the cobalt sky.

'Is this not what you had expected?' Nero demanded as Bella exclaimed with pleasure as she trailed her fingertips across some clusters of blossom.

Of such a hard, rugged man? 'No,' she admitted. 'I don't know what I expected, really.'

'So what do you think now?'

'That you have mastered the art of living in harmony with your surroundings,' she said honestly.

Nero seemed pleased by this analysis and introduced Bella to María, his cook and housekeeper, and María's sister, Concepcion, both of whom were waiting to greet him outside the door. The older ladies' faces were wreathed in smiles. They were so obviously delighted to see him Bella could only conclude Nero must have been an engaging child.

Perhaps she was being a little unfair to him, Bella conceded as the women bustled ahead, turning constantly to check that Nero hadn't left them again. The large hallway was paved in fabulous terracotta marble, softened by cinnamon-coloured rugs. The walls, painted a warm cream, were hung with antique mirrors and pictures. Probably family heirlooms, Bella guessed, apart from a painting of a wild horse, which was more recent and drew her attention immediately.

'Do you like it?' Nero asked, noticing her interest.

'I love it,' she enthused. Gadamus was an American artist noted for his freestyle technique with an airbrush and there was nothing cosy about this picture. There was nothing cosy about her life any longer, Bella thought as she glanced at Nero.

'So, what do you like about it?' he probed.

'The brutal realism,' she said, holding his gaze.

'You're drawn to danger and risk?' Nero suggested.

'It appears so,' Bella agreed coolly. She refused to be over-faced by all this quiet money, or by a man of such power and charisma.

'We'd better not keep María and Concepcion waiting,' Nero pointed out, making her a mocking bow.

They understood each other completely, Bella thought, though her confidence in handling Nero was short-lived. His touch on her arm shot the breath from her lungs as he held the door for her and they traded the shady lobby for an interior courtyard.

She quickly recovered to take in the peaceful haven

where the only disturbance was the sound of water gushing in the fountain to a background of birdsong. The air was scented with blossom, which reminded Bella that Christmas in Argentina was very different to the same season in England. The prince had warned her that she would be leaving the cold northern hemisphere for something very different. How right he was. This was another world altogether…

'You have a beautiful home, Nero.' And she was allowing herself to invest far too much interest and emotion.

The interior of the house made it even harder for Bella to disengage her feelings. There was a grand hall with a sweeping staircase, and the lake they had flown over was the focus of all the main rooms. From the windows of each elegant salon she could see beautifully tended lawns sweeping away to a golden beach and, in the far distance, snow-capped mountains.

'Do you approve?' Nero demanded dryly.

'I've never seen anything like it,' Bella admitted. 'But I'm here to work,' she managed in a firmer tone.

'Of course.'

Nero held the door for her and as she passed in front of him he made her feel so very small and vulnerable. Why must every part of her respond to him so urgently? Her mind must remain set on business, she told herself firmly.

'This is my den,' Nero explained, showing her into a smaller wood-panelled room. 'But you must make yourself at home here.'

Bella felt her smile must be little short of incredulous. Making herself at home here would take a little longer than she intended to spend in Argentina. 'I don't know how you can ever bear to leave,' she exclaimed impulsively.

'That's only because you haven't seen my place in Buenos Aires yet,' Nero informed her dryly.

And was never likely to, she thought. Hey ho.

CHAPTER SEVEN

'You must be hungry,' Nero suggested, leading the way to the kitchen. 'I know I am,' he said.

Nero's lips were pressing down so attractively she would have followed him anywhere, Bella mused wryly.

The kitchen took up a large part of the ground floor, and was another design triumph. State-of-the-art appliances sat comfortably next to well-worn settles and pieces of riding equipment. And, judging by the boots, gloves and polo helmet resting on a small side table next to an easy chair, this was the heart of the home and Nero's preferred space. The seat and the back of the chair wore the imprint of his body, Bella noticed, dragging her gaze away.

'What do you think?' Nero asked.

Censored. Dreams she could have, but she wasn't sharing them with him. 'Something smells good,' she said, inhaling appreciatively. And such smells they were—aromatic broth steaming busily on top of the old range cooker, the scent of freshly baked bread and ground coffee. Bella's mouth was watering by the time María and Concepcion had invited them to sit at the large scrubbed table.

'Perhaps you would like María to show you to your

bedroom first—so you can freshen up before you eat?' Nero suggested. 'Whenever you're ready, come down, we'll eat and then I'll take you on a tour of the stables.'

'Perfect. Though the bunkhouse would suit me fine,' Bella protested as María led the way into the hall.

'The bunkhouse?' Nero raised an amused brow. 'I'm not sure the gauchos would take too kindly to you moving in. And how could I deny María and Concepcion the pleasure of your sunny nature?' he added dryly.

Was she really such a stuck-up, starchy old maid? She must appear so, Bella realised. If only she could learn how to relax without giving Nero the wrong idea.

Her bedroom was beautiful, full of the scent of flowers freshly picked from the garden and deliciously feminine. She would never have indulged herself to this extent with all the lace and frills and flowers at home. It proved to be another occasion when she had to drag herself away.

She hadn't realised how hungry she was and devoured the delicious meal María placed in front of her. When she finally sat back with a contented sigh she noticed Nero watching her.

'Ms Wheeler?' he said formally, standing to hold her chair. 'Would you care to see the stables now?'

She flashed him a quick smile. 'Thank you, Señor Caracas. I would love to see the stables…'

The prince hadn't exaggerated. Nero's stables were unlike anything she'd seen before—six-star accommodation for horses with amenities second to none. For a moment Bella almost lost her confidence. Everything she was used to back home was so low-key compared to this. Nero's yard was the Bugatti Veyron Super Sport to her banged-up Mini of a polo yard.

But she produced great horses, Bella reminded herself.

It was Nero who shook her out of these concerns when he reminded her that the youngsters would be arriving soon, and that Ignacio wanted to show Bella the ponies he thought suitable for novices. These were retired ponies who couldn't take too much weight and whose exercise regime had been drastically reduced. 'As long as we make sure their mouths can't be dragged—and I have a cure for that,' Bella said, explaining her process with the reins to Nero. Before she knew it, she was right back where she belonged, chatting easily to him about horses. This was one area at least in which there were no tensions between them.

The stables were cleaner than many hotel rooms Bella had stayed in; sweet-smelling hay was banked high and her imagination took flight in the shadowy stall. 'We'd better get on,' she said abruptly, giving Nero one of her tight-lipped smiles.

'Why so tense, Bella?'

'I'd like to see the clinic,' she said, concerned that Nero could read her mind.

He shrugged. 'As you wish.'

Nero's shadow fell over her as he opened the stable door. He made her feel so small and feminine, which was something quite new for Bella. And she would ignore it, she determined.

And that was easy, Bella thought wryly as Nero led the way across the yard. He had changed out of his casual travel clothes into close-fitting breeches, which he was wearing with a deep maroon polo top. The contrast of colours against Nero's tanned skin made for a compelling picture. The wide spread of his shoulders and the hard, tanned chest just visible at the neck of his top didn't hurt either. And she wouldn't have been looking at his breeches if she hadn't been admiring his fabulous knee-length black leather boots. She noted with concern than the placket at the front of his breeches appeared to be under some considerable strain...

'This way,' Nero prompted.

'Of course,' she said, tipping her chin at a professional angle as she followed him.

'I have a polo match next week.'

'Next week?' So soon? And the children were arriving when?

She could cope. She would cope.

'Ignacio thought you would enjoy preparing the ponies with him.'

'I would,' Bella agreed, quickly burying her concerns. 'That's what I'm here for.' She thrilled at the challenge.

'I want the kids to get straight into it as soon as they arrive,' Nero explained, 'and this friendly match with a neighbouring *estancia* will be their first proper introduction to polo, so everything must go smoothly.'

'And it will.' She only had one concern left. Did Nero know the meaning of a *friendly* match? Somehow, Bella doubted it. 'A week isn't a lot of time to prepare the ponies.'

'My ponies are always ready.'

She didn't doubt it. Proud. Hard. Driven—didn't even begin to describe this man. Competition was everything to Nero and, just as she had suspected, this would be anything but a friendly match—and those ponies had better be ready.

It wasn't just the way Nero looked, it was the way he

moved, Bella reflected, allowing him to walk ahead of her so she could assess him like prime breeding stock. She might be the Ice Maiden, happily set on her spinster ways, but that was no curb on admiring a perfect male physique. She was a professional, wasn't she? Bella thought as Nero turned to flash a quick glance her way to make sure she was following. What else did she do all day at work if not stare thoughtfully at muscle and flesh to make sure the beast in question was in tip-top form and had the stamina to do what was required of it without injury? This beast was definitely at the peak of fitness, and Nero's stamina had never been in question.

'That was a heavy sigh,' Nero commented, hanging back to keep pace with her. 'Not tired already, I hope, Bella?'

'Not tired at all. In fact, I can't remember feeling quite so energised.'

'Excellent.' Nero's lips pressed down with approval. 'The pampas air is obviously good for you.'

Something was, Bella thought as her mouth formed the Ice Maiden line.

'This is the hospital and recovery block,' Nero explained as they approached a smart white building.

He held the door open and she walked in under his arm. Heat curled low inside her in a primitive response to Nero's size and virility. The untamed pampas had loosed something elemental inside her. It was just as well the facilities inside the clinic were exceptional and she could quickly become absorbed in these.

'We can carry out operations here if we have to,' Nero explained. 'Vets live on site. There is also a doctor and a nurse in residence to care for the two-legged members of the team. The distances are so vast here we can't rely on help reaching us in time.'

Wasn't that the truth? she thought.

'Bella?'

'Wonderful,' she said, refocusing. 'May I see the facilities for the children now?'

'I can assure you they will be well catered for.'

Bella met and held Nero's proud gaze. 'I wouldn't be doing my job if I left out one of the most crucial parts of it.'

'As you wish.'

Even Nero's back had something to say about her thoroughness. Nero was a fierce, passionate man to whom pride meant everything, and he didn't take kindly to having his establishment judged by anyone, especially her. But pride was important to Bella too, at least where doing the best job possible was concerned.

'I trust this meets with your approval?' he said, opening the door to the first wooden chalet.

How prim and boring he must think her, Bella realised as she took a look around. If she were a child staying here she would be in seventh heaven—there was even a view of the ponies grazing in the paddocks through the windows. 'It's wonderful.' She turned to find Nero with his arms braced either side of the doorway, displaying his formidable physique as he leaned into the room. 'Did you plan the finishing touches while we were in Buenos Aires?' she said, noticing the recent magazines and the latest teen films stacked by the TV.

'I had nothing better to do.'

Nero's tongue was firmly planted in his cheek, Bella suspected. 'What?' she demanded when he raised a brow. 'I didn't spend all my time in Buenos Aires learning to dance the tango…'

'How very noble of you, Bella. And how reassuring for me to know our evening out wasn't wasted.'

She groaned inwardly. What a dull companion he must think her. 'I'll take some shots for the prince,' she said, finding her phone.

'I trust your report will be favourable?'

'How could it not be when you've thought of everything—even fire extinguishers.'

'You won't need one,' Nero murmured under his breath.

The Ice Maiden had never regretted her tag more— and this time there was plenty of room for her to pass Nero at the door without touching him. He was standing well clear.

'Would you like to see the ponies we have chosen for you to look at?'

'I'd love to.'

'So you do trust our judgement?'

'Ignacio's reputation precedes him.'

'As does mine, I have no doubt,' Nero observed dryly as they walked along the dusty path together.

This time she thought it better to say nothing.

CHAPTER EIGHT

As BELLA had expected, Nero and Ignacio had judged the ponies perfectly. 'These will be a match made in heaven,' she said, 'and will give the kids loads of confidence.' She was conscious of Nero brooding at her side and wondered what was on his mind.

'We'd better go,' he said, pulling his booted foot from the fence rail. 'The first group of kids will be arriving soon, and I've no doubt you'll want to settle them in.'

'It's you they'll want to see,' Bella pointed out. Whether he chose to accept it or not, Nero was a national hero. 'It's no secret that half the kids we're expecting to join the scheme would have scoffed at the idea of leaving the city for the wilds of the pampas if there hadn't been a certain attraction named Nero Caracas waiting here for them.'

'Are you attempting to flatter me?' Nero laughed. 'I should warn you, I am immune to it.'

In the same way that familiarity bred contempt? Bella thought. 'I'm merely stating a fact.'

'Then allow me to reassure you,' Nero murmured as they walked back to the hacienda side by side, 'I'll be with you every step of the way.'

Oh, good, Bella thought wryly as her glance crashed into Nero's. 'I'm sure the children will appreciate that.'

'And you will too, I hope?'

The mocking note in Nero's voice hadn't escaped her. 'That goes without saying,' she said.

'Your wish is my command, Bella.'

And if she believed that then she was well on her way to becoming a doormat. Nero would tolerate her involvement at Estancia Caracas for the sake of his scheme and the prince's goodwill—and nothing more. She would have to work harder than she ever had in her life to make this work, Bella realised as Nero snapped his whip against his boots. At least she'd be too tired to dream about him at night. If brooding Nero intended to shadow her she would just have to act out a part—someone confident in her personal as well as her professional life—someone sophisticated who could handle Nero's high-powered sex appeal and take it all in her stride.

Someone else?

There was no one else. There was just Bella Wheeler, the Ice Maiden, and Nero Caracas, the Assassin. Oh, good.

They parted in the kitchen to shower and freshen up. When Nero came downstairs again it amused him to see María stuffing *empanadas*, the delicious little stuffed pastries, inside Bella's mouth as she crossed the kitchen on her way out, and pressing even more pastries into her hands as she tried to get through the door. Someone had made a friend.

'Sorry,' Bella garbled, chewing down a mouthful as he left the house to join her.

'Don't apologise,' he said, stealing a pastry from her hands. 'Hmm, delicious,' he agreed, smacking his hands together to get rid of the crumbs.

She risked a smile.

'What are you wearing?' he demanded.

'Dungarees—I thought, settling kids in, carrying cases…'

He shrugged.

'You don't agree?'

'There are others here who can carry cases. Wasn't it you who said we're the inspiration? And, as in this instance, I agree you're right, and so I dressed the part.' Nero ran a hand down his black polo shirt with the team emblem—The Assassin's skull and crossbones boldly embroidered in white on black over his heart. His hand moved on down his close-fitting breeches, tough riding boots and the knee protectors he customarily wore during a match. 'This is all about first appearances, you said—give the kids something to remember?'

'I see what you mean…' She frowned, but swiftly rallied. 'I suppose none of them would have a clue who you were if you were waiting for them wearing jeans.'

He met the innocent look with the faintest of smiles. 'You're probably right,' he agreed mildly.

'So, as I'm short of a Hammer House of Horrors polo shirt, what do you suggest I wear?' she asked.

Holding the concerned gaze, he put a curb on his amusement. 'What would you think if you were greeted by a woman in dungarees?'

Bella shrugged. 'The grooms were too busy caring for the horses to hang around waiting for my coach?' she suggested, reasoning that the grooms were all young—and, however scruffy they got in the course of their work, all attractive. The kids would only think an older woman in dungarees a poor substitute who probably knew nothing about horses, anyway.

'And?' Nero pressed, dipping his head to stare her in the eyes.

'The owners and trainers had better things to do?'

'And how would that make you feel?'

'Okay,' she agreed. 'You've made your point.'

'As you made yours,' Nero pointed out wryly.

He was right. If Bella had been one of the kids arriving on the coach she would like to think her arrival counted for something—enough, at least, for the people who ran the course to be waiting to greet her. 'I'll go and put something else on.'

Nero glanced at his watch. There was just enough time for Bella to change her clothes. He watched her return to the house, straight-backed, with a brisk stride. He anticipated the transformation with interest.

'Much better,' he approved when she cocked a brow before mutely running her hands down her neatly packaged frame.

Much, *much* better, he thought as his body responded with indecent enthusiasm to Bella's transformation. This was far better than dungarees, and a vast improvement on her working breeches. It was even better than Bella in a straight-laced evening dress.

'Would you like me to do a twirl?' she asked with a heavy dose of sarcasm.

'I've seen you dance, remember? So I know twirls aren't your strength.' He held her gaze. He loved holding her gaze. And so they stared at each other—staring into each other's eyes, neither one of them prepared to back down.

Until the sound of a coach approaching forced them both to glance away. But even as he stood ready to welcome the children he was keenly aware of the extremely attractive woman standing at his side dressed in no-nonsense breeches and a crisp white tailored shirt.

* * *

The children were settling in, but there was no time to relax. While his team of gauchos took the children through safety procedures and introduced them to the ponies, it was time for Nero and Bella to turn their thoughts towards the polo match. 'Let's get started, shall we?' he said, heading off towards the stables.

Bella pulled a wry face as she tucked a strand of rebellious hair back into position. 'I hope you don't live to regret involving me in this.'

He did too.

'Are you sure you're not going to find this too much? Teaching reckless kids and even wilder ponies?' He stared into her eyes, wanting to study Bella more deeply. He was a practical man. Sometimes lust intruded. Usually he would take a practical view of what was on offer—make his decision—yes or no, and then move on. Bella was too vulnerable for that. She might be acting the role but, like any actress, Bella's woman-of-the-world façade came off with the costume.

'I'm sure,' she said, meeting his gaze confidently. 'I have some experience of…coping.'

She spoke without emotion, and then he remembered Bella had three younger siblings—brothers, none of whom were interested in horses or their father's yard, and all of whom had gone on to university, thanks to Bella's riding boot up their backside. The children had lost their mother at an early age, and when their father had gone to pieces it had been left to Bella to set things on an even keel. There was more to this Ice Maiden than most people even guessed at and, remembering what he'd seen of her other side on the dance floor, he said, 'I hope you'll make time for your tango lessons. Or will they have to be put on hold for now?'

Her timing was perfect. There was a short pause,

and then, 'Why should they be put on hold?' she asked, 'Ignacio has promised to hone my technique, so the next time you and I hit the dance floor, I'll be ready for you.'

'Oh, will you?' he said.

So Ignacio was going to teach Bella the tango, was he? First María, and now Ignacio—what was happening here? 'You want to watch Ignacio,' he said, narrowing his eyes in mock suspicion. 'Many a good tune is played on an old fiddle.'

Bella laughed, letting herself go for the first time in a long time, but then she angled her chin to stare into his eyes. 'Are you jealous, Nero?'

He huffed and turned away.

'Could we have a drink before we start thinking about the polo match?' she asked, catching up with him in the yard.

'Water okay for you?'

'Perfect,' she said.

He led the way into the barn. Opening the door, he let it swing shut behind them. They were instantly enclosed in warm silence. Walking over to a sink in the corner, he filled a container with the crystal-clear water that flowed straight from the glacier via an underground stream to the hacienda. 'We'll take this with us,' he said, offering the container to Bella first.

She drank deeply and then handed it to him. He did the same. As he wiped the back of his hand across his mouth he caught her staring at him. His mouth curved with amusement as he read her thoughts. They had shared a drink from the same container. It was the closest their mouths had come to touching—up to now.

She was within touching distance of Nero. There was something magical about a hay barn. Perhaps it was the mountains of dried grass soaking up the sound, or the dust motes floating on sunbeams giving the impression of a shimmering golden veil between them. It was a soft—a ridiculously soft—frame, in which Nero appeared violently masculine.

'Bella?' he murmured.

'Could I have another drink?' She reached for the canister. Their fingers touched as Nero handed it to her and a bolt of electricity shot up her arm.

'We'd better fill it again before we leave,' he said as she lowered the container from her lips. Holding her gaze, he removed it from her hand and placed it on the side. She drew in a sharp breath as Nero's hands rested lightly on her arms.

'What are you frightened of, Bella?'

She couldn't look at him even though the temptation to let go just this once was overwhelming. 'I'm not frightened.'

'Prove it,' Nero said quietly, and behind his customary irony Bella sensed a deeper layer of concern.

'Shouldn't we be getting on?' She glanced across the honeyed space—the chasm between them and the door. Nero was like a sleeping tiger, breathing steadily and yet keenly aware at the same time. She had never played the mating game before, but she knew the signs. The look in Nero's eyes—the attractive tug at one corner of his mouth. Nero liked her. No. It was a lot more than that...

'Bella, Bella,' he murmured.

She swayed a little closer.

But something was wrong...something was out of sync. It felt as if she was edging along a tightrope with the promise of the most wonderful reward at the end of it with snapping sharks waiting in the waters below. At no point had Nero touched her—in fact, he had pulled back, and now one brow was raised in sardonic enquiry. 'What was that about?' he said.

Softening had been an insane lapse of judgement on her part—that was what it had been, Bella thought. She shared a professional relationship with Nero and that was all.

Until he dragged her close and rasped, 'You have no idea what you're playing with.' And, as she stared up at him in mute bewilderment, he added, 'I advise you very strongly to think before you act, Bella. You think you know me? You think you can play your schoolgirl games with me?'

'Don't worry,' she flashed, bouncing back onto the attack as she broke free. 'There's not the slightest chance I will ever play games with you.' And, when Nero laughed, she added, 'You're not as irresistible as you seem to think you are.' And that was meant to be her exit line, but Nero snatched her back again. 'Let go of me,' she warned him.

'You don't want this?' Nero smothered her cry of protest the most effective way he could. Brushing his lips across hers until the need poured out of her in whimpers of anger and frustrated tears, he took possession of her mouth in a fierce salty kiss.

Balling her hands into fists, she thrust them against his chest. She soon learned that fighting Nero was pointless. She should have hated him for this victory, but how could she when she wanted him, and when every encounter in the past was as nothing compared to this? The taste of him…the spice and scent of warm clean man…the feelings flooding through her veins…the heat pooling in her heart, her body, her senses…the need building up inside her…the urge to claim him as her mate.

When Nero kissed her the world and all its complications fell away. There was nothing left but sensation and the absolute conviction that this was right.

'*Dios*, Bella!' He thrust her away.

Shaken to the core, she was panting, while Nero towered over her, looking down as if he hated her. 'What if I was a different man, Bella? Don't you know what a dangerous game this is?'

'It's a game you're playing too,' she whipped back, hand across her mouth as if that could hide the proof of her arousal. She had to turn away to catch her breath before she could come back at him. Gripping the edge of the sink as if her life depended upon it, she drew a deep calming breath. Nero was right. They were both equally to blame for this. She had wanted him, but this was wrong. They were both wrong.

On the outside at least, she was utterly calm by the time she turned round again. 'We shouldn't keep Ignacio waiting,' she said coolly.

Nero opened the barn door and she walked through. And now it was back to business, Bella told herself firmly. She must forget this as if it had never happened. Or lose her credibility.

Her work provided the lifeline. The sound of churning water saved her. It distracted her and she exclaimed with interest when their route to the polo yard took them past the hydrotherapy spa. 'Can I take a closer look?'

'Of course.' Nero hung back while she went to watch the pony having its treatment. Rubber matting on the floor and side walls prevented accidental injury, and the spa stall was just large enough for the horse to feel safe as the healing salts in the chilly water bubbled around its legs. 'This is fantastic,' she commented.

'The low temperature increases the pony's circulation

and speeds up the curative process,' Nero explained, coming to stand beside her.

She breathed a sigh of relief. Thank goodness they had found something of interest in common that didn't put either her reputation or her heart at risk. 'I don't have anything like this in England.' She flashed a glance at Nero, and then remembered how things stood between them.

'I'm sure you'll find everything you need here, Bella.'

'I'm sure I will,' she said, determined to ignore the shiver of arousal that rippled down her spine.

CHAPTER NINE

As PART of the final matching process between horse and rider for the upcoming polo game, Nero was mounted and ready to give a riding demonstration. This was primarily for Bella so he could show her each pony's paces and quirks, though the newly arrived youngsters from the city had been invited to watch too.

This was why they were here, Bella thought as she watched the rapt faces around her. Nero might look like a movie star, but they all knew he wasn't playing a role, and he was doing more than show the paces of each horse. He was making the kids hungry—making them aspire to do better—to be the best they could be, so they could make a difference in the world in which they lived. But for now, Nero could turn a polo pony on a sixpence. He could gallop, skid to a halt in a cloud of dust within inches of the fence and make them all scream. He could prompt a pony to weave and turn, back up, rear round and change direction constantly, without appearing to move a muscle. And he did all this with the nonchalance of a Sunday ride in the park.

Nero was cool—really cool. He wasn't just the master of the game or even the horse he happened to be riding. Nero was master of himself, and that was sexy. He was powerful, and yet he coaxed a wild animal to be part of a team, and to do that he had to be sensitive and almost primal in his understanding of the relationship between two living things—and almost preternaturally refined in the delicacy of the adjustments he made to draw differing responses from the horse. It didn't take much to start wondering how that sensitivity of his might translate in bed.

And she had to stop thinking like that right away. She joined in the applause when Nero cantered round the ring acknowledging the appreciation of his audience with one hand raised. Staring at his strong tanned hand and imagining how it would feel resting on her naked body—firm, yet light and intuitive when it came to dealing pleasure. She had to stop that too.

'Did you draw any conclusions?' Nero demanded, reining in his horse in front of her.

'Plenty,' Bella managed as her throat went suddenly dry.

'Good.' Slipping his feet out of the stirrups, Nero eased his powerful limbs. 'I look forward to hearing your comments when I've helped the boys take the ponies back.'

'Right.' She nodded as he wheeled the pony away, but she was still rather more drawn by his muscular thighs straining the seams of his breeches than by any conclusions she had made on the work front. 'Get real, Bella,' she muttered impatiently under her breath.

Nero and Ignacio received her comments with approving nods. At least she hadn't lost it where horses were concerned. But that didn't address the bigger problem, Bella mused as Nero started to walk off with Ignacio. Staying in the house with him meant she saw Nero every day. She couldn't afford to slip up again like she had in the barn. 'I'll see you later,' she called to the two men as she headed off in the opposite direction.

She could be happy here, Bella realised as she walked along the path between the paddocks and the warm breeze ruffled her hair. It was the type of life people dreamed of, with the added spice of Nero close by. Reaching the house, she was already anticipating the welcoming smiles from María and Concepcion. The warmth of family, she thought as she opened the kitchen door. Kicking off her boots, she lined them up on the mat. Walking across the room, she left her helmet and riding gloves where Nero left his. It was maybe the closest she'd come to him since their kiss...

Seeing her smile fade momentarily, the two beaming women hijacked her with a piece of chocolate cake. 'Mmm—delicious,' Bella exclaimed, biting deep.

'More,' the two women insisted, cutting her a second slice.

'I'll miss you both so much when I go home,' she told them both in halting Spanish whilst fending off their attempts to force-feed her. She'd tried to learn more of the language, wanting to get closer to the people she was living with. She had only been in Argentina a short time, but it had made a huge impression on her. It wasn't just the facilities here, or even the challenging ponies...

It must be something in the air, Bella decided wryly, sucking crumbs off her fingers as she headed for the door. Nero *and* the pampas? That was quite a combustible combination for anyone to handle...

So she'd leave it for someone with more relationship smarts than she had.

And now she was jealous of that unknown someone.

She must remember not to let her feelings show, Bella

realised as María chased her to the door in an attempt
to feed her more reviving chocolate cake. Laughing and
holding up her hands in submission, she took the cake,
dropped a kiss on María's cheek and ran upstairs to her
bedroom.

Trailing her fingertips across the beautiful hand-
worked quilt, Bella's gaze was drawn as it had been the
first time she'd walked into the room, to an oil painting
over the fireplace. Bella's mother had been soft and
kind, but the woman in this portrait had Nero's fierce
stare and was dressed like a gaucho in men's clothes.
The only nod to femininity was the froth of chiffon at
her neck.

Bella lay on the bed, staring at the portrait. The strong
character of the woman in the painting blazed out at her.
That must have been one formidable lady, Bella thought,
taking in the determined set of the woman's jaw, the
unflinching gaze, and the line already cutting a cruel
furrow down one side of her full red lips. The likeness
to Nero was uncanny. And I bet she had a sardonic smile
too, Bella mused. The woman in the painting looked as
if she could cut any man down to size with either a whip
or her tongue. It pleased Bella to recognise the countryside in the background, though the *estancia* appeared
much smaller. No wonder the ranch had grown, she
thought, smiling as she took in the woman's planted fist
on top of the sturdy fencing. The portrait spoke volumes
about Nero's ancestry and why he was so attached to
the *estancia*. With people like that in his family, how
could he not be?

Nothing much had changed, Bella reflected as she
went to take a shower. Estancia Caracas might be huge
now and home to a very rich man, but Nero was as
much a warrior as the woman in the painting. Had no

softening influences touched him? What about his parents? Had they been written out of the picture? He never spoke about them. What sort of childhood had he had? And would she ever know?

It seemed unlikely, Bella thought as she soaped herself down. Nero wouldn't confide in her, and she could hardly question his staff.

One idyllic day melted into another, with Bella growing ever closer to Nero's staff until she felt like a real member of the team, and the youth scheme was going even better than she had dared to hope. Ignacio lightened everything, making her laugh and drip-feeding her information about Nero, as if the elderly gaucho wanted her to know what made his boss tick. The portrait in her bedroom was Nero's grandmother, he explained.

No surprise there, Bella thought dryly. She only had one regret left. She hardly saw Nero. They ate at different times, and he never seemed to be around when she was teaching. Whether he was too busy preparing for the polo match or whether he was avoiding her, she had no idea. It was none of her business what Nero was doing with his time. If she had any sense at all, she wouldn't miss him.

But she did.

The night before the ponies were due to arrive from England Bella slept fitfully. When she did manage to doze off, the young woman in the portrait seemed to come alive. With a fist planted on her hip and her strong jaw jutting at a determined angle, it felt as if she was sizing Bella up.

At one point Bella shot up with a start and switched the lights on. The room was empty. Of course it was empty, but when the cockerel crowed she realised it was time to get up. Leaping out of bed, she pushed back the heavy curtain. Excitement flashed inside her at the sight of a dust cloud that could only herald the horseboxes arriving from England.

Nero was already out in the yard.

If there was one thing guaranteed to bring Nero out, it was horses.

Heedless of how she looked or what she was wearing, Bella tugged her old dungarees over her pyjamas, adding a baggy sweater for extra warmth. There was no time to scrape her hair back, though she did pause in the bathroom to run a toothbrush over her teeth before racing out of the room and pelting downstairs. Tearing through the kitchen, startling María and Concepcion along the way, she burst through the door just in time to jog alongside the lead vehicle until it slowed to a stop in the stable yard.

'Leave this to the drivers, Bella,' Nero said sharply as she began to reach for the locks.

She was elated at the sight of Nero and feeling purposeful at the thought of the horses so close at hand. And determined to have her own way.

'I said leave it,' Nero snapped.

Moving in front of her, he said, 'This is men's work.'

'Men's work?' Bella demanded. 'Would your grandmother have said that?'

Nero's face froze and in that split second Bella said firmly, 'Excuse me, please,' and moved past him.

Bella was certain his expression could put a layer of ice on the lake, but Misty was in the back of this transporter and no one was getting in her way.

'Why don't you go back to the house and let us handle this?' Nero suggested in a more persuasive tone. She looked at his hand covering hers. 'I'll let you know when Misty's settled.'

'I'd like to do that myself. I want to welcome my own horse and check her over. I won't be going back to the house until I've checked all the ponies over,' she assured him. Planting her fists on her hips, she stared at him and he stared at her, neither of them moving.

'Shall we get on with this?' Nero suggested dryly as the back of the trailer was unhitched.

'Together,' she insisted.

Nero's lips tugged a little as he stretched the ironic stare. 'Together,' he agreed finally.

Good. This might be Nero's *estancia*, but the ponies were her responsibility too. They'd had a long drive, and a transatlantic flight and—

And standing up to Nero excited her. Her heart was pounding. And, much as she loved her work, she couldn't put all this excitement down to the arrival of her favourite horse.

Nero took charge of the lead horse, a towering bay called Colonel, one of his favourites, Bella remembered, while she took happy charge of Misty. It was inevitable they walked to the stables together—or, more accurately, walked to the small paddock outside the clinic where the ponies would wait their turn to be checked over by the vet.

'They'll be here for a few days of observation,' Nero explained as Misty whickered and nuzzled Bella. 'We'll keep her close for a few days, allow her to get acclimatised, and then you can ride her whenever you want.'

Bella's jaw must have dropped. It was the first time anyone had ever stepped in and told her what she could or couldn't do with her ponies. 'When I judge it right, I'll ride her.'

'With the vet's approval.'

'In consultation with the vet.' She had her hand balled into a fist, Bella realised, and it was resting on the top of the fence in a disturbing mirror pose of the woman in the painting in her room. And, just like Nero's grandmother, she wasn't about to back down.

The sight of Bella, even in those wretched dungarees, stirred all sorts of unwelcome feelings inside him. Those feelings had only increased when she'd drawn battle lines between them. Why must Bella make his life so complicated? Why couldn't she just fall into line?

Like the girls who put him to sleep? The girls who had nothing to talk about? The girls who might as well have lived on another planet? Was that the type of person he would like to change Bella into?

Okay. He'd felt her passion in the barn. It was all or nothing for Bella. Sex without commitment would never be enough for her. Sex with commitment was something he had never contemplated. That didn't stop his happy contemplation of her naked body beneath the shapeless clothes as they led the horses towards the veterinary station. On the surface, Bella was ignoring him, but there was a current snapping between them as she whispered sweet nothings in her pony's ear. She was probably instructing Misty to obey no one but Bella—

And who could he blame for bringing Bella here?

No one but himself.

By the eve of the polo match all the horses had passed the vet's stringent tests, which was a relief. Bella had taken it upon herself to exercise Misty the moment the small mare was given the all-clear and now Nero was down at the corral with the other men, with his boot lodged on one of the wooden struts of the enclosing fence as he watched some of the new yearlings being put through their paces. He was aware of Bella coming up on his right. He felt her presence the moment she left the house and walked across the yard. He could feel her quiet determination and confidence. Both were justified. When it came to her job, Bella had no equal—other than himself, and Ignacio, of course. When it came to caring for the ponies, Bella's energy, intuition and love for them was second to none—except, perhaps, his.

He could see her now without turning—her hair would be scraped back beneath a net under the hard hat she always wore for riding. He turned his head to confirm he wasn't wrong—giving himself the excuse that he didn't want any injuries on his conscience...

Of course she was wearing a hard hat. Perversely, he wanted to see her with her red hair flowing free now.

'Nero.' She acknowledged him briskly without breaking step.

He dipped his head briefly in response. He wouldn't see her again until she supervised the quick changes from one pony to the next between the chukkas that divided the game. Bella would be working with Ignacio, which was a great honour for her. Ignacio traditionally worked alone. But Bella was different, his elderly friend had told him.

'She has the heart of a gaucho—'

He looked at Ignacio, standing by his side.

'She reminds me of your grandmother...'

Nero hummed and curbed his smile. Those few words were probably the longest speech he'd ever heard from Ignacio on any subject that didn't include a horse. They were both staring at Bella, but he was remembering the grandmother who had brought him up, and whose portrait now hung in Bella's bedroom. In her youth,

Annalisa Caracas was said to possess the beauty of a pampered aristocrat. Nero knew she had the courage of a frontierswoman and rode like a man. Born to great wealth, Nero's father had considered a life of ease his natural right and had allowed the *estancia* to slip into ruin, forcing his own mother to come out of retirement and turn it round. It was lucky for him *and* the ranch that his grandmother had stepped in, and Annalisa Caracas was firmly placed on a pedestal in his mind.

Yes, Annalisa Caracas had been quite a woman.

He was jolted out of these thoughts by Ignacio nudging him. Bella had just mounted up and was turning her small mare towards the freedom of the pampas. He shook his head and huffed a laugh as the gauchos cheered when she set Misty at the fence instead of taking her through the gate. The small mare sailed over and then tossed her head, and in spirit so did Bella.

This was the first time in a long time, Nero realised, that he had stood with the other men to watch a woman ride.

CHAPTER TEN

THE polo match loomed ever closer and excitement was reaching fever pitch on the ranch. But it was more than excitement, Bella realised. It was as if they were preparing for the battle of the century. No piece of turf or rail had been left unchecked and her young charges were bursting with excitement. A sense of purpose had gripped everyone on the *estancia*—yet these were people whose world revolved around horses and polo, and who should surely take this *friendly* game in their stride?

Friendly game? Some hope, Bella mused. The team representing the neighbouring *estancia* were also world-class players, and although she didn't usually get worked up where testosterone-pumped males indulging in feats of macho lunacy were concerned, this was different. This was polo. But today even her great love for the game wasn't enough to stop her being anxious for Nero.

As the day wore on people arrived from far and wide. The match had brought the great and good of Argentina in helicopters, private jets and impressive cars, but there was also a large contingent of unsophisticated vehicles—trucks, horseboxes, battered Jeeps, cars with cracked suspension, rusting wheel arches and dubious paint jobs, along with a clutch of horse-drawn carts, as well as whole families riding in convoy on their ponies, trailing mules behind them, loaded with supplies. Polo meant fiesta on the pampas. It was both an excuse for a party as well as an all too rare get-together for far-flung families. All these people needed shade and water and food, as well as the other facilities associated with a small mobile city, and Bella and the rest of the staff had worked tirelessly to ensure that the event was a success. She was thrilled to think that everyone had come to see Nero Caracas, their national hero, lead his team. Nero represented everything that was proud and fine and wonderful about Argentina—her adopted country, Bella reflected as she stared out across the pampas. That was exactly how she felt about Nero's homeland—as if she belonged here.

And that was enough daydreaming when there was work to be done. The air of expectation gripping the crowd had made the ponies skittish—particularly Colonel, the pony on which Nero had decided to finish the match. In Bella's opinion, it would have been better to use Colonel in the first, or at least one of the earlier chukkas, rather than keeping the high-spirited horse until the end of the match, but Nero had overruled her saying his old faithful only needed time to calm down.

If only she could learn to calm down when it came to Nero, Bella reflected as he strode towards her down the pony lines. Surely, she should have got used to how he looked by now, but the sight of him still thrilled her—she still filled her eyes with him as she might have feasted them on a work of art. Nero was brutally beauti-ful, but he was more than that, she thought as her heart banged painfully in her chest. Oh, to hell with it—he was the sexiest man alive!

'Ready?' he said briefly.

'Ready,' Bella confirmed.

They had both checked the ponies numerous times. They were both professionals doing the job they did best, but that didn't cut off the electricity between them, or reduce her concern for Nero's safety in what was certain to be a fiercely competitive match.

And then the polo groupies arrived. Argentina was no different to the UK when it came to girls managing to look as if they had just stepped out of the fashion pages of some glossy magazine in this most workmanlike of settings. And here they were, complete with high heels and short flirty skirts, picking their way across a carpet of cobbles and horse manure. If she'd tried wearing shoes like that she'd have been up to her ankles in muck by now. She had to hand it to them, Bella thought as they clustered round Nero, the girls were groomed to the max. She couldn't blame them for their fascination. Polo was a savage game for rugged men, and horses as high-spirited could be found anywhere in the world. But as the girls fluttered round, and Nero, the king of the game, continued to ignore them and got on with his swift, practised preparations, she almost felt sorry for them. Almost, but not quite. Bella understood the tensions of the match and didn't expect Nero to pay her any attention, but the girls didn't understand that and thought all they had to do was look pretty and stick around long enough for Nero to turn and reward them with a smile…

He'd better not reward them with anything, Bella thought, feeling unusually moody as Nero turned to ask her for his stick. She passed it to him and, resting it over his shoulder, he cantered away without another word.

Taking her heart with him.

Don't be ridiculous, Bella told herself sternly. What was the point of giving her heart to Nero when he'd sooner have a bag of carrots for his ponies?

There was a tense air of expectation around the field of play. Everyone was geared up for action at the highest possible level and the game promised to be riskier than Bella had imagined. It soon became clear that, as she had suspected, this was no civilised knock-about between old friends, but a long-standing grudge match with no quarter offered by either side. There was battle fever between the players and, though Bella expected to feel on edge, she had not imagined longing for the match to finish so she could be sure Nero was safe.

Just let them all get through it in one piece, Bella thought as her gaze fixed on Nero. More the warrior than ever, with his tanned face grim beneath his helmet and his thick black hair curling beneath it, his muscles pumped and flexing and his strong hands on the reins, Nero looked invincible as he cantered round the field. That light grip was so deceptive. There was such power and certainty in it...and his powerful thighs, so subtly yet firmly controlling and directing his pony's movements.

She was jealous of a horse now?

The referee was speaking to each team. Silence fell other than the champing of bits. Anthems were played. The ball was positioned. Ponies jostled, and Nero hooked the first play clear.

The players thundered down the field with Nero taking an early lead. He was easily the most skilful rider. But even Nero wasn't invulnerable, and he couldn't evade all the opposing team's dirty tricks.

The other team's sole aim appeared to be to ride Nero off the field, and when two horses came cannoning towards him Bella screamed out a warning along with the rest of the crowd.

Nero would never risk his horse. Nero would rather risk himself—

A collective sigh rose from the crowd as Nero corkscrewed out of trouble, but it had been a narrow escape and, as the game continued, Bella grew increasingly anxious. The opposition wasn't interested in playing the game, they just wanted to create havoc with Nero in the centre of it. This wasn't about an elbow in the ribs or a well-placed knee in an attempt to unseat him, every action they took was designed to put Nero Caracas out of the game for good.

Yet Nero had never appeared stronger or more in control, Bella thought, taking comfort from his confidence as he leapt effortlessly from the back of one pony to the next between chukkas. This required split-second timing between groom and rider, with the groom having the next pony ready when the tired pony came cantering in, and no way was she going to let anyone have this responsibility—this was hers, and for once in his life Nero didn't have time to argue with her.

There was no basis for her sense of dread, Bella reasoned sensibly as the next chukka got underway. This was sport at the highest level and she couldn't expect it to be soft or easy. She should just relax and enjoy it. To see Nero at full stretch like this was a rare indulgence. She was watching out for risks around him, anticipating trouble even before it occurred. Nero shared this sixth sense and he used it to wheel and dodge his way out of trouble, while he controlled the field of play and kept his pony safe.

She was beginning to relax and enjoy the match, and shouted herself hoarse with the rest of the crowd when Nero whacked a ball halfway down the pitch and went charging after it. The other riders were in hot pursuit, but not fast enough to stop Nero smacking a goal between the posts. Rapturous applause greeted him as the teams changed ends, and within moments Nero had galloped in at the end of the chukka to change his shirt. Tugging it over his head, he displayed an obscene wealth of muscle to which Bella had to appear unmoved. And as if that wasn't bad enough, she now had to tell Nero something he wouldn't want to hear. 'I've substituted Colonel.'

'No—' Nero was scowling at the horse whose reins she was holding. 'Colonel doesn't have many matches left in him and I won't deny him this game.'

'But he's in a lather, Nero.' She shot an anxious glance towards the big bay it was taking two men to hold.

'It's your job to calm him down.'

And while she was still absorbing this piece of arrant nonsense, Nero mounted up.

'Colonel has been waiting for this moment, haven't you, boy?' he crooned, and she had to grit her teeth as the pony became both instantly alert and instantly cooperative.

'You'll never tame him, Bella.'

Was Ignacio talking about Nero or the pony? she wondered. 'It's a fantastic match,' she said distractedly. Even with Ignacio at her side, she had to brush off her growing sense of unease.

'Don't look so worried,' Ignacio said, following her gaze onto the field. 'Nero and Colonel have a special bond.'

She hoped so.

'I just wish this game didn't have to be quite so violent,' she confessed, voicing her fears.

'When you have some of the best players in the world on the field, competition is only to be expected,' Ignacio told her with a shrug.

Yes, but this was more than competition, Bella thought. This was war.

She'd never had this much invested in a match before, Bella reasoned as she leaned on the fence to watch. Ignacio had remained with her as if he sensed she needed company. There was only one man Ignacio was interested in watching, and that was Nero. She realised Ignacio couldn't have cared more deeply for Nero if he had been his own son.

'We're ahead,' Ignacio cheered as Nero swung his polo mallet and fired off another goal. The applause was deafening, but this became the cue for the game to become even rougher, and the crowd groaned when one of the riders was unseated.

Bella stared anxiously onto the field and only relaxed when she could see that both pony and player were unharmed. Her gaze flew to Nero, whose expression was thunderous beneath his helmet. She guessed he was furious at the risks the opposing team were taking with their horses. He glanced towards her and patted Colonel's neck as if he wanted to reassure her that they were both okay. She had to admit Colonel had never looked more alert or more impatient to enter the fray again. And Colonel's rider had never looked so savage, or so brutally attractive. She found a smile, though her eyes must have betrayed her concern and, with a brief nod, Nero wheeled away.

They were well into the first play when the ball

changed direction suddenly and a tightly bunched group of riders came thundering down the field towards Bella and Ignacio. Everything happened so fast—Ignacio grabbed her arm and threw her clear but, in doing so, he lost his balance as well as valuable seconds, while tons of horseflesh continued crashing towards them. Nero rode straight into the melee to save them. People were screaming as Bella went back to catch hold of Ignacio. Shoving him to the ground beneath her, she protected him with her body. For a moment it was all a terrible confusion of flailing hooves and rearing horses, with the additional obstacles of boots, feet, thighs, bridles and polo mallets. How they survived it, Bella would never know. Her first clear thought was seeing Ignacio safe on the other side of the fence as Nero swept her from the ground and threw them both clear of the mayhem. 'Thank God,' she gasped against his chest.

When she turned to look, everything was slowly returning to normal. Reins were being gathered up, boots stuck back in stirrups and horses were being turned by their riders to calm them and give each other space. It was only then that Bella realised Colonel was still on the ground. 'I told you not to ride him,' she cried out as grief and shock exploded inside her.

Dumping her on her feet, Nero returned to his horse. 'Get away from him,' he snapped when Bella would have joined them.

Ignoring Nero's instruction, she quickly checked Colonel over. 'I think he's winded.'

'And you know this for sure?' Nero's voice was ice. His eyes were unforgiving.

For some reason, Nero blamed her for this, Bella realised. 'I'm using my professional judgement,' she said as calmly as she could.

He flashed something at her in Spanish that sounded ugly. It didn't need a translation. She understood him perfectly.

'Get out of my way,' he snarled, moving to block her out.

'We should help Colonel up as soon as we can,' she said, glancing around to enlist the help of Ignacio and the other gauchos.

'Are *you* going to lift him?' Nero rapped without turning to look at them as he knelt at his horse's head. 'Where's the vet?'

'Coming—he's coming,' Ignacio soothed in their own language.

Bella looked round with relief as the vet came running up.

Ignacio grabbed her arm. 'I want to thank you, Bella, for what you did—'

'Thank you,' she replied, holding Ignacio's gaze. 'We helped each other. It could have been so much worse—' Though she doubted Nero would see it that way, Bella thought, staring at him, shoulders hunched and tense as he crouched over his horse.

The game had been suspended and uneasy murmurs swept the crowd while the vet made his examination. When he had finished, Nero drew him aside so they could talk in private.

Knowing no boundaries when it came to the animals under her care, Bella followed them. She waited until there was a pause in the conversation, and then she touched Nero's arm. 'This wasn't your fault, Nero.'

The look Nero gave her should have warned her to leave it, but she was too upset by the fact that Nero had risked Colonel by riding the horse into the collision to save her. 'Thank you.'

'For what?' Nero's fierce black eyes drilled deep into her confidence.

'For saving me.'

The aggressive stare narrowed. Did Nero regret his actions? Turning away, he resumed his conversation with the vet in rapid Spanish, leaving Bella on the sidelines until Ignacio offered to translate for her.

Thank goodness Colonel wasn't so badly injured he would have to be destroyed. For all their power and bulk, horses were such fragile animals, but iced bandages followed by a stint in the hydrotherapy unit would be enough on this occasion.

They all stood round as a team, supervised by the vet, arranged a sling to hoist Colonel onto the recovery vehicle. Nero stood apart from the rest as the transport drove slowly away. The space between them might as well have been a continent, Bella thought.

Once the field was clear the game would be restarted. It was good news for a crowd relieved to discover there had been no serious casualties. Applause followed Colonel in his transporter across the field, though Nero remained staring after it with an expression that suggested the sky had just fallen in. 'It will be his last match,' he said to no one in particular.

And Nero blames me for that, Bella realised.

CHAPTER ELEVEN

'THE game is about to restart, Nero,' Bella prompted gently.

Nero didn't turn until the transporter had disappeared and then he said, 'Where's my next horse?'

She flinched at the tone of his voice. There wasn't an ounce of compassion in it. Nero was angry with himself, but he blamed both of them for bringing Colonel's career to an abrupt close.

And she was also badly shaken, Bella realised as she offered to bring a fresh horse up. A near fatal accident had almost taken out Ignacio, an elderly man she considered her friend now. Waiting for the vet's verdict had left her in pieces. *And the children!* How must they be feeling? 'I'm sorry—you'll have to excuse me,' she said, waving to one of the grooms.

'Where the hell do you think you're going?' Nero rapped. 'Do you have any idea what just happened?'

'Yes, and I'm sorry, but the kids from the scheme have been watching all this and they will be just as shocked as we are.' Without waiting for Nero's reply, she left him and ran. The sooner the children were reassured, the sooner she could get back to work.

Every cloud had a silver lining, Bella thought as she returned to the pony lines. None of the kids had realised the dangers of polo, and those who had dismissed the sport as girlie had been transformed into fervent fans, insisting polo was every bit as dangerous as motor racing and a lot more exciting to watch. Strange how fate worked sometimes, she thought wryly. And now there was just Nero to deal with. Her smile faded as she started to run.

'So you've turned up at last,' he said as he checked the bridle on the grey.

'Didn't the groom look after you?' Bella shot a quick smile of reassurance at the hapless girl whose bad luck it was to have her good work double-checked by Nero.

'You're in charge, Bella,' Nero said sharply, springing into the saddle. 'You should be here to supervise the grooms. This is not what I expect of you in a top-class game.'

'What else could I do?' Her voice was raised to match Nero's.

Grooms turned to stare as Nero demanded harshly, 'What were you doing on the polo field in the first place? This isn't a walk in the park, Bella, as you should know. How could you, of all people, be so irresponsible? What kind of example do you think you're setting for those kids you care so much about?'

She realised Nero couldn't have seen what had happened. He didn't know that Ignacio had almost been trampled. From Nero's angle as he rode up to save her, he would only have seen Bella staggering back as the group of horses collided with the fence, and had formed his own opinion. She was hardly going to mention that she had pushed Ignacio clear. She would just have to take this unfair reprimand on the chin. And smile sweetly. Until Nero turned his back.

'I'm not interested in excuses,' he barked, clearing

a space around them as he turned his horse to keep the high-spirited animal's energy in play. 'You never go near the fence again—and that's an order. And from a purely common sense point of view,' he added in a scathing tone, 'if you see horses galloping towards you, you back away. You don't rush to meet them!'

The air of battle was on him. She understood that. After a lifetime in polo, Bella knew that what appeared to be a society sport was, as the children from the city had so correctly identified, dangerous and demanding, and the top-class athletes who played the game were as driven and as fiercely competitive as their ponies.

So she'd make allowances. But she wouldn't be a doormat. 'I can only apologise,' she said, wanting to cool things down before Nero galloped off again. 'I'll go now and make sure that your next pony is properly warmed up.' The words were compliant, but there was something in her voice that warned Nero to drop it. Having said her piece, she spun on her heel and strode away.

He had felt stirred up in the middle of a match before, but never like this. But then he had never knowingly risked a horse before. And, of all horses, it had to be his old faithful, Colonel. His anger followed Bella to the pony lines, where he watched her working with her usual efficiency as if nothing untoward had taken place. Even that infuriated him. She was like no woman he had ever known before. He had risked everything for her. Why?

Bella's reckless behaviour had forced his hand. If she wanted to risk her life that was up to her, but in future he'd keep his horses safe. He galloped grim-faced onto the field. Defeat wasn't an option. Blaming Bella for her reckless actions wasn't enough. He blamed the opposing team for riding their loyal ponies as if they owed them nothing, but, most of all, he blamed himself.

Raising his helmet in a salute to the crowd, Nero acknowledged the applause as he led his team on the winners' gallop round the field. Only loyalty to the fans and to his team-mates was keeping him back. He badly wanted to be in the equine clinic with Colonel. He was desperate to check that everything possible was being done for the horse—and that shock hadn't set in.

Bella was waiting as he cantered off the field. She looked as cool as ever, while he was in turmoil. Kicking the stirrups away, he threw his leg over his pony and sprang down, thrusting the reins into her hand in the same movement. 'Ice immediately,' he ordered.

'I know,' she soothed.

The grooms were already waiting, he noticed, with iced bandages to cool the pony's overheated muscles. It was a pity they couldn't cool his overheated mind at the same time.

'Nero, you must take a drink too,' Bella insisted, holding out a water bottle with the tempting bloom of ice still visible on its surface.

Ignoring her, he moved past her.

She chased after him and thrust it into his hands. 'Drink,' she insisted, glaring at him.

'Can't you take a hint?' he demanded roughly, but he drank the water all the same.

He could feel Bella's concern following him all the way to the clinic. He'd told her from the outset that life here was tough. She knew the game. She knew the risks—

But she had never seen him like this before. *Too bad.* There was no room on the *estancia* for passengers. His grandmother had taught him that at a very young age.

'Nero, wait!'

Bella was running after him?

She not only ran after him, she ran ahead of him and stopped in front of him. 'What the hell?' He raked his hair.

'You won't do Colonel any good if you blaze into his stable in this state of mind.' She stood unmoving, glaring at him. 'I won't let you go in there.'

'Oh, won't you?' he said roughly, reaching out to move her away.

She slapped his hands down. 'Don't you dare touch me,' she raged at him white-lipped. 'While I'm here, those ponies are my responsibility as much as yours and I won't let you visit the clinic while you're like this!'

'Are you questioning my judgement?' he roared.

'Right now?' she roared back at him. 'Yes, I am.'

He walked round her. Had he really expected the Ice Maiden to tremble and quake like a virgin?

'I know why you're angry, Nero,' she said, running to keep up with him.

'Oh, do you?' he said.

'Colonel was reaching the end of his playing days, and you think you hastened that...' And when he made a sound of contempt it only prompted her to add fiercely, 'You did no such thing, Nero. You rode into danger to save the situation.'

'I had no option,' he flashed. 'I did what anyone else would have done under the same circumstances.'

Bella very much doubted it.

'If you will excuse me, I have an injured horse to check up on.'

'Then I'm coming with you,' she insisted, chasing after him.

'You've done enough damage for one day,' Nero

rapped, barging through the gate without holding it open for her. 'May I suggest you go back to the pony lines and confine yourself to bathing legs? Just make sure you don't get kicked by the ponies when you do so. We don't need any more slip-ups today.'

She fell back, allowing Nero to stalk off. He was without doubt the most obnoxious, pig-headed, arrogant man she had ever met. There wasn't a soft bone in his body or a kind thought in his head. Nero cared for nothing but his horses. He was truly incapable of a single caring feeling for his fellow man.

Which should have made him correspondingly unattractive, but unfortunately it had no effect in that direction.

It just made him more of a challenge, Bella realised, pulling out her phone and calling ahead to give the clinic a storm warning. Nero, a challenge? Yes, and professionally she could handle him, but in every other way Nero was destined to torment some other woman with more experience than Bella would ever have.

Having reassured himself that all was well with Colonel and that the horse was resting quietly, Nero returned to the *estancia* to eat and freshen up. There was no sign of Bella. He glanced up from the dining table every time he heard a door open or close. María and Concepcion were unusually subdued, as if the drama on the pitch had affected them too. He still couldn't work out why, for the first time in his life, he'd risked a horse. He ended up with the only answer he found palatable—he would have done the same for anyone. Human life was worth any risk he could take. There was nothing remotely personal about it. The fact that Bella was involved was mere coincidence.

He was in the shower when Ignacio rushed to tell him that Colonel had developed potentially fatal colic. He ran straight from his shower to the stable, barely pausing to dry himself, pulling on his jeans as he ran.

Bella had taken over the vigil in Colonel's stable from Nero the moment he had left the yard. He didn't know she was there. She wanted no fuss. And she certainly didn't want another row with him. She had agreed with Ignacio that, for all their sakes, it was better if she did this discreetly. And so it was Bella who had called the vet and sent for Nero. There was nothing more she could do, Bella realised, leaving a bowed and shaking Colonel in the care of Ignacio and the vet. Walking swiftly from the yard to avoid a confrontation with Nero, she saw him running from the house. She doubted he would even have noticed her.

She called in on Misty and spent some time with her own pony. The yard was quiet and there was no way she could know what was going on. When she left Misty's stable, she leaned her face for a moment against the cool stone wall. It was so peaceful in the stable yard after the high octane drama on the polo field. Squeezing her eyes tightly shut, she knew it was ridiculous to feel this way. She had too much emotion invested in a man who didn't have the slightest interest in her beyond her knowledge of horses. When he'd sucked that dry Nero would be happy to let her go.

And these tears were for Colonel, Bella thought impatiently, dashing them away. Straightening up, she lifted her chin. She'd check on her human charges next. The kids knew nothing of what was happening to Colonel at the clinic, and Ignacio had asked her to keep it that way. 'Not everyone has our resilience, Bella,' her elderly friend had counselled her gently. 'We don't know these children like you and I know each other, and we can't risk undoing the work we've already done with them.'

She'd felt proud at that moment, and touched that a man she admired had included her in his summary. Events had thrown her together with Ignacio and in a short space of time they had become close friends. The gaucho's friendship warmed her now and gave her courage. And Ignacio was right about the children, Bella thought as she walked briskly towards their chalets. Normally, she wouldn't dream of keeping anyone in the dark and would have come straight out with it, but these kids had a lot on their plates already, and it was up to everyone on the *estancia* to introduce them to different types of hardship sensitively. A party had been arranged for them tonight and she didn't want to spoil that for them. Without knowing the outcome of Colonel's colic, she had to consider that a drama on the pitch was one thing, but a tragedy might ruin the children's adventure on Estancia Caracas almost before it had begun. She'd tell them when she had some firm news.

The children greeted her warmly and she left them in the best of moods with the young counsellors the authorities had chosen to accompany them. She had another cause in mind now. Leaning back against the smooth sweet-smelling wood of the chalet she had so recently visited with Nero, she stared down the road leading to the clinic wondering what was happening with the sick pony.

What gave her the right? Bella thought. She was hardly qualified to offer therapy to anyone. She hadn't felt like this for years—so defensive. Perhaps she should take her own advice and leave Nero to it. This was a deeply personal crisis for a cold, sardonic man to whom horses meant everything. She really shouldn't intrude.

Nero had made it clear that he didn't welcome her interference.

It wasn't like her to give up either, Bella thought as she walked back to the house in the darkest of moods. Nero's feelings were standing in her way, and she was still fighting with herself when she pushed open the door of the hacienda. She'd have an early night. Things would look better in the morning. Whatever was going to happen with Colonel would happen, with or without her intervention.

She took a bath and went to bed, burying her head under the pillows, refusing to think about anything. At least that was the theory, but she was restless and sleep eluded her. She shot up with a start and glanced at her watch. 3:00 a.m. Whatever was going to happen to Colonel would have happened by now. She just had to know what that was. Nero would have been in bed hours ago.

Now the decision was made, she was filled with a sense of urgency. Not even waiting to tie her hair back, she tugged on a pair of jeans and a warm sweater and ran through the house, pulling on her boots at the door.

The clinic was unlocked and she took the narrow corridor with its faint smell of disinfectant and wet animals leading to the yard. Colonel's stable was easy to find. It was the only one with a dim light burning inside and the half-door left open. 'Hello, Colonel.' Bright eyes and pricked ears told her all she wanted to know. Colonel had recovered. And then something else stirred in the stable. She peered in cautiously. Nero was asleep on the hay, sprawled out with two dogs and the stable cat curled up alongside him. Her heart stirred. She pulled away as quietly as she could, not wanting to disturb him. Pressing her back against the door, she closed her eyes tightly. A man with so much love to give couldn't be all bad, could he?

She just didn't know when to give up, Bella thought as she walked back to the house. But why should she give up? A girl could dream, couldn't she? she mused, climbing the stairs. Nero was a product of his environment as much as she was of hers. So what if he was cranky? She was cranky herself. Add defensive, mistrustful, wary and aloof—oh, yes. She was a barrel of laughs.

First thing in the morning, she tacked Misty up and walked her round to the clinic yard, just to see, Bella told herself. There was no sign of Nero, and the veterinary nurse told her that Colonel had been released into the small paddock attached to the clinic where they could keep an eye on him. Colonel's leg was still strapped but the colic had passed, and the vet thought it best to keep him moving.

Thanking the nurse, she kept Misty on a loose rein and walked her as far as the boundary fence to stare out across the pampas. During her stay Bella had grown accustomed to its wild splendour, but today it looked so empty and not enticing at all. Take the romance out of it, and it was just mile upon mile of flat, open countryside, ringed with white-capped mountains showing faintly purple in the distance.

She turned at the sound of a horse's hooves. If there was one thing she should be accustomed to by now it was the sight of Nero on horseback. So why was her pulse going crazy? He'd been monstrous to her yesterday!

He had slept with his sick horse, she remembered, and was wearing the red bandana of a gaucho tied around his forehead, which was a very sexy look indeed with all that thick black hair tumbling over it.

'Where are you going?' he demanded, reining to a halt. 'Or are you just coming back?' His dark glance ran over her breeches which, clean of dust and mud, gave him the answer. Resting his fists on the pommel of his saddle, Nero raised an imperious brow. 'So where are you going?'

'Good morning to you too,' she said, turning Misty.

'Wait—'

The small mare recognised the note of command in Nero's voice even if Bella was determined to ignore it and Misty stopped dead, waiting for her next instruction. Not wanting to confuse her, Bella turned a cool glance on Nero's face. 'Yes?' she said.

'You need to be careful of the *yarara* if you're thinking of riding out,' he said in a voice devoid of emotion.

'The *yarara*?' Bella frowned, thinking only of the safety of her pony now.

'Poisonous snakes. It's the season for them,' he said before turning away.

'Wait,' she called after him.

Nero turned his horse. 'They won't bite unless you frighten them, but they will spook the horses.'

'Thanks for the warning.'

'Don't mention it,' he said. 'Just be sure you don't linger by any low-lying shrubs, or go rooting under rocks.'

'Is that it?'

'Should there be more?'

They confronted each other as if they were squaring up for a fight. Bella broke the silence first. 'If you've got something to say to me, Nero, just spit it out. It won't take me long to pack.'

'Pack?' he demanded with an angry gesture. 'Your work isn't finished here.'

Before she had a chance to react to that, Nero ground his jaw and finally admitted, 'I was wrong yesterday.' He raised a brow as if daring her to disagree, while she waited for a chorus of angels singing *Hallelujah!* 'I shouldn't have shouted at you,' he said, 'especially after Ignacio told me what you had done. That was very brave of you, Bella.'

'I don't want your praise!'

'Well, you shall have it.'

'I'll be sure to keep away from the *yararas*,' she said, turning Misty abruptly.

'Bella—'

She ignored him and the moment they were through the gate she urged Misty into a gallop. Nero caught up with her easily. 'You know emotions are heightened on the polo field.'

'I also know that's no excuse,' she called back. 'Your rudeness to me—'

'My rudeness?' Nero refused to take offence as he cantered easily alongside.

'You shouted at me!'

'And you shouted back.'

She rode without speaking, but all she could think about was Nero sleeping in the stable with his motley crew of animals and his sick horse.

'You came to find me in the stable,' he said, riding with all the nonchalance of a gaucho born in the saddle, 'so I can't have been so bad.'

'I was worried about your horse.'

'And me, just a little bit?'

'Not at all.' And, with a shout of encouragement, she gave Misty her head.

'But you will agree that it's good news about Colonel?' Nero caught up with her again and rode alongside as if they were trotting sedately in Windsor Park rather than indulging in a flat-out gallop across the pampas.

'It is good news,' she said. 'The best.' And there was only so long she could hold the frown for. 'Did you get much sleep?' she asked, trying not to sound too interested.

'Not much,' Nero admitted, slowing his horse. 'You?'

'Some,' Bella admitted, walking Misty towards the welcome shade of some trees. 'I woke in the night and wanted to check up on him. I thought you'd be asleep in bed,' she confessed.

Reaching for his water bottle, Nero took a long, thirsty slug. 'Do you have water?' he said, holding the canister out to her.

She wasn't falling for that again. 'I do,' she said, patting her saddlebag.

'Hey,' Nero called after her as she nudged Misty forward to hide her glowing cheeks. 'You forgot to tie your hair back, Bella.'

She was already feeling for the hairband on her wrist when it occurred to her he was teasing.

'What are you frightened of?' Nero challenged as she tied it up again, bringing his horse level with Misty. 'Are you worried you might show a softer side?'

'I'm only worried about getting my hair tangled when I ride,' she said mildly. 'And you're hardly in a position to talk about a softer side.'

Nero acknowledged this with a shrug. 'But I'm not frightened,' he said.

And she was? Yes, she was, Bella acknowledged silently—of some things, some men, but most of all she was frightened of losing control—of letting go. She hid these thoughts behind a counter-attack. 'You're the Assassin, remember. What do you know about fear?'

'Only a fool doesn't know fear,' Nero countered, 'but I'm not afraid. There's a big difference, Bella.'

With those dark eyes searching hers, she was glad of her shirt buttoned to the neck and the severe no-nonsense cut of her riding breeches. No way could this encounter be mistaken for anything other than it was—a purely chance meeting of the world's top polo player riding out on his ranch with a visiting professional who would soon be returning home.

CHAPTER TWELVE

FULFILLING her role as a professional judge of horse-flesh, Bella turned her attention from Nero to his horse. He was riding a magnificent black stallion, far bigger than any of the polo ponies in his yard. She guessed this must be a descendant of the Spanish war horses Nero had told her about. His mount certainly looked pretty impressive with its fancy scarlet saddlecloth, silver bit and the silver headband to keep its thickly waving fore-lock back. Nero wore silver spurs, and when the horse danced impatiently as he turned it in circles to calm it she saw that his belt was decorated with silver coins, and the typical gaucho dagger Ignacio had told her was called a *facon* was firmly secured in the back. More interestingly, Nero hadn't shaved and looked more dangerous than he ever had.

'How about a race?' he challenged with a curving grin.

'You are joking. Misty barely reaches the withers of that fire-breathing monster.'

'Then I'll give you a head start,' he said.

'Don't patronise us, Caracas.'

Nero's answer to this was a tug of his lips and a Latin shrug. 'If you're not up to it—'

Bella barely needed to touch Misty with her heels. The mare got the message and bounded forward.

A contest? Bella thought with relish. She was up for that. Let the best horse win!

'Hey,' Nero shouted after her as he took up the chase. 'Your hair's come loose, Bella!'

Bella's hair would feel like skeins of silk beneath his hands and her kisses hot. The thought of challenging the Ice Maiden to a race had got his juices flowing, Nero realised, reining back to slow his stallion. It would be the easiest thing in the world to overtake her, but that would mean the end of the chase—and, as any hunter knew, the thrill of the chase was everything—something to be drawn out and appreciated, so that the final outcome might be relished all the more. And seeing Bella crouched low over her pony as she rode with absolute determination to win this contest made him think the final outcome mustn't be too long coming.

They rode like the wind with no boundaries in front of them other than the snow-capped mountains more than half a day's ride away. The thrill of the chase excited Bella and, as the wind blew her hair back from her face, she felt this was the first time she had felt completely free since landing in Argentina—maybe the first time she had ever felt so free. The thunder of hooves warned her that Nero was close behind, the challenge in his eyes that if he caught her she would pay the consequences. She wouldn't give up without a fight. Goaded into renewed effort, she crouched low over Misty's neck as they streaked like an arrow across the pampas, but it was only a matter of time before the renowned agility of her polo pony lost out to the brute strength of Nero's stallion. Feeling the hunter relentlessly closing the distance between them stopped the breath in her throat.

There was something so controlled about it—so confident. Hot, hectic panic overwhelmed her and blazed a trail down her spine that spread across her back like cracking glass. There was nowhere to run—nowhere to hide—just miles of flat plain ahead of them. She would need a half mile head start to get away from him, and any moment now Nero would gallop past them. The anticipation of that was infuriating, and terrifying, and thrilling.

But Nero didn't overtake her. He must be holding back, Bella realised. Misty was fast but the polo pony was a sprinter, while a long gallop like this was little more than an easy hack for Nero's stallion. He should have disappeared ahead of them in a cloud of dust by now. Beneath her, Misty was straining to gallop faster. Having the stallion so close behind had unleashed a primitive flight mechanism in the mare. Misty's flared nostrils and laid-back ears were as telling as the arousal flooding Bella when she realised Nero had no intention of riding past her; he was wearing her down, knowing she was as unlikely to put her horse at risk as he was. Nero understood her a little too well.

Feeling Misty starting to flag, she steered her towards a covert of some gum trees. It was still a victory, Bella reasoned, slapping Misty's neck in praise as they slowed down. They had still won the race, and she had decided the finish line.

She was shivering with excitement by the time she reined to a halt. At least she'd made a good choice in stopping here—not only was it cooler, but an underground stream had thrust its way through the soft, fertile earth so the horses could drink their fill. Kicking her feet free of the stirrups, Bella dropped to the ground. She heard the chink of a bridle close behind her and then heard Nero spring down to the ground close by. 'Well?' she demanded, swinging round, hands on hips. 'Are you going to congratulate me?'

'You have my respect,' Nero conceded in a husky tone. 'You have a good pony, Bella, and you have trained her well.'

'Well, thank you, kind sir,' she said dryly. 'Forgive me if I'm wrong, but something in your tone suggests you believe you could have overtaken me any time.'

'And you don't think that's the case?' Nero raised one sweeping ebony brow.

A rush of excitement thrilled though her. She loved this game, loved the opponent best of all.

'You surely don't think you could outrun me?' Nero mocked.

She countered this with an amused huff. 'I did outrun you.'

'And now you want me to grovel in defeat?' Nero suggested.

Her gaze dropped to his lips, adrenalin still raging through her. 'No. I want more than that.'

She thought she was safe taunting him? Nero's head only dropped minutely, as if he were thinking about this. The next thing she knew, she was in his arms.

The heat of the chase had made her crazy, Bella concluded as Nero's mouth crashed down on hers—crazy for Nero. A lifetime of wondering and longing, and ultimate disappointment and embarrassment, was all worth it for it to end like this in a fierce pampas kiss—not a vain old man's kiss, but a gaucho's kiss—a real man's kiss—a kiss that was certain and firm, and teasing, and exciting, and so much more than she had ever dreamed a kiss could be.

Fire met fire. They should have burned each other

out. Not a chance. Sharp black stubble scored soft, pale skin. Pain was pleasure. The hot, experienced South American and the cool, inexperienced Englishwoman. Surely, it should have been unmitigated disaster—it wasn't. It was fire and ice, heat and need, action and pressure, gripping, grasping, seizing, holding, punctuated by groans of ecstasy and growls of intent. And all the time the heat was mounting. Even the horses had moved away. Who'd have thought it? The Ice Maiden had finally melted and met her match.

No... No!... *No!* What was she thinking? Theirs was a professional relationship. She had to recover the situation somehow!

Which hardly seemed likely when her body was an out of control, wanton, craving force. And if she was any other woman, it might be possible to go right ahead with this and deal with the consequences later, in a cool and professional manner. But she would never recover her self-respect if she didn't get out fast. She didn't have the savvy, the nous, the tools...

'Please—' Pulling away, she combed her hair with her fingers into some semblance of order. 'Forgive me...' She added a light laugh that sounded as insincere as it was. 'I don't usually get carried away like this.' All this in a cut-glass accent as foreign to her as Nero's South American drawl. 'The excitement of the chase...' She glanced at Nero to judge his reaction, only to find she had missed the mark by a mile or so. His face was a mask of sardonic disbelief.

'You'd like to talk about the scheme now?' he suggested.

'Yes, yes, I would,' she exclaimed with relief, blanking the sarcasm in his voice.

There was time to see little more than a flash of

movement—amused eyes and a tug of Nero's lips—
before she was in his arms again. 'I don't want to talk,'
he murmured. To prove the point, he teased her with
his tongue and with his teeth, brushing the swell of
her bottom lip with kisses until she was struggling to
breathe and arousal hit every erotic zone at once, leaving
her whimpering with need, and longing for release. But
he hadn't taken possession of her mouth yet and, when
he did, plunging deep into her moist warmth in a blistering approximation of what he could be doing to her, she
responded as he must have known she would, by arcing
upwards, seeking contact in a frenzy of excitement.

And Nero's answer to this loss of self-control?

He pulled away, leaving her in a daze.

She had been dazzled by the master of control. It was
this foreign land and their exotic surroundings, Bella
reasoned, the unfamiliar trees rustling a very different
tune, and the small, angry stream bursting through the
ground on its way to the sea. She was lost in a terrifyingly wild open space on a scale she couldn't even begin
to describe.

All this was her fault, Bella convinced herself, tying
her hair back in a signal to them both that this mistake
was well and truly over.

Who was she trying to kid? She certainly wasn't fooling Nero who, having had time to process the data, was
now regarding her with barely controlled amusement.
'Don't tie your hair up on my account,' he said.

'Lady Godiva of the pampas?' Bella grimaced as she
pretended to consider this. 'I don't think so, do you?'

'Depends on whether you think I want to see you
naked.'

She flinched inwardly. 'Believe me, you really don't.'

Nero knocked some dried grass from his breeches. 'Concerned you might disappoint me?'

'Concerned?' She laughed it off. 'Why should I be? And, anyway, as you won't get the chance to find out…'

'You're supposing I want that chance.'

But he did, Bella thought as she went to find Misty. And, more worrying that that, so did she.

She drew a sharp breath as Nero caught hold of her arm. 'Why do you always pull back from the brink, Bella?'

'I don't.'

'Don't lie to me—I sensed the change in you while I was kissing you.'

Her hand was already at her mouth. 'The change in me?' she repeated, pretending surprise though the proof that she had been violently aroused was emblazoned on her lips.

'You know what I mean,' Nero insisted.

Brazening it out and holding his gaze, she snapped, 'Do I?'

'I've seen you on the dance floor, Bella, and I've seen you retreat into your shell. What I don't understand is why you don't just let go for once—take a risk, taste life,' Nero tempted, refusing to have his good mood squashed by Bella's sudden change of heart.

'And if I did?' She laughed. 'I only get it wrong.'

'Do you think you're the only one who makes mistakes, Bella?' Nero demanded.

She had just thrown the reins over Misty's head and was about to put her foot in the stirrup when Nero held her back. 'When I was a little boy, idiot was my middle name. I was always getting into trouble. I never did what I was told.'

'Am I supposed to be surprised?' Bella said wryly, leaning back against Misty's flank. 'From what I can see of your grandmother from her portrait and from what Ignacio told me about her, I'm guessing she soon sorted you out.'

Nero laughed. 'You could call it that. She warned me that if I was determined to run wild, I should have a real challenge.'

Bella stroked Misty's neck. 'How old were you?'

'I was about nine when my grandmother took me for this particular ride on the pampas. We were both riding crazy horses.'

'Do you breed any other type?' Bella laughed.

'We didn't take a lot of food.' Nero's eyes grew thoughtful. There was a self-deprecating curve to his lips, as if he couldn't believe how badly he'd been sucked in. 'You think you know everything when you're nine— you're immortal and invincible.' Refocusing, he went on. 'Grandmother told me she wouldn't be out long enough for us to need much in the way of food.'

'I bet she did,' Bella said, her eyes twinkling. 'And you weren't suspicious?'

'Why should I be?' Nero frowned. 'This is my grandmother we're talking about.'

'Exactly,' Bella said wryly.

And now Nero was laughing too. 'I should have known when she asked if I had plenty of water with me, but I was very trusting in those days.' His lips pressed down as he rasped his chin.

'I guess we were both destined to learn our lessons young,' Bella commented. 'So your grandmother abandoned you on the pampas?'

'Yes, she did,' Nero confirmed. 'We made camp. She made sure I had something to eat, and then, while

I was lying back relaxing, no doubt planning my next mischief, she sneaked off.'

'And you didn't hear her ride away?'

'My grandmother had learned the ways of the gaucho. She tied cloths over her horse's hooves and led him away. By the time I looked around and wondered where she'd gone she was probably back at the ranch.'

'How long did it take you to find your way home?'

'Two days.'

'And what did your grandmother say when you finally turned up?'

'We never spoke of it—she wasn't exactly noted for showing her feelings.'

Like Nero, Bella thought.

'But she had—shown her feelings, I mean,' he murmured as he thought about it. 'In her way.' He grinned. 'Anyway, after that, Ignacio started playing a larger part in my life, or perhaps I started listening. I knew now that I would need all the tricks Ignacio could teach me to make sure I was never caught out again—like knowing where to find food and water on the pampas. How to catch a runaway horse. How to understand women...'

'Ah, the hardest lesson of all.'

'And one I'm still brushing up on,' Nero admitted with an engaging grin.

'And were you still a bad boy after this period of study?'

'What do you think?'

'I think you channelled your energies in a different direction.'

Nero shrugged and grinned back. 'I couldn't possibly comment.'

'So Ignacio has played a really crucial role in your life.'

'Ignacio and my grandmother were my formative influences. Everything I am, I owe to them. And that's enough of me,' he said. 'I want to hear more about you. I want to know if you mean to live up to your Ice Maiden tag for the rest of your life, Bella.'

'Maybe.' Bella shrugged. 'It hasn't done me any harm so far.'

'Hasn't it?' Nero challenged. 'Why would you choose to be that way, Bella, when there's so much life to live?'

She thought about it for a moment, 'Because I feel safer.'

'Safer?' Nero demanded. 'What happened to make you feel unsafe?'

'It was nothing,' she insisted with a flippant gesture.

'Nothing? There must be something to make you so defensive.'

'It's just so stupid,' Bella exclaimed with frustration, not wanting to talk about it. 'And the more time goes by, the harder it is to get past it.'

'Try me,' Nero said.

'It's not that easy,' Bella said wryly, twisting with embarrassment.

'It's never easy to open up and share things you hide deep inside. And if you've held on to something for a long time you can't expect it to come pouring out. Everyone fears they'll be judged, Bella, or that they're making too much of what happened, but that can't be the case with you, because you're so strong in every other area of your life except this.'

'All right,' she blurted suddenly, as if he'd lanced a wound. 'If you must know, when I was a teenager one of my father's friends made a pass at me.'

'And you kept it quiet all these years?'

'No one likes to be made a fool of twice. I didn't think anyone would believe me.'

'Why not?'

She shrugged unhappily, forced to remember. 'He had status. I had none.'

'Status?' Nero demanded as if the word had burned his tongue.

'I was just a kid around the stables back then. I'd always thought of myself as one of the boys. I grew up with brothers, remember, and so all that girlie stuff passed me by. I wasn't sure how to dress or to put make-up on without feeling silly, so my confidence wasn't exactly sky-high to start with.'

'What you're telling me sounds more serious than make-up and clothes, or even an acute lack of self-confidence. This sounds more like a breach of trust with long-reaching consequences,' Nero argued firmly.

'Anyway,' Bella continued offhandedly, 'when he left me he spread a rumour around the polo club that I was frigid. People started laughing at me. I didn't know why at first, but when it finally dawned on me...'

Nero cursed viciously beneath his breath. 'Forget him. Forget all those people. They're not worth remembering, Bella.'

'How can I forget them when that's my world?'

'That's your workplace. Your world is something different. At least,' Nero added wryly, 'I hope it is. What happened wasn't your fault, Bella. You were young and naïve, but you got over it. You're a survivor and you're strong. You built something wonderful with the legacy your father left you. I think you can afford to give yourself some credit for that.'

'You make it all sound so romantic—so excusable,

but I must have led that man on for him to try in the first place.'

Nero interrupted her with a vicious curse. 'How did you lead him on?' he demanded. 'With your youth? With your innocence? The man who did this to you isn't worthy of being called a man. His behaviour is not excusable. And being strong isn't romantic, Bella, it's a necessity. Being strong is what life requires and demands of you. When you're pushed to the limit you grow stronger and, whether you know it or not, that is what has happened to you, so instead of letting the past drag you down, take a look at what you have learned from it, and how it has lifted you up.'

'I couldn't fight him,' she said, lost in the past now. 'He was so much stronger than I was…'

'You don't need to tell me any more.'

'In the end he gave up.'

'Not for want of trying,' Nero said angrily. Bella's bewildered gaze had shocked him and the realisation of what she had been hiding all these years cut him like a knife. 'You must have been terrified.'

'Terrified? Yes,' she said faintly as she thought back. 'When he started laughing at me and calling me frigid and ugly, I was at my lowest point—beaten. But later, when I got over the shock of what had happened, I felt angry. When people joined in with his mocking comments—laughing about me and my father—it changed me for good, Nero. It turned me into a fighter. It made me determined that no man or woman would ever control me. And when my father's business failed I went to work for him. I wanted to help him rebuild—not just the business, but his good name. I wanted to prove to the world that Jack Wheeler still counted for something.'

'The Wheeler name counts for a lot,' Nero cut in.

'And that's thanks to you, Bella. Whatever problems your father had in the past have been eclipsed by your work in his name.'

He took her in his arms, feeling instantly protective, along with a whole host of less worthy feelings towards the man who had assaulted her. Without a mother to advise her, or close female friends to coax her out of her defensive shell, she had battled this nightmare alone. No wonder she found it so hard to trust anyone. Bella was the most thoughtful person he knew and only her complete lack of vanity and self-absorption had allowed so much time to pass before she unburdened herself. He was touched and honoured that she had chosen him when she chose to do so.

'Nero?'

He stared down into her wounded eyes. 'I wish I'd known all this before, Bella.'

'Well, you know now,' she said with the same flippant gesture, still trying to make light of it.

Speaking gently, he captured her hand and held her close. 'I want you to promise that you're going listen to what I'm going to say to you, because you need to hear this.' He waited until she relaxed. 'While you were struggling to take control of your life, you imposed sterner rules on yourself than anyone else would have done. You've been unforgiving where Bella Wheeler is concerned and you need to ease up. Let the past go, Bella. Let the bad parts fall away. You've got too much to give to keep yourself imprisoned in this Ice Maiden cage.'

She was hugging herself, Bella realised, releasing her arms. 'How can I do that when it still hurts every time I remember?'

'It will hurt less now you've told someone,' Nero promised.

'But it hurts now.'

'These are old wounds, Bella, and you just poked them with a stick.'

She had never felt able to share the past with anyone, or to talk freely about herself before, yet Nero had made her do that, Bella realised. For all his savage masculinity, he possessed some deep curative power. He was using it now to calm Misty. The little mare was impatient to leave and was showing off in front of Nero's stallion with head tosses and jaunty prancing, but one quiet word from Nero and she was still.

Bella was so busy admiring Nero's horse-whispering technique, he surprised her. Instead of mounting up, he turned his back and, ripping his shirt free of his gaucho breeches, he loosened his belt and pulled the waistband of his breeches down revealing the most terrible scars.

'Oh, my God,' Bella exclaimed in shock. 'Who did that to you?' The cruel score of whip marks was livid red and unmistakable. This was calculated cruelty on a scale that made her own long-held internal wounds pale into insignificance.

'This is my father's work,' Nero said without emotion. Adjusting his clothing, he fastened his belt. 'I was eleven years old before the beatings stopped.'

Around the time his parents had been killed and Nero's grandmother had moved in to take care of him, Bella realised. No wonder Nero had pushed himself and the ranch to the limit. Nero was as driven as she was in his own way. 'Your grandmother must have been horrified to discover what had been happening to you in her absence.'

'It was something we never talked about.'

'But it must have hurt her terribly if she loved you—'

'Love?' Nero murmured, appearing distracted for a moment. 'I adored my grandmother, but love was something else we never discussed,' he admitted wryly.

That made her sad. The way Nero dismissed love was an ominous sign, Bella thought, even if it was understandable. As a child, he had been denied love by his violent, drunken father and, with a child's stoical acceptance of what couldn't be changed, had learned to live without love.

'Things happen,' he said with a shrug. 'I'm only showing you these scars to let you know they haven't changed me—my father hasn't won, and neither must you allow what happened to you to rule your life and hold you back.'

'You can't compare what happened to me with someone beating a child!'

'And, bad as that was, somewhere out there will be children beyond number who have suffered far worse. That is why we are launching our schemes, Bella. You may not have thought it through as I have and come to that conclusion, but that is why you and I are so driven, and why you must use the past as a stepping stone rather than a barrier.'

The past hadn't changed him, Bella realised as Nero turned away to check the girth on his horse, but it had formed the man he was. Would Nero ever settle down, or would he never be able to trust enough to take the risk of loving anyone?

It all made sense now, Bella thought as she calmed Misty—her chats with Ignacio and the gaucho's closed face whenever she'd tried to ask him about Nero's father.

Estancia Caracas was a closed community where everyone knew everything that was going on.

'Bella?'

Refocusing, she put her foot in the stirrup and swung lightly into the saddle. 'Nothing's easy, is it, Nero?'

His mouth curved into a grin. 'You want easy, you could always go back to England.'

She shot him a level stare. 'And leave a job half-done?'

'Follow me back to the *estancia*, Bella.'

'Until we reach the straight,' she agreed. Challenging glances met and held. They had learned a lot about each other in a very short time, Bella thought, which, if they were to work together successfully, was no bad thing. 'Well?' she pressed. 'What are you waiting for?'

'I'm giving you a head start,' Nero told her with an ironic look. 'It's only fair.'

'Fair?' She laughed. 'I'll give you fair. I'll have a cup of coffee waiting for you when you get back.'

'Do you seriously think you're going to arrive before me?' Nero vaulted onto his horse. '*Hasta la vista*, Bella. I'll be in the bath by the time you get back.'

He stayed just far ahead of her to know she was safe. There was no point exhausting the horses, and he had nothing to prove. Neither did Bella. She had more than proved herself, Nero thought wryly. Everything he had sensed about Bella was true—except that her hunger for fulfilment went even deeper than he had thought. That was one problem he could solve. Her hair had felt like heaven beneath his hands—and her body, neatly packaged in practical yet severe riding clothes, had given him a provocative hint of the softly yielding flesh beneath.

She had stopped him because of lack of confidence,

he knew that now. Confidence could make a person, just as the lack of it could break you, he mused, easing the pace when he heard her pony falling back.

He liked her all the more for her unflinching acceptance of his scars. But Bella was as stubborn as the grandmother who had raised him. Like his grandmother, Bella would never admit to any inner weakness, believing it made her seem less in control. Unfortunately for Bella, he'd grown up with a woman like that. He knew what was going on.

He slowed the stallion to a brisk trot as they approached the yard. He didn't want to hurt Bella, but nothing had changed. He still wanted her.

CHAPTER THIRTEEN

SHE blamed it on the tango. Her neatly ordered life had always made sense before, but the tango made her confront her passions and accept that she was human. And it did all that—with a little help from Ignacio—in the first thirty-two bars. She wasn't exactly a new person by that stage, but she had certainly loosened up, and by the end of the dance Ignacio had managed to prove to her that as much as control was necessary to succeed, so was passion.

As in tango, so in life? One thing was certain, she couldn't go on the way she had been, marking time.

A number of parties had been arranged for the days following the polo match, and so she didn't lose face completely, Ignacio had agreed to tutor her in private dance lessons. The barn had a number of uses, Bella had discovered, and not all of them contained the dangers inherent in meeting Nero alone there. Ignacio came equipped with an ancient portable machine to play their music and proceeded to train her with the same mixture of firmness and patience with which he schooled the polo ponies. She'd never be an expert, she accepted, but she was a lot better than she had been by the time Ignacio had finished with her.

'Don't be frightened to let yourself go, Bella,' Ignacio

advised. 'And then the contrast when you draw yourself back will be sharper. You'll have people trembling on the edge of their seats,' he assured her when she laughed at her pathetic attempt. 'Bravo!' he exclaimed with gusto when she got it right.

Would Nero tremble on the edge of his seat? Somehow, Bella doubted it.

Nero felt her arrive at the party and his gaze followed her across the room. She looked incredible. The transformation from Ice Maiden to Tango Queen was complete, and was all the more impressive because of the contrast it drew between cool Bella and too-hot-to-handle Bella.

Too hot for any other man to handle, Nero determined, making his move. He bridled when he noticed the hungry stares of all the men present following her across the room. 'Bella.' He ground his jaw as one of the good-looking young stable lads got there first and led her onto the floor. He narrowed his eyes when he noticed Ignacio raise a glass to him at the far side of the room. Ruthless old rogue.

Nero grinned and then he laughed. It appeared Ignacio still had some lessons to teach him. And he'd obviously been busy with Bella too—boy, could she dance. They were queuing up to dance with her—boys who had hardly started shaving, some of them. And, of course, Bella being Bella, was only too happy to dance with all of them. She had so much joie de vivre waiting to burst out of her—something he'd only caught a glimpse of at the polo party in London. He raised a glass to Ignacio, who bowed his head in acknowledgement of the praise as Bella continued to dance with boys from the project, boys from the stable.

Men too.

He was at her side in moments.

She stared up at him. Her lips were full and red. Lipstick she never wore outlined them, enhanced them, made them gleam. 'Nero,' she murmured provocatively.

Her hair was severely drawn back, but he would forgive her that at a tango party, as the style was appropriate for the occasion. Her eyes were smoky and made even more lustrous by make-up. She looked and smelled fabulous—like a warm pot of passion just waiting for him to drown in. And the dress… What a dress. Low-necked and split to the thigh in shimmering silver, it was an exquisite example of the type of dress a professional tango dancer would wear.

María's daughter, he thought immediately. Carina was a famous tango dancer in Buenos Aires and about the same size as Bella. He had already noticed that María had made sure all the girls on Bella's scheme had the prettiest dresses to wear, and Bella's outfit was yet another example of his staff showering approval on her. He'd heard rumours that Ignacio had been teaching Bella to dance, and knew for a fact that Ignacio had found smart clothes for all the city boys to wear. But it was Bella, and only Bella, he was interested in now. There was a new confidence in her eyes, and the outfit, with those fine black stockings with the sexy seam up the back, had changed her, like an actress walking onto a stage she owned. If he waited for Bella to be without a partner, he'd be waiting all night.

And so he cut in. 'I'm claiming the winner's prize,' he told Nacho, owner of the neighbouring ranch, who just happened to be the most notorious playboy in Argentina and who was still stinging from losing the polo match to

Nero. Their black stares met in a fierce, no-holds-barred challenge.

'Would you like a partner who can show you how it's done?' Nero demanded when Bella hesitated.

'Get in line, Caracas,' she told him with a glint of humour in her seductive, smoky eyes.

'Nero doesn't wait for anything,' Nacho murmured, yielding as good manners dictated he must.

Nero stared with triumph into Bella's eyes. Remembering their last outing on the dance floor, he offered benevolently, 'I'll lead.'

'Into trouble?' she murmured.

Those lips!

Those lips were his. Firing one last stare at Nacho, he led her onto the floor.

It was like holding an electric current in his arms— dangerous, hot and impossible to contain or let go. 'Don't worry,' he soothed in a soft, mocking voice as she looked up at him, 'I'll be gentle with you.'

'And I with you,' she assured him as they waited for the music to begin.

He noticed how poised she was. She was a very different woman to the one who had taken the floor so awkwardly with him in Buenos Aires. Could this be the same woman who was almost, but not quite touching her flattened palm to his?

It was only Bella's hand, but he wanted it. He wanted her hand in his… He wanted all of her.

She evaded him as the music began and, with a provocative flash of her emerald eyes, she whipped out of his reach in a turn he wouldn't have imagined her to be capable of executing. He snatched her back again and held her close, staring down, imposing his will.

Raising a brow, she thrust him away.

His eyes assured her that he accepted the challenge and, when he drew her close this time, she had no option but to move with him. She fought him at first, and then she relaxed. They were attracting attention, he noticed. Or, rather, Bella was attracting interest. She was his perfect partner. The fact that they were dancing together, and quite so intensely, was drawing a lot of attention. He noticed Ignacio watching them from the shadows. The jigsaw didn't take much piecing together. Ignacio knew Nero had finally met his match and had enjoyed tutoring Bella so she could more than hold her own when they next met on the dance floor.

Hold her own? Bella was incredible. She set the air on fire, and everyone had gathered round to watch. Sensually and emotionally, she was transformed. It was like dancing with a different Bella—a confident woman who had found herself and knew what she wanted out of life—and she wanted more than polo. There were other gaps in Bella's education, gaps that only he could fill.

'Where are we going?' Bella demanded as Nero strode with her across the yard. She dug her heels in, refusing to go another step with him until he explained why he had taken her away from the party.

'I don't care to play out my private life in front of an audience.'

'I thought you didn't care what people thought.' She fought him, but his grip only tightened on her arm.

'I don't.' Nero stopped dead, his breathing heightened as he stared down at her. 'You look fabulous tonight, Bella.' And just when her eyes widened at the thought that he was paying her a compliment, he added, 'You could hardly think you were going to fade into the background in a dress like that?'

'Are you jealous, Nero?'

'Jealous?' Heat rose in his eyes.

'Do you regret dancing with me when there were so many more important women at the party?'

'What?' Nero looked genuinely bemused.

'Or don't you like my dress?'

'It certainly draws attention.'

A glint of humour was in his eyes and the glance he lavished on her now made the blood sizzle in her veins.

'And men were staring at me?' She struck a pose to stir him even more. As if she was on a mission to push Nero to his limits, she couldn't stop. Even his growled response and his grip on her arm had no effect. 'You were happy to call me the Ice Maiden along with everyone else, but now I show another side and you don't like it.'

'That's not true,' Nero said huskily, 'I like it a lot.'

'How much?' She shivered deliciously as Nero's thunderous expression changed to a challenging smile. He was playing with her, Bella realised as he released his grip on her arm. He was treating her like one of his ponies in the corral—drawing her to him, then casting her into the void without him so she craved nothing more than his attention. 'I'm going back to the party.'

'I don't think so.'

Balling her hands into fists, she thrust them against his chest, but from the waist down they were connected. There was so much passion between them now they could set the barn on fire. Had Nero planned to goad her all along? He did very little in life without a very good reason. Nero was the consummate seducer—of horses, women—everyone he met. Ice Maiden? Nero cared nothing for that tag. He had always known how to make her burn.

They should have made it to the house—to a bed-room—to a bed.

They'd made it halfway across the stable yard when Nero dragged her close and trapped her between his hard body and the barn door. With his hands planted flat on the door either side of her face, he nuzzled her ears, her lips, her cheeks, her neck, sending heat shooting through her veins to her core. Her breasts felt heavy and a pulse throbbed hungrily between her legs. And when she managed to focus at all it was only to see all sorts of wickedness in Nero's eyes.

She was drowning in arousal by the time Nero dipped his head to brush her bottom lip with his mouth. As his warmth and strength enveloped her, all it took was his lightest touch to fire her senses. The will to move—to leave him—the will to do anything remotely sensible had completely deserted her. She claimed one small victory, hearing him groan deep in his chest when he deepened the kiss and her tongue tangled with his. A lifetime of avoiding men had left her hungry, and now she found it ironic that the most masculine man she had ever met had freed something inside her, allowing her female powers to have their head.

Their kisses grew more heated, more urgent, until the barn door creaked behind them. Shouldering it open, Nero drew her inside. The silence was intense. It shielded them from the noise of the party, and when he dropped the great iron bar across the door she knew that no one could disturb them.

Kissing her, Nero backed her towards the sweet-smelling bed of hay. She kept hold of his shirt as she sank down, dragging him with her. This might be a dream that lasted one night, but she had no intention of waking yet. She softened as Nero pressed her to the

ground. Each of his touches was a caress, and each
glance a promise to keep her safe…

Unfastening the straps on her dancing shoes, he
tossed them aside.

'I'm not wearing very much beneath my dress,' she
explained haltingly, having a sudden fit of the same
self-consciousness that had dogged her all her life.

'Excellent,' Nero approved, lowering the zip on her
dress.

'Nero—' She flinched as he pushed her bra straps
down.

'You're not frightened of me, are you?'

'You? No,' she answered. She was more frightened
of the way she felt about him. 'I'm not frightened of
anything.'

'Only a fool doesn't know fear,' Nero reminded her
as his kisses moved to her shoulder and then the swell
of her breast. And when she sighed in his arms, he took
her bra off and tossed it away. 'If I ruled the world—'

'You'd be unbearable?' she suggested, rallying determinedly between gasps of pleasure.

'It would be a crime to construct lingerie out of reinforced canvas,' Nero advised her as he teased her nipple
with the tip of his tongue. 'How did you fit that ugly
contraption beneath this divine dress?'

'With the greatest difficulty,' Bella admitted.

'Are you a virgin?'

'What sort of question is that?' she demanded.

'It's a perfectly reasonable question. And if you are,
now would be a good time to tell me. Come on, Bella,
your answer can only be yes or no—'

'Or yes…and no,' she said, stalling.

Nero frowned as he shifted position. 'I think you'd
better explain.'

When had she ever found it easy to discuss intimacy—or met a man who cared enough to ask? 'Of course I'm not a virgin. At my age?' she added with an awkward laugh.

Nero shrugged this answer off. 'Plenty of women your age are virgins—they haven't met the right man—they're flat-out not interested. It isn't a crime, Bella.'

Right. But she hadn't thought to hear Nero say it. She had always believed it was almost as taboo for a woman to admit to being a virgin at her age as it was to admitting she slept around.

'So what's your reason?' he prompted gently.

Surrender. That was Bella's reason. Loss of control. Putting her trust in someone else. She had never trusted anyone enough to be able to completely let go. But how to tell Nero that? 'People can control your life,' she murmured.

'Only if you let them,' Nero murmured between tender kisses. 'I would never do that. I have too much respect for you, Bella.'

She searched his eyes as Nero stroked her hair back. 'You have to let the past go,' he insisted gently. 'Learn from it, by all means, but move forward.'

'I have moved forward,' she said fiercely.

'Hey.' Nero was laughing softly as he brought her into his arms. 'No one's achieved more than you, tiger woman.'

'I had to…I had to defend my father.'

'Your hero?' Nero prompted, understanding.

'He was always my hero,' Bella admitted, eyes shining as she remembered all the wonderful times she had shared with a man who was flawed in the eyes of the world, but just about perfect where she was concerned. 'I had to stand my ground.'

'And fight?' Nero supplied. 'I know something about that,' he said wryly.

'I had to show all those people, Nero.'

'And you did,' he reassured her. 'Now it's time for you to think about Bella Wheeler for a change...'

And as he kissed her she thought that might, at long last, be possible—except there would always be that same thing holding her back—Bella's hidden flaw. 'I can't,' she said, pulling free from Nero's embrace.

'You can't?' Nero's ebony brows rose, though his eyes were as warm and as passionate as they had ever been.

'You asked me if I was a virgin,' she reminded him. 'And I don't know how to answer you because if I say I am, I'm not... What I mean is, I have and I haven't...'

'And when you did it was a bad experience—and that's what you remember?'

'Enough not to try it again,' Bella admitted, trying to be wry and funny at the same time, with the inevitable result that she ended up stumbling over the words. Her cheeks were glowing redder by the second. Closing her eyes, she tried again. 'What I'm trying to say and not making a very good job of is that I have...once, but I've never reached the ultimate conclusion that everyone else raves about.' She opened her eyes again. 'So you tell me, Nero. What does that make me?'

'A woman I want,' he murmured, drawing her into his arms. 'And if you haven't had an orgasm before, you're about to. So buckle your seat belt, Ms Wheeler—you're coming with me.'

And when she made some mild protest, Nero ignored her and removed her dress as if they had all the time in the world, and every inch he brought it down he replaced the whisper of silky fabric with his sensitive hands, or with his lips, or the nip of his teeth. Naked and exposed, her heart opened but, vulnerable though she was, she had gone too far now to turn back. The truth was, she didn't want to turn back.

Cradling her in his arms, Nero freed her hair and arranged it around her shoulders so that it framed her face. 'You're beautiful, Bella Wheeler,' he murmured.

She wasn't, but Nero made her feel so, and for the first time in her life she felt like a desirable woman. That feeling gave her strength and, unbuttoning his shirt, she pushed it from his shoulders, pausing only to admire the firm tanned flesh. At what moment had this hard, rugged face become hers to kiss? She brushed the curve of her smooth cheek against Nero's sharp black stubble and shivered with the promise of all the knowledge in his dark eyes that he would use to bring her pleasure.

Dipping his head, he took her lips again. 'No doubts?' he murmured, making her quiver as his hot breath touched her ear.

'None,' she said shakily. Torn between passion and fear of the past coming back to haunt her, she blocked out her past experiences and believed only in a very different future with the man she loved. Lacing her fingers through Nero's hair, she bound him to her.

Sensing her disquiet, Nero soothed her with a kiss, and when that kiss became heated he turned her, bringing her across his thighs so he could kiss his way up the back of her knees, her thighs and her buttocks until he reached the small of her back. As he cupped them, her buttocks responded with delight to each kiss and nip and stroke. She groaned with anticipation, forgetting everything but this, and even opened her legs a little to encourage him. Nero turned her so he could watch the pleasure building in her eyes as he stroked her into a frenzy of arousal. His hand found her heat and moved with an exquisite understanding of her need, but he drew it away, smiling faintly when he saw her disappointment. 'Not yet,' he cautioned.

'But soon,' she begged, writhing against him.

Nero suckled first on one breast and then the other. The heat of his mouth, the lash of his tongue and the rasp of his stubble all conspired to heighten sensation until she was completely lost in the moment. Laughing softly, Nero kissed the corner of her mouth until she turned to look at him, when he deepened the kiss and, drawing her into his arms, lay down with her on the hay.

'Now,' she begged him, easing down on the hay so that his kisses must find her belly and now the inside of her thighs. Shameless and determined, she thrust her hips towards him in a blatant invitation, crying out in triumph when Nero parted her legs with the wide spread of his powerful shoulders. Throwing her head back she gasped with approval.

But it still wasn't enough.

'I submit,' Nero murmured, when she moved over him and held him down.

'That's good,' she said, kissing his face, his neck, his shoulders, and then his chest.

'Don't stop now,' he teased her.

She had no intention of doing so, though she felt a jolt when she kissed the hard planes of his belly. He was so toned, so perfect. Nero was a playground of pleasure. And it was his turn to exclaim softly when she stroked his thighs, before cupping the swell of his erection beneath the straining fabric of his breeches. She measured and nursed it, and wondered if she could encompass it in one hand. There was only one way to find out…

'Feel free,' Nero murmured as she trailed one finger-tip down the cool steel zip.

'Shameless,' she mocked him softly as he locked his arms behind his head.

'You'd better believe it.'

Freeing the fastening at the top of his zip, she eased it down and he sprang free. Question answered: two hands. Lowering her head, she closed her mouth around him.

CHAPTER FOURTEEN

FOR a moment Nero was completely lost. He couldn't move, he couldn't think; the pleasure was far too intense. Bella had really surprised him. She was bolder than he had imagined, and instinctively sensual. She traced the acutely sensitive tip with her tongue, sucking and licking until he was forced to move—had to move if he wanted to please her.

Without losing the delicious contact of Bella's mouth on him, he kissed his way down her body until he reached the plump swell of her arousal. When she whimpered and threw herself back in the hay he stripped off the last of his clothes. Spreading her thighs wide, he found the heat at her core again and, laving it delicately with his tongue, he gradually increased the pressure. She was already moist and so swollen with arousal that when he parted her plump lips to claim the most intimate part of her, she widened her thighs and urged him on. When Bella's mouth and tongue began their work again, the exchange of pleasure between them was like nothing he had ever known.

Nero brought her to the brink so many times she wondered how he knew when to draw back. Was it second sight? Intuition? Whatever it was, she was pleased he possessed the skill. And, as for her fears of falling short as a woman—what fears? By the time Nero moved over her she couldn't have taken fright if she'd tried. She had never felt anything like this—had never thought herself capable of such intense sensations. Could it really get any better?

Nero brought her beneath him, positioning her as he teased her with just the tip of his pulsing erection. She loved the way he cushioned her buttocks with his hands. 'Oh, please,' she begged him. 'Don't make me wait this time.'

She heard herself add to this a brazen request in words that to her knowledge she had never spoken out loud before. Nero didn't seem shocked. He stared into her eyes and kissed her as he eased inside her, filling her completely. 'Yes, oh, yes,' she cried as he stretched her beyond what seemed possible. He waited until she relaxed before he moved again, and when he did she whimpered with surprise that such pleasure was possible as he thrust deeply before slowly withdrawing again.

'No,' she cried out, ordering him back immediately.

Nero laughed softly as her fingers bit into his shoulders and her teeth closed on his skin. She was soon gasping for breath as he started moving to a steady and dependable rhythm, taking her higher and closer to the promised goal with each firm stroke. Could it be possible to hover so near the edge and still feel safe? The tango might have brought her here, but this was the best dance on earth. She was rocking on a plateau of pleasure with a great dam waiting to burst behind her eyes and in her mind.

'Look at me, Bella,' Nero commanded.

As he claimed her attention she obeyed, and with one final thrust he gave her what she had waited a lifetime to achieve. Briefly, it took her out. Shooting stars invaded her head as pleasure exploded inside her. Sensation ruled and she embraced it hungrily, screaming out her release as the violent spasms gripped her, and they went on and on until she was completely spent and left to float gently on a tide of lazy waves.

'More?' Nero suggested dryly.

'Why are you smiling?' Bella demanded groggily, barely able to summon up the strength to speak.

'Once is never enough,' Nero murmured against her lips.

'You're so right,' she agreed on a contented breath. 'That was so good, I think you'd better do it all over again just so I can be sure I wasn't dreaming.'

Laughing softly, he brought her on top of him. 'It's your turn now. Ride me, take your pleasure. Use me as you will.'

She laughed into his eyes, feeling safe and strong—so safe she missed the flicker of something out of sync in Nero's eyes. She was still buzzing with how it felt to be liberated sexually—to be free and fulfilled. Nero had shown her that this was how it should be—and how it would be from now on. He was unique. Fate had brought them together. They shared so much—and not just this, she thought as she began to rock to a primal rhythm. They shared careers, and a whole raft of other interests... Nero was a friend she trusted, and now he was her lover. Could anything be more perfect?

Bella sucked in a sharp breath as Nero's hands began to control her movements. While one guided her hips, encouraging her, the other moved skilfully at pleasuring her. Her mouth opened in a gasp of surprise as Nero quickly brought her to the brink again. Lost to all rational thought, she allowed him to finish what he had so expertly begun and in the final moment before she took the plunge into pleasure she screamed out his name, and might even have whispered that she loved him.

Holding her safe in his arms, Nero stroked her hair until she fell into a contented sleep, while he stared unseeing into the shadows at the far end of the barn.

Bella slept soundly until a sharp ray of sunshine breached her closed eyelids. Stretching contentedly, she reached out a questing hand. The prickle of hay greeted her. It took her a moment to get her thoughts in order to process this. Party... Nero... Last night... Incredible.

And all these disjointed thoughts were bound by one certainty. She was in love. Nero was the man she loved. Thanks to him, she was transformed from Ice Maiden into something unimaginably different, Bella thought with a happy sigh, and last night Nero had put the seal on her love by proving that he felt the same. They had laughed and learned about each other and, trusting each other completely, had made the most spectacular love together.

So where was he?

She called his name, not really expecting a reply. Nero would be down at the stables with the horses. Considerately, he'd left her to sleep. He'd even brought a blanket from the house to cover her. Drawing it close, she sighed a second time. Did life get any better than this? She moved with remembered pleasure, but found it impossible to settle. The silence hung heavily all around her, making the barn feel incredibly empty, making her feel shut out.

So it was time to get up, she reasoned sensibly. She couldn't lie here all day with just a blanket covering her. Nero had folded her clothes. They were so neatly stacked there was something alarming about it. She couldn't put her finger on it exactly, but it could be interpreted as making order out of chaos. Last night had been chaotic and passionate—and amazing. Did Nero think so too? Or was he trying to make sense of the passion that had consumed them both?

And now she was overreacting as usual, Bella reassured herself. The Ice Maiden with her frozen shell and vivid inner life—she could put all that behind her now. Last night had changed everything—and she refused to think anything bad. Sitting up, she dragged the blanket round her and smiled like a contented kitten. She ached all over—in the most pleasant way. The impossible had happened. She had something going on with Nero, something deep and special. She felt like a real woman for the first time in her life, well loved and completely fulfilled. The Ice Maiden had gone for ever. Bella Wheeler had a new life now. Hurrying to get dressed, she threw on her clothes, brushed off the hay and didn't even bother to tie back her hair. What was the point when she'd leap straight in the shower when she got back to the house? And, anyway, well-loved women didn't bother with scraping their hair back. Flinging open the barn door in this new mood of abandon, she closed it quickly and then opened it a crack. Nero had his back to her and he was discussing something with a couple of gauchos. One of them was holding Misty, saddled and ready for him to ride.

Well? That was part of the deal. She brushed off any lingering qualms.

Once Nero gets used to riding Misty, he will never be able to let the pony go.

Nero should ride Misty—she wanted him to ride her pony. He'd been far too considerate so far, never trespassing on her enjoyment of riding her favourite horse—always giving way while she had been staying on the *estancia*.

Stealing another look out of the door, Bella's heart picked up pace. Nero was so poised, so utterly in command. The dark blue top emphasised his tan, and he was freshly showered with his hair still damp. Clean breeches, highly polished boots, and muscular legs it seemed incredible to her now she had been kissing only hours before. The conversation in rapid Spanish was indecipherable but, judging by Nero's gestures, he was telling the gauchos to take Misty back to the stables and get the mare ready for *Inglaterra*—she could hardly mistake that.

To hell with what people thought of her. Quickly, she slung the high-heeled sandals over her wrist and left the barn barefoot in her tango dress to confront Nero.

The men had gone, taking Misty with them. Nero was standing alone with one hand on the back of his neck and his head bowed as if the woes of the world were on his shoulders.

Swallowing deep, she could feel her own life splintering in front of her eyes. There was no pretending she didn't know what was going on. They had grown too close for the smallest nuance in Nero's behaviour to escape her. Her time in Argentina was at an end. They had always known this was a temporary arrangement. The scheme for the children was a success—they all wanted to come back and had promised to recommend the project at Estancia Caracas to their friends, which was all Nero or Bella had wanted. The prince would be pleased too, Bella told herself numbly. She had fulfilled her duty. 'Nero… Good morning,' she said lightly.

'Bella.' He turned, but the light in his eyes was swiftly dimmed.

He had made her strong, and now it was time for her to be strong for Nero—for both of them. 'So the time has come,' she said without emotion, angling her head to one side. Damn it, the smile wouldn't come. 'It's been—'

'Don't,' he said shortly.

'It's time for me to go, Nero,' she said as if she were encouraging him. She turned then and walked towards the house without a backwards glance. She had always known, deep down, Nero wasn't going to ask her to stay. Nero Caracas was a free spirit whose life had taught him that he could only be happy on his own. He had given her all that he could.

And that was a lot, Bella reflected as the shadow of the hacienda fell over her. Nero had made her believe in herself and in her inner strength, and in the beauty that came from a woman who was happy in her own body, and he had cemented that belief by making love to her. Nero Caracas, the Assassin, polo hero, national icon, the world's most eligible bachelor and most beddable man, the heartbreaker of Argentina. Why was she surprised that it hadn't worked out? She was a professional career woman, Bella told herself firmly, ignoring the tears battering the back of her eyes. Tilting her chin at a determined angle, she told herself firmly that polo was her life, not polo players—whoever they were, they were incidental—*which wasn't enough to stop her heart feeling as if someone had smashed it into tiny pieces with a polo mallet.*

She just needed a minute to settle her thoughts and then she'd get on with the rest of the day. The rest of the day? What about the rest of her life?

* * *

Nero spent the rest of the morning arranging transport to England for Bella and her horse. They'd use his private jet, of course, and with one of his own vets in attendance. He couldn't do more for Bella. He could never do enough for her.

And thoughts like those were where it all started to go wrong. He could see the future in Bella's eyes, while his was firmly lodged in his head. It was the same plan he'd had all along—be the best, make his grandmother and Ignacio proud—there was no room in his life for anything but the ranch and polo.

Nero's eyes softened briefly, and then grew resolute again when he remembered the hearts and flowers in Bella's eyes and the cold, clear thoughts in his. Rather than soften towards him, she would have done better to remain the Ice Maiden, for his heart was still the same piece of stone. He'd seen what families could do to each other—and knew he didn't want that. He wouldn't inflict that on any woman. What? And break her like a horse? Would he strip away Bella's successful career and dim that flare of emerald fire in her stare? What gave him the right to do these things when she had done everything he and the prince had expected of her and more? Could he take her pony? No.

Could he love her?

The only thing he knew about love was that it was corrosive and destroyed everything in its path. He refused to even think about it. He and Bella had enjoyed a great short-term professional relationship and that was it.

He should never have seduced her. He should never have enjoyed her. He would never stop thinking about her. His only option was to send her away before he wrecked everything for her. She must go back to

England, where she could continue her valuable work and pick up her successful career. Work was something he understood. Work meant building, as he had rebuilt the ranch. Love destroyed. These were some lessons a boy growing up never forgot. He wanted Bella, but what could he offer that wouldn't take her from the life she had built for herself half a world away?

Nothing more needed to be said, Bella reflected, which was both strange and sad. She had to go and Nero had to stay. She had started her packing straight after her shower. By the time she went downstairs Nero was in the kitchen drinking coffee as if it were any other day. It was every other day, but it was radically, horribly changed by the unbearable tension between them. She felt fresh and clean, neatly ordered and ready for work—with a yawning hole in her chest where her heart used to be.

'Thank you, María,' she said with a warm smile when Nero's housekeeper passed her a steamy cup of freshly brewed coffee. She turned away fast. She couldn't bear to see that look in María's eyes. How did María know? Was everyone on the pampas psychic?

This definitely wasn't the usual relaxed morning in the kitchen, Bella registered, feeling the tension rise to unsustainable levels. Nero finished his coffee. Putting his newspaper down, he stood, reminding her of how small she'd felt in his arms, and how protected.

'When you've got a minute, we should discuss your travel arrangements,' he said.

'Of course,' she said briskly, 'but I want to talk to the children first. And Ignacio. I want them to hear I'm leaving from me.' She swung round, conscious of María standing close behind her as if hovering, waiting to give comfort. 'And of course I'd really appreciate a few minutes of your time, María—I'm going to miss you all so much.'

Instead of answering this, María enveloped Bella in a hug.

And now they both had tears in their eyes.

'I'll be at the stables,' Nero said as he wheeled away.

As the jet soared into the sky Bella stared out of the window, feeling as though she was joined to Argentina by an umbilical cord and that cord was being stretched tighter and tighter until finally it snapped. There was just a solid floor of cloud beneath her now. She could have been anywhere—going anywhere.

Turning away from the window, her throat felt tight as she answered politely when the flight attendant asked her if she had everything she needed. Not nearly, Bella thought. The man quickly left her, as if he could sense that she was nursing some deep wound.

She stared unseeing at the dossier in front of her. These were the papers and photographs and the quotations from the children, which she had collected to show the prince. She could have sent most of it by e-mail, but wanted…needed, maybe, concrete evidence of her time in Argentina.

She'd miss the children, Bella thought, focusing on a group shot. She'd miss everyone. Ignacio, dressed for the occasion in full gaucho rig, positively exuding a sense of adventure and exoticism. The kids with their cheeky grins—long-time enemies, some of them, with their arms around each other, smiling for the camera—teams now, not gangs. María and Concepcion, their laughing faces so kind and smiling. And Nero. Nero towering over everyone in his polo rig, looking every bit the glamorous hero with the wind ruffling his thick black hair and his fist planted firmly on the fence beside him. No wonder control was so important to him. He'd seen where the lack of it had led, and what restoring it and going forward could achieve.

And she wasn't going to cry.

Who knew bottled up tears could hurt so much?

Picking up the champagne the flight attendant had poured for her, she raised a glass to absent friends.

CHAPTER FIFTEEN

LIFE went flat the moment Bella left Argentina. The atmosphere inside the *estancia* was instantly sombre, and the mood in the stable yard was scarcely any better.

'Everyone misses her,' Ignacio complained, stating the obvious.

'Do I need telling this?' Nero scowled at his old friend, who simply shrugged.

The last of the children in this year's scheme had just left, and the two of them had stayed behind to wave them off, but all the children had wanted to know was: Where was Bella? When was Bella coming back? Would she be here next year?

'Maybe,' was the best he could offer them, swiftly followed by, 'she's very busy.'

It had felt like a cop-out to him and he hadn't fooled anyone. To make things worse, Bella had left a jokey video for them all to watch. It had made the children laugh—and not just because of Bella's halting Spanish. He had stood at the back with his arms folded and his eyes narrowed as Ignacio ran the film—preparing to close a chapter and turn the page, but even he had smiled. No, it was more than that. He'd been drawn in. He'd grown wistful. He'd wanted things he couldn't have.

And now he felt wretched. The moment the lights had

come up he had acted as if this was just another day. But nothing would ever be the same again. Who could have predicted Bella would remember her first uncertain days on the *estancia* and could communicate the mistakes she'd made in such a hilarious and self-deprecating way in order to make the kids feel better?

Bella had given them all something to think about, Nero reflected, turning for the stables to saddle up his horse.

He stopped dead inside the stable yard. 'Ignacio. Is something wrong?' He had never seen his old friend dumbstruck before. Ignacio was known for being taciturn but nothing like this. Nero's heart raced with apprehension. 'Which horse is it?' he demanded, expecting the worst.

'You'd better see for yourself,' Ignacio told him, standing back.

'She left you a note,' one of the grooms told him, pressing a letter into his hand.

'Not now,' he said, in a rush to see whichever horse had succumbed to illness or injury. But then he halted. 'Who left me a note?'

'Bella,' the young lad said.

Ripping the envelope open, Nero scanned the contents rapidly: *She'll have a better chance with you—a better life.* Both the letter and the envelope drifted to the ground as he threw the stable door open. 'Misty...'

The sight of the little horse in his stable overwhelmed him. Sentiments he had never allowed himself to feel came flooding in. Bella had sacrificed part of her heart for him—and for the little horse she loved. 'How did this happen?' he asked Ignacio with a tight throat. 'How could the transporter leave my yard with the wrong horse?'

'Bella?' Ignacio said wryly. 'Bella insisted on overseeing all the arrangements for Misty's transport personally.'

'Of course she did…' A faint smile broke through Nero's frown. And she would have done so knowing that no one would argue with that.

'No. I can't do it.' Bella shook her head.

'But you must,' Bella's second in command insisted.

Agnes Dillon was an older no-nonsense woman who had worked for Bella's father as a young girl and now worked for Bella. 'The British team has asked for you by name. The prince has too. You're going to be supervising the royal stable yard, for goodness' sake, Bella—doesn't that mean anything to you?'

For the England-Argentina international? Yes, that meant something to her. All she could see in her head was Nero—the same man who had sent her a cryptic message saying: *Bella, what have you done?* But there was nothing to be done about it now. Staying longer than she had intended in Argentina meant she had come straight back home to a match. 'I suppose I could take the day off sick,' she mused out loud.

Agnes's wiry grey bun bobbed. 'You're never sick,' she pointed out, rejecting this idea.

'Then I'll take a holiday.'

'On the day of the most crucial match in the polo calendar?'

'Okay, I don't do either of those things,' Bella conceded while Agnes shoved her hands into the pockets of her faded raspberry-coloured cords and waited. 'I'll work in the background.'

'People expect to see you, Bella. Your place is on the

pony lines at an international. What's the matter with you?' Agnes demanded. 'You haven't been the same since you came home.'

No. She had been restless and anxious and angry that Nero hadn't sent her more news about Misty. She couldn't bring herself to phone him, but her call to Ignacio had confirmed that Misty was in the best of spirits and was being ridden every day in preparation for the season. And, yes, Nero would be riding her. Misty would be his first choice in all the matches. It would have been nice to hear this from Nero.

'Did something happen in Argentina, Bella?'

Bella looked long and hard into Agnes's eyes. 'No. Nothing,' she insisted fiercely, as though trying to convince herself.

Agnes shrugged in the way people did when they knew not to press.

'Okay, we've got work to do.' Bella shut her mind to everything else. 'I should get my horse ready. I'm planning to ride one of the newly trained horses in the last chukka in the women's match.'

Bella could feel Agnes's concern on her back as she walked away. If only the older woman knew! How would she handle seeing Nero again when she'd thought of him every waking moment since leaving Argentina?

She'd handle it because that was her job, Bella told her herself impatiently, mounting up. Her team was at the top of the tree when it came to horse management. Man management she'd leave to the specialists, Bella concluded, seeing a group of stick chicks wandering off to the bar. They had no interest in watching women play, but when the Argentinians arrived, like the answer to every woman's sex-starved dream, they'd be back.

* * *

The Argentinian contingent rolled into town like a conquering army—four-wheel drives with blacked-out windows, vans, trucks, flashy sports cars with exotic-sounding names, a couple of fire-fed motorbikes and what seemed like a constant parade of sleek new horse transporters. The glamour quotient in the prince's polo yard shot into the stratosphere as the polo guys and their skimpily clad groupies emerged to stroll nonchalantly about while the polo ponies with their massive entourage decanted exuberantly from their motorised stalls, tossing their heads as if to say, *Clear a path; we're the real stars of the show!*

With so much testosterone flying about, it was no wonder Bella had her work cut out keeping her young grooms in check. The brash new Argentinian horse transporters were like nothing they had ever seen before. The Argentinian horses breathed fire. And the men…

The less said about the men, the better, Bella thought, heart thundering as the swarthy marauders with their flashing eyes, deep tans and athletic frames took possession of every inch of space. Even Agnes had come over all coy and girlie.

Whereas she was attending solely to business, Bella reassured herself, checking each horse into the yard on her clipboard, ignoring the fact that her heart was beating a frantic *so-where-is-he?* tattoo. She was doing very well until a deep voice penetrated her thoughts.

Whirling around, she saw him at once. Nero must have been riding shotgun at the back of the parade, but now he had moved in to help bring a particularly fractious pony down one of the transporter ramps. Seeing him with his muscles pumped at full stretch kept her rooted to the spot for a moment. Nero was so much more than she remembered. He meant so much more to her than she had even realised.

But when a horse threatened to run amok, safety was paramount. With the carefully choreographed re-union between one professional and another that she had planned forgotten, Bella dropped her clipboard on the ground and ran to help.

Everyone else had backed away when she ran in. Corded muscles stood out on Nero's arms. He had looped the rope around his waist but, as the horse shrieked its disapproval and reared up again, something in Nero's stillness caught its attention. Rolling white eyes fixed on Nero's while flattened ears pricked up as Nero began crooning reassurances in his deep, husky voice. It was a sound that touched not only the horse, but Bella somewhere deep too. She loved this man. Love wasted, maybe, but she would always love him. She drank in Nero's resolute face and loved him all the more. Her heart and her eyes were full of him. Nothing in her life had ever come close to this feeling.

Finally, the horse was calm enough to lead away. Nero would allow no one but himself to take the risk of leading her and Bella hurried ahead of him to open the stable door. Her heart was stripped bare for Nero to trample on and only her professionalism allowed her to put her own feelings to one side and do what her train-ing, her life had taught her. It was cool and shadowy inside the stable. She had prepared everything for just this eventuality. There was always one horse, sometimes more than one, spooked by the journey and the new sur-roundings, and Bella's aim was to soothe the frightened animal with the fresh sweet scent of hay and clean, cool water. Nero was also the consummate professional and, having seen his troupe safely into the yard, he wouldn't allow himself to acknowledge the world outside until everyone was safe.

Slipping the harness off the horse, he handed it to her. They hadn't spoken a word to each other yet, but there was an incredible level of tension between them. It was like an electric current joining them. They didn't need to speak, Bella realised as they quietened the highly strung horse between them. In this area of their lives, at least, they would always be as one.

Satisfied that the horse was calm, they left quietly. Bella turned for one last look over the top of the stable door.

'All's well that ends well. Isn't that what you say in your country, Bella?'

Nero's muscular forearms were resting on the lower half of the door as he turned to look at her. Holding his luminous gaze, she sensed rather than saw the hard mouth soften. 'Hello, Nero.'

Warmth stole into his eyes. 'Hello, Bella…'

Their naked arms were almost touching, but while Nero might have stepped straight out of the pages of a fashion magazine and smelled divine, Bella was conscious that she smelled of horse and in her workmanlike outfit of faded top and muckers—the boots she wore around the stables—with hoof oil smeared across her stable breeches, she was hardly a contender for groupie of the year. She hadn't wanted to look as if she was trying too hard when Nero and the Argentinians arrived, but there were degrees, she realised now.

'How are you, Bella?'

How was she? She had planned to be calm and professional. 'I'm well… And you?' Such few words to express a whole world of feeling.

'I'm very well, thank you,' Nero replied formally.

Nero hadn't moved. He was just staring at her as if he wanted to imprint every fraction of her face on his mind. 'Bella, what you did—'

'I should go. I have all your documentation here,' she said, clinging to business. She handed him the pack she had prepared earlier. He didn't even look at it. 'I'll come down to the stables later when you've had time to settle in,' she said, turning to go. 'If you need anything at all before then, please don't hesitate to call me. You'll find my number in the folder, along with all the others I thought you might find useful.' She was looking into his eyes. She should have seen. She should have known.

The breath caught in her throat as Nero put his hands on her shoulders. 'No more talking, Bella.'

She weakened against him. When Nero kissed her it felt so good, so right. The scent of him, the touch, the taste, the strength. She felt protected all over again.

And knew how dangerous that could be. It was better, safer, to be alone.

'No,' Nero exclaimed fiercely when she tried to pull away. 'I won't let you go this time. I've missed you too much, Bella. I didn't know what I was losing, or what I stood to gain,' he added with a glint of the old humour.

She would not—could not—give way to the maelstrom of feelings boiling inside her. 'You thought I was teaching you something?' Nero murmured, staring deep into her eyes. 'But you taught me more, Bella. You made me realise how proud my grandmother would be of the ranch as it is now, how the team she founded has gone on and prospered.'

'How proud she would be of you,' Bella amended softly. 'Don't put yourself down, Nero.'

'Says the expert on such matters,' Nero observed

huskily, brushing her lips with his mouth. 'You showed me that history doesn't have to repeat itself, and that a life alone is a lonely life.'

'I've missed you,' she breathed, nuzzling into him.

'Of course you have,' Nero agreed with all the old confidence, dropping another kiss on her mouth. His eyes were dancing with laughter and the familiar crease was back in his cheek.

'You're impossible,' she said.

Nero shrugged. His mouth curved. 'I won't deny it, but I've missed you, Bella—more than you know.'

For the first time in his life he felt a little up in the air. He'd put his heart on the line and Bella had been called away. He knew she wasn't a woman to be ordered around or someone who would fit in to suit—not that he wanted that, but Bella was at the other extreme. This was a woman with her life totally mapped out.

Was there a place for him in that life? He had never thought to ask the question before. It was clear that Bella belonged here as much as he belonged in Argentina. Could two lovers half a world apart ever be together for longer than the polo season? With a vicious curse under his breath, he watched her stride away. And then he shook his head a little ruefully. She was cool. He had to give her that. He admired her composure, just so long as the Ice Maiden didn't make a bid to come back.

'Hey, Ignacio,' he called. His face lit up at the sight of his closest ally and dearest friend.

'Can't stop,' Ignacio informed him in rapid Spanish. 'I'm going to see Bella. Can't be late; she's expecting me!'

He was jealous of Ignacio now? He felt shut out, Nero realised as Ignacio hurried off in the same direction

Bella had taken. At least he knew where he stood in the pecking order now. Try nowhere for size.

'Can I help you?'

He looked down into the concerned face of an older woman he remembered from previous visits. 'Agnes,' he said, remembering her name. They shook hands. 'It's good to see you again. Bella has made sure I have everything I need, thank you.' Except for the one thing he wanted, Nero thought as his glance strayed after Bella.

He was still grinding his jaw with frustration when he went to check on the ponies. He had wanted to say so much more to Bella, but she hadn't given him the chance. He had wanted to thank her for the movie she'd left for the kids and tell her how they had used it for each new intake—and that they would need a new film for next year. He had thought about their reunion constantly since she'd left, but he had pictured something very different—fireworks, not business. It was always duty first for Bella.

But now duty called him too. Work soothed him. The ponies always soothed him. And Bella would be back at his side as soon as she had finished whatever it was she had left him to do.

Bella wasn't back at his side, later that day or the next. Having made discreet enquiries, he learned she was evaluating the fitness of borderline match-ready ponies. Ignacio was his usual taciturn self and, in spite of Nero's subtle and not-so-subtle prompting, Ignacio refused to let anything slip about his own reunion with Bella. So had they talked about him at all? Or was work really all that mattered to Bella? And why was he feeling so indignant when it was the same for him? He had a week of non-stop training and preparation until the match ahead of him.

The day of the game matched his mood, with grim grey skies and rolling clouds of ink-lined pewter. He had only dozed on and off through another lonely night. How was Bella? Had she slept well? Selfishly, he hoped not. He hoped, like him, she hadn't slept properly all week.

Peering out of the window of his hotel, which was located on the fringes of the polo club, he had a good view of the pitch. Slippery, he determined, and the weather wasn't going to get better any time soon. He let the curtain fall back.

Drying off after an ice-cold shower, he switched on the news in time to catch the weather forecast. Thunder predicted later. Brilliant. Just what the horses didn't like. Bella would need all the help she could get to keep them calm. Sensing electricity in the air, they would be restless. It was one thing staying out of Bella's private life, but where work was involved her safety was his concern. And at work was the only time he'd seen her this week, at a joint team briefing. And each time when tension snapped between them she found some excuse to hurry away.

The time had come to change that for good.

Bella enjoyed her time with Ignacio, asking him questions about Nero's wild youth. Of course, she knew there were areas where she shouldn't trespass. Nero had told her about his parents—his father, in particular, and she wouldn't stretch the elderly gaucho's patience by delving into a past that he wouldn't care to remember, but he did give one reason why Nero had difficulty expressing his feelings. 'It's the gaucho's way,' Ignacio told her.

Ignacio had been a huge influence on Nero's life, stepping in and teaching him all his grandmother's tricks, as well as a few of his own. But there were other reasons for Nero's solitary path through life, his horrific childhood for one. When he should have known love and protection, Nero had faced cruelty and uncertainty. But if she could put her past behind her—

'Are all the ponies match-ready?'

She jumped guiltily at the sound of Nero's voice. 'All the ponies on this side of the yard have been passed by the vet.'

Without a word, Ignacio gathered up his grooming tackle and left them.

'What do *you* think, Bella?' Nero pressed.

'I think the weather conditions are treacherous and likely to get worse,' she said, holding Nero's fierce stare. 'I think the ponies are in great condition, but you need to take care. The ground will be slippery and your ponies don't like the wet, whereas our English ponies are used to damp conditions.' Her heart was pounding with concern and with longing.

'And your English ponies are unlike every other breed on the planet in that they're used to thunder, are they?' Nero demanded. With a sceptical huff, he flicked a look at the sky.

'We'll just have to hope the storm holds off.'

'Well, whatever happens, no more heroics from you. No more straying onto the pitch. For whatever reason,' Nero insisted, dipping his handsome head to stare her in the eyes. 'Do you understand me?'

'I thought we had that squared away.'

'We have, but I haven't forgotten.'

She let out a shaking breath as he strode away. Would things ever be relaxed and easy between them again?

Since his return it felt as if Nero had seized hold of her life and tossed it into the path of a hurricane.

Yes, and when he left she'd be in the doldrums again. Even if they hardly spoke now, she dreaded him leaving. She dreaded facing another endless span of unbearable longing. Resting her face against the warm, firm neck of the pony she'd been grooming, Bella vowed not to waste another second of her life thinking about Nero. Time was such a fragile, fleeting thing, and he would soon be going home to Argentina.

CHAPTER SIXTEEN

THE thunder held off, though Bella had been right about the ponies. The ground was wet and more than one pony had gone lame after skidding to a halt. The pony Nero was riding in this chukka had cast a shoe. 'Where is she?' he demanded when he rode in. 'Where's Bella?'

'She's with the grooms, warming up the ponies,' Agnes explained as he swung down from the saddle.

'She should be here.' He gazed up and down the pony lines, searching for her. 'It's her job to be here.' He pulled off his helmet as the horn sounded, announcing the end of the first half.

Meanwhile, Agnes was wringing her hands, which was most unlike her. 'What's the matter, Agnes?'

'We're short of horses, or I'd have another one brought up for you right away.'

'Don't worry; it's not your fault. These are unusual weather conditions. The match should have been cancelled.'

'Such an important match?' Agnes appeared horror-struck.

'Why not?' he said. 'It's only a game.' Words he thought he'd never hear himself say twice in one lifetime. He turned to see Bella leading Misty towards them. 'What are you doing?' he said suspiciously. 'I heard you'd run out of horses.'

'Not quite,' Bella said as she patted the pony's neck.

'You have to be joking. I'm not risking Misty. I brought her back to England where she belongs—with you. Have you seen the weather conditions? It's carnage out there.' And his emotions were all over the place. Bella was offering him her pony, a symbol of everything she cared about. 'I won't ride her,' he said decisively.

'She's equal to anything out there.'

'The brutality?'

'She'll keep you safe, Nero.'

There was so much in Bella's steady gaze, he seized her in front of everyone and brought her close. They stared into each other's eyes for a moment, for a lifetime, for eternity. 'Don't you ever stay away from me again,' he ground out.

'It's been a week,' she teased him.

'A week too long,' he argued, kissing her with hungry passion. He cursed impatiently as the horn sounded, calling him back onto the field.

'I'll be waiting for you,' she called after him, levelling that same steady stare on his face.

'I'll take care of her,' he promised, vaulting onto Misty's back. As he settled his helmet on his head he was suddenly aware that Bella and he were the focus of everyone's attention, from the grooms to Ignacio, and from the stick chicks to the prince, who had come to inspect his horses. 'I love you, Bella Wheeler,' he called out as everyone cheered. 'I've always loved you and I always will.' And he didn't care who heard.

'I love you too,' she said, her face as bright as the sun peeping through the clouds. 'Stay safe!'

Removing his helmet, he saluted her with a bow. He'd

won the only match he cared about. He hadn't a clue
how Bella and he were going to make it work; he only
knew they would.

They drank a toast to the victory of Nero's team. It was
a massive victory, as the prince was the first to admit.
He could hardly blame Bella for allowing the captain of
the Argentinian team to ride her best pony, when it was
the prince who had suggested that the best polo player in
the world ought to be matched with Misty. He just hadn't
factored the timing into his thinking, the prince admitted wryly. Just as he hadn't realised what a wonderful
job Bella had done in Argentina, he added, thanking
her for the portfolio of her stay she'd compiled for him.
'You must go back there,' the prince insisted. 'Agnes
and my team can hold the fort for you here.'

'You're too kind, Sir,' Bella said, glancing at Nero.

The moment the prince's back was turned, Nero
grabbed hold of her hand. 'You, me. Quiet time, now,'
he insisted, leading Bella away. 'You can't refuse a royal
command,' he reminded her, tongue in cheek, 'though
I don't need the prince to prompt me.'

Bella curbed a smile. 'I've got something for you,'
she said softly.

'And I've got something I want to tell you,' he said,
drawing her to a halt in the grand, ornately plastered
hallway of the Polo Club.

'Present first,' Bella insisted. Ignacio had told her
that although Nero was the most generous of men, he
frowned on his staff spending their hard-earned money
on him. And, as he had no living relatives, Nero didn't
exactly get a full Christmas sack. Bella intended to
change that.

Nero looked suspicious. 'Is Ignacio in on this?'

'If he is I wouldn't tell you.'

'Will I like it?'

'Oh, I think so,' she said confidently.

He must be patient, Nero thought as Bella led him back across the polo ground towards the stables. What he had to say to her had waited long enough—it could wait a little longer. Bella touched him more than any woman ever had. Like now, when she was clutching her breast above her heart as she took him across the yard towards an emerald-green paddock that stretched down to the river. The paddock was home to a herd of spirited young colts, currently racing around, testing each other.

'The grey,' Bella said, pointing. 'That's Misty's first colt. He was born before I even met you, but he's two years old now, ready to start polo training.'

She stared up at him. 'He's a fine pony.' Nero's eyes narrowed as he watched the young horse go through his paces. 'A little wild, but courage and daring is what I always look for.' His gaze was drawn to Bella. 'You've done well,' he said, 'really well.'

'I named him Tango. For you.'

He inhaled sharply. 'For me?'

'It's my gift to you,' she explained, 'for your...hospitality in Argentina.'

He was incredulous. No one had ever given him anything of such great value before. He threw her a crooked smile. 'I'm glad you enjoyed yourself.'

'Oh, I did. And now at least you can breed some decent animals from those Criollas of yours,' she teased him, tilting her chin at the familiar challenging angle.

'Cheeky,' he warned, but he was laughing too. He wondered if he had ever been so happy in his life.

'Hopefully, a few years down the line your polo

ponies will be able to keep their feet when they come to England.' She turned serious. 'Tango has a great bloodline, Nero, and I think he'll be happy with those pretty mares of yours on the pampas.'

'Bella, I don't know what to say.'

'Don't say anything.'

'What can I give you in return?'

'I don't want anything in return—I never have.'

'May I give you my heart?' He stared down, realising that this was the single most important question he had ever asked in his life, and that Bella's answer would change both their lives for ever.

The solution was simple. The solution had been in front of them all the time, which was probably why they hadn't seen it and the prince had, Bella realised as she tried on the wedding dress in the thirty-third shop in at least the sixth country on the polo tour. But this one was perfect, which was just as well, since it was essential she found one before Nero came back to drag her out of the shop. Patience was not one of his virtues. A special licence and the two of them was all that was required—Bella had different ideas. She wanted photographs for their children to remember. So here she was in the most exclusive wedding store in Rome.

As the murmuring attendants fussed around her, Bella allowed herself a moment of quiet reflection. After their wedding, she would be back in Argentina with Nero in time for the new intake of children on the scheme and for the polo season there. They would then both travel back to the northern hemisphere in time to manage Bella's projects. But, more important than all of this, Nero insisted, was the life they built together. Remembering the portrait of his grandmother, Bella knew she would be following her heart to the pampas, just as Nero would be following his head when he came to England to play polo for the prince.

She was jolted out of these thoughts by Nero throwing the assistants into a panic by striding unannounced into a wedding boutique that suddenly seemed far too small to hold both Nero Caracas and the chosen wedding dress. Barring the entrance to her cubicle, the brave women held him at bay.

'Get me out of this,' Bella exclaimed, already tearing at the laces.

The women only just managed to remove the gown in time and hide it as Nero threw back the curtain.

'Don't test me, Bella.'

The women scattered, leaving them alone.

Bella levelled a stare on Nero's face as his fierce expression mellowed into a lazy gaze. 'Do you like it?' she asked, modelling the new underwear he'd bought her.

'It's a great improvement on industrial weight serge and heavy engineering.'

And she would never have bought such inconsequential scraps of lace for herself, or dreamed of wearing such things before she met Nero but, thanks to him, the damage of the past was nothing more than a reminder of how lucky they were to have found each other.

'We are in the city of lovers,' Nero murmured, running the knuckles of one hand very lightly down her cheek, 'so I shall test you later, to see if the new lingerie is having the required effect.'

'Excellent,' Bella agreed softly. 'The Ice Maiden is already melting in anticipation of your prolonged attention.' Catching hold of his hand, she kissed it whilst holding his gaze.

'You're my world, Bella,' Nero said, turning suddenly serious as he cupped her face between his hands. 'And after this tour we're going to stay home in Argentina and raise ponies together.'

'*What?*' And then she saw the laughter in his eyes.

'Did I say ponies?' Nero murmured.

'You know you did. Nero—stop,' she begged him as his kisses migrated from her mouth to her neck and from her neck to her breast. 'We're not alone.'

'When in Rome...' he murmured, clasping her to him.

'But the women in the shop...'

'Have seen it all before.'

'We can't.'

'No, you're right,' Nero agreed, leaving her weak and trembling as he removed his hand. 'We may need some time, so I'm going to make you wait until we get back to the hotel. All those years of work and no play have made Bella a very naughty girl indeed.'

'And you, of course, are absolutely innocent,' she commented wryly.

'No, *chica*,' Nero murmured against her mouth, 'I'm a very bad man indeed.'

All Bella could hear was the beating of her heart. 'Yes, yes...*Yes*!' she agreed in a heated whisper, 'Promise we can keep it that way...'

* * * * *

DAMASO CLAIMS
HIS HEIR

ANNIE WEST

For Ana Luisa Neves.
With heartfelt thanks for your patience and
Portuguese language expertise.

CHAPTER ONE

DAMASO SAW HER and his breath snagged in his lungs.

He who'd had women dancing to his tune well before he made his first million.

How long since one had quickened his pulse? He'd known divas and duchesses, models and Madonnas. In the early days there'd been tourists by the armful, and one memorable tango dancer whose sinuous body and blatant sexuality had made his teenage self burn with need. None had affected him the way she did—without effort.

For the first time she was alone, not laughing with her coterie of men. He was surprised to see her crouched, photographing flowers on the rainforest floor. She was so engrossed, she didn't notice him.

That was new for Damaso. He'd grown used to being watched and avidly sought after.

It pricked him that she was oblivious to him while he was hyper-aware of her. It infuriated him that his eyes strayed to her time and again, yet she had done no more than gift him with the dazzling smile she awarded so indiscriminately.

Damaso moved closer, intrigued. Was she really unaware or was she trying to pique his curiosity? Did she know he preferred to be the hunter, not the prey?

Beautiful blondes were commonplace in his world. Yet from the first day, watching her radiant face as she'd emerged drenched but undaunted from white-water rafting, Damaso had felt something new. A spark of connection.

Was it her unbounded energy? The devilment in her eyes as she risked her pretty neck again and again? Or that sexy gurgle of laughter that clutched at his vitals? Perhaps it was the sheer courage of a woman that didn't baulk at any challenge on a trek designed to spark the jaded interest of the world's ultra-wealthy.

'Marisa. There you are. I looked for you everywhere.' Young Saltram blundered out of the undergrowth to stop beside her. A computer geek who looked about eighteen, yet was worth upwards of seven figures annually, he was like an over-grown puppy salivating over a bone.

Damaso's jaw tightened as Saltram ate her up with his eyes—his gaze lingering on the delectable peach ripeness of her backside as she squatted with her camera.

Damaso stirred, but stopped as she turned her head. From this angle he saw what Saltram couldn't: her deep breath, as if she'd mustered her patience before turning.

'Bradley! I haven't seen you for hours.' She gave the newcomer a blinding smile that seemed to stun him.

That didn't stop him reaching out to help her rise, though it was clear she didn't need assistance. Damaso had never seen a woman so agile or graceful.

Saltram closed his hand around her elbow and she smiled coquettishly up at the youth.

Amazingly, Damaso felt something stark scour his belly. His fingers twitched as he resisted the urge to march across and yank the boy away.

She was laughing, flirting now, not at all perturbed that Saltram was breathing down her cleavage.

She wore shorts and hiking boots and her toned legs drew Damaso's gaze like a banquet set before a beggar. He swallowed, tasting his own hunger and the sharp, pungent tang of green apples.

Scowling, he recognised it was her scent filling his nostrils. How could that be? Standing in the shadows, he was too far away to inhale her perfume.

She turned and let Saltram guide her down the track, her long ponytail swaying across her narrow back. For a week Damaso had wanted to stroke that shining fall of gold and discover if it was as soft as it looked.

Yet he'd kept his distance, tired of dealing with fractious women who wanted more than he was prepared to give.

But she wouldn't make demands, the voice of temptation whispered. *Except in bed.*

For Princess Marisa of Bengaria had a reputation with a capital R. Pampered from birth, living carelessly off inherited riches, she was a party girl extraordinaire. The tabloids branded her wilful, reckless and as far from a demure, virginal princess as it was possible to get.

Damaso had told himself he was sick of high-maintenance women. Yet a week in her vicinity had given him a new perspective. She might be feckless but she wasn't needy.

She'd flirted with every man on the trek. Except him. Heat drilled through his belly as the significance of that hit.

She was *exactly* what he needed. He had no interest in virgins. A little wildness would add spice to a short vacation liaison.

Damaso smiled as he sauntered down the track after her.

Marisa turned her face to the waterfall's spray, grateful for its cooling, damp mist in this sultry heat. Her blood pumped fast and her limbs felt stretched and shaky from fatigue and adrenalin as she clung to the cliff face.

Yes! This was what she wanted. To lose herself in the challenge of the moment. To put aside all the—

'Marisa! Over here!'

She turned her head. Bradley Saltram watched her

from a perch well away from the waterfall. His grin was triumphant.

'Hey, you did it! Great going.' Bradley had confided his fear of heights. Even his relatively straightforward climb was a momentous achievement. No wonder he wore full safety harness and had Juan, their guide, in close attendance. 'I knew you could do it.'

But it was hard meeting his bright eyes, almost febrile with excitement and pleasure.

A hammer blow struck her square in the chest and she clutched at her precarious handhold. When he smiled that way, with such triumph, she remembered another smile. So radiant it had been like watching the sun's reflection. Eyes so clear and brilliant they'd been like the summer sky. Happiness so infectious it had warmed her to the core.

Stefan had always been able to make her forget her misery with a smile and a joke and a plunge into adventure, making a nonsense of the joyless, disapproving world that trapped them.

Marisa blinked, turning away from the bright-eyed American who had no idea of the pain he'd evoked.

A lump the size of Bengaria's cold, grey royal palace settled in her chest, crushing the air from her lungs and choking her throat. Her breath was a desperate whistle of snatched air.

No! Not now. Not here.

She turned back to Bradley, pinning a smile on her features. 'I'll see you at the bottom. I just want to check out the falls.'

Bradley said something but she didn't hear it over the drumming pulse in her ears. Already she was moving, swinging easily up, shifting her weight as she found new foot- and hand-holds on the slick rock-face.

That was what she needed, to concentrate on the challenge and the demands of the moment. Push away everything but the numbness only physical exertion brought.

She was high now, higher than she'd intended. But the rhythm of the climb was addictive, blotting out even Juan's shouted warning.

The spray was stronger here, the rock not merely damp but running with water.

Marisa tuned in to the roar of the falls, revelling in the pounding rush of sound, as if it could cleanse her of emotion.

A little to the left and she'd be at the spot where legend had it one brave boy had made the impossible dive into the churning pool of water below.

She paused, temptation welling. Not to make a name for herself by a daredevil act, but to risk herself in the jaws of possible oblivion.

It wasn't that she wanted to die. But dicing with danger was as close as she'd come lately to living, to believing there might possibly be joy in her life again.

The world was terminally grey, except in those moments when the agony of grief and loneliness grew piercingly vivid. Those moments when Marisa faced the enormity of her loss.

People said the pain eased with time but Marisa didn't believe it. Half of her had been ripped away, leaving a yawning void that nothing could fill.

The pounding of the falls, like the pulse of a giant animal, melded with the rapid tattoo of her heartbeat. It beckoned her, the way Stefan had time and again. When she closed her eyes she could almost hear the teasing lilt in his voice. *Come on, Rissa. Don't tell me you're scared.*

No, she wasn't scared of anything, except the vast aloneness that engulfed her now Stefan was gone.

Without thought she began climbing towards the tiny ledge beside the fall, taking her time on the treacherously wet rock.

She was almost there when a sound stopped her.

Marisa turned her head and there, just to her right, was

Damaso Pires, the big Brazilian she'd been avoiding since the trek had started. Something about the way he watched her with those knowing dark eyes always unsettled her, as if he saw right through what Stefan had dubbed her 'party princess' persona.

There was something else in Damaso's gaze now. Something stern and compelling that for a moment reminded her of her uncle, the all-time expert in judgement and condemnation. Then, to her amazement, he smiled, the first genuine smile he'd given her.

Marisa grabbed at the cliff as energy arced through her body, leaving her tingling and shaky.

He was a different man with that grin.

Dark and broodingly laconic, he'd always had the presence and looks to draw attention. Marisa had surreptitiously watched the other women simper and show off and blatantly offer themselves to him.

But when he smiled! Heat slammed through her in the wake of a dazzling blast of raw attraction.

His dark hair was plastered to his skull, emphasising the masculine beauty of his bone structure. Tiny streams of water ran from his solid jaw down his strong throat.

It was only then that Marisa realised he wasn't wearing a safety helmet.

It was the sort of thing Stefan would have done in one of his wilder moments. Did that explain the sudden tug of connection she felt?

The Brazilian jerked his head up and away from the falls, his ebony eyebrows rising questioningly.

Following his gesture, Marisa remembered Juan telling them about a lookout beyond the falls and a rough track that curved down from it to the valley floor.

She met those fathomless eyes again. This time their gleam didn't disturb her. It beckoned. Her body zinged with unexpected pleasure, as if recognising an equal.

With a nod she began to clamber up and away from the

sheer plunge of water. He climbed beside her, each movement precise and methodical, till in the end she had to make a conscious effort not to watch him. Weary now, Marisa needed all her concentration for the climb. The spurt of energy that had buoyed her had abated.

She was almost at the top, her vision limited to the next tiny hold, her breath ragged in her ears, when a hand appeared before her. Large, well-kept but callused, and bearing the silvery traces of old scars, it looked like a hand you could rely on.

Arching her neck, Marisa peered up and met liquid dark eyes. Again she felt that jolt of awareness as heat poured through her. Heat that had everything to do with the sizzle in Damaso Pires's gaze as he stood above her on an outcrop of rock.

Marisa hesitated, wondering what it was about this man. He was different from the rest. More…real.

'Take my hand.'

She should be used to that rich accent now. It was a week since she'd arrived in Brazil. But, teamed with Damaso's dark, velvet voice, the sultry seduction of it made something clutch inside.

A quiver rippled through her. She ignored it and made herself reach for his hand, feeling it close hard around her fingers. His strength engulfed her. As she watched, his lips curved in a smile of pure satisfaction.

Awareness pulsed through their joined hands and Marisa knew something like anxiety as his expression sharpened. For a moment he looked almost possessive. Then he was hauling her up, not waiting for her to find the purchase of another foothold.

His display of macho strength shouldn't have made her heart hammer. When she'd been in training she'd known plenty of strong, ultra-fit men.

But not one of them had made her feel as feminine

and desirable as she did now, standing, grubby and out of breath, before this man.

His eyes held hers as he deftly undid her helmet and drew it away. The breeze riffled her damp hair, tugging strands across her face. She knew she looked a mess, but refused to primp. Instead she returned his stare, cataloguing achingly high cheekbones set aslant an arresting face of dark bronze, a long nose with more than a hint of the aquiline, a firm mouth, unsmiling now, and heavy-lidded eyes that looked as if they held untold secrets.

The way he looked at her, so intent, so direct, made her feel like he saw *her*—not the celebrity princess but the woman beneath, lost and alone.

No man had ever looked at her like that.

His gaze dropped to her mouth and her lips tingled. She swallowed hard, unprepared for the sexual need that swamped her as she inhaled his scent—clean, male sweat and something else—soap, perhaps—that reminded her of the sea.

'*Bem vinda, pequenina*. Welcome, little one. I'm glad you decided to join me.'

She stood, looking up at him, her chin tilted, revealing the slender line of her pale throat. Her eyes, the purest azure he'd ever seen, held his, unblinking. And all the while his body tightened, impossibly aroused by the touch and sight of her.

How would she taste?

The question dried his mouth and set his libido spinning.

'Is this the lookout Juan spoke of?' She didn't move away but slipped her hand from his as she turned to admire the view. It was stupendous, the sort of thing people travelled continents to experience. Yet Damaso suspected she used it as an excuse to avoid him.

Too late for that. He'd felt the throb of mutual awareness.

He'd recognised desire in her eyes even as she'd clung like a limpet to the vertical rock.

There would be no more avoiding what was between them. The time for that was past.

'What were you doing, over by the falls?' The words shot out—an accusation he hadn't intended to voice. But the memory of fear was a sharp tang on his tongue. It had sent him swarming up the cliff face without bothering with safety gear.

There'd been something about the way she'd climbed— a determination—as she'd headed for the exposed, most dangerous part of the cliff that had sent a chill scudding down his spine.

What *had* she been up to?

The shadowed, almost dazed look in her eyes when she'd turned to face him on the cliff had shot a premonition of danger through him. Growing up where he had, Damaso had a well-honed instinct for danger in all its forms. He hadn't liked what he'd read in the princess's eyes.

She shrugged. 'Just looking.' Her tone was off-hand, as if she hadn't just risked her life on one of the country's most notoriously treacherous climbs. 'I remembered Juan talking about that boy's dive into the pool.'

Anger stirred at her recklessness. Damaso opened his mouth to berate her then noticed the taut muscles in her neck and her rigid posture. She was like a guard on parade.

Or a princess deflecting impertinent questions?

She had a lot to learn if she thought he'd be so easily dismissed.

He lifted a hand and stroked long, golden strands from her cheek and back over her shoulder.

Her hair was as soft as he'd imagined.

She said nothing, didn't even turn, but he watched with satisfaction as she swallowed.

'The forest seems to go on for ever.' Her voice had a husky quality that hadn't been there before. Damaso smiled.

She was out of danger now and she was here with him. Why probe what she clearly didn't want to talk about?

'It would take days to walk out, and that's if you didn't get lost along the way.' He couldn't resist reaching out to sweep a phantom lock of hair off her cheek. Her skin was hot, flushed with exertion, and so soft he wanted to slide his fingers over all of her, learning her body by touch before testing it with his other senses.

A pulse throbbed at the base of her neck, like a butterfly trapped in a net.

Heat drove down through Damaso's belly as he imagined licking that spot.

Her head jerked around and he was snared by her electric-blue gaze.

'You know the forest well, Senhor Pires?'

She sounded like a courtier at a garden party, her tone light with just the right amount of polite interest. But the cool, society veneer merely emphasised the hot, sexy woman beneath. The fact she was dishevelled, like a woman just risen from her lover's arms, added a piquant spice.

Damaso was burning up just looking at her.

And she knew it. It was there in her eyes.

Awareness sizzled between them.

'No; I'm city bred, Your Highness. But I get out to the wilderness as often as I can.' Damaso always allowed himself one break a year, though he took his vacation checking out one of his far-flung companies. This year it was an upmarket adventure-travel company.

He had a feeling the adventure was just about to start.

'Marisa, please. "Highness" sounds so inflated.' A spark of humour gleamed in her bright eyes. It notched the heat in his belly even higher.

'Marisa, then.' He liked the sound of it on his tongue, feminine and intriguing. 'And I'm Damaso.'

'I don't know South America well, Damaso.' She paused

on his name and a shiver of anticipation raced under his skin. Would she sound so cool and composed when he held her naked beneath him? He didn't know which he'd prefer, that or the sound of her voice husky with pleasure.

'I haven't visited many of the cities.' She reached out and picked a leaf off his open collar. The back of her fingers brushed his neck and his breath stalled.

A tiny smile played at the corner of her mouth. Her eyes told him the lingering touch had been deliberate. Siren!

'My birthplace isn't on anyone's must-see list.' Now *there* was an understatement.

'You surprise me. I hear you're something of a legend in business circles. Surely they'll be putting up a sign saying "Damaso Pires was born here"?'

He plucked a twig from her hair and twirled it between his fingers. No need to tell her no one had any idea where exactly he'd been born, or whether there'd even been a roof for protection.

'Ah, but I wasn't born with a silver spoon in my mouth.'

She blinked, her mouth thinning for an infinitesimal moment, so that he wondered if he'd blundered in some way. Then she shrugged and smiled and he lost his train of thought when she took the twig from his fingers, her hand deliberately caressing his. That light touch drew his skin tight across his bones as lust flared.

'Don't tell anyone,' she smiled from under veiled eyes as if sharing a salacious secret. 'But silver spoons aren't all they're cracked up to be.'

With a quick twist of the wrist he captured her hand in his. Silence throbbed between them, a silence heavy with unspoken promise. Something kindled in her eyes. She returned his hungry look, not resorting to coyness.

'I like the way you face challenges head-on,' he found himself admitting, then frowned. Usually he measured his words carefully. They didn't just shoot out.

'I like the fact you don't care about my social status.'

Her hand shifted in his hold, her thumb stroking his. It pleased him that she didn't pretend disinterest, or lunge at him desperately. The sense of a delicate balance between them added a delicious tension to the moment.

'It's not your title I'm interested in, Marisa.' Her name tasted even better the second time. Damaso leaned forward, eager for the taste of her on his tongue, then stopped himself. This wasn't the place.

'You don't know how glad I am to hear that.' She planted her palm on his shirt and his heart leapt into overdrive. It felt as if she'd branded him.

Tension screwed his body tight. He wanted her *now* and, given the way her fingers splayed possessively on him, her lips parting with her quickened breathing, she felt the same.

He wanted to take her here, hard and fast and triumphantly. Except instinct told him he'd need more than one quick taste to satisfy this craving.

How had he resisted her for a whole week?

'Perhaps you could tell me on the way back down exactly what you *are* interested in, Damaso.'

He snagged her hand in his again and turned her towards the rough track leading away from the cliff. Her fingers linked with his, shooting erotic pleasure through him that felt in some strange way almost innocent. How long since he'd simply held a woman's hand?

Marisa towel-dried her hair while looking out at her private courtyard in the luxurious eco-resort. A bevy of butterflies danced through the lush leaves.

She tried to focus on how she'd capture them on film but all she could think about was Damaso Pires. The feel of his hand enclosing hers as they'd clambered down the track. The wrench of loss when he'd let her go as they'd approached the others. The way his burning gaze had stripped her bare.

No wonder she'd avoided him.

But now she craved him. She, who'd learned to distrust desire!

Yet this was something new. With Damaso Pires she sensed a link, a feeling almost of recognition, that she'd never experienced. It reminded her a little of the very different bond she'd shared with Stefan.

Marisa shook her head. Was grief clouding her thoughts?

Physical exertion, even danger, didn't ease her pain. Since Stefan's death she'd been shrouded in grey nothingness, till Damaso had reached out to her. Could she do it? Give herself to a stranger? Excitement and fear shivered through her. Despite what the world believed, Marisa wasn't the voracious sexpot the press portrayed.

Then she remembered how she'd felt trading words with him, their bodies communicating in subtle hints and responses as ancient as sex itself.

She'd felt happy. Excited. That aching feeling of isolation had fled. She'd felt alive.

A knock sounded on her door, reverberating through her hollow stomach. Second thoughts crowded in, old hurts. Marisa glanced in the mirror. Barefoot, damp hair slicked back from a face devoid of make-up, she looked as far from a princess as you could get.

Did he want the real woman, not the royal? She wavered on the brink of cowardice, of wanting to pretend she hadn't heard him. She'd taken chances on men before and been disappointed. More, she'd been eviscerated by their callous selfishness.

The knock came again and she jumped.

She had to face this.

With Damaso, for the first time in years, she dared risk herself again. That tantalising link between them was so intense, so profound. She *wanted* to trust him. She wanted desperately not to be alone anymore.

Her heart pounded as she opened the door. He filled the space before her, leaning against one raised arm. His eyes looked black and hungry in the early-evening light. Her stomach swooped.

With a single stride he entered the room, closing the door quietly behind him, eyes holding hers.

'*Querida.*' The word caressed her as his gaze ate her up. If he was disappointed she hadn't dressed up, he didn't show it. If anything his eyes glowed warm with approval. 'You haven't changed your mind?'

'Have you?' She stood straighter.

'How could I?' His smile was lop-sided, the most devastating thing she'd ever seen. Then one large palm cupped her cheek and he stepped close. His head lowered and the world faded away.

CHAPTER TWO

'*MALDIÇÃO!* WHAT YOU do to me.' Damaso's voice rumbled through her bones, his hands gripping tight at her hips as his mouth moved against her ear. Marisa shivered as her hyper-aware nerve endings protested at the sensory overload.

She'd never felt so vulnerable, so *naked*. As if their lovemaking had stripped her bare of every shield she'd erected between herself and a hostile world.

Yet, strangely that didn't scare her. Not with Damaso.

Marisa clutched his bare back, sleek and damp, heaving slightly as he fought for breath. His chest pushed her down into the wide mattress and she revelled in the hard, hot weight of him, even the feel of his hairy legs imprisoning hers.

All night Damaso had stayed, taking his time to seduce her, not just with his body but with the fierce intensity he'd devoted to pleasing her. He was a generous lover, patient when unexpected nerves had made her momentarily stiff and wooden in his arms. She'd been mortified, sure he'd interpret her body's reaction as rejection. Instead he'd looked into her eyes for an endless moment, then smiled before beginning a leisurely exploration of every erogenous zone on her body.

Marisa shivered and held him tight. Holding him in her arms felt...

'I'm too heavy. Sorry.'

Before she could protest, he rolled over onto his back,

pulling her with him. She clung fast, needing to maintain the skin-to-skin contact she'd become addicted to in the night.

Marisa smiled drowsily. She'd been right: Damaso *was* different. He made her feel like a new woman. And that wasn't merely the exhaustion of a long night's loving speaking.

'Are you all right?' She loved the way his voice rippled like dark, molten chocolate in her veins. She'd never known a man with a more sensuous voice.

'Never better.' She smiled against his damp skin then let her tongue slick along the solid cushion of his muscled chest. He tasted of salt and that indefinable spicy flavour that was simply Damaso.

He sucked in a breath and her smile widened. She could stay here, plastered to him, for ever.

'Witch!'

His big hand was gentle on her shoulder, lifting her away. After lying against the furnace of his powerful body, the pre-dawn air seemed cold against her naked skin. She opened her mouth to protest but he was already swinging his legs out of bed. She lifted a hand to catch him back then let it drop. He'd be back once he'd disposed of the condom. Then they could drowse in each other's arms.

Marisa hooked a pillow to her, trying to make up for the loss of Damaso. She buried her nose in its softness, inhaling his scent, letting her mind drift pleasurably.

They had another week left on the tour. A week to get to know each other in all the ways they'd missed. They'd skipped straight to the potent attraction between them, bypassing the usual stages of acquaintanceship and friendship.

Anticipation shimmied through her. The promise of pleasure to come. Who'd have thought she could feel so good when only yesterday...?

She shook her head, determined to enjoy the tentative optimism filling her after so long in a grey well of grief.

Marisa looked forward to learning all those little things about Damaso—how he liked his coffee, what made him laugh. What he did with his time when he wasn't looking dark and sulkily attractive like some sexy renegade, or running what someone in the group had called South America's largest self-made fortune.

A sound made her turn. There, framed in the doorway, stood Damaso, watching her.

The first fingers of dawn light limned his tall body, throwing his solid chest, taut abdomen and heavy thighs into relief. The smattering of dark hair on his chest narrowed and trickled in a tantalising line down his body. Marisa lay back, looking appreciatively from between slitted eyes. Even now, sated after their loving, he looked formidably well-endowed. As if he was ready to…

'Go to sleep, Marisa. It's been a long night.' The dark enticement of his voice was edged with an undercurrent she couldn't identify.

Shoving the spare pillow aside, she smoothed her arm over the still-warm space beside her.

'When you come back to bed.' She'd sleep better with him here, cradling her as before. It wasn't sex she craved but his company. The rare sense of wellbeing he'd created.

Damaso stood, unmoving, so long anxiety stroked phantom fingers over her nape. Almost, she reached out to drag up the discarded sheet. She hadn't felt embarrassed by her nudity earlier, when he'd looked at her with approval and even something like adoration in his gaze. But this felt different. His stare was impenetrable, that tiny pucker of a frown unexpected.

The silence lengthened and Marisa had to clench her hands rather than scoop up the sheet. She'd never flaunted herself naked but with Damaso it had felt right. Till now.

He prowled across the room with a grace she couldn't

help but appreciate. He stopped at the edge of the bed,
drawing in a deep breath. Then he bent abruptly to scoop
something off the floor—his discarded jeans. He dragged
the faded denim up those long thighs.

Surely he had underwear? she thought foggily, before
the implication struck.

Her gaze met his and rebounded from an impenetrable
black stare. Gone was the spark of excitement in his gaze,
the wolfish hunger that should have scared her yet had
made her feel womanly and powerful. Gone was the sizzle of appreciation she'd so enjoyed when they'd sparred
verbally.

His eyes held nothing.

'You're leaving.' Her voice was hollow. Or was that her
body? Ridiculously, she felt as if someone had scooped
out her insides.

'It's morning.' His gaze flicked to the full-length window.

'Barely. It's still hours till we need to be up.' How she
spoke so calmly, she didn't know. She wanted to scuttle
across the bed and throw herself into his arms, beg for
him to stay.

Beg... Marisa had never begged in her life.

Pride had been one of her few allies. After years facing down family disapproval and the wilder accusations
of the ravenous press, she'd been stripped of everything
but pride. Now she was tempted to throw even that away
as desperation clutched at her.

'Exactly. You should get some sleep.'

She blinked, confused at the hint of warmth in his voice,
so at odds with his unreadable expression. She felt like
she'd waded into knee-deep water and suddenly found herself miles out to sea.

More than ever Marisa wanted to cover herself. Heat
crept from her feet to her face as his hooded gaze surveyed
her. Was that a flicker of regret in his eyes?

'It's best I go now.'

Marisa bit down a protest. Perhaps he was trying to protect them from gossip, leaving her room before even the staff were up. But since the pair of them had missed dinner last night it was probably too late for that.

'I'll see you at breakfast, then.' She sat up, pinning a bright smile on her face. There would be time enough to spend together in the next week.

'No. That won't be possible.' He finished the buttons on his shirt and strode to the bedside table, reaching for his watch.

'It won't?' She sounded like a parrot! But she couldn't seem to engage her brain.

He paused in the act of wrapping his watch around his sinewy wrist.

'Listen, Marisa. Last night was remarkable. *You* were remarkable. But I never promised you hearts and flowers.'

Indignation stiffened her spine, almost dousing the chill dread in her veins. 'I hardly think expecting to see you at breakfast has anything to do with *hearts and flowers,* as you so quaintly put it.'

Damn him! She leaned down and grabbed the sheet, pulling it up under her arms. At least now she wasn't quite so naked.

'You know what I mean.' The hint of a growl tinged his deep tone and Marisa felt a tiny nub of satisfaction that she'd pierced his monumental self-assurance. For that was what it was—that unblinking stare from eyes as cool and unfeeling as obsidian.

'No, Damaso, I don't know what you mean.' She regarded him with what she hoped looked like unconcern, despite the fact she was crumbling inside.

'I gave no commitment.' As lover-like statements went, this one hit rock bottom.

'I didn't ask for any.' Her voice was tight.

'Of course you didn't.' Suddenly he looked away, intent

on his watch. 'You aren't the type. That's why last night was perfect.'

'The type?' Out of nowhere a chill crept over her bare shoulders.

'The type to cling and pretend a night in bed means a lifetime together.'

His eyes met hers again and she felt the force of desire like a smack in the chest. Even as he rejected her the air sizzled between them. Surely she didn't imagine that? Yet the jut of his jaw told her he was intent on ignoring it.

There she'd been, daydreaming that this might be the start of something special. That, after a lifetime of kissing frogs and finding only warty toads, she might actually have found a man who appreciated her for herself.

She should have known better. Such a man didn't exist.

Marisa's stomach plunged, reopening that vast chasm of emptiness inside.

'So what did it mean to you, Damaso?' She clipped the words out.

'Sorry?'

He looked perplexed, as if no woman had ever confronted him like that. But Damaso was an intelligent man. He knew exactly what she was asking.

'Well, clearly you don't want me expecting a repeat of last night.' Even now she waited, breathless, hoping she was wrong. That he *did* want to spend more time with her, and not just for sex. Marisa wanted it so badly that she discovered she'd curled her hands into hard fists, the nails scoring her skin.

'No.' He paused, his face very still. 'This can't go anywhere. There's no point complicating things further.'

Complicating? Now there was a word. The sort of word men used to denigrate what made them uncomfortable.

'So, out of curiosity…' She kept her voice even with an effort. 'What was last night to you? Did you make a bet with the others that you could get me into bed?'

'Of course not! What sort of man do you think I am?'

Marisa raised her eyebrows, surveying his shocked expression with a dispassionate eye even as hurt carved a channel through her insides. 'I don't know, that's the point.'

She'd vowed never to be burned again. Yet here she was, regretting the impulse that had made her open herself to him.

Marisa had been so sure that this time she'd found a man who at least had no hidden agenda. How many times did she have to learn that particular lesson? Bitterness soured her tongue.

'So it was the princess thing, was it? You'd never done it with a royal?'

He loomed over her, his jaw set.

'Why are you being deliberately insulting?'

And it wasn't insulting, the way he was shoving her aside once he'd had what he wanted, without as much as a 'good morning' or a 'thank you' or even a 'see you later'?

Bile burned in the pit of her stomach and she swallowed hard when it threatened to rise. She wouldn't give him the satisfaction of seeing how he'd hurt her. She'd finally reached out to someone, trusted herself with a man…

Marisa bit her cheek, cutting off that train of thought. She'd been right to hesitate when he'd held out his hand to her on the climb. If only she'd followed her instinct and not touched him.

'I merely want to get it clear in my mind.' She rose and wrapped the sheet around her. She still had to look up at him but at least she wasn't sitting like a supplicant at his feet.

'It was sex, great sex. That's all.' Suddenly there was fire in his eyes and a frisson of angry energy sparked from him. 'Is that what you needed to hear?'

'Thank you.' She inclined her head, wondering how she'd managed to invest simple animal attraction with such significance.

Because she was so needy?

Because she was so alone?

What a pathetic woman she was. Maybe her uncle was right after all.

'Marisa?'

She looked up to find Damaso frowning. This time it was concern she read on his features. He'd even moved closer, his hand half-lifted.

Marisa stiffened. She didn't need anyone's pity, especially this man who'd seen her as perfect for just a night, no strings attached. No doubt, like too many others, he saw her as a woman who wouldn't mind being bedded then shunned.

Her skin crawled and pain stabbed hard between her ribs. It was all she could do not to clutch at her side, doubled up at the force of what she felt.

'Well, if we've finished here, you might as well go.' She looked past him to the bathroom. 'I have a yearning for a long, hot shower.' She wished she could scrub away the hurt that welled as easily as she could wash away the scent of his skin on hers. 'And don't worry; I won't look out for you at breakfast.'

'I won't be here. I'm leaving.'

Marisa blinked and looked away, making a production of gathering up her robe where it had been discarded last night.

So there'd never been a chance for them at all. Damaso had always planned to leave and hadn't had the decency to tell her.

That, as nothing else, clarified exactly what he thought of her. She'd never felt so bruised by a man, so *diminished*. Not since the night Andreas had admitted he'd bet his friends he could get her into bed.

Pain swelled and spread, threatening to poleaxe her where she stood. She had to get away.

Marisa drew herself up and headed for the bathroom.

She paused in the doorway, clutching it for support, and looked over her shoulder.

To her surprise, Damaso hadn't moved. He watched her with a scowl on his face. A scowl that did nothing to reduce the magnetism of his honed features.

He opened his mouth to speak and Marisa knew she couldn't bear to hear any more.

'I wonder if that makes me a notch on your belt or you a notch on mine?' Her voice was a throaty drawl, the best she could manage with her frozen vocal chords.

Then, with a flick of the trailing sheet that only long hours' practice in a ball gown and train could achieve, she swept into the bathroom and locked the door behind her.

'It's a pleasure to have you visit, sir.' The manager smiled as he led the way.

Damaso strode through the lodge, his gaze lingering approvingly on the lofty spaces, the mix of local stone, wood and vast expanses of glass that gave this mountain eyrie an aura of refined, ultra-modern luxury. He'd been right to build it, despite the problems constructing on such a site. Even after a mere six months the place had become a mecca for well-heeled travellers wanting to experience something different.

Beyond the massive windows the vista was stunning as the setting sun turned the jagged Andean peaks and their snowy mantle a glowing peach-gold. Below, even the turquoise surface of the glacier-fed river was gilded in the last rays of light.

'Your suite is this way, sir.' The manager gestured Damaso and his secretary forward.

'I'll find it myself, thanks.' Damaso's eyes remained fixed on the remarkable view.

'If you're sure, sir.' The manager paused. 'Your luggage has been taken ahead.'

Damaso nodded dismissal to both men and headed into

the main lounge. Something about the stillness and the feeling of being up above the bustle of the world drew him. Not surprising, given he'd worked like the devil for the last month, his schedule even more overloaded than usual.

Yet, no matter how frenetic his days or how short his nights, Damaso hadn't found his usual pleasure in managing and building his far-flung empire.

Something niggled at him. A sense of dissatisfaction he hadn't the time or inclination to identify.

He looked around, surprised to find the vast room empty. Turning, he strolled towards a door through which came the hum of voices. The bar was this way. Perhaps he'd have a drink before dinner. He had a full night ahead with his laptop before tomorrow's inspection and meetings.

Laughter greeted him as he stepped across the threshold, halting him mid-stride. Rich laughter, infectious and appealing. It coiled through his belly and wrapped tight around his lungs.

His pulse gave a hard thump then took off.

He knew that laugh.

Damaso's neck prickled as if delicate fingers brushed his nape, trailing languidly and drawing his skin tight with shivering awareness.

Marisa.

There she was, her golden hair spilling around her shoulders, her smile pure invitation to the men crowded close. Her eyes danced as she spoke, as she leaned towards them as if sharing some confidence. Damaso couldn't hear what she said over the thunder of blood pounding in his ears.

But there was nothing wrong with his eyes. They traced the black dress that hugged her sinuous curves. The hemline hovered high above her knees, making the most of the contrast between sparkly black stretch fabric and shapely legs that would make grown men sit up and beg.

He should know. He'd spent hours exploring those legs along with every inch of her delectable body. Everything about her had enthralled him, even the long, curving sweep of her spine had been delicious. *Was* delicious.

A wave of energy surged through him. He found himself stepping forward until his brain clicked into gear. Did he mean to stalk across and rip her away from her slavering fans? What then? Throw her over his shoulder and take her to his room?

A resounding *yes* echoed through his whole being.

That stopped him in his tracks.

There'd been a reason he'd left her so abruptly a month before.

Left? He'd run as fast as he could.

It had nothing to do with business commitments and everything to do with the unprecedented things she'd made him *feel*. Not just desire and satiation, but something far bigger.

He'd got out of her bed with every intention of returning to it then had realised for the first time in his life there was nowhere else he wanted to be.

The idea was utterly foreign and completely unnerving.

That was when he'd decided to order a helicopter back to the city. Not his finest moment. Even with his date-them-then-dump-them reputation, he usually displayed far more finesse in leaving a lover.

Even now part of him regretted leaving her after just one night. What they'd shared had been amazing.

Marisa's gurgle of laughter floated in his ears. Damaso swung round and walked back the way he'd come.

Once was enough with any woman. This…reaction to Princess Marisa of Bengaria was an anomaly. He didn't do relationships. He couldn't. Nothing would ever change that.

He strode up the stairs and along a wide corridor to the owner's suite.

She was nothing to him. Just another party girl. Had she even gone home after the rainforest vacation? Probably not. She was probably whiling away a couple of months in

exclusive resorts at her nation's expense while trying out
some new lovers along the way.

His teeth ground together and his pace picked up.

There was a tap on the conference-room door before a
concerned-looking staff member entered.

'I'm sorry to interrupt.' Her eyes shifted from the manager to Damaso, his secretary and the other senior staff at
the large table.

'Yes?' the manager asked.

She shut the door behind her. 'One of the guests has
been taken ill on the slopes. They're coming back now.'

'Ill, not an accident?' Damaso heard the note of worry
in the manager's voice. Illness was one thing; an accident
under the supervision of the lodge's staff was another.

'It sounds like altitude sickness. She only arrived yesterday.'

'She?' Damaso surprised himself by interrupting.

'Yes, sir.' The woman twisted her hands together, turning back to her boss. 'That's why I thought you should
know. It's Princess Marisa.'

'You've called a doctor?' Damaso found himself standing, his fists braced on the table.

'Don't worry, there's one on staff,' the manager assured
him. 'Only the best for our clients, as you know.'

Of course. That was what set Damaso's hotels apart—
attention to detail and the best possible services.

'The doctor will be with her as soon as she arrives,' the
manager assured Damaso, nodding dismissal to the staff
member, who backed out of the door.

Damaso forced himself to sit but his focus was shot. For
the next half hour he struggled to concentrate on profits,
projections and the inevitable glitches that arose with any
new enterprise. Finally he gave up.

'I have something to attend to,' he said as he stood and
excused himself from the meeting. 'You carry on.'

He knew he was behaving inexplicably. Since when did Damaso Pires delegate anything he could do himself? Especially when he'd crossed the continent to take these meetings personally.

Five minutes later he was stalking down a quiet corridor, following a nervous maid.

'This is the princess's suite, sir.' She gestured to the double doors with their intricately carved rock-crystal handles. Tentatively she knocked but there was no answer.

Damaso reached for the door and found it unlocked. 'It's okay,' he murmured. 'I'm a friend of the princess.' Ignoring her doubtful gaze, he stepped inside and closed the door behind him.

'Friend' hardly described his relationship with Marisa. They didn't *have* a relationship. Yet curiously he hadn't been able to concentrate on the business that had brought him here till he checked on her himself.

The sitting room was empty but on the far side another set of double doors was ajar. He heard the murmur of a woman's voice followed by the deeper tones of a man.

'Is it possible you're pregnant?'

CHAPTER THREE

'No!' THE WORD jerked out in shock. 'I'm not pregnant.' Still shivery from nausea, Marisa squinted up at the doctor.

Her? A mother? Why would she bring a child into the world when she couldn't get her own life on track?

She could just imagine her uncle's horror: impulsive, unreliable Marisa who frittered her time away with unsuitable interests rather than knuckling down to the role she was born to. Not that he had faith in her ability to perform that role.

'You're absolutely certain?' The doctor's gaze penetrated and she felt herself blush as she hadn't since she'd been a teen.

She waved one hand airily. 'Technically, I suppose it's possible.' She drew a slow breath, trying to ease her cramped lungs as images she'd fought hard and long to obliterate replayed in her head. 'But it was just one night.'

'One night is all it takes,' the doctor murmured.

Marisa shook her head. 'Not this time. I mean we…he used a condom. Condoms.' The blush in her cheeks burned like fire. Not from admitting she'd been with a man; after all, she was twenty-five.

No, the scorching fire in her face and belly came from the memory of how many condoms they'd gone through— just how insatiable they'd been for each other. Until Damaso had said he wanted nothing more to do with her.

'Condoms aren't a hundred per cent effective, you

know.' The doctor paused. 'You're not using any other contraceptive?'

'No.' Marisa's mouth twisted. All those years on the Pill while she'd been in training and now... Should she have kept taking it?

'Forgive me for asking but how long ago was this night you're talking about?'

'Just over a month ago. A month and a day, to be exact.' Her voice sounded ridiculously husky. She cleared her throat, telling herself to get a grip. Her periods weren't regular—the time lapse meant nothing. 'But I've had no other symptoms. Surely I would have? It has to be altitude sickness. That's what the guide thought.'

Even now the room swooped around her when she moved.

The doctor shrugged. 'It could be. On the other hand, your nausea and tiredness could indicate something else. It's best we rule out the possibility.' He delved into his bag and held something out to her. 'Go on, it won't bite. It's a simple pregnancy test.'

Marisa opened her mouth to argue but she was too wrung out to fight. The sooner she proved him wrong, the sooner he'd give her something to make her feel better.

Reluctantly she took the kit and headed to the bathroom.

Damaso stood unmoving, staring blindly at the sunlight pouring across the richly carpeted floor.

He didn't know what stunned him more—the possibility of Marisa being pregnant, or the fact he'd been her only recent lover.

When he'd left her in the rainforest he'd expected her to find someone else to warm her bed. The way she'd teased those guys in the bar just last night—pouting and showing off that taut, delectable body—he'd been certain she'd ended the night with a man.

If the press was to be believed, she had no scruples about sharing herself around.

Yet she'd been so certain there'd only been him.

That was why Damaso had stayed where he was during the conversation. Eavesdropping wasn't his style, but he was no fool. His wealth made him a target for fortune hunters. It had seemed wiser to wait and hear what she admitted to the doctor in case she tried to bring a paternity suit.

His mouth tightened. He was no woman's easy prey.

But then he recalled the raw shock in her voice. She wasn't playing coy with the doctor—that much was clear. She'd been speaking the truth about the date. If anything there'd been a tremor almost of fear in her voice at the thought of unplanned pregnancy.

A month and a day, she'd said. So precise. Which meant that if she *was* pregnant it was with Damaso's baby.

Shock rooted him to the spot. He was always meticulous about protection. Inconceivable to think it had failed this time.

Even more inconceivable that he should have a child.

Alone almost from birth, and certainly for as long as he could remember, Damaso had turned what could have been weakness into his greatest strength—self-sufficiency. He had no one and needed no one. It had always been that way. He had no plans for that to change.

He plunged his hand through his hair, raking it back from his forehead. He should have had it cut but this last month he'd thrown himself into work with such single-minded focus there'd been no time for fripperies.

A month and a day. His gut churned.

A murmur of voices dragged his attention back to the other room. In two strides he was there, arm stretched out to open the door.

Then his arm fell as the unthinkable happened.

'Ah, this confirms it, Your Highness. You're going to have a baby.'

* * *

Marisa wrapped her arms around herself as she stared out at the remarkable view. The jagged peaks were topped with an icy covering that the setting sun turned to candy pink, soft peach, brilliant gold and every shade in between. Shadows of indigo lengthened like fingers reaching down the mountain towards her, beckoning.

Realisation struck that this was one invitation she couldn't take up. No more climbing for her, no skydiving or white-water rafting if she was pregnant. All the activities she'd used to stave off the grimness of her life were forbidden.

For the hundredth time Marisa slipped her palm over her belly, wonderment filling her at the fact she was carrying another life inside her.

Could the doctor be wrong?

Marisa felt fine now, just a little wobbly and hollow. She didn't *feel* as if she was carrying a baby.

She'd head to the city and have another test. After all, the kit wasn't infallible.

Marisa didn't know whether to hope it was a mistake or hope it wasn't—she was too stunned to know how she felt.

One thing she was sure of, though—she wouldn't be raising any baby of hers within sight of Bengaria's royal palace. She'd protect it as fiercely as any lioness defending her cub.

'Excuse me, ma'am.' Marisa turned to find a smiling maid at the open door from the suite out to the private terrace where she sat. 'I've brought herbal tea and the chef has baked some sesame-water crackers for you.' She lifted a tray and Marisa caught the scent of fresh baking. Her mouth watered. She hadn't eaten since breakfast, worried about bringing on another bout of nausea.

'I didn't order anything.'

'It's with the hotel's compliments, ma'am.' The maid

hesitated a moment then stepped out onto the terrace, putting her laden tray on a small table.

'Thank you. That's very thoughtful.' Marisa eyed the delicate biscuits and felt a smile crack her tense features. The doctor must have organised this.

Leaving the edge of the balcony, she took a seat beside the table. An instant later the maid bustled back, this time with a lightweight rug.

'It's cooling down.' She smiled. 'If you'd like?' She lifted the rug.

Silently Marisa nodded, feeling ridiculously choked as the downy rug woven in traditional local designs was tucked around her legs. How long since anyone had cosseted her? Even Stefan, who'd loved her, had never fussed over her.

She blinked and smiled as the maid poured scented, steaming tea and settled the plate of biscuits closer.

'Is there anything else I can get you, ma'am?'

'Nothing. Thank you.' Her voice sounded scratchy, as if it came from a long distance. 'Please thank the chef for me.'

Alone again, Marisa sipped the delicately flavoured tea and nibbled a cracker. It tasted divine. Or perhaps that was simply because her stomach didn't rebel. She took another bite, crunching avidly.

She needed to make plans. First, a trip to Lima and another pregnancy test. Then... Her mind blanked at the thought of what came next.

She couldn't bear to go back to her villa in Bengaria. The memories of Stefan were too strong and, besides, the villa belonged to the crown. Now Stefan had gone, it belonged to her uncle and she refused to live as his pensioner. He'd demand she reside in the palace where he could keep an eye on her. They'd had that argument before Stefan had been cold in his grave.

Marisa drew the rug close. She'd have to find a new home. She'd put off the decision for too long. But where?

Bengaria was out. Every move she made there was reported and second-guessed. She'd lived in France, the United States and Switzerland as a student. But none were home.

Marisa sipped her tea and bit into another biscuit.

Fear scuttled through her. She knew nothing about being a mother and raising children. Her pregnancy would be turned into a royal circus if she wasn't careful.

Well, she'd just deal with that when and if the time came, and hope she was more successful than in the past.

'Marisa?'

Her head swung round at the sound of a fathoms-deep voice she'd never expected to hear again. Her fingers clenched around delicate bone china as her pulse catapulted.

It really was him, Damaso Pires, filling the doorway to her suite. He looked big and bold, his features drawn in hard, sharp lines that looked like they'd been honed in bronze. Glossy black hair flopped down across his brow and flirted with his collar, but did nothing to soften that remarkable face.

'What are you doing here?' She put the cup down with a clatter, her hand nerveless. 'How did you get in?'

'I knocked but there was no answer.'

Marisa lifted her chin, remembering the way he'd dumped her. 'That usually means the person inside wants privacy.'

'Don't get up.' He stepped onto the terrace, raising his hand, as if to prevent her moving.

She pushed the rug aside and stood, hoping he didn't see her sway before finding her balance. The nausea really had knocked the stuffing out of her.

'I repeat, Senhor Pires, why are you here?' Marisa folded her arms. He might top her by more than a head but she knew how to stand up to encroaching men.

'Senhor Pires?' His brows drew together in a frown that

made her think of some angry Inca god. 'It's a little late for formalities, don't you think?'

'I *know*,' she said, stepping forward, surging anger getting the better of her, 'that I've a right to privacy.'

Her stomach churned horribly as she remembered how he'd made her feel: an inch tall and cheap. She'd have thought she'd be used to it after a lifetime of not measuring up. But this man had wounded her more deeply because she'd been foolhardy enough to believe he was different.

He digested her words in silence, his expression unperturbed.

'Well?' Marisa tapped her foot, furious that her indignation was mixed with an unhealthy dollop of excitement. No matter how annoyed she was, there was no denying Damaso Pires was one fantastic looking man. And as a lover…

'Let me guess. You discovered I was here and thought you'd look me up for old times' sake.' She drew a quick breath that lodged halfway to her lungs. 'I'm afraid I'm not interested in a trip down memory lane. Or in continuing where we left off.'

She had more self-respect than to go back to a man who'd treated her as he had.

She stepped forward. 'Now, if you'll excuse me, I'd like to be alone.'

Her steps petered out when she came up against his impassable form. His spread legs and wide shoulders didn't allow space for her to pass.

Dark eyes bored into hers and something tugged tight in her belly. If only she could put it down to a queasy stomach but to her shame Marisa knew she responded to his overt, male sexuality. A frisson of awareness made her nape tingle and her breasts tighten.

Surely a pregnant woman wouldn't respond so wantonly?

The thought sideswiped her and her gaze flickered from his. Today's news had upended her world, leaving her feeling adrift and frail. What did she know about pregnancy?

'Marisa.' His voice held a tentative edge she didn't remember. 'Are you all right?'

Her head snapped up. 'I will be when I'm allowed the freedom of my own suite, *alone*.'

He stepped back and she moved away into the sitting room, conscious with every cell in her body of him looming nearby. Even his scent invaded her space, till she had to focus on walking past and not stopping to inhale.

She was halfway across the room, heading for the entrance, when he spoke again. 'We need to talk.'

Marisa kept walking. 'As I recall, you made it clear last time I saw you that our…connection was at an end.' Valiantly she kept her voice even, though humiliation at how she'd left herself open to his insulting treatment twisted a searing blade through her insides.

'Are you trying to tell me you thought otherwise?'

Her steps faltered to a halt. If she'd truly been unaffected by his abrupt desertion, she wouldn't be upset at his return, would she? She certainly wouldn't show it. But it was beyond even Marisa's acting powers to pretend insouciance. The best she could manage was haughty distance.

She needed him out of the way so she could concentrate on the news she still had trouble processing. That she was probably pregnant—with *his* child.

Marisa squeezed her eyes shut, trying to gather her strength. She'd face him later if she had too. Now she needed to be alone.

'I didn't think anything, *Damaso*.' She lingered over his name with dripping, saccharine emphasis. 'What we shared is over and done with.'

Her fingers closed around the door handle but, before she could tug it open, one long arm shot over her shoulder. A large hand slammed palm-down onto the door before her, keeping it forcibly closed. The heat of Damaso's body encompassed her, his breath riffling her hair as if he was breathing as hard as she.

'What about the fact you're carrying my child?'

She gasped. *How did he know?*

Marisa stared blankly at the strong, sinewy hand before her: the light sprinkling of dark hairs; the long fingers; the neat, short nails.

She blinked, remembering how that hand had looked on her pale breast, the pleasure it had wrought. How she'd actually hoped, for a few brief hours, she'd found a man who valued her for herself. How betrayed she'd felt.

'Marisa?' His voice was sharp.

She drew a jagged breath into tight lungs and turned, chin automatically lifting as he glowered down at her from his superior height.

The sight of him, looking so lofty and disapproving, stoked fire in her belly. She'd deal with him on *her* terms, when *she* was ready.

'I don't know what you think gives you the right to come here uninvited and throw your weight around. But it's time you left. Otherwise I'll have the management throw you out.'

Damaso stared into blazing azure eyes and felt something thump hard in his belly. Energy vibrated off her in waves. Just meeting her stare sent adrenalin shooting into his bloodstream.

His body tensed, his groin tightening at the challenge she projected.

She tempted him even as her disdainful gaze raked him. But it wasn't only dismissal he read in her taut features. The parted lips, the throbbing pulse, the fleeting shadow in her bright eyes gave her away.

He aroused her. He sensed it as surely as he recognised the symptoms in his own body. He hadn't got her out of his system even now.

Without thinking, he put his hand to her face, cupping her jaw so that a frantic pulse jumped against his skin. His fingers brushed her silk-soft hair.

She felt every bit as good as he remembered. Better than he'd allowed himself to believe. He leaned towards her, lowering his head. Discussion could wait.

Sudden pain, a white-hot flash of agony, streaked up his arm.

Stunned, Damaso saw she'd fastened on to a pressure point in some fancy martial arts manoeuvre. He sucked in a breath, tamping down his instinctive response to over-power her. He'd never learned to fight by any code of rules. Where he'd grown up, violence had been endemic, brutal and often deadly. In seconds he could have her flat on her back in surrender. He forced himself to relax, ignoring the lancing pain.

'I'm calling the management.' She breathed heavily, as if it was she, not he, in agony.

'I *am* the management, *pequenina*.'

'Sorry?' Her fierce expression eased into owlish dis-belief.

'I own the resort.' Damaso tried to move his fingers but another dart of pain shot through him. 'You can let me go,' he said through gritted teeth. 'I promise not to touch you.'

'You own it?' Her grip loosened and he tugged his hand free, flexing it as pins and needles spread up his arm. For an amateur, her self-defence skills were impressive.

'I do. It was my team of architects who designed it. My builders who constructed it.'

'The staff report to you?' Her tone was sharp. 'That explains a lot.' Her mouth tightened. 'I don't see why the doctor should run to you with news of my health, even if you employ him. What about patient confidentiality?' She didn't raise her voice but the way she bit out the words, as if chipping off shards of glacial ice, spoke volumes.

Damaso shook his head. 'He didn't breathe a word.'

At her frown he explained, 'I was here, in the suite, when he confirmed your test results.'

She stared up at him, her eyes bright as lasers, and just

as cutting. Damaso felt his cheeks redden, almost as if he blushed under her accusing stare.

It was impossible, of course. Embarrassment was a luxury denied those who'd survived by scavenging off others' refuse. Nothing fazed him, not even the shocked accusation in her glare. He didn't care what others thought.

Yet he looked away first.

'I'd heard you were ill and came to see how you were.'

'How very considerate.' Her hands moved to her hips, pulling the fabric of her designer T-shirt taut over those delectable breasts. Belatedly, Damaso tore his gaze away, only to find himself staring at her flat stomach. She cradled his baby there. The shock of it dried his throat. He wanted to slip his hand beneath the drawstring of her loose trousers and press his palm to the softness of her belly.

The snap of fingers in front of his face startled him.

'Being the owner of this place doesn't give you the right to pry into my private life.'

'It was unintentional. I was coming to see you.'

'That's no excuse for spying on what is my affair.'

'Hardly spying, Marisa.' Her flashing eyes told him she disagreed. 'And this *affair* affects both of us.'

Colour streaked her cheekbones, making her look ridiculously young and vulnerable.

He softened his voice. 'We need to talk.'

She shook her head, her bright hair slipping like spun gold across her dark shirt. With quick grace she turned and crossed the room to the vast windows framing the view of the Andes. She stood rigid, as if his presence pained her.

'A month and a day, remember, Marisa? This is as much my business as yours.'

She didn't move, not so much as a muscle. Her unnatural stillness disturbed him.

'When were you going to tell me?'

Still she said nothing. Damaso's skin tightened till it felt like hundreds of ants crawled over him.

'Or weren't you going to? Were you planning to get rid of it quietly with no one the wiser?'

Damaso grimaced at the pungent sourness filling his mouth. Had she decided to get rid of his child?

His child!

He'd been stunned by the news he was to be a father. It had taken hours to come to grips with the fact he'd have a child—blood of his blood, flesh of his flesh.

For the first time in his life, he'd have family.

The idea astounded him, scared him. He, who'd never expected to have a family of his own. Yet to his amazement part of him welcomed the idea.

He didn't know exactly how he expected this to play out. But one thing was absolutely certain: no child of his would be abandoned as he'd been.

No child of his would grow up alone or neglected.

It would know its father.

It would be cared for.

He, Damaso Pires, would make sure of that personally. The intensity of his determination was stronger than anything he'd known.

He must have moved for he found himself behind Marisa. Her hair stirred with each breath he exhaled. His fingers flexed, as if to reach for her hips and pull her to him, or shake her into speech.

'Say something!' Damaso wasn't used to being ignored, especially by women he'd known intimately. Especially when something as profoundly important as this lay between them.

'What do you want me to say?' When she turned, her eyes were wide and over-bright. 'No, I hadn't planned an abortion? No, I hadn't decided when I'd tell you, if at all? I haven't had time even to get my head around the idea of being pregnant.'

She jabbed a finger into his sternum. 'I don't see this being as much your business as mine.' Her finger stabbed again. '*If* I'm pregnant, I'll be the one carrying this baby. *I'll* be the one whose body and life and future will change irrevocably. Not you.'

Her finger wobbled against his chest; her whole hand was shaking, Damaso realised. He wrapped his hand around hers but she tugged loose from his hold and backed away as if his touch contaminated her.

Too late for that, my fine lady.

Marisa watched his harsh mouth curve in a smile that could only be described as feral. He looked dangerous and unpredictable, his eyes a black gleam that made her want to step back again. Instead she planted her feet.

How had he turned the tables, so his intrusion on her privacy had become a litany of accusations against *her?* Enough was enough. She was tired of being bullied and judged.

'Obviously you've had time to jump to all sorts of conclusions about this pregnancy, if there is one.' She fixed him with a stony gaze.

'You deny it?' He scowled.

'I reserve judgement until I've got a second opinion.' She braced her hands on her hips, refusing to cower before his harsh expression. 'But obviously you've gone beyond that stage.'

'I have.' His gaze dropped to her stomach and she felt a hot stirring inside as if he'd touched her there. Abruptly, his dark eyes locked on hers again. 'There's only one sensible option.'

'Really?'

'Of course.' His brooding features tightened, a determined light in his eyes. 'We'll marry.'

CHAPTER FOUR

MARISA COULDN'T PREVENT the ripple of laughter that slipped from her mouth.

'Marry?' She shook her head. Astonishment punctured the bubble of tension cramping her chest. 'You've got to be kidding. I don't even know you.'

His downturned mouth and furrowed brow told her he didn't appreciate her levity. Or maybe he didn't like the panicked edge that see-sawed through her laughter.

Marisa didn't like it either. She sounded, and felt, too close to the edge.

'You knew me well enough for us to create a baby together.' His deep voice held a bite that eradicated the last of her semi-hysterical laughter. It brought her back to earth with a thump.

'That's not knowing. That's sex.'

He shrugged, lifting those broad shoulders she'd clung to through their night together. She'd dug her nails into his flesh as ecstasy had consumed her. She'd never wanted to let him go and had snuggled against his solid shoulder through the night.

Until he'd made it clear he wanted nothing more to do with her.

'You've changed your tune.' Did he hear the echo of hurt in her tone? Marisa was beyond caring; she just knew she had to scotch this insanity.

'That was before there was a child, *princesa*.'

She stiffened. 'There still may not be one. I won't be sure till I've had another test. It could have been a false positive.'

Damaso tilted his head, as if examining a curious specimen. 'The idea of a child is so horrible to you?'

'No!' Marisa's hand slipped to her stomach then, realising what she'd done, she dropped her arm to her side. 'I just need to be sure.'

He nodded. 'Of course. And when we are sure, we'll marry.'

Marisa blinked. Why did talking to Damaso Pires feel like trying to make headway against a granite boulder?

'This is the twenty-first century. People don't have to marry to have children.'

He crossed his arms, accentuating the solid muscle of his torso beneath the pristine business shirt, reinforcing his formidable authority. Wearing casual trekking gear, he'd been stunning, but dressed for business he added a whole new cachet to the 'tall, dark, handsome' label.

If only she didn't respond at that visceral, utterly feminine level. She couldn't afford to be distracted by such rampant masculinity.

'We're not talking about *people*. We're talking about us and our child.'

Our child. The words resonated inside Marisa, making her shiver. Making the possibility of pregnancy abruptly real.

She put out a hand and grabbed the back of a nearby settee as the world swam.

Suddenly he was there before her, his hand firm on her elbow. 'You need to sit.'

It was on the tip of her tongue to say she needed to be alone but she felt wobbly. Perhaps she should rest—she didn't want to do anything that might endanger her baby.

And just like that she made the transition from protest to acceptance.

Not only acceptance but something stronger—something like anticipation.

Which showed how foolish she was. This situation had no built-in happy ending.

Marisa let Damaso guide her to a seat. The pregnancy no longer felt like a possibility, to be disproved with a second test. It felt *real*. Or maybe that was because of the way Damaso held her—gently, yet as if nothing could break his hold.

She lowered her eyes, facing the thought of motherhood alone. Learning to be a good mother when she had no idea what that was. The only things she'd ever been good at were sports and creating scandal.

Marisa bit down a groan, picturing the furore in the Bengarian royal court, the ultimatums and machinations to put the best spin on this. The condemnation, not just from the palace, but from the press.

In the past she'd pretended not to feel pain as the palace and the media had dealt her wound after wound, slashing at her as if she wasn't a flesh-and-blood woman who bled at their ferocious attacks.

'I'll get the doctor.' Damaso crouched before her, his long fingers still encircling her arm.

'I don't need a doctor.' She needed to get a grip. Wallowing in self-pity wasn't like her and she couldn't afford to begin now. More than ever she had to find a way forward, not just for herself, but for her child.

'You need someone to care for you.'

'And you're appointing yourself my protector?' She couldn't keep the jeering note from her voice.

For the first time since he'd shouldered his way into her suite, he looked discomfited. Eventually he spoke.

'The baby is my responsibility.' He spoke so solemnly, her skin prickled.

'Sorry to disillusion you but I don't need a protector. I look after myself.' She'd learned independence at six, when her mother had died. Now she only had vague memories of warm hugs and wide smiles, of bedtime stories and an exquisite, never-to-be-repeated certainty she was precious.

'Reading the press reports about your activities, I can see how well you've done that.'

Marisa's chin shot up, her furious gaze locking with his. 'You shouldn't believe everything you read in the press.'

Except everyone did, and eventually Marisa had given up trying to explain. Instead she'd been spurred to a reckless disregard for convention and, at times, her own safety.

That stopped now. If there was a baby…

'So I should give you the benefit of the doubt?' He leaned closer and her breath snared in her lungs. Something happened to her breathing when Damaso got near.

'I don't care what you think of me.' In the past that had worked for her. But with Damaso things were suddenly more complicated.

'I can see that. But I also see you're unwell. This news has come as a shock.'

'You're not shocked? Just how many kids do you have littered around the place?' Marisa strove for insouciance but didn't quite achieve it. Absurdly, the thought of him with a string of other women made her stomach cramp.

'None.'

Ah. Maybe that explained his reaction.

'Let me propose an interim arrangement.' He sat back on his haunches, giving her space.

It was a clever move, she realised, as her racing pulse slowed.

'Yes?'

'You want a second pregnancy test. Let me take you to the city and arrange a medical examination. Then, if the results are positive, we talk about the future.' He spread his hands in a gesture of openness.

Yet the glint in his dark eyes hinted things weren't so simple.

But what did she have to lose? He only proposed what she'd already decided. And, as owner of the lodge, he could get her out of here quickly, without waiting for a scheduled flight.

'No strings?'

'No strings.'

Doubt warred with caution and a craven desire to let someone else worry about the details for once. If he tried to trample her, he'd learn he was messing with the wrong woman.

'Agreed.' She put out her hand, using the business gesture to reinforce that this was a deal, not a favour. A tiny bubble of triumph rose at his surprised look.

But, when his hand encompassed hers, engulfing her in its hard warmth, her smile faded.

Marisa twisted in her seat as the helicopter's rotors slowed. Damaso saw anger shimmer in her eyes as she glared at him. 'You said we'd go to the city.'

'São Paolo is inland, not too far away.'

'You lied to me.' Her mouth set in a mutinous pout that made him want to pull her close and kiss those soft, pink lips till all she could do was sigh his name.

Damaso stared, grappling with both his urgent response and surprise at her vehemence.

'I said I'd take you to have your pregnancy confirmed.' Even now, after a day to absorb the news, he felt a pooling of emotion at the thought of the baby they'd created.

'In a city. That's what we agreed. That's why I agreed to come to Brazil with you. I thought when we transferred from the plane we were going into São Paolo.'

'I've organised for a doctor to visit you here, in my private residence.'

Marisa's gaze roved the view beyond his shoulder, past the ultra-modern mansion looking over a pristine beach and aquamarine water to the tangle of lush forest rising up the slope beyond. 'It's secluded,' he murmured. 'I own the whole island.'

'You think that's a recommendation? I have no interest in your *private* estate.' Her jaw clenched, as if she read what he'd tried to suppress—the physical hunger that still plagued him.

From the moment he'd seen Marisa, he'd wanted her. One night in her bed had only sharpened his appetite, and not just for her lithe body. He wanted to possess all of her: her quicksilver energy; her laughter; her earthy, generous sexuality and that feeling she shared some rare, exquisite gift with him. Even arguing with her was more stimulating than sealing a multi-billion-dollar deal.

This craving disturbed him. Usually he found it easy to move on from a woman. But then, he'd never had one carry his child before. That must be why he couldn't get her out of his head.

'Lots of women would give their eye teeth to be here.'

She looked at him with a supercilious coolness that made him feel, for the first time in years, inferior. 'Not me.'

The smack to his lungs, the hot blast of blood to his face, shocked him to the core.

He was Damaso Pires, self-made, successful, sought after. He bowed to no one, gave way to no one. He'd banished the scars of childhood with the most convincing cure of all: success. Inferiority was a word he'd excised from his personal lexicon years before.

'You're not impressed, *princesa?*'

Her eyes widened a fraction. Because he'd called her 'princess', or because he'd growled the words between gritted teeth?

'It's not about being impressed.' She spoke coolly. 'I simply don't like being lied to.'

Damaso drew a slow breath and unclicked his seat belt. 'It wasn't a lie. I often commute to the city from here.' He put up his hand before she could interrupt. 'Besides, I thought you'd appreciate the privacy of my estate, rather than go to a clinic or have an obstetrician visit you in a city hotel.' He stared into her sparking blue eyes. 'Less chance of the paparazzi getting hold of the story, since my staff are completely discreet.'

He watched her absorb that: the quick swallow, the rushed breath through pinched nostrils.

Ah, not so superior now. Obviously she didn't want news of her condition made public.

'Thank you.' Her quick change of tone surprised him. 'That's thoughtful of you. I hadn't considered that.' She fumbled at her seatbelt so long, he looked down and saw her hands were unsteady. He wanted to reach out and do it for her but her closed expression warned him off.

At last the seatbelt clicked open and she pushed it away. 'But don't ever lie to me again. I don't appreciate being lured here under false pretences.'

It was on the tip of Damaso's tongue to say he wasn't interested in luring her anywhere. But that was exactly what he'd done, because it suited his purposes. Much as it went against the grain to admit it, she had a point.

'Very well. In future you will be consulted.'

Her perfect dark-gold eyebrows arched. 'In future,' she corrected in a voice of silk-covered steel, 'I *decide*.'

In one easy movement she swung her legs out of the door, held open by one of his staff, and strode away from the tarmac of the landing pad without waiting to see if he followed.

She walked like a princess, head up, shoulders straight, with a firm gait that wasn't a stride but somehow conveyed her absolute confidence that the world would rearrange itself to fit her expectations.

He told himself she was spoiled and wilful. Instead, he found himself admiring her. He wasn't used to having his arrangements questioned.

Her thanks for his thoughtfulness had surprised him.

Her firm insistence on making her own decisions was something he understood.

He watched the cream linen of her trousers tighten around her shapely backside with each step, watched the way her hair, a thick curtain of gold, swung between her narrow shoulder-blades.

In future he'd remember to take the time to convince Princess Marisa to agree to his decisions before he put them into action.

Damaso's mouth curved in a rare smile as he got down from the chopper and followed her. Persuading Marisa presented all sorts of interesting possibilities.

Marisa strode from the house mere moments after the doctor had left her. Not just any doctor, but the region's best obstetrician, apparently, and a woman to boot. Damaso had thought of everything.

No doubt he was closeted with the doctor, receiving confirmation of the pregnancy.

Marisa's step quickened till she reached the soft, white sand of the beach where she tugged off her sandals.

She wanted to sprint down the beach till her lungs burned, swim out into the impossibly clear depths of the bay till she was totally isolated from the luxury mansion full of staff. Climb the rocky headland that jutted at the far end of the beach.

Anything to feel free again, if only briefly.

Marisa sighed. She needed to be more cautious now she was pregnant. She could sprint, of course, but the security guard trailing her would think she was under threat. If she explained, he'd feel obliged to race up the beach beside her, destroying her enjoyment.

Reluctantly she looked back and there he was: a bulky figure trying, ineffectually, to blend into the foliage just above the beach.

Even in Bengaria she'd had more freedom!

Marisa waded into the warm shallows till she was up to her calves, letting the tiny waves lap against her legs. She breathed deep, trying to feel at one with the gentle surge and wane of the water, focusing on slowing her pulse.

It was years since she'd practised the techniques she'd used to prepare herself for a gymnastics competition. If ever she'd needed to feel grounded, it was now.

She was going to be a mother.

Joy, mingled with fear, spilled through her veins. Despite the circumstances, she couldn't regret the child she carried. Did she have what it took to raise it and care for it the way it deserved?

She had no one to turn to, no one to trust, but Damaso: a stranger who saw this baby as a responsibility.

Fleetingly, Marisa thought of the others who'd claim a say in her child's future.

Her relatives. She shivered and wrapped her arms around her torso. No matter what it took, she'd keep her child safe from them.

The advisors of the Bengarian Court. No, they'd simply follow her uncle's lead.

Her friends. Marisa bit her lip. She'd given up seeking real friends long ago—after the few she'd had were ostracised by the palace for being too uncultured and common for her to mix with.

Which left her alone.

Her smile was crooked as she gazed towards the mainland. She'd always been alone, even when Stefan had been alive. There was only so much he'd been able to do to support her. He'd had his own troubles. She'd been lucky—as a mere princess, she was window dressing, for she'd never inherit the crown. Poor Stefan, as crown prince, had borne the brunt of everyone's expectations from birth.

'Marisa.'

She swung around to see Damaso at the water's edge. In lightweight trousers and a loose white shirt, sleeves rolled up past his elbows, he looked too sexy for her peace of mind.

Her heart crashed against her ribs and her lungs tightened, squeezing the air from her body till she felt breathless and light-headed. Her skin tingled as his dark gaze slid over her. She was burning up, a pulse throbbing between her legs.

'We need to talk.'

'You don't waste time, do you?' She crossed her arms.

'What do you mean?'

'You've come straight from the doctor, haven't you?' He'd said they'd find out if she was pregnant then they'd talk about the future. 'Can't you give me some breathing space?'

She hadn't meant to say it aloud but she felt hemmed in by news of the pregnancy, by the security guard, by the fact she'd have to tell her uncle. Above all, by this man, who for reasons she didn't understand made her *feel,* right to her core.

'I'm not going to hurt you.'

Marisa sucked in a breath. 'I'm not afraid of you, Damaso.' How dared he even think it? She, who'd never turned from a physical challenge in her life.

'No?' She supposed that tightening of his mouth at one corner was supposed to be a smile. She didn't see anything funny about the situation.

'Absolutely not.' Facing down a sexy Brazilian with an ego the size of Rio's Sugarloaf Mountain was nothing compared with what she'd dealt with before.

Yet she didn't move to join him. Instead he waded out to meet her, the water covering first his bare feet then soaking his trousers. Marisa's mouth dried as if she hadn't tasted water in a week.

He stopped a breath away, his scent mingling with the salt tang of the water.

'How do you feel?'

'Fine.' It was true. She'd been sick again this morning but tea and dry toast in bed and a slow start to the day had made the nausea easier to handle.

'Good. We need to talk.' His intent scrutiny made the hairs stand up on the back of her neck. Some sixth sense told her he wasn't here to continue an argument about marrying for the baby's sake.

'What is it?' She'd received bad news before and, attuned after Stefan's recent death, she knew Damaso would rather not break this news. 'Is it the baby?' Her voice was a hoarse whisper. 'Did the doctor tell you something she didn't tell me?'

He took her elbow as she lunged towards him, her heart pounding frantically. 'It's not the baby. Nothing like that.'

Instinctively Marisa planted her hand on his chest, needing his support. She felt the steady thud of his heart beneath her palm and managed to draw a calming breath. She pushed down a moment's terror that there'd been something the doctor hadn't shared.

'What, then? Tell me!'

His mouth thinned to a grim line. 'It's the press. There's been a report that you're pregnant.'

'Already?' Her head swung towards the multi-level residence commanding the half-moon bay.

'It wasn't one of my staff. No one here would dream of going to the press with a story about a guest of mine.'

'How can you be sure?' Something passed across his face that Marisa couldn't fathom. 'For the right sort of money...'

He shook his head. 'My people wouldn't betray me.'

Fleetingly, Marisa wondered what bond could possibly be so strong between a billionaire and his paid staff.

'It was someone from the hotel in Peru. One of the kitchen staff. They overheard my request for something to settle your morning sickness.'

'*Your* request?' Marisa dragged her hand back from his

chest as if scalded. She'd thought the doctor had ordered tea and crackers for her.

The thought of Damaso leaving her room and heading to the kitchens to make a personal request on her behalf made her still. It didn't fit with the way he'd treated her. But, now she considered it, since learning of her pregnancy he'd been intent on looking after her.

She'd been too annoyed at his high-handed actions to acknowledge it, possibly because his way of helping was to try taking control.

'It was a new staff member. Now an ex-staff member. They won't work in any of my enterprises again.' The steely note in his voice made Marisa feel almost sorry for whoever had thought to profit from gossiping to the press.

'I thought I'd have a little more time before it became public.' She tried for nonchalance, though an undercurrent of nerves made her body tense. Once the news was out…

'It's an unconfirmed rumour. Nothing they can prove.'

'I suppose I've weathered worse.'

Memories rose of being pilloried at just fifteen. Someone on the gymnastics squad had leaked the fact that Marisa was on the Pill and it had been splashed across the press, along with photos of her partying.

No one had been interested in the fact she'd been prescribed the medication to help deal with periods so painful they'd interfered with her training, or that the parties were strictly chaperoned. Everything had been twisted. Innocent glances in photos turned into lascivious stares, smiles into wanton invitations. They'd portrayed her as a little slut, precocious, uncontrollable and without morals.

Once typecast by the paparazzi, there'd been no way to turn the tide of popular opinion.

The palace had been ineffectual. It was only years later she'd begun to suspect the palace had left her to fend for herself—a brutal lesson in dancing to her uncle's tune or else. Eventually, after years fighting the tide, Marisa had given up and begun to take perverse pleasure in living down to expectations.

She breathed deep and stepped back, registering anew the gentle swish of water against her legs.

'At least I don't have to worry about the press here.' She pasted on a smile. 'Thank you, Damaso. It seems you were right. If I'd stayed in a hotel, I'd be under siege.'

Was it her imagination or did his gaze warm a fraction? 'In the circumstances, I'd prefer not to have been right.'

It was tempting to bask in the fragile sensation of being looked after. But she couldn't afford to get used to it.

They walked side by side up the beach, scooping up their discarded shoes and turning towards the house.

They'd just stepped onto the cropped emerald turf when a white-coated servant appeared and spoke to Damaso in swift Portuguese.

'What is it?' Marisa sensed the instant change in him.

'A message for you. You had a phone call and they're calling back in fifteen minutes.'

'Who was it?' But already Marisa felt her stomach plunge like a rock off a precipice. She knew exactly who it had been.

His words confirmed her fears. 'The King of Bengaria.'

CHAPTER FIVE

DAMASO PACED THE shaded loggia, the tray of coffee and his laptop forgotten. Through the full-length glass he had a perfect view of Marisa.

He'd begun to wish he hadn't given her privacy to take her call. Not when instinct urged him to march in and rip the phone out of her hand.

That, by itself, gave him pause.

He didn't interfere in the lives of others. He was never interested enough to do so. But, watching Marisa stand to attention beside the desk in his study, Damaso knew an inexplicable urge to break the habit of a lifetime.

What was the King saying? As far as he could see, she hadn't had the chance to say much. Yet her body spoke volumes. Her spine was ramrod-stiff and she paced with military precision, like a soldier on parade. Her mouth was a flat line and her shoulders inched high towards her ears.

She wore the figure-hugging white capri pants and yellow crop top from the beach. There she'd looked like a sexy embodiment of the summer sun—bright and vibrant. Now, with her pinched features, she seemed like another woman.

To hell with it. He strode towards the glass doors that separated them.

Then he stopped, for now Marisa was talking.

This close he heard her voice, though not the words. She spoke crisply, with definite emphasis. Her chin lifted and she looked every inch the pure-bred aristocrat: haughty and regal.

She paused, as if listening, then spoke sharply, her arm slicing the air in a violent sweep. She turned and marched across the room, her toned body taut and controlled, ripe with pride and determination.

Damaso stared, unable to believe the visceral stab of desire that hit him as he watched her lay down the law. A woman in control—that had never been his fantasy. Always he was the hunter, the master, the one who set the rules.

Was that what had made their night together so cataclysmically memorable? The sense of two matched people coming together as equals, neither in control?

If that was so, why this unfamiliar urge to protect her? It had to be because of the baby. Since he'd learned of her pregnancy she'd become the centre of his thoughts—a rival even to his business empire, which had given him purpose and identity all his adult life.

Damaso breathed hard, aware he was on unfamiliar ground.

It took him a few moments to realise she'd ended the call. Now she stood, shoulders slumped, hands braced wide on the desk. As he watched, her head bowed in a move that spoke of a bone-deep weariness.

Something stirred in Damaso's belly. That tickle of concern he'd first felt the morning he'd left her in the jungle. When, despite her anger and her hauteur, he'd sensed something out of kilter in her queenly dismissal of him.

'Marisa?' He was through the door before he had time to reconsider.

Instantly she straightened. If he hadn't been looking, he'd never have seen the strain etching her face before she smoothed it.

'Yes?'

Damaso stared, confronted by a cool, self-contained princess, the hint of a polite smile curving her soft lips.

Only the glitter of strong emotion in her eyes, now darkened to midnight sapphire, belied that regal poise.

'What did he want?'

Her delicate eyebrows arched high, as if surprised at his temerity in questioning her. That cut no ice with Damaso.

Silently he waited. Eventually her gaze skittered from his. She shrugged. 'King Cyrill wasn't pleased when his public relations advisors told him there were rumours I was pregnant.'

'They were quick off the mark!'

Her mouth tightened. 'They're always careful to keep tabs on me.' Did he imagine an emphasis on 'me'?

'And what did you say? Did you confirm the pregnancy?' Damaso wished he knew more about the Bengarian monarchy. He'd had no interest in the small European kingdom till someone on the trek had pointed Marisa out as the infamous party princess he'd vaguely heard about. How close were she and the King? Obviously their conversation had taxed Marisa's strength, despite her show of unconcern.

She half-turned and stroked a finger idly along the gleaming surface of his desk. 'It's none of his business.' Defiance edged her tone. 'But then I realised there was nothing to be gained by waiting. I'd have to face the flak sooner or later.'

'Flak? Because you're not married?' He knew next to nothing about royals—except that their lives seemed steeped in tradition.

She laughed, the sound so bitter he wondered if it hurt. 'Not married. Not in a relationship. Not seeing a man vetted and approved by the palace. Not doing what a Bengarian princess is supposed to do. Take your pick.'

Damaso stepped closer, drawn by the pain in her voice. 'What is it you're supposed to be doing?'

Marisa's head lifted, her chin angling, as if facing an opponent.

'Being respectably and sedately courted by a suitable prince, or at least a titled courtier. Keeping out of the press, except in carefully staged set pieces arranged by the palace. Not causing a scandal, particularly now.'

'Now? Why now?' Why hadn't he taken time to find out more about Marisa's European homeland?

Because his focus was and always had been on building his business. That was what he lived for. What made him who he was.

Marisa straightened, but once again refused to meet his gaze. 'I'd like to say it's because the country is still in mourning for Stefan. But it's because Cyrill doesn't want any scandal in the lead up to his coronation.'

At Damaso's enquiring look, she explained. 'Cyrill is my uncle, my father's younger brother. My father was king and after my father died Cyrill was Regent of Bengaria for eleven years, till Stefan came of age at twenty-one.' She sucked in a breath and for a moment he thought she'd finished speaking. 'Stefan was my twin brother and King of Bengaria. He died in a motorboat accident two months ago.'

Two months ago? Damaso frowned, searching her face. Her brother had been barely cold in his grave when Damaso had met Marisa. She hadn't acted like a woman grieving the loss of a loved one.

Yet what did he know of grief or loss? He'd never had so much as a best friend, let alone family.

'You don't like your uncle?'

Marisa turned startled eyes on him, then laughed again, the sound short and sharp. 'I can't stand him.' She paused. 'He was our guardian after our father died and to all intents and purposes King.' Her voice held a sour note that told far more about their relationship than her words. 'Even when Stefan was crowned, Cyrill was there in the background, trying to manipulate opinion whenever Stefan dared to instigate change.'

'But now you're free of him.'

Marisa turned to stare out across the lawns to the sandy crescent of Damaso's private beach. It looked so peaceful, so perfect. But the sight did nothing to calm her. Not after Cyrill's threats.

The last day and a half, she'd been in a state of shock. And now this... Once more her uncle threatened to turn her life inside out.

'It's not that simple.' Foolishly, she'd thought it was. With Stefan gone, Marisa had no interest in Bengarian politics. She just hadn't counted on the fact that Bengaria wasn't ready to wash its hands of her. A fact her uncle had been at pains to point out.

'Marisa? What is it?' Damaso's voice deepened and she forced herself to look up, only to find herself pinioned by his questioning gaze. Between Damaso and her uncle, she had no chance of peace! What she needed was time to sort herself out, away from domineering men. Even if one of them made her question her need for solitude.

'Are you going to tell me or will I ring your uncle?'

Shock warred with laughter at the idea of anyone calling Cyrill on the spur of the moment. Who would win? Her uncle, with his smug self-importance and devious ways, or Damaso with his my-way-or-the-highway approach?

'He wouldn't talk to you.'

'No one is that inaccessible, Marisa.' Damaso crossed his arms, one slashing dark eyebrow lifting in enquiry. He didn't bluster but there was such innate determination in his stance, his expression, she had no doubt her uncle would come off the worse in a contest of wills. 'Why aren't you free of him?'

With a sigh, she sank into a nearby armchair. 'Because he holds the purse strings. As simple as that.' And, fool that she was, she hadn't seen it coming. How could she not have thought of it earlier?

Because she'd been wiped out by grief, grimly battling to face each new day after Stefan's death and not to wear her pain publicly. She'd actually thought she could break her ties with the palace. How naïve, especially after experiencing her uncle's Machiavellian ways first-hand.

Every penny she had was now sequestered by royal command. How was she going to find herself a home and provide for her child when everything she owned no longer belonged to her? Marisa bit her cheek hard as she felt her mouth tremble.

She'd thought she was adrift and rudderless without Stefan, but now...

'He's threatened to stop your allowance?' Damaso's tone was casual.

'Yes, he's stopping my *allowance,* as you call it—the money invested for me by my parents.' She drew a deep breath. 'He's also threatening to freeze my assets, including my personal bank account.'

Fire kindled in Damaso's eyes. 'By what right?'

'By right of the sovereign. In Bengaria, that means everything. He has control over all members of his extended family if he chooses to use it.' She sank back in her seat, weary beyond reckoning. It was a power even her strict father wouldn't have invoked. 'It's legal. Just not ethical.'

That was Cyrill all over. Anything to get his own way.

Who'd have thought his plans would still include her after the breach between them? She shuddered, wondering if he really wanted her back in Bengaria, or whether this was an elaborate tactic to make her suffer for repudiating him.

Damaso sank down before her, his gaze capturing hers. 'You'll want for nothing now you're with me.'

He meant it. It was there in his steady stare.

'Except I'm not *with* you! I haven't agreed to marry you.' Her heart hammered high in her throat as she read his implacable expression.

He didn't say anything. He didn't need to. This was a

man used to giving orders and having them obeyed. Right now he wanted her.

Correction: *he wanted her baby.*

Chilled to the marrow, Marisa crossed her arms, shielding her child.

Damaso and Cyrill both wanted to control her for their own ends. Both wanted her child—Damaso for reasons she didn't fully understand, Cyrill because her baby had royal blood, making it a potential pawn in his elaborate schemes to extend the power of the crown.

'So, go out and get a job. Support yourself.' Impatience edged Damaso's tone. Marisa had heard it before from people who didn't know her but believed all they read in the press.

About to hide her feelings behind the usual show of casual disdain, something stopped her.

Damaso's good opinion shouldn't matter. He'd already shown how little he thought of her. Yet she paused. She was tired of being judged and found wanting.

'You think I haven't tried?' At the surprise in his eyes, she turned away, hunching her shoulder against his disbelief. 'Who'd take me seriously, especially when the press start hounding me, pestering my employer and other staff? Making bets on how long I'll stick it out?'

She shuddered, remembering how her naïve optimism had been shattered again and again. Failure had bred failure. Her reputation hung like an albatross around her neck: dilettante; party girl; frivolous, unable to stick to anything. How many times had she tried to do something worthwhile, only to have the opportunity snatched away?

Last time the press had camped outside the special school where she'd volunteered until both staff and children had become unsettled and nervous. Finally the director had asked her not to come any more.

'I've tried. Don't think I haven't.' Marisa heard the shaky echo of defeat in her voice. It scared her. All she had left was her independence. She'd fought so long for that and she had to be strong now.

Instantly she was on her feet, needing to move, to think.

But Damaso was before her, his large hand wrapping around her wrist before she could take a step.

He looked down into her pale face, her wide eyes, shadowed now instead of bright, and felt the tiniest tremor ripple under her skin. Slowly she lifted her chin as if distancing herself from him. Was it an unconscious gesture, that superior set of the head, or a practised move designed to scare off plebeians such as himself?

Yet, holding her slender wrist, it struck him that behind the air of well-bred hauteur lurked a world of pain.

Damaso was an expert at reading people. It was a skill he'd cultivated and exploited even as a child, gauging which adults would respond to a skinny kid's wide-eyed hungry look with an offer of food and which with a swift kick. But in all his years his understanding had rarely turned to empathy.

Yet, what other explanation could there be for this protectiveness? This need to wrap his arms around her and hold her close?

There were violet smudges under her fine eyes and she couldn't quite disguise the way her lips trembled. She did a magnificent job of hiding it but once more he recognised a vulnerability about Princess Marisa of Bengaria that went far deeper than the mere loss of funds.

His hand gentled on her arm.

'Whatever he does, he can't touch you here.'

It was meant for reassurance, but he felt her stiffen.

'But I haven't said I'd stay.'

Sharp heat twisted in Damaso's belly. He refused to countenance a future where his child grew up without him.

His child.

The words were like a beam of light, illuminating a hollow in the dark void of his soul he'd never known till now.

He'd never thought to belong to anyone. Yet he knew with deep gut instinct that he had to be part of his baby's life. His child would have a father, a family, such as he'd never known. His child would never be alone and frightened. It would never want for anything.

Damaso's hand tightened around Marisa's.

He wasn't the sort to step back from what he wanted. He'd never have survived the slums if he hadn't learned early to take life by the throat and hang on tight.

But there was more than one way to get what he wanted. He was fast learning Marisa wasn't the two-dimensional party girl the world thought she was. He'd seen hints of it from the first. Her revelations about her uncle and her distress when Damaso had snapped that she should get a job had shattered that image.

'Let me go, Damaso. You're hurting me.'

Yet she stood stock still, too proud to fight his hold. Unexpectedly, his chest squeezed at her defiant posture. Holding her as he did, he felt her tremble.

'Am I?' He slid his fingers down to wrap around hers and lifted her hand, inhaling the tang of her skin's scent. Slowly he lowered his head and pressed his lips to the inside of her wrist. Instantly her pulse flickered hard and fast. He kissed her again and heard her swift intake of breath.

'Damaso. Let go of me.' Her voice had a distinct wobble. It reminded him of her broken cry of ecstasy the first time she'd climaxed beneath him. Heat saturated his skin as his libido shifted gear, rousing in an instant.

'What if I don't want to?' Her fingers twitched in his hold as he kissed her again.

Damaso didn't look up. Instead he held her hand and laved the centre of her palm, feeling her tiny shudder of reaction and its echo in the tightening of his groin.

It was a warning that the seducer could also be the seduced. But Damaso had no doubt who was in control. He'd keep Marisa here by whatever means worked—by force, if necessary—but far better to convince her she wanted to remain exactly where she was.

'*I* want you to stay.'

'Really?'

He tugged her hand and she stumbled a half-step closer. Damaso took advantage of her momentum to wrap his other arm around her and draw her close. Slowly, with a thoroughness designed to break the strongest will, he pressed his lips to her wrist again, then higher, planting firm kisses along Marisa's forearm. When he got to her elbow she jerked in his hold, her breath a soft gasp.

Instantly the heat drenching his skin stabbed deep into his belly, igniting a fire that spread to his groin.

He wanted her.

Just like that, he wanted her again. Not only the baby—but Marisa, lithe and sexy, in his bed.

From her elbow he took his time tracing a path up her soft flesh till he reached her bare shoulder. He felt her choppy breathing flutter over his throat, the gentle softening of her body in his hold, and triumph filled him.

She'd stay, and on his terms.

Damaso nuzzled the pulse point at the base of her neck and she arched back, giving him unfettered access.

His groin was rock-hard as he gathered her in and kissed his way up her neck to the corner of her mouth.

Desperate hunger rose. Despite the carnal intimacies they'd shared, he'd yet to taste her lips. She'd always distracted him with her body, her caresses. He intended to remedy that.

He turned his head to take her mouth but she wrenched away. Taken by surprise, he wasn't quick enough to catch her back. She broke free and stood, breathing heavily, one palm pressed to her chest as if fearing her heart might catapult free.

Damaso was about to reach for her when his vision

cleared and he read her expression: confusion, desire and fear, all etched starkly on features drawn too tight.

An iron fist crushed his chest, forcing the air from his lungs.

She looked so weary. Yet she drew herself up, as if to repel a hostile takeover. Her chin angled proudly in that familiar tilt, but her face was flushed, and one hand twisted the edge of her top.

Damaso could seduce her. He'd felt her tremble on the brink of surrender. But at what cost?

For the first time in his life, Damaso pulled back from the edge of victory. Not because he didn't want her but because Marisa wasn't ready.

He breathed deep, stunned at the decision he'd made without thinking—putting her needs before his.

Somehow he managed a smile. He watched her eyes widen.

'I have a proposal, Marisa.'

Instantly she stiffened.

'Stay here while we get to know each other. Relax and recuperate till the morning sickness passes. Take the time to rest and don't worry about your uncle. He can't reach you here.' He swept an arm towards the windows. 'Swim, eat, sleep and take all the time you need. Then later we'll talk. In the meantime treat this as a private resort.'

'*Your* private resort.'

He nodded, barely stifling impatience. 'I'll be here. It's my home.' He neglected to mention his apartment in the city and the other residences scattered around the globe. He had no intention of leaving Marisa. How could he seduce her into staying permanently if he wasn't here?

Eyes bright as lasers sized him up and he had the unexpected sensation Marisa knew exactly what he intended. His hands clenched as she surveyed him. Patience wasn't his strong suit.

Finally, she spoke. 'I have one condition. There'll be no

coercion.' Her eyes flashed. 'As your guest, I expect you to respect my privacy. When I want to leave, you won't try to prevent me. I'm here of my own free will. I refuse to have my movements curtailed.'

Damaso inclined his head, wondering how long it would take to convince her it wasn't privacy she craved.

CHAPTER SIX

A SHADOW BLOTTED the sun and Marisa opened her eyes, squinting up from the sun lounger.

'You'll burn if you stay there any longer.' Damaso's voice turned the warning into a seductive samba of delicious sound. That deep, liquid, ultra-masculine voice, the lilt of his accent, sent her nerves into overdrive.

Immediately her drowsy comfort vanished as her heart took up a wild percussion rhythm. Even after weeks on his island she wasn't immune to the sheer sensual appeal of the man. And she'd tried. How she'd tried!

Her mouth dried as she saw he'd stripped off his shirt, his skin dark-gold in the afternoon sun. The board shorts he wore rode low over his hips, drawing the eye to the sculpted perfection of taut muscle.

A whorl of sensation twisted between her legs, making her shift uneasily.

'I put sunscreen on just a while ago.' Her voice sounded reedy, and no wonder. She'd never met a man as physically compelling as Damaso. Despite her efforts to blot their night together from her memory, she remembered exactly how it had felt, pressed up against that glorious body, embraced by those powerful arms.

She'd never thought she'd regret the end of her morning sickness, but after mere weeks it had waned and without its distraction Marisa found herself conscious of Damaso at a deep physical level that disturbed her.

'Here.' Damaso held up a tube of sunscreen, squirting some onto his palm. 'Let me protect you.'

'No!' Why did his words make her think of another sort of protection altogether? One that had already failed?

Heat scored Marisa's cheeks as she reached out and took the tube from him. 'Thanks, but I'll do it myself.' She did *not* need Damaso's hands on her.

Their time on his island had only escalated her awareness of him. He hadn't touched her, but the intensity in his dark eyes whenever they rested on her was proof he hadn't forgotten their night together either. And, despite the way her thoughts chased round in her head as she tried to plot a future for herself and her baby, Marisa found herself too drawn to this almost-stranger.

The last thing she needed was to give up her independence and allow another man power over her. She would rely only on herself now her baby was on its way. She was determined to protect her child from the negative influences she'd experienced, overbearing men included.

At least Damaso hadn't crowded her during these last weeks. Unlike her uncle, whose constant phone and email messages unsettled her.

Marisa slapped the cream on her arms, across her cleavage and down to her midriff and legs.

Still Damaso stood, unmoving. She felt him watching every slide of her palm and felt heat build deep inside. It was as if he was the one touching her flesh, making her nerves tingle in response to his heavy-lidded stare.

'What about your back?'

For answer, Marisa shrugged into a light linen turquoise shirt.

Was that a smile tugging his mouth at the corner?

'You're a very independent woman, Marisa.'

'What's wrong with that?' In her uncle's book, 'independent' had been synonymous with 'troublesome'.

'Absolutely nothing. I admire independence. It can make the difference between life and death.'

Marisa opened her mouth to ask what he meant when he dropped to his knees beside her, hemming her in. They hadn't been this close, close enough for his body to warm hers, for weeks.

Instantly, sexual awareness hummed through her body and effervesced in her bloodstream. The shocking intensity of it dried her automatic protest.

'You missed a bit,' he murmured, bending close.

Then he was touching her, but not in the long, sensuous strokes she'd expected. Instead his brow furrowed with concentration as he painted sun cream across her nose in gentle dabs, as if she were a child.

She didn't feel in the least childlike.

Damaso's eyelashes were long and lustrous, framing deep-set eyes dark as bitter chocolate. The late sun burnished his face and Marisa's breath hissed between her teeth at the force of the longing that pooled deep inside.

For she wanted him. She wanted his touch, his body, and above all his tenderness, with an urgency that appalled her.

Oh yes, he could be tender when it suited him. But she hadn't forgotten how he'd dismissed her after their night together, when she'd begun to wonder if she'd finally found someone who might value her.

Marisa sat back, jerking from his touch.

Never had she craved a man like this. Was it pregnancy hormones, playing havoc with her senses?

He surveyed her steadily, as if she wore her thoughts on her face. But surely he had no idea what she was thinking? She'd learned to hide her thoughts years ago.

Slowly Damaso lifted his hand but this time he swiped the remaining sun cream across his chest in a wide, glistening arc. Marisa swallowed and told herself to look away. But her fascination with his body hadn't abated. How could it, when in the late afternoon light he looked like some gilded deity, an embodiment of raw masculine potency?

'What's that scar?'

If he noticed the wobble in her voice, he didn't show it. Instead he looked down at the neat line that curved at the edge of his ribs.

'A nick from a knife.' His tone was matter-of-fact, just like his shrug.

Marisa tried not to cringe at the idea of a knife slicing that taut, golden flesh.

'And that one?' She'd noticed it the night they'd spent together: a puckered mark near his hip bone that had made her wince even though it was silvered with age.

'Why the curiosity?'

'Why not?' It was better than dwelling on how he made her feel. With him so close, she couldn't get up and move away, not without revealing how he unsettled her. It was a matter of pride that she kept that to herself.

The gleam in his eyes made her wonder if he knew she was looking for distraction. But he didn't look superior, or amused. Instead, he met her regard steadily.

'You want me to marry you but I don't know anything about you,' she prompted.

It was the first time marriage had been mentioned since she'd arrived, as if by common consent they'd agreed to avoid the matter. Marisa wondered if she'd opened a can of worms by mentioning it again.

Would he try to force her hand now she'd brought it up? That was her uncle's tactic—bulldozing through other people's wishes to get what he wanted.

Damaso crossed his arms over his chest, as if contemplating her question. The movement tautened each bunching muscle, highlighting the power in his torso.

Marisa kept her eyes on his face, refusing to be distracted.

'It was another knife.'

'Not the same one?' She frowned.

'No.'

So much for explanation. This was like drawing blood from a stone. 'You got yourself into trouble a lot when you were young?'

Damaso shook his head. 'I got myself *out* of it. There's a difference.'

At her puzzled look, he shrugged and Marisa swallowed quickly. Did he realise how tempted she was to reach out and explore the planes and curves of his naked torso?

Of course he knew. He watched her like a hawk, seeking signs of vulnerability.

'I'm a survivor, Marisa. That's why I'm still here—because I did what it took to look after myself. I never started a fight, but I ended plenty.'

There was no bravado in his words. They were plain, unadorned by vanity.

The realisation sent a trickle of horror down her spine. She'd had her troubles but none had involved fighting for survival against a knife attack.

'It sounds like life was tough.'

Something flickered in his eyes. Something she hadn't seen before. Then he inclined his head a fraction. 'You could say that.'

Abruptly he moved, rising in a single, powerful surge. He leaned down, reaching to help her up, but Marisa looked away, pretending she hadn't seen the gesture.

She'd never been a coward but inviting Damaso's touch was asking for trouble. She stood unaided then turned back to him, putting a pace between them as she did so. Nevertheless, her skin tingled from being so close.

'What about you? What's the scar at the back of your neck?'

Marisa's head jerked up. He couldn't see the scar now; it was covered by her single thick plait. Which meant he'd noted and remembered it from the night they'd spent together. Heat fizzed from her toes to her breasts as their gazes locked. Damaso had spent his time that night learning her body with a thoroughness that had undone her time and again.

'A fall off the beam.'

'The beam?' One eyebrow arched.

'In gymnastics we sometimes perform on a beam, elevated off the ground. This—' her hand went automatically to the spot on her nape just below her hairline '—was an accident when I was learning.'

'You're a gymnast?' He looked at her as if he'd never seen her before.

'Was. Not any more.' Bitterness welled on her tongue. 'I'm too old now to be a top-notch competitor.' But that wasn't why she was no longer involved in the sport she'd adored, why she wasn't even coaching it. She'd come to terms with that years before, so the sudden burst of regret took her by surprise.

Could pregnancy make you maudlin?

Despite her physical wellbeing after these weeks of rest and privacy from prying eyes, Marisa was unable to settle. Her emotions were too close to the surface. Perhaps all those years repressing them were finally catching up with her.

'I think I'll stretch my legs.' She turned and wasn't surprised when Damaso fell into step beside her, shortening his stride to fit hers.

In silence they walked along the soft sand of the beach. Surprisingly, despite the tug of awareness drawing her belly tight, Marisa felt almost comfortable in his company. If only she could forget about Damaso as a lover.

They'd reached the end of the beach when the thoughts she'd been bottling up demanded release.

'Why, Damaso?' She swung round to find him watching. 'Why do you want marriage?' Though he hadn't raised the idea recently, it still pressed down on her. 'Lots of parents don't marry.'

'Yours were married.'

'That's no recommendation.' She didn't bother to hide her bitterness.

'They weren't happy?'

She shrugged and bent to pick up a shell, pearly-pink and delicate on her palm.

'No, they weren't.' She paused, then sighed. Why not tell him? Then maybe he'd understand her reluctance to marry. 'It was an arranged marriage, made for dynastic reasons. My mother was beautiful, gentle, well-born—and rich, of course.' Her mouth twisted. Bengaria's royal family always looked for ways to shore up its wealth. 'My father wasn't a warm man.' She bit her lip. 'They weren't well-matched.' At least, not from what she remembered and the stories she'd heard. Her mother had died so long ago, she only had a few precious memories of her.

'That doesn't mean all marriages are doomed to failure.'

'So, were your parents happy together?' If he'd grown up in a close-knit, loving family, that might explain why he insisted on marriage.

Damaso watched her in silence so long, she felt tension knot between her shoulder blades.

'I doubt it.'

'You don't know?'

'I don't remember my parents.'

'You're an orphan?'

'No need to sound so shocked. I've had a long time to get used it.' His smile was perfunctory, not reaching his eyes.

'Then why marriage? Why not—?'

'Because I *will* be part of my son's life. Or my daughter's. I'm not interested in child support by proxy. My child will have *me* to support them.' His face was tight and implacable.

Marisa shivered. The way he spoke, all their child needed

was *him*. Where was she in his grand scheme? She intended to be there to protect her baby, come what may.

'You don't trust me to be a fit mother, is that it?' Pain bruised her chest as she thought of the scandal that dogged her. These past weeks had opened up emotional wounds she'd thought long buried. 'You're judging me on what you've read in the press.'

Sure, she'd done her share of partying, but the reality wasn't anything like the media's lurid reports. Her notoriety had gained a life of its own, with kiss-and-tell stories by men she'd never even met.

Damaso shook his head. 'I'm not judging you, Marisa. I'm simply saying I won't settle for a long-distance relationship with my own flesh and blood.' She heard the echo of something like yearning in his deep voice.

Was that it? Did he *want* their child, rather than just feel responsible for it? The idea held a powerful appeal. Already she knew she'd do whatever was needed to ensure her baby's well-being. Marisa blinked up at his stern face, looking for signs of softness.

If only she could read him. It was rare that she sensed the man behind his steely reserve. She saw only what he allowed.

How could she trust a man she didn't know?

'What sort of man would I be to walk away from our child and leave all the responsibility on your shoulders?'

He had no idea how much she wanted support now. But responsibility without caring was a dangerous combination. That was how Cyrill had been with her and Stefan and it had poisoned their lives. She had to protect her baby.

'Doesn't our child have a right to both parents?' His eyes searched hers. She felt the force of his stare right to her toes. 'Doesn't it deserve all the security we can give it?'

'Yes, but—'

'There are no buts, Marisa.' Suddenly his hands were on her shoulders, drawing her close enough to feel the ripple of energy radiating from him. 'I refuse to abandon my child to make its own way in the world. I want to keep it safe, nurture it, care for it and protect it from all danger. I want it never to feel alone. Is that a crime?'

Suddenly, it was as if the rigid blankness of a mask had been ripped aside, revealing a man who, far from being cold and remote, was racked by strong feeling. A man whose hands shook with the force of stark emotion she saw in eyes that glittered almost black.

Is that what had happened to him? Had there been no one to protect and care for him?

Marisa thought of the knife wounds. His previous iron-hard composure. His talk of independence as the difference between life and death.

Horror and pity welled. What had this man survived? How long had he been alone as a child?

But she knew better than to ask. Damaso Pires was many things but an open book wasn't one of them. He'd revealed what he had grudgingly, presumably to convince her to accept him.

'Of course it's not a crime.' Her voice held a husky edge as her see-sawing emotions overcame her diffidence. She lifted a hand and planted it on his chest—to comfort and reassure, she told herself. Yet the sharp thud of his heart beneath her palm told her it would take more than that to calm him. She tried not to react to the erotic pleasure of hot, male flesh and crisp chest hair against her palm.

'So you agree.' Triumph blazed in his face. 'Marriage is the only option.'

'I didn't say that.' Marisa backed away, or tried to. His hold on her shoulders stopped her. Those hard fingers flexed and drew her closer, till her hand on his bare torso was all that separated them. His heat encompassed her; the subtle tang of his skin invaded her nostrils, making her recall the salt taste of him the night they'd been lovers. She quivered as a blast of longing rocked her.

'I could persuade you.' His voice dropped to a deep timbre that brushed like raw silk across her skin. His hands softened, smoothing her shoulders and back in a caress that spoke of easy expertise. Marisa bit her lip as her body arched greedily under his touch.

He bent his head, his mouth brushing her hair, his breath hot on her forehead. 'You've kept your distance since we came here, and I've let you pretend, but we both feel the connection. You can't deny it. It's there every time you look at me, every time I look at you. It hasn't gone away.'

His marauding hands swept the curve of her spine and out to her hips. He dragged her close and her breath stopped when she felt his arousal hard against her belly.

She closed her eyes, willing her trembling body to move away. His hold was firm but not unbreakable. She could escape. If she wanted to.

Instead she pressed closer, rising on her toes, bringing them into more intimate contact.

Damaso's breath hissed and Marisa might have felt triumph if she hadn't been swamped by hunger.

He was right. She'd tried to ignore it but this was why she'd been restless. Not just her pregnancy and the quandary over her future. Those were problems for later, eclipsed by the immediacy of her desire for Damaso.

Seeing him daily but keeping her distance had been an exercise in futility. What control she'd clung to now shattered in response to his potent charisma.

Her neck bowed back as he dropped his head and kissed her throat.

'You'd like me to persuade you, wouldn't you? It will be a pleasure for us both. A pleasure we've denied too long.' His mouth, hot and sensual, moved up her neck, kisses becoming tiny, erotic nips that tightened her skin and puckered her nipples. Her hands slid across the planes of his chest, raking slick skin and coarse hair.

Then his hand slid round her hip, delving unerringly in

one quick, sure motion to her feminine core. His fingers
pressed hard against the fabric of her bikini bottom, making a pulse thud hard and quick between her legs.

Her breath snagged again and a wisp of sanity invaded
her clouded mind. It would be so easy to give in. But something about the knowing ease of his action evoked a memory: Andreas, with his practised seduction technique that
she'd been too naïve to recognise. Andreas, who'd used
her for his own ends.

Damaso's mouth dipped from her ear to the sensitive
point at the corner of her jaw, sending every nerve into
tingling ecstasy. Marisa felt him smile knowingly against
her skin.

He knew precisely how to seduce her.

One desperate shove and a backward step and she was
free, her chest heaving, her legs wobbling as if she'd run
for her life. Shock hit her that she'd actually broken away.
Her body screamed with loss now he wasn't touching her.

Marisa watched unguarded emotion flit across Damaso's
features: shock, anger and desire. Determination.

Her heart sank. If he touched her again, she'd be lost;
even knowing his every move was carefully orchestrated
to make her putty in his hands.

It wasn't his seduction she fought but herself. Her face
flamed.

He moved towards her and she shrank away.

Instantly he stopped.

In the silence all she heard was the thunder of blood in
her ears and his ragged breathing.

'Don't.' Her voice was choked and thick. She swallowed
hard. Her gaze dipped to the reddened streaks on his heaving chest. Her nails had scored him.

Marisa's scalp tightened as she saw that reminder of
her unbridled response. It was one thing to give in to lust
when they'd come together as equals. It was another to let

herself be coaxed by a man ruthlessly assessing her weakness to achieve his own agenda.

'Please.' She gasped as the word slipped out, but her pride was already in tatters. Her vision glazed and she wanted to hide her face, ashamed at how easily she'd responded.

Forcing her eyes up, she met his slitted gaze. Marisa drew a shuddering breath. 'If you have any respect for me at all, if you want any possibility of a future together, don't *ever* do that again. Not unless you mean it.'

CHAPTER SEVEN

'DAMASO! IT'S BEEN an age.' The once familiar, sultry voice made him turn. It had been months since Adriana had shared his bed but, looking into her exquisite, model-perfect face, it felt like far longer.

Once he'd been eager to accept the invitation in her sherry-gold eyes. Now he looked and felt nothing, not even an echo of past satisfaction.

She was stunning, from her glossy fall of black hair to her ripe curves poured into a flame-coloured dress that looked like liquid fire in the mood lighting. Even the memory of her enthusiasm for pleasing him did nothing to ignite his interest.

'Adriana.' He inclined his head. 'How are you?'

'All the better for seeing you.' Her smile was a siren's, her hand on his jacket proprietorial.

Annoyance tracked a finger down his spine and he shifted, watching her frown as her hand dropped.

'You're not happy to see me?' Her lips were a seductive scarlet pout.

'It's always a pleasure.' Or it had been, until she'd started hinting about staying in his city penthouse and asking about his movements. Possessive women were guaranteed to dampen his libido.

'But not enough to call me.' Damaso opened his mouth to terminate the encounter but she spoke again, pressing close. 'Forgive me, Damaso. I didn't mean that.'

'There's nothing to forgive.' Yet he didn't respond to the blatant offer in her gaze or the way her body melted against his. He stood straighter. She was beautiful, but...

'I see you have a new friend.' Her voice dipped on the word. 'Aren't you going to introduce me?'

He turned to see Marisa threading her way through the throng. Her gold hair was piled elegantly high, adding inches to her small frame. Or maybe it was the way she held herself. The frothy skirt of her scant, sapphire-blue dress swung jauntily above her knees as she walked, drawing covetous glances.

She looked right at home among Brazil's elite as they celebrated. Marisa was chic, gorgeous and effervescent, thriving on the attention of so many besotted men.

She stopped to exchange a laughing comment with a debonair man in exquisitely tailored formal clothes. A man who obviously cared about looking good at Fashion Week's premier event. He might have been a model with that chiselled jaw shadowed with designer stubble.

The stranger reached out and touched Marisa lightly on the hand.

Damaso felt heat ignite deep inside, sparks shooting through his bloodstream. His fingers tightened on his glass as Marisa smiled at the man now blocking her path.

'Although it seems she's otherwise occupied.' Adriana's voice filtered through the fog of pulsing sound in his ears. 'Your princess appears to know a lot of people.'

Across the room she drew yet another slavering admirer into the conversation. She positively sparkled at the epicentre of male attention.

Damaso slammed his glass onto a nearby table, his fingers flexing.

Marisa was *his*. She mightn't admit it yet but she soon would. He could have forced her to do so just days ago on the island. But that haunted look, her desperate dignity when she'd pleaded to be left alone, had stopped him.

Crazy, when he knew she wanted him.

Now the sight of another man, other *men*, fawning over her made him want to smash his fist into one of them. All because of a woman!

'Damaso? Are you okay?' Adriana touched his hand. 'You're burning up! Are you unwell?'

He wrenched his gaze away to focus on Adriana. She looked worried. Perhaps because it was the first time she or anyone had seen him lose his cool.

He'd brought Marisa to the city to keep her occupied while he worked through what had happened that day on the beach. The feelings Marisa provoked scared Damaso as nothing had since he'd been fifteen and he'd taken on the pair of knife-wielding thugs who'd ruled his squalid neighbourhood.

No other woman got to him the way she did.

His jaw tensed and seconds later he was looming over Marisa's admirers. Conversation faltered and they melted away.

'Damaso.' The husky way Marisa said his name, the way her eyes darkened as she looked up at him, made him want to hoist her over his shoulder and forget any pretensions at being civilised. 'I'm glad you're here.'

'Are you? You seemed to be enjoying yourself.' His jaw clenched.

She shrugged, her smile dying as she read his face. What did she see there? Anger? Possessiveness?

Marisa turned away but he wrapped his fingers around her chin, tipping it so he could read her expression. Long lashes veiled her eyes but her lips trembled. The animation bled from her face and he read weariness there, the hint of shadows beneath her make-up.

'Marisa?' Something swooped in his chest. 'What's wrong? I thought you were enjoying yourself.'

If anything was guaranteed to satisfy the party-girl princess, it was this, one of São Paolo's most chic, most exclusive parties. The guest list was a who's who of beautiful people and the music was an enticing pulse-beat of good times.

'It's…nice. I'm just tired.'

'Tired?' The woman who thrived on celebrations? 'I thought you loved this sort of thing.'

'Sometimes.' Marisa's smile was perfunctory. Damaso stared at the taut line of her bare shoulders. Stunned, he realised she was anything but happy.

She broke his hold and turned away, lifting an outrageously decorated cocktail to her lips.

His hand shot out, grasping her wrist. 'Alcohol isn't good for the baby. Especially the potent cocktails they serve here.'

Marisa's mouth flattened. The hairs at his nape rose as her eyes narrowed to needle sharpness.

'You don't think much of me, do you? Here.' She shoved the fruit-laden cocktail towards him so hard it sloshed over the edges, dripping onto her wrist and down her dress. She paid no heed. 'Go on, taste it.'

Dimly he was aware of the buzz of conversation, the curious stares.

'Go on!' Her lips twisted derisively. 'Or are you afraid it's too strong for you?'

Her eyes blazed as she pushed the neon-tinted straw to his lips. Reluctantly he sucked and swallowed.

'Fruit juice!'

'Amazing, isn't it? Imagine me drinking anything but alcohol, when all the world knows I only quaff champagne.'

Abruptly she let go of the glass and he grabbed it before it fell and shattered. Cold, sticky juice dribbled down his hand.

'I didn't have so much as a sip of wine the whole time I was on your precious island.' Her voice was an acerbic hiss as she leaned close. 'Yet you assume I can't control myself as soon as I hit a party.'

A smile curved Marisa's lips but her eyes were flat. 'I see my reputation precedes me.' She drew in a breath that pushed her breasts high and her shoulders back. 'What else did you think—that I'd be off having sex with some man in a dark corner while you chatted with your friends?' She paused, her eyes widening. 'Or, let me guess, with a couple of men? Is that why you looked like some Neanderthal, stomping over here?'

Damaso stared. The whispered vitriol was so at odds with the smile on her delicate features. Anyone watching would think she was playing up to him rather than tearing strips off him.

It hit him with the force of a bomb exploding that Marisa was an expert at projecting an image. Suddenly his certainties rocked on their foundations.

How real had her enjoyment been when she'd laughed with those guys? Had she been putting on a front?

'I came because I wanted to be with you.'

'I'm sure you did.' Her saccharine tone told him she didn't believe a word. 'You had to tear yourself away from your girlfriend. I assume she *is* a girlfriend?'

Damaso stiffened. 'This isn't the place.' He explained his private life to no one, especially to a woman who somehow managed to make him feel in the wrong. It wasn't a familiar sensation and he didn't like it.

'Of course she is.' Abruptly Marisa dropped her gaze. 'Well, far be it from me to play gooseberry. No doubt I'll see you tomorrow.' She turned away. 'Goodnight, Damaso.'

Her arm was supple and cool beneath his palm as he wrapped his hand around it.

Her eyebrows arched in a fine show of hauteur, as if he defiled her with his touch. She looked as she had the day in the jungle when she'd dismissed him so disdainfully. It irked now as it had then.

He didn't give a damn how superior she acted. He wasn't releasing her.

'Where do you think you're going?'

'Back to your city apartment. Where else?'

She looked like an ice maiden, ready to freeze any male foolish enough to approach.

As if that would stop him! She could pretend all she liked but he knew better.

'Good.' Damaso said. 'I'm ready to leave.'

He tucked her hand through his arm and strode out, oblivious to the curious crowd parting before them.

The short helicopter ride to his penthouse was completed in silence. Marisa sat with her face turned, as if admiring the diamond-bright net of city lights below, her profile calm and aristocratically elegant.

She ignored him, as if he was far beneath her attention. Anger sizzled. He wasn't the ragged kid he'd once been, looking in on society from the outside. He was Damaso Pires. Powerful, secure, in command of his world.

Yet he'd watched those men eat her up with their eyes and rage had consumed him. Rage and jealousy.

The realisation hit him with full force.

He didn't do jealousy.

Damaso shook his head.

He did now.

Is that why he'd been so tactless? He had a reputation for sophistication but tonight he'd felt out of control, trapped in a skin that didn't fit.

The chopper landed and soon they were alone in his apartment.

If he'd thought she'd shy from confrontation, he was wrong. Marisa swung around, hands on hips, before he'd done more than turn on a single lamp. In her glittering stilettos, with sapphires at her throat and her short, couture dress swinging around her delectable legs, she looked like any man's dream made flesh.

But it was her eyes that drew him. Despite their flash of fury, he saw shadows there.

He'd done that.

'I'm sorry.' He'd never said that to any woman. Even now he couldn't quite believe he'd spoken the words. 'I overreacted.'

'You can say that again.' Absurdly her combative attitude made him want to haul her close and comfort her. In the past, he'd have walked away from a woman who wasn't totally compliant. But Marisa hooked him in ways he didn't understand.

'I didn't think you'd been drinking or having sex.' Damaso paused. He could have phrased that better.

'And I'm supposed to be impressed by that?'

'No.' He ploughed a hand through his hair, frustrated that for the first time the words hadn't come out right. Usually persuading a woman was easy.

'I'm tired, Damaso. This can wait.' She turned away.

'No!' He lowered his voice. 'It can't. On the island, we got on well.'

'And?'

'And I want to understand you, Marisa.' It was true. For the first time in his life, he wanted to know a woman.

What did that mean?

'I want you to trust me.' That was better. Women loved talk of trust and emotions.

'Trust?' Her voice was harsh. 'Why should I trust you? We spent one night together. I don't recall *trust* being high on your agenda then.'

She clasped her hands, fingers twisting. The movement made her look young despite her expression of bored unconcern, making him recall his suspicion that she threw up defences to hide pain.

'Your eagerness to leave once you'd had your fill was downright insulting.' Her jaw angled high but didn't disguise the flush of colour across her cheekbones.

An answering rush of heat flooded his belly. Shame? He wasn't familiar with that emotion either.

Whenever he remembered that dawn confrontation, he focused on her disdain. It was easier to concentrate on that than the fact he'd bolted out of her bed, scared by the unaccustomed yearning that had filled him. It wasn't pressing business that had moved him, but the innate knowledge this woman was dangerous to his self-possession in ways he hadn't been ready to confront.

He hadn't stopped to think of her. Now he did.

'I shouldn't have left like that.'

A quick shrug told him it didn't matter to Marisa, but instinct told him she hid her feelings.

'I made a mistake.' Bright blue eyes locked with his and he read her shock, almost as strong as his own, that he'd admitted such a thing. 'But circumstances have changed. It's in both our interests to understand each other better.'

'Like you did at the party when you thought I was boozing and—'

'I was wrong.' His voice grew loud in frustration and he hefted in a deep breath, willing himself to be calm. This was unfamiliar territory but he was determined to see it through. Whatever it took to secure his child.

'I know you hide behind that smile of yours.' As he said it, Damaso realised it was true. How often on the trek had he seen her dazzling her audience with a smile? Yet when she was alone there was an air of sadness about her.

'You're an expert on me now, are you?' Her tone was accusatory but Damaso didn't take the bait. He had her measure, realising instinctively she'd try to alienate him rather than let him close.

But he wanted to be close. How else could he get what he wanted?

'No,' he said slowly, feeling his way. 'But I know the woman the press talks about isn't the real you. I know that far from being shallow you have unplumbed depths.'

It had taken him too long to realise that. His thinking had been muddled by emotion—something new and unfamiliar. Now the inconsistencies that had puzzled him coalesced into a fascinating whole.

How would a woman who was nothing but a shallow socialite have the patience for painstaking photography? He'd seen it engross her in the rainforest and again on his private estate.

Why would such a woman be upset at not being able to work if all she wanted was to party?

Above all, why hadn't she jumped at the chance to marry a billionaire who could buy and sell her quaint little kingdom several times over?

He should have wondered about that when she'd had two full days in the city to shop and had come back to the apartment with just one purchase: the dress she wore tonight.

'I don't claim to know who you are, Marisa.' His voice was raspy with self-disgust at his slowness. 'But I want to.'

'You have a strange way of showing it.' Her clipped words bit into what passed for his conscience. 'You left me as soon as we got to the party.'

It was true. He'd thought it wise to give her space. He'd kept his distance, more or less, these last weeks because crowding her would be counterproductive. Look what happened that afternoon on the beach.

'You were nervous?' He frowned. Marisa was so confident, used to being at the centre of a throng.

'Not nervous. But it would have been nice…' She shrugged, her gaze sliding away. 'Forget it.'

'No.' He paced closer. 'Tell me.'

Her head swung up, her stare impaling him. 'Let's just say fielding pointed questions about our relationship and the pregnancy isn't the best way to relax among strangers.'

'Someone had the gall to ask you about that?' He'd been so caught up in his strategy of giving her the illusion of space he hadn't considered that. He'd believed her status as his guest would protect her.

Guilt squirmed anew in his belly.

What was wrong with him? Usually he was ahead of the game, not six steps behind.

'Not directly.' Her mouth and nose pinched tight. 'But indirectly…' She shrugged, stress plain in her taut frame. 'It wasn't the most comfortable evening.'

'I shouldn't have left you.'

One pale brow arched as if she didn't believe him, then she looked away. 'The fact you took me there, then ostentatiously left me to fend for myself, sent a very particular signal.' Her tone was bitter.

Damaso scowled. '*Who* dared to insult you?'

Her head jerked round and he caught a flicker of surprise in her stare.

'There was no insult,' she said, her voice clipped and her chin high. 'But some of the men—'

'I can imagine.' Damn it. He could imagine all too well.

He swiped a hand round the back of his neck, massaging knotted muscles. If he'd been thinking instead of trying to find the best way forward with Marisa he'd have realised: he'd inadvertently signalled she was fair game for any man on the prowl for a quick fling with a gorgeous woman.

And she was gorgeous. He couldn't drag his eyes from her.

But she wasn't available.

She was *his*.

'I'm sorry.' Ineffectual as they were, he couldn't stop the words rising again to his lips. 'I should have been with you.'

He wasn't used to taking responsibility for anyone but himself. Now he cursed his failure. This woman made him re-evaluate so much he'd taken for granted. It was discomfiting.

Marisa walked to the window, her straight back and

shoulders telling their own story. 'I'm used to fighting my own battles. Tonight was no different.'

But it was—because he'd put her in that situation.

He'd never known guilt or regret before Marisa.

He'd never felt half the things he felt around her.

The laugh would be on him if she knew. She thought his embrace on the beach had been a tactic to seduce her into marrying him.

The truth was he'd wanted Marisa since the day they'd met. He wanted her with a sharp, stabbing hunger that grew daily.

He wanted her body. But he wanted her company too. Her smile. Her attention.

He wanted to keep her safe.

He wanted…

'I'm not used to apologising.' His voice came from just behind her and she shivered as its dark richness slid through her, making a mockery of her defences. 'But, for what it's worth, I really am sorry. For *everything*.'

If she wasn't careful, Damaso would overwhelm her. Over the past weeks she'd seen glimpses in him of a man she could come to care for. Marisa fought desperately to keep her distance but part of her wanted to surrender, give up the fight and be persuaded to trust him.

His hand on her shoulder was firm but gentle and she found herself turning at his insistence. In the soft lighting his eyes were unreadable yet the intensity of his stare made something in her chest tumble over.

'I should never have put you in that situation.' His lips twisted in a grimace. 'I thought to give you a treat.'

'A treat?' Marisa breathed deep. 'I'm not a child.'

But that was how he viewed her. Not surprising, given her reputation. She'd been maligned and vilified and she hadn't exactly led the life of a nun. There'd been a time when living up to her reputation of partying every night had been her life. But she'd bored of it quickly.

'Believe me, Marisa.' His accent thickened deliciously as he stepped squarely into her personal space. 'I know you're not a child.'

Lightning jagged through her at the rough, seductive timbre of his voice. At the feel of his hand warm on her shoulder. He seduced her so easily. Desperation rose. How could she resist him when she wanted so badly to give in?

'I'm not an easy lay, either.' The words shot out as she fought the sizzle of excitement in her blood. If he'd had a fight with his girlfriend, he needn't think he could turn to Marisa to warm his bed.

'I know, *querida*.'

'You're just saying that. At the party—'

'At the party I couldn't see straight for jealousy.'

'Jealousy?' The word stunned her, stealing her voice.

To be jealous, he'd have to care about her. She'd done her homework via the Internet and knew Damaso had a notoriously short attention span when it came to lovers. He thrived on pursuit. He certainly didn't stick around long enough for possessiveness. Yet the idea of him caring, just a little, cracked open a frozen part of her heart. 'You don't have a jealous bone in your body.'

'Don't I?' His mouth turned down in a tight grimace as he loomed close, hemming her in.

'What about this one? It's held you close.' Damaso picked up her hand and placed it on his forearm. She felt his heat through his clothes.

'Or this one.' He slid her hand up his arm and across to his collarbone. Her palm tingled at the contact and tiny ripples of delight fluttered up her arm. 'You slept there, do you remember? Your head on me, your leg over my belly.'

Damaso's voice was hypnotic, drawing her into a place where nothing existed beyond the pair of them and the haze of desire clouding her mind. No, not just desire. A longing for the warmth and…contentment she'd found so briefly with him. She swallowed hard, feeling herself weaken.

'Don't, Damaso.' She yanked but he wouldn't release her hand. Her heart hammered high in her throat as she fought panic.

'Why don't you go to your girlfriend?' Marisa hated the tell-tale way her voice wobbled. It revealed how much she cared.

'She's not my girlfriend.' His ebony gaze captured hers and her breath stalled. 'She stopped being that before I met you. Besides, I have no desire for any other woman.' The way he said it, as if the truth throbbed in his husky tones, made Marisa's knees turn to water.

'Stop it! Don't play these games.' She hated that he could make her feel so vulnerable, so hurt. So needy.

His other hand cupped her jaw, his touch gentle.

'I never play games, Marisa. Ever. Ask anyone—it's not my way.'

'Of course you do.' Her voice was half an octave too high. Was it his touch that did that? Or the fixed way he stared at her mouth? Or the searing tide of need rising inside? She jutted her chin.

'You tried to seduce me just days ago so I'd agree—'

His hand slid over her lips. She breathed in the fresh, salt scent of him, tasted it on her tongue when she swallowed. Why did it affect her so?

'And you told me not to touch you unless I meant it.'

Finally he dragged his hand away but, instead of releasing her, he spread long fingers over her throat, down to her collarbone, where her pulse hammered unevenly.

'I want you, Marisa.' He leaned in so the words caressed her face. 'You have no idea how much.'

She planted both hands on his wide chest and pushed. Nothing happened except her palms moulded to the solid shape of his torso.

'Don't lie. You only want me because I'm carrying your baby.' She'd never found a man she could trust. They were all out for something. And now it wasn't just her wellbeing at stake, but her unborn baby's. She had to keep a clear head for its sake and make the right decisions for its future. 'You want to secure me, that's all—trap me into marriage.'

Something dark and untamed glimmered in his eyes and Marisa's heart leapt against her ribs. Slowly, infinitesimally slowly, his lips curved into a smile that turned her insides to liquid fire. His hands slipped to her shoulders and, despite her caution, his touch on her bare skin melted another layer of her defences.

'It's true that I find the fact you're carrying my child unbelievably erotic.' His voice was husky and inviting. She'd never heard anything so mesmerising.

Damaso moved, one thigh wedging hers apart and pushing up against her. She gasped as she came in contact with his erection. Her inner muscles clenched needily, making a lie of her resistance.

His Adam's apple rose and fell as if he was nervous. Yet she was the one whose nerves were stretched to breaking.

'I mean it this time, Marisa. I want you. I've wanted you from the moment I saw you.' His chest rose as he drew in a shuddering breath. 'This is about more than the baby, or what the world thinks. This is about me and you. Right now, all I care about is how you make me feel, and how I make you feel.'

Despite everything, she wanted to believe him. How she wanted to!

He plucked one of her hands from his chest and planted a kiss at the centre of her palm. Her knees buckled as he sucked at her flesh, sending waves of weakness through her.

'Can't we forget tonight and start again?' His voice was dark, liquid temptation.

'Why?' Marisa clung to his shoulder for support, trying to shore up the distrust that would keep her and her child safe. 'What is it you want?'

'I want us to be just Damaso and Marisa. Simply that.'

Did he have any idea how perfect that sounded? How *real* and uncomplicated? How tempting?

Damaso's head swooped low and, with a sigh, Marisa gave up the battle she'd been losing for so long.

CHAPTER EIGHT

THIS TIME WHEN Damaso bent to kiss her, Marisa lifted her mouth to him, desire filling her. For the first time she didn't turn aside so his lips brushed her face, her throat or the sensitive point behind her ear.

The sensation of his mouth on hers, sure and hard, demanding the response she could no longer stop, blasted her into another world.

Wave upon wave of pleasure crashed through her. She clung to broad shoulders as his marauding mouth demanded more, ever more. Her surrender elicited a growl of satisfaction from Damaso that she felt right through her core as he gathered her close.

She needed this, him, filling her senses, as she couldn't remember needing anything in her life.

Even the night they'd shared—giving in to instinct and reaching out to Damaso in the hope he was different from the rest—Marisa had shied from this particular intimacy. She'd shared her body but kissing on the mouth had been a step too far. It was a boundary she hadn't crossed since Andreas had seduced and betrayed her. In her mind, it had become a symbol of gullibility and defeat.

Yet now she revelled in Damaso's hot, delving kiss, the tangle of tongues and hot breath, the flagrant openness and hunger.

There was no trace of bitterness, only the spicy, addic-

tive taste of Damaso spinning her senses out of control
and a thrill almost of triumph in her effervescent blood.

There was something else she couldn't name, something
strong and pure, that filled her with elation and wonder.

This felt *right*. More than right.

She gave up trying to put a name to it as her mind
fogged.

Marisa clamped her hands to the back of Damaso's head,
revelling in the tangle of his thick, soft hair between her
fingers. She angled her head to give him better access as
he devoured her. His big hands held her close, his body
anchoring her.

If this was defeat, it was glorious.

This kiss wasn't like Andreas's practised moves. Nor
was it like Damaso's earlier attempt to seduce her into
compliance. It was potent, hungry, untamed and it affected
them both equally.

She felt the shudders rake Damaso's big frame as she
moved against him; heard the raw delight in his gasp as
she licked into his mouth; registered the convulsive tightening of his hands at her waist as she pressed even closer,
trying to meld herself with him.

The air sizzled with the charge they generated.

Marisa wasn't surprised when a flash of light flickered
across her closed eyes and a boom that could only be thunder ripped open the night. It was as if the elements had been
triggered by the force of passion unleashed when Damaso
set his mouth on hers.

Something cool and hard hit her bare shoulders; Damaso held her pinioned against the reinforced glass wall
that gave such a spectacular view of the city. The cool glass
made her even more aware of the intense heat of Damaso's
aroused body. He was like a furnace.

Greedily, she wanted that heat for herself.

She dropped her hands to his shoulders and pushed his
jacket back. He growled again, low in his throat, as if an-

noyed at the interruption, but let her go long enough to shake free of the jacket.

When he reached for her an instant later his hands moulded her breasts and she choked on a sigh of satisfaction.

'Yes! That!' Her head arched back against the glass, her breasts thrusting up into his palms as he caressed her, gently at first, then demandingly.

A guttural murmur broke from Damaso's throat. She didn't understand the Portuguese but her body responded to the urgency in his voice.

Her fingers fumbled at his collar, yanking at buttons till her hands met hard flesh. She wanted to bury her face there and taste the salty tang that rose sharp in her nostrils. She was wrestling with another button when Damaso's hands dropped away and she had to bite down hard to stop the mew of disappointment that rose on her lips.

She needed his touch on her body.

She wanted...

With one tremendous heave of shoulders and arms, Damaso ripped his shirt wide, buttons spattering to the floor. In the semi-dark Marisa watched the play of heavy muscles, the ripple of movement all the way down his dark, gold torso as he fought to tear the sleeves away.

Then he was bare-chested, snatching her hands in his and planting them high on his solid pectorals. Her palms tingled as hot flesh and the brush of body hair tickled.

'You're stunning,' she murmured. 'How did you get to look so good?'

He shook his head, his features taut as if fired in metal. 'It's you who's stunning, *querida*. I've never known a more perfect woman.'

'I'm not—'

Damaso's index finger closed her lips and it was a sign of her need that her tongue streaked out to taste him. His eyelids drooped as she licked him and the flesh beneath her hands rippled in spasm.

She did that to him so easily?

'You're perfect for *me*, Marisa.' His voice, thick with that sexy accent, brooked no argument. 'You're exactly what I want.'

Why that statement stilled her soul, Marisa didn't know.

Surely this was about lust? But when Damaso watched her like that, spoke of wanting her and only her, her heart gave a strange little leap. That look, those words, spoke to a part of her she'd kept hidden most of her life—the part that craved love.

'Stop thinking,' he growled, but his touch was gentle as he raised his hands and pulled the pins from her hair so it fell around her bare shoulders, a sensual caress that made her shiver. 'This is just you and me—Marisa and Damaso. Yes?'

His breath warmed her face; his hands dropped to her shoulders then down to the exquisitely tender upper slopes of her breasts. His fingertips traced the sweetheart neckline of her strapless dress, centimetre by slow centimetre, till she could take no more and clapped her hands over his, dragging them down to cup her breasts as she leaned close.

'Say yes, Marisa.'

She licked dry lips and through slitted eyes saw his gaze flicker.

'Yes, Damaso.'

It didn't matter whether she was saying yes to his statement that he wanted her, or his demand to stop thinking. Or whether she was simply urging him not to end the magic shimmering like stormy heat between them.

Whatever this was, she needed it, treasured it. For the first time in her life she felt not just passably pretty but beautiful, inside and out. No one had ever made her feel like this.

She blinked, her mouth hitching up in a tremulous smile

as a glow filled her that had nothing to do with the warmth of Damaso's body or the sultry night.

'Marisa.' His lips touched hers. Outside another crash of thunder shook the air, but it was the tenderness in Damaso's bass voice that made her quake. She leaned into him, her face upturned, her mouth clinging to his. He plunged one hand into her hair, holding her to him as he slowly, thoroughly, savoured the taste of her.

How could a kiss make her weak at the knees? She wobbled in her high heels, clutching Damaso for support.

She half-expected to see a satisfied smile at her reaction when he drew back. Instead she read nothing but taut control that made his features severe.

Then he was gone, dropping silently to his knees before her, hands knotting in the spangled froth of her skirt. She shivered as his hands slid up her bare legs, pushing the fabric up and up. Ripples of excitement shivered along her thighs. She pressed them together as she felt a rush of liquid desire.

Damaso lifted her shirt higher, then higher still, pausing when he saw the little silk bikini panties in aqua that she'd chosen to go with her new dress.

The sight of his dark head close enough for his breath to heat her skin like a phantom touch made excitement twist inside.

He pushed the fabric right up to her breasts, baring her to his gaze.

Marisa's breath laboured. There was something indescribably erotic about the way Damaso knelt at her feet, studying her so intently.

One large hand spread across her stomach, gently stroking till the tide of pleasure rose even higher.

'You're carrying our child in there.' He looked up, midnight eyes transfixing her. Before Marisa could think of anything to say, he leaned in and pressed a kiss to her flesh, then another and another. And all the while his eyes held hers.

She felt…treasured, vulnerable, different. The look on his face, the tenderness of his touch, the raw curl of arousal in her belly, created a moment of rapt awareness. She was a goddess come to life, the embodiment of femininity: creator, mother and seductress combined.

In that moment she felt awe at the miracle happening inside her and an unexpected sliver of hope. Damaso's reaction was genuine. Could this pregnancy really help them forge a relationship?

Damaso's mouth curved up in a smile. His eyes glittered in the soft light as he slid his hand down to the delicate silk of her panties, then with one swift tug dragged them down.

Over the sound of her gasp Marisa heard the whisper of tearing silk. Soft fabric fluttered down her legs.

'They were new!' Could he tell that was a gasp of anticipation, not outrage?

Damaso's smile widened. 'They were in the way.'

Before she could think of a retort, he dipped his head and her body convulsed as he pressed his lips to the centre point of every nerve. One stroke of his tongue and the trembling in her legs became a quaking shudder.

'Damaso!' Her fingers knotted in his hair, holding on, torn between wanting to pull him away and wanting him never to stop. For the storm was inside her now, the blasts of white-hot light jagging right through her again and again until, with a sob of shock, she shattered.

Marisa was tumbling, falling through a darkened sky lit by flashes of brilliant sparks. But she didn't fall. She was cushioned, wrapped close, gentled as she shuddered again and again, her body strung out on ecstasy.

A hand brushed her face and, dazed, she felt wetness. Marisa gulped in air and realised there were tears trickling down her cheeks.

She felt like she'd never recover from the surge of energy that had wracked her. More than delight, this was euphoria.

'I've never...' Her throat closed. How could she explain the depth of what she'd felt—the combination of sensual pleasure and emotional crisis that had created a perfect storm?

'Shh, *minha querida*. It's all right. I have you safe.'

And he did. Even in her bemused state she knew he protected her. Damaso's warmth and strength encompassed her, cocooning her. She burrowed closer, hands clinging.

She sank into soft cushions and Damaso eased away.

'No!' She clutched at him, hands sliding on his solid shoulders. 'Don't leave me.'

'I don't want to crush you.'

Marisa tried and failed to find the energy to lift her eyelids. 'I need you.'

Had she really said that?

For a moment there was no response. Then her limp body was picked up again and she found herself draped across Damaso. He was long and hard and spectacularly aroused.

'Sorry.' Her leg brushed his erection through his trousers and he tensed.

'It's okay. Just relax.'

That was new in her experience of men, she realised foggily. He really *was* putting her first.

She snuggled closer and he tensed, his hands clamping tight as if to stop her moving. Her head was pressed to his chest and she inhaled the delicious scent of his skin. She pressed a kiss there and felt a quiver ripple through him.

Marisa's exhaustion ebbed. She opened her eyes to a close-up view of Damaso's shoulder and taut biceps as he cradled her. She touched the tip of her tongue to his skin, tasting that curious combination of potent male and sea spice.

'Don't!'

'Why not?' She slipped her hand down to cover the heavy bulge in his trousers. His guttural response was part protest, part approval as he jerked hard beneath her.

'Because you're not ready.'

Marisa looked down to see his hand hovering over hers, as if he wanted to pull her away but couldn't quite manage it. She rubbed her hand up his length and saw his fingers clench. Beneath her ear, Damaso's heartbeat quickened.

She smiled. Now the power was hers. 'Let me be the judge of that.'

Deliberately she leaned over and licked his nipple, drawing it into her mouth.

Seconds later she was flat on her back on the sofa, pressed into the cushions by Damaso's big frame. Between them his hand scrabbled at his belt and zip. His other hand caught one of hers above her head.

His mouth closed with hers and this kiss was hunger and heat. It was utterly carnal, Damaso's tongue thrusting and demanding as he pushed her down into the soft upholstery. Wild elation rose as Marisa met each demand and added her own.

She needed Damaso to make her whole. Despite her shattering climax, there was an emptiness at her core only he could fill.

She was gasping when he surged back, rising to strip the last of his clothes and kick his shoes away.

Deep within, every muscle tightened as she surveyed Damaso, bronzed and powerful. Then he moved, shoving her legs wide, settling between them; his arms braced beside her, his breath warm on her lips, his eyes glittering as they ate her up.

He lay still so long she wondered if he'd changed his mind. Or was he waiting to see if she had?

Marisa reached down and took him in her hand, hot silk over rigid strength, and he shuddered.

In one fluid movement he dragged her hand away and

thrust slowly to the place she needed him. Her breath expelled in a sigh.

He moved again, sure and unhurried, as if savouring every sensation.

Next time he withdrew, Marisa tilted her hips, but instead of pressing deeper or harder Damaso took his time, centimetre by slow centimetre.

He was killing her. From complete satiation just minutes ago, remarkably now Marisa trembled with the need for more. She opened her mouth to urge him on then shut it as she registered his knotted brow, hazed in perspiration, the tendons tight to snapping point in his neck and arms, his gritted teeth.

This was killing him too!

'I won't break,' she gasped as he eased away and stroked gently back, teasing her unbearably with the need for more.

His eyes snapped open and she wondered if he saw her clearly. His gaze looked blind.

She planted her hands on his buttocks, feeling the twitch and bunch of muscle as she tried to draw him close, yet he resisted.

His eyes focused and her heart thudded at the look he gave her. Slowly he shook his head. 'The baby.'

He was afraid for the baby?

Marisa blinked. Emotions surged, engulfing her in a pool of warmth. At first she'd told herself she wasn't ready to have a child. More, she was scared about the responsibility of motherhood. But now she knew a certainty as deep as primitive instinct—that she wanted this child and would do anything to protect it.

And so would Damaso. This was connection at a visceral level, more profound than anything she'd ever expected.

He genuinely cared. He'd opened his heart to their unborn baby.

Could he open his heart to her too?

Something fluttered in her chest, her heart throbbing

too fast. A wave of emotion swept her, tumbling her into depths where the only anchor point was Damaso.

Hers. A voice in the deep murmured he was hers.

'The baby will be fine,' she whispered, wondering at the enormity of what she felt.

'How do you know?'

From instinct as old as time.

Marisa guessed he wouldn't be convinced by that. She focused on something more tangible. 'The doctor told me.'

Damaso breathed deep, his body sinking into hers. 'Still…' He shook his head, moving so slowly it was exquisite torture.

He was so obstinate, yet how could she protest when he thought to protect something so precious?

Marisa slipped her hands to his shoulders and hauled herself higher, nuzzling his jaw, kissing his ear, feeling the friction of his chest against her tender breasts. His breathing drew ragged

'I want you now,' she whispered, and bit down hard at the curve between his tanned neck and shoulder.

Damaso juddered, surging hard and high.

'Yes, like that.'

'Marisa.' It was a warning that became a groan as she wrapped her legs tight around him. For an instant he held strong, then his control broke and he surged into her, driving them hard and fast in a compulsive rhythm.

Marisa hugged him tight, filled with a feeling of openness, of protectiveness, as the big, powerful man who'd taken over her world let go and gave himself up to the force of passion.

Sex with Damaso had been spectacular.

Making love with him was indescribably better.

Marisa cradled him, overwhelmed by the belief they had shared something profound. Then, as their rhythm spun out of control, he bent to suckle her breast and both shattered in a climax that tumbled them into a new world.

CHAPTER NINE

THE STORM HAD PASSED, and the steady drum of rain should have lulled Damaso to sleep, yet it eluded him.

Staying with Marisa was too distracting. The rumpled disarray of the guest bedroom, the first one he'd staggered to with her in his arms, proved that.

He'd promised himself he wouldn't touch her after that cataclysmic coming together in the sitting room. He'd assured himself he could hold back from the need to imprint himself on her, taste and hold her. But his willpower had snapped when she'd turned to him again.

He hoped she and the doctor were right. Logic told him sex wouldn't harm the baby, yet he'd felt a profound fear of doing the wrong thing until Marisa had touched him.

He flung up an arm over his head, staring at the dark ceiling. His resolve had been renowned, and unbreakable, until her.

How had she done it? How had she overridden his determination to be gentle?

This wasn't what he'd planned. Granted, he'd wanted her in his bed. What better way to bind her to him than with sex? He'd use any tactic he could to convince her marriage was best.

But now he had her where he wanted her, Damaso realised things weren't so simple.

Tonight hadn't felt like any sex he'd had before.

It hadn't felt like he was in control.

On the contrary, his loss of control had been spectacular.

Then there was the way he'd *felt*. When he'd realised he'd hurt Marisa with his easy assumptions. When he'd knelt and kissed the woman who carried his baby. When she'd come apart so completely, her vulnerability had unravelled something inside, something he couldn't mend.

Each time he'd climaxed, it seemed he'd lost a little of himself in her.

He shifted. That was nonsense.

'Damaso?' Her drowsy voice was like rich, dark honey, sweet and enticing, making his mouth water.

He remembered being twenty-two, a kid from the slums who'd dragged himself into the commercial world with a mix of relentless determination, hard work and luck. He'd put his past behind him and thought he knew it all: how to turn a quick deal, where to find profits, how to satisfy a woman, how to protect himself on streets so much safer and more respectable than the ones he'd known.

He'd been in a breakfast meeting at a hotel. Damaso had followed the other man's lead, eating as they talked so as not to look too eager. He'd taken a bite of bread slathered in honey and had been instantly addicted.

Such a simple thing that most people took for granted. Yet just a taste had the power to drag him straight back to his past, deprived and wanting. To a time when honey had been a luxury he'd only heard of.

'Damaso?' Her hand touched his chest. 'What's wrong?'

He mentally shook himself out of abstraction. 'Nothing.' He paused, realising how abrupt he sounded. 'You must be tired. You should sleep.'

Her hand shifted, fluttering over his ribs, and he sucked in a breath as arousal stirred.

'Would you hold me?' She sounded tentative, unlike the feisty woman who'd faced him down time and again.

Did the past haunt her too?

How little he knew of her.

Silently he reached out and dragged her close, hoisting her leg over his and pushing her head onto his chest. Then he pulled the sheet over them both.

Holding her in his arms felt surprisingly satisfying. She was soft and serene and fitted snugly against him, as if designed for this. His breathing evened to a slow, relaxed rhythm.

'I should never have left you alone at the party.' Naked against him, he realised how tiny she was. She might have energy to burn, and an attitude the size of São Paolo, but that didn't mean she could take on the world alone.

'You've already said that.' Her mouth moved against his chest.

He had, hadn't he? It wasn't like him to dwell on mistakes. Yet he couldn't shake the guilt that he'd made her a target for unwanted attention.

'Nevertheless, I'm sorry. You—'

'Forget it, Damaso. I handled it.'

Damaso firmed his mouth rather than blurt that she shouldn't have needed to handle it.

'I'm sorry I lost my temper with you in public.' She puffed out a breath that warmed his skin. 'That will just fuel public interest.'

An apology from Marisa, too? Perhaps they *were* making progress. Damaso stroked a hand along her spine, enjoying its sensuous curve and the way she arched ever so slightly in response.

'Don't apologise. I should have known better.'

'What? Known I wasn't busy seducing other men and generally behaving badly?' Marisa's voice was a whisper yet he heard the tinge of bitterness she couldn't conceal. 'How could you? That's what everyone expects. It's in all the gossip magazines.'

She lay taut in his arms, that delicious lassitude replaced by tension. Damaso wished now he'd never raised the subject. But he owed her.

'The magazines are wrong.'

'I'd rather not discuss it.' She shifted as if to pull away and he wrapped both arms around her, holding her gently but firmly.

'I *know* they're wrong.'

Marisa stilled. 'You can't know that.'

'But I do.'

'Don't!' She twisted in his hold and he saw her pale face look up at him in the darkness. 'You don't need to pretend.' Her voice was scratchy and over-loud and it made something inside him ache.

'I don't know the details, Marisa. Only you do. But I do know you're not the woman the media paints you.' He paused, wondering how much he should admit. Then he registered the tiny shivers running through her taut frame and went on. 'I believed it at first but the more time I spent with you the more I came to realise you're someone quite different.' He ventured a caress along her bare shoulder. 'Someone I want to know.'

It was true. Marisa intrigued him. More than that, he'd discovered he *liked* her, even when she was prickly and refused to give in to his wishes.

'Why don't you tell me about it?' he murmured.

'Why would I do that?' No mistaking the wariness in her voice.

'Because you're hurting, and talking about it might make you feel better.'

His words surprised even himself. Not that he didn't mean them. It was how much he meant them, how much he wanted to help, that made him frown.

Since when had he been there for anyone? He was a loner. He'd never been in a long-term relationship. He didn't dwell on feelings. Yet here he was, offering a sympathetic ear as if he was the go-to guy for emotional support.

Yet he was sincere.

Another first.

If he wasn't careful this woman would change his life. Already she had him re-thinking so much he'd taken for granted.

'Why? Because you're such a good listener?' Marisa forced lightness into her tone but it didn't quite mask her pain. Her restless fingers moved over his rib cage until he clamped his hand over hers, spreading it wide against his chest. He liked her touch on him.

'I have no idea.' He didn't bother to add he'd never been anyone's confidant. 'Why don't you try me?'

He said no more but waited, slowly stroking the luxurious softness of her hair from her head down her back.

Marisa's words, when they came, surprised him.

'I was fifteen when the press came after me the first time.' Her voice was firm but a little breathless, as if she couldn't fill her lungs. Damaso forced himself to keep up the rhythm of his long strokes.

'There'd been press attention before then, of course. It was inevitable, with us orphaned when we were only ten. Every time we appeared in public they went into a frenzy— the poor little orphan royals.' Bitterness laced her words. 'Not that anyone cared enough to check we were all right.'

Damaso digested that in silence. He knew Marisa's relationship with her uncle, the current king and former regent, was poor, but better not to interrupt her with questions.

She drew a slow breath. 'Things eased a little over the years. Stefan and I got used to the media presence. Then at fifteen I was trying out for the national gymnastics team and suddenly I was in the spotlight again, initially because of the novelty of me competing with "ordinary" girls, and then…'

Damaso waited.

'Someone with an axe to grind fed them a story that I was a slut, partying all night with one guy after another, then playing the privileged prima donna among the rest of the competitors by day.'

'Who was it?'

'Who was what?'

'The person who invented the story.'

She lifted her head and even in the darkness he knew she searched his face. 'You believe me?'

'Of course.' It hadn't occurred to him she might lie. Everything about her, from her repressed emotion to her obvious tension, proclaimed the truth. 'Besides, I doubt you'd have the energy for bed hopping during the competition. Plus, you're anything but a prima donna, despite your pedigree.'

He'd watched her play the icy aristocrat when it suited, but he'd also seen how open and accessible she was to everyone on their tour. In his home she treated his staff with courtesy and genuine friendliness.

Marisa fisted one hand on his chest and propped her chin on it, staring.

'What?' He couldn't read her expression, but felt her gaze like the rasp of sharp metal on his flesh.

'You're the first person apart from Stefan and my coach to believe me.' Her voice had a curious, flat tone that he knew hid more than it revealed. He wondered how it had felt being vilified so publicly at such an age.

At least she'd had her brother.

'Surely your uncle's PR people would have helped?'

Marisa turned, lying again on her side, her face obscured. 'You'd have thought so, wouldn't you?'

Damaso waited, curious.

'They were spectacularly ineffective. But my uncle had never approved of my passion for gymnastics. He thought it unladylike and definitely not suitable for a royal. He disapproved of me being seen in leotards, getting sweaty and dishevelled in public, and especially on live TV. And as for competing with commoners!'

'He ordered his staff not to support you?' Damaso frowned. He knew how hard elite athletes worked. One of his few peers to succeed and, like him, make a life outside the slum where they'd grown up had gone on to represent Brazil at football. He'd seen how much dedication and hard work that took.

Marisa shrugged, her shoulder moving against his chest. 'I never found out. Eventually the gymnastics committee decided it was too counter-productive having me on the team. The press attention was affecting everyone. A week after I turned sixteen, I was dropped from the squad.'

Damaso fought the urge to wrap his arms tight around her. The fact that her voice was devoid of emotion told its own story. His chest tightened.

'Mighty convenient for your uncle.' Had he used the negative press stories to push his own ends?

'That's what Stefan said.' Bitterness coloured Marisa's words. 'But we could never prove anything, no matter what we suspected.'

Damaso stared into the darkness, putting two and two together. He recalled her hatred of the current king, the way even talking with him on the phone had sapped her energy. He remembered her comment about no one bothering to check she and her brother had been well-cared-for once Cyrill had become their guardian. That level of resentment must have deep roots. Was it possible her uncle had actually fostered the press stories?

'It's too late to worry about that now.' She did a good job of sounding matter-of-fact but he heard the undercurrent in her voice.

'Because the damage is done?'

'Sometimes it doesn't matter if a reputation is deserved. It takes on a life of its own.' She shifted against him. 'You'd be amazed how much difference a provocative caption can make to an innocent photo. Anything that didn't fit was seen as me or the palace trying to put a good face on things.'

'So you couldn't win.'

Abruptly Marisa tugged her hand free of his grip and

sat up, her back to him. She anchored the sheet beneath her arms and took her time pushing her hair back from her face.

'I survived.' Her tone was light. 'In fact, being known as a party girl made it easier to flout convention when the fancy took me, which it did. Eventually I learned to enjoy the benefits of notoriety, so it's not all bad. I always get invited to the most *interesting* parties.'

Damaso propped himself on one elbow, trying to read her profile in the darkness. He guessed her physical withdrawal meant he was getting too close for comfort.

Instinct told him Marisa wasn't used to sharing confidences either. She was strong and self-reliant in a way he recognised in himself, despite their dissimilar backgrounds.

Which meant it was time to back off. She didn't want him probing further.

Fat chance. He wanted to know all there was to know about her.

Besides, despite her tone of unconcern he sensed a fragility that intrigued him.

'Except you wanted something more. You said the other day you'd wanted to work but the press exposure stopped you.'

Had she stiffened or did he imagine it?

Her shoulders rose and fell in what passed for a shrug. 'It wouldn't have worked out anyway. I don't have any qualifications or useful skills.' Her chin lifted, reminding him of that morning in the jungle resort when she'd turned from beddable siren to haughty empress in the blink of an eye. Now, he'd swear it was a self-protection mechanism. Had it been that, then, too?

Marisa spoke, distracting him. 'I'm not academically minded. I barely made it through high school. Unless an employer wants someone who can make a perfect curtsey, or chat aimlessly with doddering aristocrats and bland-faced diplomats, my skills aren't exactly in demand.'

'Putting yourself down before someone else does it for you?'

That drew a reaction. She whipped round to face him, her hair flaring wide around her shoulders.

'Just facing facts, Damaso. I'm a realist.'

'Me too.' And what he saw was a woman who'd been badly hurt time and again but conditioned herself not to show it.

He should be grateful she didn't cry on his shoulder.

But he wasn't. Something wild and dark inside clawed with fury at the way she'd been treated. The way she'd been judged and dismissed.

He wanted to grab her uncle and the media piranhas by their collective throats and choke some apologies out of them.

He wanted to crush Marisa in his arms and hold her till the pain went away. She'd probably shove him aside for his trouble. Besides, what did he know of offering comfort?

'Let's end this conversation, Damaso. I've had enough.'

Yet he couldn't leave this.

'So you played up to your reputation. Who wouldn't in the circumstances? But we've already established you're not as promiscuous as the world thinks.'

'Don't forget the drug-taking and high-stakes gambling.' Even in the gloom he saw her chin jut higher.

Damaso tilted his head. Why was she raising those rumours? It was as if she'd changed her mind about sharing herself with him and took refuge instead in her reputation for licence.

'And did you? Snort coke and lose a fortune gambling?'

'I lost my driver's licence just two and a half months ago doing twice the speed limit on the hairpin bends above the palace.'

Two and a half months ago. 'After your brother died?'

'Leave Stefan out of this.' Marisa swung her legs out

of bed but Damaso's hand on her arm shackled her so she couldn't move.

'Let me go. I told you I'd had enough.' Her voice was clipped and condescending and a frisson of long-forgotten shame feathered his spine—as if he was still a ragged slum kid who'd dared to touch a princess with his dirty paw.

His hand gentled.

'You're too fit to be a regular drug user, Marisa. I've seen too many of them to be fooled. And as for gambling… You've had ample opportunity since you arrived but you've shown no interest.' He paused. 'That leaves your reputation with men.'

'I'm hardly a virgin, Damaso.'

For which he was grateful. Sex with Marisa was one of life's high points.

'So how many have there been, Marisa?'

She tugged at his arm but he held firm.

'You can't seriously be asking that.'

'I seriously am.'

For four pulse beats, five, six, she stared him down. Then she leaned towards him, her free hand sliding from his thigh to his groin, closing around his already quickening shaft.

'Enough.' Her voice was a throaty murmur that turned his bones molten.

'Convince me.'

For a flicker of a moment she hesitated. Then she shoved him back on the pillow and bent her head. Long tresses of silk caressed his skin. Her lips were hot and soft, wickedly arousing on his burgeoning flesh.

But something was wrong. Damaso felt the tension in her frame, as if her nerves had been stretched to breaking point.

With a groan of disbelief at what he was about to do, Damaso pushed her away, rolling her onto her back and imprisoning her with the weight of his body.

They lay so close he saw the over-bright glitter of her fine eyes and the uneven twist of her lips.

'Don't *ever* do that unless you want it too.' The idea of her servicing him rather than acting out of shared arousal left a bitter taste on his tongue. For that was what she'd been doing, he was sure of it—trying to distract him.

Slowly, tenderly, he leaned down and planted a kiss at the corner of her mouth, another near her nose, then across her cheek to follow a leisurely trail down her neck. By the time he reached the base of her throat, her pulse was frantic. He kissed her there, ridiculously reassured by this proof of her response.

Marisa wanted him. Had wanted him all along. It was just that she'd tried to side-track him to avoid answering questions.

His hand slipped between her legs as he moved lower to kiss her nipple. With a sigh she tilted her hips and he pressed harder, rewarding her responsiveness.

'How many men, Marisa?'

She stiffened, her indrawn breath a hiss in the darkness.

Damaso feathered teasing kisses across her breast, his fingers delving into her most sensitive place. Marisa's hands threaded through his hair, holding him close.

When she was soft again beneath him he stopped.

'How many?'

'You're a devil, Damaso Pires.'

'So I've been told.' He nipped gently at her breast and watched her arch high. 'How many?' Deliberately he lifted his hand away. Still Marisa didn't admit defeat.

It took ten minutes of delicious pleasure before she finally gave in, by which time Damaso was close to losing the last of his own control.

'Two,' she gasped, her body writhing beneath his.

'Two?' Damaso couldn't believe his ears. Only two men before him?

'Well…one and a half.' She drew him down till he sank between her thighs.

'How can there be a half?' He groaned when he found his voice. She was slowly killing him.

Marisa's eyes opened and for a moment he could have sworn he read pain in her eyes, though it should have been impossible in the darkness.

'The first one seduced me so he could brag about it to his friends. After that…' She looked away. 'After that I found it hard to trust, so the second one didn't get as far as he expected.'

Damaso braced himself high and joined them with one easy move that took him home. 'Not this far?'

'No.'

'But you don't mind…with me?'

Slowly she smiled and the tightness banding his chest fell away.

'I don't mind.' She gasped when he moved and clutched his upper arms. 'I could even…come to quite enjoy it.'

Quite enjoy it!

There was a challenge if ever he'd heard one.

Damaso made absolutely sure she'd more than 'quite enjoyed' herself before he was finished.

Finally she lay limp against him, curled up with her head tucked beneath his chin, her knee between his and her hand flung across him where it had fallen when he'd rolled onto his back.

Her breathing was deep and steady, and he told himself if she dreamed it was of something pleasant, not the disappointments and pain of her past.

Damaso was sure he had only half the story. But that was enough. Duped and betrayed by her first lover, hung out to dry by the uncle who should have protected her, scorned by the world's press… Who'd been on her side?

Her twin, Stefan, who'd died just months ago.

Damaso had assumed the passion he'd shared with

Marisa that first night was the product of two healthy li-
bidos and a wildfire of mutual attraction. Yet he recalled
the blind look on Marisa's face as she'd tackled that notorious climb on the trek. She'd been lost in her own world
and the blankness of her stare had scared him. Had that
been grief driving her?

Had grief pushed her into his arms?

He swallowed and turned his gaze to the first grey fingers of dawn spreading across the sprawling city.

She'd had only one real lover before him.

One!

Damaso would love to think it was his sheer magnetism
that had made her walk into his arms. But did that ring true
with a woman who'd guarded her lack of sexual experience under the eyes of the gloating world press? Who, even
when she partied all night, kept herself apart from casual
sexual encounters?

There'd been a wealth of pain in Marisa's voice as she'd
spoke of the man who'd betrayed her. It made Damaso want
to commit violence.

What had it done to her?

He'd thought Marisa sexy and alluring with a feisty,
'don't give a damn what society thinks' attitude that
matched his.

Instead he'd discovered she was a woman who needed
careful handling. She had so much front it was hard to tell
where the public persona ended and the real woman began.
One thing he knew for sure—behind her masks of hauteur
and unconcern was a woman who felt, and hurt, deeply.

His fingers twitched as she shifted, her breath hazing
his skin. He wanted her again with a hunger he found almost impossible to conquer.

If she'd been the woman he'd first thought, he'd have
had no qualms about waking her.

Instead Marisa was a unique mix of fragility and

strength. A woman who, instinct told him, needed the sort of man he didn't know how to be.

For the first time in years, he felt inadequate. Tension made his jaw ache as he contemplated the tangle that was their relationship.

Damaso wasn't equipped to deal with the nuances of emotional pain. He'd experienced and witnessed so much trauma as a kid he'd all but excised feelings from his life until he'd met Marisa.

He didn't know how to give Marisa what she needed.

Her vulnerability made him feel like a clumsy lout who'd blundered in and smashed what was left of her fragile peace by getting her pregnant.

A better man would regret that.

A better man would support her yet let her go.

Damaso had never been anything like a good man. He was too used to getting his own way. He'd been driven solely by the need to survive, then thrive.

He couldn't bring himself to wish Marisa's pregnancy away. He was too selfish for that.

He wanted his child.

He wanted Marisa.

His hand tightened on her hip and he smiled grimly when she snuggled closer, as if this was where she wanted to be.

Who was he kidding? He'd seduced her, taking advantage of her vulnerability after the stress of the party. He'd used his superior sexual experience to make her open up to him, physically and emotionally.

And he'd continued to push his way into her life, inveigling her to become part of his.

A better man...

No, he'd never be a better man. He was hard, bent on winning at all costs.

His one concession would be that from now on, knowing what he did of Marisa's story, he'd treat her gently, give her space and time to adjust to her new life with him.

He'd learn what he needed to protect her and keep her with him till she wanted to stay by choice.

Even if it meant keeping his distance till she did.

CHAPTER TEN

'BUT YOU CAN'T have considered, Your Highness!'

Marisa leaned back in her cushioned seat and raised one eyebrow, knowing her silence would be like a red rag to a bull. She seethed at the superior attitude taken by the Bengarian ambassador. He was her uncle's crony, and no doubt Cyrill's belief that he could command and she'd obey had rubbed off.

'Think of the publicity,' he urged. 'Think of the gossip. You *have* to be there for the King's coronation.'

'I don't recall anything about that in the constitution.' She should know; she'd been force-fed the document as a child, reminded again and again of her royal obligations and all the ways she didn't measure up.

Languidly she crossed one leg over the other. The ambassador's gaze dropped to her bright sandals, then up past her linen trousers to the gauzy top in tropical shades of lime-green and vivid yellow that she'd picked up just last week in the markets.

No wonder he pursed his lips and frowned. She looked good, she reminded herself. In fact, she looked blooming. Obviously the early stages of pregnancy agreed with her now the sickness had passed. But, though she was dressed with casual chic, she'd refused to don the staid, formal clothes expected of a Bengarian princess.

She wasn't in Bengaria and had no intention of returning.

'If I may say, princess...' he paused long enough for

her to feel bile rise at that unctuous tone '…you have an obligation not only to your country but to your uncle, who sacrificed so much for you. Remember that he raised you.'

'And I'm the woman I am today because of him.' Let him chew on that for a while. When the ambassador simply frowned, she added, 'We've never been close. He'll hardly miss me in the throng.'

No doubt Cyrill would be surrounded by sycophants, people who had feathered their nests from the royal coffers.

'If I may say, Your Highness, that's a very…' He read her expression and paused. 'Unhelpful attitude.'

If he expected that to convince her, he had a lot to learn.

'I wasn't aware anyone expected me to be helpful.' She leaned forward a fraction. 'In fact, I seem to recall being advised months ago that it would be to the country's benefit if I left as quickly and quietly as possible.'

He had the grace to blush.

'Now.' She rose to her feet. 'Thank you for your visit. As always, it's a delight to be brought up to date with the news from Bengaria. But I'm afraid I've another appointment.'

'But you can't just—' She watched him swallow, his Adam's apple bobbing in that scrawny throat. She'd feel sorry for him if she didn't know him for one of Cyrill's yes-men who'd made Stefan's life and her own a nightmare obstacle course of deliberate disruption and sabotage. 'I mean.' He fiddled with his tie as if it were too tight. 'The baby.'

'Baby?' Marisa surveyed him with a glacial stare that would have done Cyrill himself proud.

'Your baby.'

Marisa said nothing. She had no intention of discussing her pregnancy with her uncle's envoy.

'King Cyrill had hoped… That is to say, he's already making arrangements…'

Arrangements to do what? Adopt out her child? Force her to have an abortion? Marisa's flesh crawled.

In the innermost recesses of her heart lurked a fear she might not have what it took to be a good mother. That she might let her child down. But despite her doubts Marisa would face down the King of Bengaria and the whole of his parliament before she let him lay a hand on her child.

'As ever, I'm fascinated by my uncle's plans.' She forced the words beyond the knot of fear in her constricting throat. 'Do tell.'

The ambassador shifted and cleared his throat.

Finally he spoke. 'The King has graciously decided to negotiate a royal match that will give your child legitimacy and save your reputation. He's been in discussion with the Prince of—'

Marisa flung up a hand and the ambassador lapsed into silence. Her stomach heaved as his words penetrated like arrows. This time it took almost a minute before she could speak.

'With someone who is willing to overlook the little matter of another man's child,' she murmured. 'In return for my uncle's help in shoring up his social position.' Her mouth twisted. 'Or is it his wealth? No, don't tell me, I really don't want to know.'

Cyrill must be desperate to contain any possible damage to the royal family's reputation. Or, just as likely, to have some positive media to counteract the negativity his harsh rule was attracting. There was nothing like a royal wedding and a royal baby to turn the tide of public opinion.

But not *her* baby!

Marisa would do anything to ensure her child wasn't a royal pawn. It would grow up as far from palace machinations as possible.

She was determined her child would have what she hadn't: love and a nurturing environment. She'd even begun to wonder if perhaps marriage to Damaso might provide that. He didn't love *her* but she had no doubt he cared for their baby.

Marisa drew a slow breath and dredged the depths of her strength. She felt ridiculously shaky but determined not to show it.

'You can thank my uncle for his concern but I'll be making my own arrangements from now on. Good day.'

Without a second glance, she turned and swept out of the room, the ambassador's protests a vague background babble over the sound of her rough breathing and the blood pulsing in her ears. If she didn't get to the bathroom soon…

'Madam, are you all right?'

It was Ernesto, Damaso's butler-come-bodyguard, assigned to accompany her whenever she went out. For the first time, she was truly thankful for his enormous height and sheer bulk.

'Please make sure the ambassador is escorted from the apartment.' She swallowed convulsively, feeling her insides churn uncomfortably, and pressed her hand to her mouth.

Ernesto hesitated only a split second, concern in his shrewd, dark eyes, then swung away.

'And make sure he doesn't return,' Marisa gasped.

'You'll never see him again, madam.' The bass rumble was ridiculously reassuring as she stumbled to the bathroom.

When she emerged Ernesto appeared with a laden tray.

'Thanks, but I'm not hungry.'

'If you've been unwell you need to replace your fluids. The mint tea will make you feel better.'

At Marisa's stare, he shrugged and put the tray on the coffee table. 'So Beatriz says.'

Great; he and the housekeeper were discussing her health now.

Yet the knowledge soothed rather than annoyed her. Ernesto and Beatriz, like Damaso's staff on the island, were unlike any servants she'd known. They genuinely cared about their employer and, by extension, her.

She wasn't used to being cared for. Stefan and she had shared a bond nothing could sever, but each had had their own pursuits and, once he'd become King, Stefan shouldered new responsibilities.

As for Damaso, Marisa was sure he cared. Look at the way he personally escorted her now to restaurants, dance clubs and parties, never leaving her side. Every night his tender seduction drew her more and more under his spell.

Damaso cared, all right. But whether for her or her baby, she wasn't sure.

She'd spilled her secrets to him, revealing details she'd never shared, and he'd held her and made love to her in such a way, she'd swear he understood.

And yet…

Marisa chewed her lip, confronting the doubts that had racked her since that memorable night when she'd given herself to him again. She'd opened up to Damaso in ways she never had with any man. The catharsis of reliving her past, and giving herself so completely, had left her limp and drained, yet more whole than she'd felt in years. Even the devastating loss of her twin seemed more bearable.

The next morning she'd woken with scratchy eyes and heavy limbs but to a sense of renewed hope. Until she'd found Damaso had left her to sleep late while he went to work.

What had she expected? That he'd stay with her, sharing his own secrets as she'd done hers?

She wasn't so naïve. Yet she'd hoped for *something*. Some breaking down of the barriers between them. At a physical level, the barriers had shattered, but emotionally? It felt like Damaso had retreated even further. She was no closer to knowing him than she'd been a month ago.

Oh, he was tender in bed, and solicitous when they went out. Her mouth twisted as she remembered how he'd staked his claim over her just last night at another exclusive party. Marisa wanted to believe it was because he felt something for her. But more likely he was doing what was necessary to get what he wanted—access to their baby.

The trouble was she longed to trust him as he urged, not just with her body but with her future and her child's. Even with her heart.

She sucked in a sharp, shocked breath.

How could she think like that? She'd loved two people in her life, her mother and her brother, and their deaths had all but shattered her. Loving was far too dangerous.

'Madam?'

Ernesto held out a steaming porcelain cup in his massive hand.

Dragged from her circling thoughts, Marisa accepted the cup. She was too wired to sit and eat the pastries Beatriz had prepared, but she'd learned to appreciate Brazilian mint tea. She lowered her head and inhaled, feeling a modicum of calm ease her tense body.

'I'll go out when I've had this.' She was too restless to stay indoors.

Ernesto nodded. 'By helicopter or car?'

It was on the tip of Marisa's tongue to say she wanted to walk, blocks and blocks through the teeming city. Anything to numb the pain and the trickle of fear the ambassador's words had stirred. Anything to blot out the fear that she was in danger of swapping one gilded cage for another.

She was safe from her uncle's machinations—he couldn't force her into an arranged marriage—but the fact remained she'd let weeks race by without coming up with a plan for her future and the baby's. She needed to decide where they'd live, not drift aimlessly.

A vision of Damaso's private island swam in her brain and her lips curved as she imagined splashing in the shallows with an ebony-haired toddler.

Marisa blinked and sipped her tea. Maybe it would soothe her need for action.

'Where is Damaso today?'

Stupid that her thoughts turned to him so often. He'd never pretended to care for her as anything more than the woman carrying his child. But this last week, despite logic, she'd imagined a deeper connection between them.

How could that be when he left her to her own devices all day? She told herself she was glad he found it so easy to push aside the intimacy of their nights together. Better than having him on hand, reminding her of his demand that they marry.

'He's out in the city.'

'In his office?' Damaso had pointed out the building to Marisa one night on their way to an exclusive club.

'No, madam.'

Ernesto's less than helpful answer made her prick up her ears. Or maybe it was because she sought distraction from her fears.

'I'd like to see him.' She watched over the top of the delicate cup as Ernesto's eyes widened a fraction.

'I'm not sure that's a good idea.'

'Why not?' What was Damaso doing that he wanted to keep from her? He was as close as a clam about his life.

Ernesto hesitated a moment. 'He's in one of the *favelas*.'

'*Favelas*?' Marisa was sure she'd heard the word before.

'Poor neighbourhoods. Where the houses aren't—' He shrugged, his English apparently failing him. 'A slum,' he said finally.

Marisa frowned. That was the last thing she'd expected. She put down her cup and saucer, relieved to have something to divert her from Cyrill's schemes. 'You can take me there.'

'Truly, madam, this isn't a good idea.'

Marisa smiled her sympathy at Ernesto as they negotiated a rutted dirt road, but refused to turn back. Not till she found Damaso and what had brought him here.

On either side of the track rose haphazard buildings,

some solid-looking and painted in bright colours, others looking like they'd been cobbled together with whatever materials could be salvaged. The scent of fires, spicy food and something much less savoury lingered in the air. Marisa plodded on. It wasn't the first place she'd visited that didn't have a reliable sewage system.

They approached a long building painted saffron-yellow and the bodyguards Ernesto had brought fanned out. Ernesto gestured for her to accompany him inside.

The first face she saw was Damaso's. He sat at a battered metal table with a group of men, all sipping coffee out of tiny cups, engrossed in conversation. His proud features were intent as he listened to an older man speak and he leaned back, as if fading into the background. Yet even in casual jeans and shirt he stood out from the rest.

Marisa's breath caught as she drank in the sight of him.

He didn't see her and she stopped just inside the open door, letting her senses adjust.

The building was cavernous. Over behind the men was an indoor basketball court where a bunch of gangly teens played, encouraged by catcalls and cheers.

From a door to the left came the clanging of pots and a delicious savoury scent that could only mean someone was cooking. Over on the far left, she heard music and voices, and straight ahead on a battered wall was tacked a collection of photos.

Instinctively she moved towards the photos, telling herself she hadn't lost her nerve about seeing Damaso. He was busy, and not with some dusky beauty as she'd half-feared.

Marisa wrestled with self-directed anger. Why had it been so imperative she see him? She could deal with her uncle's schemes without running to Damaso for support.

The photos ranged from ordinary snapshots to one or two that made her pulse trip a beat. That one of the skinny teenager, his eyes far too old for his face, his expression weary yet his stance all pugnacious machismo, as if he dared the world to mess with him. The wistful look on the old woman's crinkled face as she watched a young couple in bright colours dance on a cracked concrete floor, their bodies lithe and sinuous, the embodiment of sexual energy.

'What are you doing here, Marisa?'

'Admiring the art.' She didn't turn, preferring not to respond to Damaso's dark tone. 'Some of these are remarkable.'

'You shouldn't have come.' She heard him drag in a breath. 'Ernesto should have known better.'

'Don't blame Ernesto.' She turned and met his shadowed glare, wondering exactly what she'd interrupted. Damaso's tension was palpable. She'd never seen him so edgy. 'He didn't want to bring me here but his orders are to keep me safe, not a prisoner.'

Damaso's nostrils flared as he breathed deep, apparently searching for calm. He couldn't have missed the challenge in her tone. She'd agreed to stay with him, but on condition there was no coercion. Restricting her movements would violate that.

Marisa watched his hands bunch then flex, as if he resisted the urge to pick her up and cart her away. For a moment she was tempted to provoke him, break the invisible barrier that kept him so aloof while she felt impossibly needy.

Hurt and anger warred with pride. This wasn't the place.

'You think this place is safe?' Warning filled his voice.

'I have guards. Besides, you're here.' She didn't add that at least some of the locals had seemed friendly. She hadn't missed the wary looks of others and the way a few figures had skulked away into the shadows as they'd passed.

'That's different.'

Marisa tilted her head to one side, taking in his clenched jaw and the tight line of white around his mouth.

'I can see it is.' She wasn't a fool. 'But I was curious.'

'Now you've seen it, you can leave.'

That didn't even deserve a response. 'What is this place?'

Damaso shoved his hands into his pockets. 'A local gathering place. A community centre, if you like.'

'I'm sorry I interrupted your meeting.' She nodded to the group of seated men watching them.

'We'd finished. Now.' He reached out and took her arm, his hold implacable. 'It's time we left.'

'What are you hiding, Damaso?'

His head jerked back as if she'd slapped him and his gaze slid away. Marisa stared, stunned that her instinct had been right. He was concealing something.

Damaso's lips moved as if he were about to speak but he said nothing. His face took on that spare, hewn look that she'd come to suspect meant he repressed strong feeling.

Instinctively she covered his hand with her own.

'Now I'm here, won't you show me around?' She met his stare openly. 'It's important to you,' she said slowly, 'or you wouldn't be here.' For clearly this wasn't some high-powered finance meeting that would reap more profits for his ever-expanding empire. 'Please?'

His exhalation of breath was a warm gust on her face. 'You're not leaving till I do, are you?'

Marisa shook her head and felt the rock-solid muscle of his arm ease a little against hers.

'Very well.'

Damaso intended the tour to take a brief ten minutes but he'd reckoned without the inevitable interest Marisa aroused. People came out of the woodwork to see the gorgeous blonde Damaso Pires had brought into their midst.

As the clustering numbers grew, tension ratcheted up again. He couldn't believe she was in any danger with him. Yet he couldn't be comfortable with Marisa in these surroundings. It just wasn't right.

To her credit, Marisa wasn't fazed. She was interested in everything, not pushing herself forward, but not afraid to initiate conversation in her halting Portuguese that Damaso for one found endearing and sexy.

They loved her, drawn by her bright energy and enthusiasm. By the way she didn't shy from shaking hands and sharing a joke. By her interest, especially in the kids. Some girls had been having a dance class and showed what they'd learnt. When one, a little over-eager, stumbled when she attempted a cartwheel, Marisa showed her how to place her hands, shucking off her shoes and demonstrating, then helping the little one get the move right.

Damaso smothered a smile. It was the first time he'd seen his security staff lost for words. As for the kids, they regarded her with a mix of awe and acceptance that made him proud and infuriated at the same time.

'This is marvellous.' Marisa smiled up at the woman who'd served her at the large communal table and dipped her spoon back into the bowl that had been set before her. 'Tell me what it's called?'

'Feijoada—black bean stew.' Even now, with the budget to live on champagne and lobster, it was Damaso's favourite dish. In the days when he'd first eaten it, of course, there'd been very little meat to flavour the rich dish, and much more of the rice and beans.

'Do you think Beatriz would make it for us?'

He nodded. Beatriz, like he, had grown up with it.

One of the little girls sidled closer to Marisa on the long bench seat, her eyes wide. At a comment from Marisa in hesitant Portuguese, she grinned and began talking.

Damaso watched them communicate easily with so few words and felt something tighten and twist deep in his belly. He should have known Marisa would take a visit to a poor neighbourhood in her stride. As a princess, she was no doubt used to playing Lady Bountiful, bringing out that practised smile to charm the adoring crowds.

But this was something else. This wasn't stage-managed. He felt the warmth of her personality reach out and encompass him as it enthralled the little girl.

Yet some dark thing inside him rebelled at Marisa being here. It coiled through his gut, clawed through his veins and made him itch to drag her away to the world where she belonged. A world of luxury and ease, where he could take care of her while she nurtured the baby they'd created.

That was it. The baby.

She had to think of the baby's wellbeing, not salve her social conscience visiting the poor.

'It's time we left.'

He rose and held out his hand. Even to his own ears the words were abrupt and he saw startled looks directed his way.

The little girl shrank away as if he'd shouted at her and he felt heat score his cheeks as shame flared. But it couldn't counteract the terrible urgency gnawing at his innards. He had to get Marisa away from here. Now!

It took a lifetime for Marisa to move. His pulse galloped as he watched her turn and say something to the girl that made her grin shyly. Then Marisa rose from her wooden seat with all the grace of an empress. An empress who ignored his outstretched hand with a disdain that knifed right to his chest. Her gaze slid across his face before she turned and thanked first one person and then another for their hospitality.

They clustered around, responding to her warmth and sincerity, and absurdly Damaso felt locked out, as if he were alone in the darkness, cut off from a happiness he hadn't even known he'd grown accustomed to.

Absurd!

He was successful. Sought-after. He had it all, everything he'd ever dreamed of and more.

Yet when Marisa finally made a move to leave, turning not to him but to Ernesto, something fractured inside.

In two strides Damaso was at her side, tugging her arm through his. She stiffened and her smile grew fixed but she didn't pull away.

Good! He'd run out of patience.

CHAPTER ELEVEN

NEITHER SPOKE ON the journey. He was reminded of the night of the party when he'd been jealous and suspicious, when she'd stood up to him and they'd come together in such a conflagration it had melted his self-control.

But this was different. This was… He shook his head, unable to put a name to the vast, nameless void that had taken up residence in this chest the moment he'd seen Marisa in the squalor that had been the only world he'd known.

Nevertheless, he held himself in check as they entered the apartment and Marisa headed to the bedroom they shared.

Did he expect her to pack her things? Was that the source of the tension knotting his belly?

But she merely dropped her bag on the bed and headed for the bathroom. His hand on the door stopped it closing behind her.

'I'd like some privacy while I take a bath.' Her eyes fixed on his left ear and turbulent anger rose in a coiling wave. He would *not* be dismissed.

'Since when have you needed privacy for that?' Deliberately he let his gaze rove her body, lingering on the swift rise and fall of her lush, pert breasts, the narrow waist that always seemed impossibly tiny beneath his hands and the delicious curve of her hips.

'Since now, Damaso.' She turned away, unclasping her

chunky silver bracelet and putting it on a tray beneath the mirror. 'I'm not in the mood for dealing with you.'

'*Dealing* with me?'

His gaze collided with hers in the mirror and he realised when she flinched that he'd shouted.

Her chin inched up as she took a silver and turquoise stud from her ear and let it clatter onto the tray.

'Your disapproval.' Her throat worked and something dragged at his belly, like a plough raking deep and drawing blood. 'You couldn't have made it any clearer that you don't want me meeting your friends. And don't try to tell me those people aren't important to you. Anyone could see they mean more than the social set you party with.'

Her hands worked at the other stud yet she couldn't seem to drag it free.

'But if you think you can just dismiss me as not good enough because I don't have a vocation or a career, because I haven't yet made anything of my life, then you can think again.' Her voice wobbled and the raw furrow in his belly gaped wider, sucking his breath out as pain stabbed.

'I don't—'

'I don't want to hear it, Damaso. Not now.' Finally she loosened the earring and it clattered onto the tray then bounced to the floor. Marisa didn't notice. 'Not while I'm trying to decide whether to leave.'

Her gaze dropped to her watch as she fumbled with the band.

Damaso didn't realise he'd moved till he saw his hand reach out and brush her fingers aside.

He swallowed down a toxic brew of self-disgust and anger as he unclasped her watch and placed it on the crystal tray with her jewellery.

'I don't want you to leave.' For a miracle, the words emerged steadily. He told himself Marisa was grieving and insecure. She'd misunderstood his actions. There was no danger of her leaving. He'd stop her, one way or another.

She shook her head and tendrils of spun gold feathered her cheeks. 'It's too late for that.' She put a hand to his chest and shoved.

As if that would move him. For all her energy, she was tiny. He captured her hand in his, pressing it hard against his chest.

'Marisa, you've got it wrong.' Damaso searched his brain for an explanation. That was it: the child. 'You have to be careful of the baby. In an area like that—'

'Stop it! I don't want to hear any more.' The way her voice suddenly rose silenced him. He'd never heard Marisa so...desperate.

She drew a shuddering breath. 'I know the baby is ultimately all you care about, Damaso, but don't try to dress up what happened today.' Her eyes met his, boring right into his soul. 'You disapproved of me being there because you disapprove of me. It was plain as the nose on your face.'

He saw the bright sheen of her eyes and knew he was on the verge of losing her.

'Disapprove of you?' His laugh was harsh. 'You have no idea.' He crowded her back against the vanity unit, his hands running over her as if learning her body's shape all over again, or ensuring she was whole and unscarred by today's outing.

'Don't try to seduce me, Damaso. It won't work. Not this time.'

He shook his head as he searched for the right words.

'I didn't want you there. It's not safe. It's not...' The words dried as his throat constricted. How could he explain that awful blank fear that had consumed him, seeing her there? His hands balled into straining fists. 'You shouldn't be in such a place.'

'I might have been born a princess, Damaso, but I don't live in an ivory tower.'

'You don't understand.' He hefted a deep breath that didn't fill his lungs. 'It's too dangerous.'

'For the baby. So you say.'

He gripped her shoulders and her startled eyes met his. 'Not just the baby. You too.' He ground the words out past a clenched jaw. 'You have no idea what can happen in a place like that. I needed to protect you, get you away from there.'

His breath sawed loud and fast, competing with the drumming blood in his ears. He knew he held her too tight but he couldn't get his hands to relax.

'What can happen, Damaso?' Her quiet voice penetrated the thunder of his pulse. Her eyes held his and for the first time he had her full attention. Maybe she'd listen now.

Her hand touched his cheek and the delicacy of it against his unshaven jaw reminded him of all the differences between them. Differences he'd ignored until today, when their two worlds had collided with shattering impact.

The palace and the slum.

'Too much.' His voice was hoarse as he ran his hands up and down her back, reassuring himself she really was all right. 'Disease, danger, violence.'

'Those people live there every day.'

'Because they have to. You don't. You're safe here. With me.' He planted a possessive palm over her breast, feeling its warm weight, satisfaction rising at the gasp of delight she couldn't stop.

She was his and he'd protect her.

He pressed closer, his thighs surrounding her, one arm wrapping around her, drawing her to him, while the other slipped under her top and flicked her bra undone.

'Damaso!' Her voice wasn't strident this time. She wasn't fighting him any more, *graças a Deus*. But something in her tone stopped him. Her gaze was steady and serious.

'How do you know so much about the *favelas*?'

He felt his lips hitch up in a mirthless smile. No point

denying it; she'd find out sooner or later, even if it wasn't public knowledge. 'Because it's where I'm from.'

Damaso waited for the shock to show in her eyes. The disgust.

Her hand brushed his cheek again then tunnelled through his hair, pulling his head down till his forehead touched hers.

'The place where we were today?'

Slowly he shook his head and drew another breath into cramped lungs that burned as they expanded. 'Somewhere much worse. It's long gone, bulldozed and redeveloped.'

She said nothing and with each second's silence he waited for her to pull away. Now she knew what he really was.

The opinion of others had never mattered. He'd been too busy clawing his way out of poverty to care about anything but climbing each successive step to success. But Marisa's reaction mattered.

His fingers flexed against her satiny skin, his hands big and rough against her delicate, refined body.

When she did move it took a moment to realise what she was doing. She pulled back but only to haul off her top and bra. Her summer-bright eyes held his as her clothes, a tangle of bright silk, fell to the floor.

'I'm sorry I worried you.' Her voice was high and breathless, but not as oxygen-starved as he was, watching her small hands anchor his much larger ones over her delectable breasts. The warmth of her soft body melted a little of the ice in his veins. Her nipples, firm and peaked, tickled his palms, making his breath ease out on a sigh.

His brain struggled to compute what she was doing. How had they gone from his life in poverty to this?

'You could just have told me.' Her gaze meshed with his as her hand went to the zip of his jeans.

Damaso swallowed hard, giving thanks for the strange yet wonderful impulses of his reckless princess.

* * *

Damaso drowsed at her breast, his hold encompassing her even in sleep. For the first time he hadn't demurred when she'd told him to stay where he was in the languid aftermath of love-making. Instead of rolling aside, he lay spread across her, as if melding himself with her.

For that was how their loving had felt. Slow and deliberate and possessive in a way that made Marisa's throat catch and her heart drum when she remembered it.

Yet there'd been desperation too, in his eyes and in the barely contained power of his body bringing her to ecstasy again and again.

Marisa smiled against his warm skin. She was making up for all those years of sexual abstinence. Just one of the benefits of having a lover like Damaso.

Her smile faded.

What would he be like as a husband?

For the first time she allowed herself to consider the possibility dispassionately, pushing aside her anxiety at the idea of tying herself to any man. Would Damaso be any more controlling than the unknown aristocrat her uncle wanted her to marry?

Damaso was dominant, bossy, used to getting his own way. But he'd never bullied her like her uncle, and no one could accuse him of being cold like her father. The more she knew him, the more she wondered how she'd ever thought him cold. Damaso was hot-blooded and passionate. Not just in bed; when he talked of their baby the glow in his eyes revealed a depth of feeling that had at first scared her and now... Marisa blinked. It soothed her, she realised.

She *liked* him caring so strongly for their baby. It was reassuring to know that if something happened to her Damaso would be there to look after their child.

He made her feel less alone. In the past she'd had Stefan and losing him had devastated her. That tearing hurt had made her even more determined not to open herself up to anyone. But slowly Damaso had been breaking down her barriers. Now he was *there*, firmly planted in her life, pushing the yawning chasm of darkness back till she no longer felt on a precipice of pain.

He tried to protect her too. Damaso was always at her side now at any society event.

Then there was his reaction to her visit today.

Marisa's brow puckered, remembering his stark expression when he'd spoken of the danger. She remembered the scars on his body and how he'd got them. Yet instinct told her this was about more than some physical threat.

Clearly Damaso had reacted on a visceral level. Perhaps, if she understood him, she might trust him enough to accept what he offered.

Shame bit. She'd been focused on her independence and on grappling with the changes this pregnancy would bring. She'd been self-absorbed, every bit as selfish as the press painted her.

Oh, she'd been curious about Damaso, always fascinated by the man who'd slowly begun to reveal himself to her. But she'd never pushed to delve deeper. True, he was taciturn about his past, always focusing on the here and now or the future. But she could have tried harder. He'd been genuinely sympathetic when she'd told him about herself. What had she given in return?

Damaso was inextricably part of her life now. As her child's father and more, much more.

Marisa swept her hands over his broad shoulders, marvelling at the closeness she felt, the bond that wasn't just to do with the baby but with them as a couple. She hugged him tight.

A couple. It was a new concept.

Maybe for the first time she had, after all, found a man she could trust.

* * *

Her second trip to the *favela* tested his temper but not in the way she'd expected.

'I thought we'd agreed it was too risky for you to spend time there.' He stood, tie wrenched undone at his throat, shirt sleeves rolled up to reveal strong, sinewy arms and fists buried in his pockets. His brow was like a thunder-cloud as he watched her from the door to the private roof-garden.

He looked vital and sexy, and something clenched hard in Marisa's stomach as she met his scowl. Kneeling as she was, she had to crane her neck to survey his long, power-ful body but it was worth it. She had to scotch the impulse to go to him and let him kiss her. If she did there was a danger she might cave in rather than stand her ground. He was that persuasive.

'I listened to what you said, Damaso, which is why I agreed when Ernesto insisted on taking other guards.' Pri-vately she thought the security precautions overkill but she'd fight one battle at a time.

'He should never have allowed you—'

'We've been over that.' She lifted one wet hand and pushed her hair off her face with the back of her wrist. 'Don't you dare bully Ernesto. He was just doing his job. If he'd tried to stop me I'd have gone without him.' It wouldn't be the first time she'd evaded professional minders.

'I was safe. And I was welcome.' The generous welcome she'd received had been heart-warming. 'I helped a little with one of the classes and talked to the co-ordinator about reviving the photography project.'

Marisa wasn't qualified to teach but knew a little about that. Enough to foster the efforts of the few youngsters who'd taken part in an earlier program to develop photog-raphy skills. The co-ordinator had talked enthusiastically about career-building. For Marisa, though, it was about helping others find the peace and satisfaction she herself felt looking at the world through the lens of a camera.

'That would mean going there regularly!'

Marisa didn't bother answering. She'd known Damaso would be angry but she was determined to proceed. For herself, because selfishly she clung to the idea she could be useful, and for the kids.

Was it preposterous to think she also did this for Damaso? For the orphan he'd been, struggling to survive in a tough environment? Who had helped him? Ever since he'd let her glimpse the pain of his past, she'd found herself imagining him on streets like those she'd walked today. Was it hardship that had honed him into the man he was— ruthless and single-minded, guarding his heart so closely?

She groped for the soap that had fallen into the basin of warm water, feeling it slippery on her palm.

'And it doesn't explain what you're doing with *that*.' Damaso's voice dropped to resonant disapproval.

Marisa surveyed the skinny dog she held by the scruff of the neck. It trembled as it stood in the big basin of tepid water but made no move to escape.

'He needed a home.'

'Not this home.' Damaso stalked across to stand over them, his long shadow falling on the pup.

'If it's a problem, I'll take him elsewhere.' She paused, more nervous than she'd expected now it came to it. She was sure of her ground, wasn't she? Yet if he called her bluff… No, that wouldn't happen. 'I'm sure I'll have no trouble finding somewhere to stay where dogs are welcome.'

The silence was so loud it reverberated in her ears.

'Is this you making a point, Marisa?'

She looked up to see him watching her through narrowed eyes.

'No one ever accused me of subtlety. But, no, it's not.

The poor thing was in need of a home, that's all. And I...'
She shrugged and lathered the dog's fur. 'It seemed right.'

She could have said more—about how she'd always
wanted a pet, about her growing desire to care for something after being so alone. But in truth she'd looked into
those hopeful, canine eyes and felt a twang of fellow feeling. Here was another outcast, someone who didn't fit and
didn't expect to be wanted.

Damaso moved closer and the dog shivered. Marisa put
out a soothing hand to gentle it.

'I can find a good home for it. It doesn't belong here.'
His offer surprised her and she jerked her gaze back up.

'Thank you.' His expression told her he didn't want anything to do with the dog. 'I appreciate it. But I want to look
after him myself.'

If she could do a good job of looking after a dog, perhaps
she could work her way up to caring for a baby. Besides,
he trusted her; she couldn't let him down now.

Damaso's gaze shifted to the dog and Marisa sucked
in her breath at the antipathy in that stare. No wonder the
poor thing was shaking.

'You can't be serious. Look at it! It's a mongrel. If you
must have a dog, at least let me get one for you from a
breeder.'

'A pure-bred, you mean?' Her hand slowed and she put
the soap down.

'Why not? Surely that's more fitting?'

'For a princess?'

'It's what you are, Marisa. There's no point pretending
otherwise.'

'Is that what you think I'm doing? Pretending to be
someone I'm not?' Hurt scored her voice. Is that what he
thought she'd been doing on her visit today?

'Of course not.' He strode away then spun on his foot.
'Just look at it. No matter what you do, it will always be a
slum-bred mongrel.'

The words echoed in her head. Marisa read Damaso's taut features, the rigidity of his big frame. She'd only seen him like this once before, when he'd been so adamant she stay away from the *favela*.

Because he was ashamed of where and how he'd grown up?

It didn't seem possible. She'd never met a man more grounded and self-assured than Damaso.

Yet he harped so often about her royal lineage, as if that mattered a scrap compared with character.

'It's probably carrying disease too.'

Marisa shook her head and reached for a bucket of rinse water. 'I've taken Max to the vet and he's had the all clear.'

'Max?'

Marisa tipped the water gently over the dog and reached for another bucket.

'He reminds me of my great-uncle, Prince Maximilian.' Despite the tension in the air, she smiled. 'Same long nose, same big brown eyes.'

Great-Uncle Max had been a scholar, happier with his books than playing politics, but he'd always had time for Marisa, even hiding her when she'd played hooky from history classes. But then Uncle Max had had a way of bringing the past alive in a way her teachers didn't.

She blinked hard, surprised to feel her eyes prickle at the memory of those brief snatches of childhood happiness.

Damaso watched her intently from beneath lowered brows, his gaze shifting from her to the dog.

'You really do care about the animal.' There was a thread of shock in Damaso's voice.

Admittedly Max, drenched and bony, wasn't the most handsome dog around, but he had character.

Marisa shrugged and finished rinsing off the soap suds. Even she was surprised at how quickly she and Max had bonded. She couldn't send him back to the streets, not now. Despite what Damaso thought, this wasn't some deliberate

test of his forbearance. It had been an impulsive decision
that she'd known instinctively was right.

'Very well, it can stay, but I don't want to see it inside.'

Damaso turned back into the apartment before Marisa
could thank him, but a tiny glow of heat flared inside and
spread. 'Hear that, Max?' She reached for the towel Beatriz had provided and began to dry him. 'You can stay.'

They'd both found sanctuary with Damaso. His reasons
weren't purely altruistic, since he was angling to convince
her to stay long-term. But Marisa had experienced enough
duplicity to know actions did count louder than words.

She wondered if Damaso had any idea how much his
generosity meant.

CHAPTER TWELVE

'THE CITY LOOKS wonderful at this time of night.'

Damaso watched across the table as Marisa leaned back in her seat, sipping from a goblet of sparkling water as she surveyed the panorama. The view from his private roof garden had always been spectacular but he'd never found time to appreciate it until Marisa had moved in with him.

There were a lot of things he hadn't fully appreciated.

His gaze roved her golden hair, loose over her shoulders, the dreamy expression in her eyes and the ripe lushness of her breasts beneath the filmy, sea-green top.

He'd known many beautiful women but none of them had made the breath seize in his lungs or his chest contract.

'I love this city.' Her smile widened.

'You do?' He raised his beer glass to his lips rather than reveal how pleased he was by her announcement. 'Why?'

She shrugged. 'It's vibrant, so different from Bengaria. There's so much happening, and the Paulistanos have such energy.' She looked at the table between them and the remains of the meal Beatriz had served. Her hand slipped to her stomach. 'Plus, I love the food. If I'm not careful, I'll be fat as butter by the time the baby's born.'

Damaso shook his head. Only a lover would know she'd put on a mere couple of pounds during her pregnancy. As that had only made her pert breasts fuller, he wasn't complaining.

He tried to imagine her swollen with his child and a stab of possessiveness seared through him.

Just as well she enjoyed the life here. He wasn't letting her go, even if she had yet to come to terms with the fact.

'My uncle has invited me to his coronation.'

Damaso stilled, fingers tightening on his glass. 'You're not going? You hate Cyrill.'

'I don't know,' she said slowly. 'At first I didn't intend to, but I'm wondering. I don't want to see *him*, but sometimes it feels like I'm hiding here, afraid to go home and face the music.' Her jaw angled higher in that determined way she had. 'I don't like that.'

He frowned. 'I thought you told me Bengaria wasn't home.'

She shrugged. 'I wasn't happy there but it's in my blood.'

'So what are you thinking? That you owe it to your uncle to hold his hand through the coronation? You want to play happy families with him?'

Marisa's mouth turned down. 'Not that. I just wondered if it wasn't better to face them all.'

'Why?' He leaned close. 'So they can lecture you about your irresponsible behaviour in getting pregnant?'

Damaso silently cursed his straight talking when she winced and looked away. Yet everything in him rose up in protest at the idea of her leaving, even for a short visit.

If she went to Bengaria, what was to stop her staying? Certainly not love for him. They had great sex, and she seemed as content as he to spend time together, but nothing she'd done or said indicated she'd fallen for him.

His pulse quickened. Was that what he wanted—Marisa head over heels in love with him?

That would solve all his problems. Marisa in love would be a Marisa committed to staying. It would hardly matter that he didn't know the first thing about love or relationships. She had enough warmth for the pair of them, the three of them.

In his bleaker moments he wondered if he had it in him to learn how to love.

'You think going back would be a mistake?'

Damaso paused, conscious that this was the first time Marisa had asked his advice.

Was it wishful thinking, or was this a turning point?

Stifling a triumphant smile, he tempered his words, cautious not to sound dictatorial like her uncle. Marisa could be persuaded, not ordered. He'd learned that quickly. Better if she thought staying was her decision.

'I think you need to consider how your uncle will try to use your presence to his advantage. Do you want to be his dupe?'

The tightening of her lips told him he'd struck a chord. Marisa was proud. She wouldn't want to play into the hands of a man she despised.

'Why don't you decide later?' Damaso knew better than to push his advantage. 'Tell me about your day,' he urged. 'I haven't seen you for hours.'

There was another first. He looked forward to their evenings together, discussing the day's events. It was something he'd never experienced with anyone else.

'I took the kids to the gallery.' She leaned forward, her eyes shining, and he congratulated himself on hitting on something to take her mind off Cyrill. 'You should have seen how excited they were. Silvio spent a couple of hours with them and they drank it all in.'

'I'm sure they did.' He remembered the first time he'd left the neighbourhood where he'd grown up. The excitement and fear. The children Marisa had taken under her wing with her photography classes would never have dreamed of anything as plush as Silvio's gallery. As the most successful photographer in South America, and probably beyond, he could name his own price for his work.

'I have to thank you for introducing me to him.' Marisa's hand found his and he threaded his fingers through hers, marvelling again at how something so delicate and soft could be so strong. 'I've admired his work for years, but...'

'No need to thank me.' They'd been over that weeks ago, when Damaso had taken her to Silvio's gallery. She'd been in seventh heaven, so rapt in Silvio's artwork that the photographer had taken an immediate shine to her. They'd been thick as thieves ever since.

Damaso might have been jealous of the way Marisa spoke so often of Silvio, except it was his work she was interested in, and her responsiveness to Damaso was unabated.

Anything that strengthened Marisa's ties to Brazil, such as her friendship with Silvio, was something Damaso encouraged. Besides, watching her enthusiasm as she talked about how her young photographers had blossomed at this rare opportunity was like watching a flower open to the sun.

Something stirred and eddied in his chest as a smile lit her face.

She was so happy.

It was only now, seeing her excitement, hearing her enthusiasm, that he realised how she'd changed. She'd always seemed vibrantly alive. But now Damaso knew her well enough to recognise that in the past some of her vivacity had been a persona, like clothing worn to project an image.

Damaso knew about that. In the early days he'd acted the part of successful businessman even when he'd had barely enough money to feed himself. He'd poured everything into becoming the man he was determined to be. Convincing others to trust him had been part of that.

Seeing Marisa glow from within, he realised the woman he'd met in the jungle had been going through the motions, despite her bright, engaging smile. Grief had muted her.

The real Marisa was stunning, almost incandescent. The sort of woman to draw men, like moths to flame.

He'd never felt as lucky as he did now, despite the niggle

of doubt, because she hadn't yet agreed to marry him. His hand tightened on his beer and he took another swallow.

'Silvio offered to meet them again and look at their work. Isn't that fantastic?'

'Fantastic,' he murmured. 'But they're already learning a lot from you.'

Marisa's sessions with the kids had been a huge success. He'd heard from a number of sources how enthusiastically not only the teens but their parents too had responded, plus he'd seen the results.

Marisa shook her head. 'I'm an amateur.'

'A talented amateur.'

'Flatterer.' Her eyes danced and again Damaso felt familiar heat in his belly.

It still unsettled him, knowing Marisa was going to the *favela*. He wanted to lock her away so she couldn't be hurt. But seeing her now, he knew he was right to hold back.

Movement at the end of the table caught his eye as the mongrel dog sidled up to her chair. With a fond glance, Marisa reached down and stroked its head, then tickled it under the chin. The dog closed its eyes in ecstasy and leaned closer.

Damaso's mouth thinned. What did she see in it? Watching her delicate fingers ruffle its fur just seemed wrong. He could give her a dog bred specifically to be a perfect companion. Instead she settled for a ragged mongrel that looked like it belonged on the streets, no matter how much she bathed and brushed it.

Marisa caught the direction of his stare.

'Why don't you like him?' Marisa's head tilted to one side in that characteristic look of enquiry.

Damaso shrugged. 'I don't have time for pets.'

Her silence told him she didn't buy that.

'But it's not just any pet, is it? You offered to get me another dog to replace him.' She paused, studying him carefully. 'It's something about Max.'

Damaso said nothing. He'd agreed to let the animal stay. What more could she want?

'It's because of where he comes from, isn't it?' She leaned across the table. 'Is that why you can't bear to look at him?'

Marisa sank back in her chair, her fingers burrowing deep into Max's fur as understanding hit out of the blue.

She'd been in Damaso's island home, and here in his city penthouse, and only now realised that, while he didn't display his wealth with crass ostentation, everything was of the highest quality materials and craftsmanship.

Nor had she seen anything with the patina of age— no antiques, nothing second-hand. Everything was pristine, as if it had been made yesterday. Many of the pieces had been created by world-renowned artisans, from the artwork to the furniture, and of course the architectural design of the buildings.

The same applied to his luxury hotel in the Andes. Only the best, nothing ordinary or even old.

Terrible foreboding tingled down Marisa's backbone and she straightened, putting down her glass. She put both hands on the table, as if to draw strength from the polished metal.

'What is it?' No fool, Damaso had picked up her sudden mood change, from curiosity to stomach-curdling distress.

'Everything you own is top of the range, isn't it? Only the absolute best.' Even the kitchen where Beatriz presided would do a Michelin-starred restaurant proud.

'What of it? I can afford it and I appreciate quality.'

'Quality.' The word tasted bitter. It had been a favourite of her uncle's, especially when he berated her for mixing with the 'wrong' sort of people.

Marisa swallowed hard, telling herself she was mistaken. Yet nothing could dispel the suspicion now it had surfaced.

'Marisa? What is it?' Damaso's brows drew down in a

frown that, instead of marring his features, emphasised their adamantine charisma. 'There's nothing wrong with owning beautiful things.'

'It depends why you want them.'

For long seconds she fought the sickening idea, but it was no good. Finally the words poured out. 'Is that why you're so insistent marriage is our only option?'

His eyes widened. 'What are you talking about? I don't see the connection.'

'I come with a pedigree. Having a royal title means I'm *quality*.' She dragged in a breath that didn't fill her lungs and stared into his expressionless features, looking for some sign she was wrong.

'You think I'm hung up on a royal title?'

Marisa pressed her palms harder into the cool metal of the table.

'I know you want my baby.' How stark the words sounded, crashing through the truce they'd built so painstakingly. Yet she couldn't shy away from the truth. 'But maybe there's more to it.'

Inside a voice cried that she was wrong. That Damaso was different. But how could she trust her judgement on this? She'd been wrong before.

'What do you mean?' He sat so still she knew he exercised steely control.

'Your reaction to me visiting the *favela* is out of proportion to the danger, especially given the bodyguards you insist on.' Something flashed in his eyes and her heart dived. 'I think the reason you don't like Max is because he comes from a slum.'

Marisa paused and waited but Damaso said nothing. The only animation was the tic of a pulse in his clenched jaw.

'Tell me the truth, Damaso.' She sucked in an unsteady breath. 'Do you want me as a trophy to add to your collection? After all, a princess comes pretty close to the top of the heap if you care for titles and *quality*.' Try as she might, she couldn't stop herself gagging on the word.

She'd thought she knew Damaso, that they shared something fragile and precious, something that made her happier than she could ever remember being. She'd begun to trust him, to hope.

'If you want to hide from your past and pretend it never happened, saddling yourself with me isn't the way to do it. Remember, most people don't think of me as a quality item. I'm sullied goods.'

'Don't talk like that!' He lunged across the table, his hand slamming down on hers, holding her captive. His dark eyes sparked, as if she'd tapped into a live volcano. 'Don't ever say such things about yourself.'

Marisa tried to look down her nose at him. She'd learned the trick from her haughty uncle and it had proven invaluable when she'd wanted to hide private hurt. But it didn't work now. Somehow she'd lost the knack—or Damaso had burrowed too far beneath her defences.

Desperation added an edge to her voice. 'Why not? It's what everyone thinks, even if they don't say it to my face. You might consider me the royal icing on the cake of your success, something special to add to your collection.' She swept a glance beyond the exquisite hand-forged table and chairs to the sculptures scattered through his private garden that would have done any national gallery proud. She gulped, her throat raw. 'But I'm flawed, remember? That detracts from my value.'

He moved so fast, her head spun. Large hands cupped her cheeks, turning her head up to where he towered above her.

'Don't ever say that again.' He bit the words out, his face drawn as if in pain, his eyes furious. Oddly, though, his hands felt gentle against her chilled flesh. 'I won't have it, do you hear? You're so wrong.'

Damaso looked down into her wide, drenched eyes and

had never felt so furious or helpless. Why couldn't she see what he saw? A woman worthy of admiration and respect. A woman unlike any he'd known.

Marisa blinked, refusing to let the glittering tears fall. It was typical that even now she put on a show of pride.

Yet the reminder of her vulnerability tore through him. Damaso dropped to his knees beside her seat, only vaguely aware of the dog darting out of the way.

He felt as if something had broken inside him when he saw her hurting so badly.

Leaning close, he drew in the familiar scent of green apples and sweet woman. Every instinct clamoured for him to haul her to him and make love to her till he blotted all doubt from her mind. But she needed to hear the words.

He swallowed hard. 'You've begun to believe your uncle's lies.' He saw her eyes widen. 'He's always put you down, tried to restrict you and mould you, but you didn't let him. You were too strong for that. Don't let him win now by undermining your confidence.'

Damaso paused, letting her digest that.

'For the record, any man would be proud to have you as his wife. And not because of your royal blood. You're bright and caring, not to mention beautiful. You're intelligent, fun and good company. You must have noticed how everyone wants to be with you.'

It was painful to watch the doubt still clouding her eyes. 'You know how much I want you, Marisa.' He grabbed one of her hands and planted it on his chest so she could feel the way his heart sprinted.

'You want my baby,' she said slowly. 'But do you want me or the cachet of marrying into royalty? If social status is important, that would be some achievement for a boy from the slums.'

'I want us to be a family.' The words rumbled up from some place deep inside. *Family.* The strength of his need for Marisa and their child undid him. 'I want to be with our child and I want to be with *you*. You know that. You felt the chemistry between us from the first.'

'You mean the sex?' She breathed deep and he had the impression she had to force the words out. 'People don't marry for that. What other reason could you have?'

Damaso looked into those brilliant, guarded eyes and realisation slammed into him. He'd seen that yearning look before, years ago, when he'd broken off with a lover who'd begun to want too much.

Perhaps Marisa didn't know it, but it was emotion she craved from him. Shunned by her family and her country, Marisa needed love.

A lead weight plummeted through his gut.

Marisa wanted the one thing he didn't know how to give.

For a moment he thought of lying, trotting out the trite words that would salve her pain. But Damaso couldn't do it. She'd see straight through the lie and convince herself it was for the worst possible reason.

Panic rocked him. He'd do so much for her. Anything except let her go.

He had nothing to give her except the truth.

Damaso reached for her hand and closed his fingers around it. Her other hand was still plastered against his chest. Did she notice how his heart raced?

'You think I surround myself with beautiful things to escape my past?' He drew a harsh breath and forced himself to go on, ignoring a lifetime's instinct for privacy. He had to share what he'd hidden from the world or risk losing Marisa.

'You could be right,' he said eventually and heard her hiss of indrawn breath. Her hands twitched in his and he tightened his hold implacably, refusing to let her pull away. He stroked his thumb over hers where it rested on his chest.

'I started with nothing but the clothes on my back.' He grimaced. 'I was determined to shake off the dust of what passed for my home as soon as I could. By sheer hard work and some very lucky breaks I succeeded and, believe me, I never once looked back with regret. As soon as I could, I surrounded myself with the trappings of success. Sharp clothes, swanky office, beautiful women.'

At Marisa's expression he smiled, buoyed a little at what he hoped might be jealousy. 'Why wouldn't I? I'm only human.'

'I'm not judging.'

He shrugged. 'I'm not ashamed of enjoying success. My priority was always to plough back profits into the business and have enough capital to optimise any opportunity. That's how I moved from running errands to being a tourist guide and then owner of a tour company. We became known for delivering the best vacation experiences, taking people to places others couldn't or wouldn't.

'As the profits grew, my interests spread across a range of ventures. I'd always had a taste for clean clothes and comfortable housing and saw no reason not to indulge myself.'

He watched Marisa digest that. 'Along the way I developed an interest in modern art, possibly from visiting so many galleries. When I got money, I bought pieces I liked. Just as I bought cars and houses that appealed.'

Damaso paused, remembering her accusation. 'I'd never considered it before but you're right. I prefer to own beautiful things. I feel no need for external reminders of where and how I grew up. I'm surrounded by others who share similar memories, even if we don't speak of them.'

Marisa was silent for a moment. 'Ernesto?'

Damaso nodded. 'And Beatriz. All my personal staff. I didn't know them when I was a kid, but they come from similar places.'

'No wonder they think the world of you. You've given them the chance they needed.'

He shrugged. It was easy to lend a hand when you had

his advantages. Marisa made it sound like he was some sort of saviour of the slums.

He thought of her dog, rescued from a similar place, and winced. Marisa had hit the nail on the head. Whenever he looked at her petting that mutt, it highlighted the gulf between her and him: the refined princess and the rough-and-ready slum kid.

'Damaso? What is it? You're holding me so tight.'

Instantly he eased his grip. But he didn't let her go. Anxiety clutched his belly. He'd never spoken about his childhood. But if he wanted to keep Marisa…

'You think I can't bear to be reminded of where I came from, but I carry it in my bones.'

He wanted to leave it at that but Marisa needed more. At the same time, he realised this wasn't just about easing her fears. She'd cared enough to wonder about his past, not just now, but before this. How many had done that?

Pleasure and horror surged.

'Tell me.'

He let her hands go and stood, turning towards the city vista.

'I barely remember my mother and I have no idea who my father was. I didn't have a real home. I lived…' He swallowed and forced himself to go on. 'You've seen photos of ragged kids scavenging on garbage heaps? That was me.'

Suddenly he was there again, the odours pungent in the rain, the ground slippery mud and worse beneath his feet, his saturated clothes sticking to his skinny body.

Damaso felt movement and realised she'd come to stand beside him.

'Later there were charity hand-outs, but my main memory is the pain of an empty belly. All day, every night.' He blinked and the images before his eyes resolved into the downtown cityscape.

Marisa's hand slipped into his and his fingers closed around it. Strange how good that touch felt.

'You think I overestimate the danger for you. Maybe I do.' The admission cost him. Every instinct urged him to keep Marisa and their child away from there. 'But where I grew up…' He lifted tight shoulders. 'I saw too much violence to take safety for granted.'

'Those knife scars,' she said, her voice soft.

Damaso nodded. He refused to tell her the details of gang rivalries, drug dealing and more. 'I saw death up close too often. I was lucky to get out when I did. A lot of kids didn't. The neighbourhood you visit is much safer than mine, but something inside me screams out every time you go there.'

'I'm sorry.' She leaned against him, her weight warming his side.

'But you still want to help those children.' His mouth twisted. He hated her being there but how could he be anything but proud and moved that she wanted to help?

'You think I'm being selfish?' Her face turned up to his and he read her doubt.

'I think you're a wonderful, warm-hearted woman and I want you in my life.' He turned and put his arms around her, pulling her close.

'Really?'

'Absolutely. Your social status and bloodline never mattered to me. I take people as I find them— rich, poor or in between.' He lifted her face so she looked into his eyes. 'I want you for purely personal reasons and I don't give a damn what anyone else thinks. Understood?'

For long seconds she watched him silently then she stood on tiptoe and whispered against his mouth. 'Understood.'

The look in her eyes made his heart swell.

CHAPTER THIRTEEN

'You look stunning.' Damaso surveyed her appreciatively. From the top of her golden head to her jewelled stilettos, she was perfection.

Covertly he searched for some evidence of her pregnancy but even after several months she still appeared trim and taut. He looked forward to the day when it would be obvious she was pregnant.

Possessiveness raked familiar talons through his insides. He didn't want to share Marisa. He wanted to keep her with him, away from the men who slavered after her wherever she went.

'Why, thank you.' She twirled, her multi-coloured dress flaring high, revealing toned legs, lightly tanned and delectable. His groin tightened as he thought of some of the things he'd prefer to do with the evening.

But this was her night.

'I have something for you.' His voice was gruff. He told himself that just because she'd refused to accept anything but hospitality from him didn't mean she'd refuse this. He reached for the slim leather case on the bedside table. She was so stubbornly independent, who knew how she'd react?

Damaso forced a smile, feeling tense muscles stretch. What was wrong with him? He'd given women gifts before, casually lavish presents that had meant little.

But this wasn't casual. This he'd chosen personally, had had it designed specifically for Marisa.

He watched her eyebrows arch as she recognised the distinctive logo of one of the world's top jewellery designers.

'There was no need.' She made no move to reach for it and a cold feeling invaded the pit of his stomach.

'I know.' He held her eyes but for the first time in weeks had no idea what she was thinking. Had the closeness between them been a mirage?

'You admire so many Brazilian designers, I thought this would appeal. When I saw it I thought of you.' It was true. No need to reveal his long consultation with the designer about Marisa and her style.

He proffered the box and after a moment she took it. Heat swirled through him in a ribbon of satisfaction.

She didn't open the gift immediately but smoothed her hand over the embossed emblem. Finally she lifted the lid and he heard the snatch of her indrawn breath.

For long seconds she said nothing, eyes fixed on the contents, lush lips slightly parted. Then her throat worked.

Had he miscalculated? Got it wrong?

Eyes as brilliant as the summer sky met his. The way she looked at him made him feel ten feet tall.

'They're absolutely gorgeous.' The catch in her voice tugged at something inside and Damaso wanted to reach out and gather her close. He told himself to wait. 'I've never seen anything like them.'

That was exactly what he'd wanted, because he'd never met a woman like her. 'You like them?'

'*Like* them?' She shook her head, her expression bordering on dazed. 'They're fabulous. How could anyone not like them?'

'Good, then you can wear them tonight.'

Was it his imagination or did she retreat a fraction?

'Why, Damaso? Why the expensive gift?'

He stared down, willing her to accept. 'You deserve to celebrate your first public exhibition. The cost is immaterial; you know I can afford it.'

'Not *my* exhibition.' Despite the doubt in her eyes, her lips curved slightly. 'Tonight is about the kids' photography.'

'Not according to Silvio. From the way he talks, he has big plans for you.' Damaso watched as delicate colour washed her cheeks. 'As well as for your class.'

'So it's a congratulatory gift, because you think I should celebrate?'

Damaso hesitated, reading her anticipation. She wanted more but what could he say? That seeing her contentment and purpose had made him happier than he could ever remember ?

That he wanted to keep that and keep *her*?

That he wanted to put his ring on her finger and bind her to him?

He'd had enough of waiting and battled not to behave like an unreconstructed male chauvinist, forcing her to stay despite her doubts.

'You've worked hard and achieved so much,' he said at last. 'You're making a difference to those kids, giving them skills and confidence and using your connections to open up a new world to them.'

'Really?' It didn't seem possible but Marisa's eyes shone brighter.

He nodded, his throat closing as he saw how much his words meant. Marisa was so active and energetic, sometimes it was easy to forget the burden of doubt she struggled with.

'As an up and coming photographer, you need to look glamorous at your premiere.'

'Looking the part, then?' Her eyes dropped and Damaso reached out and tilted her chin up. Her soft skin made his fingers slide wide, caressing her.

'Far more than that, Marisa. I…'

She leaned towards him and he had the sudden overwhelming conviction she was waiting for him to say something deep, something about how he felt.

Damaso swallowed, knowing he was on dangerous ground.

She'd become a vital part of his future, her and the baby. They brightened his world in a way he'd never thought possible. Yet if he blurted that out her beautiful mouth would thin and she'd turn away.

'I'm proud of you, Marisa. You're a special woman and I'd be honoured if you'd wear my gift tonight.'

Something that might have been disappointment flickered in her eyes then she nodded, but her lips curved in a smile. Damaso assured himself he'd misread her.

'Thank you. I'd like that,' she said huskily.

He reached into the open box and took out the necklace, letting the fall of brilliant burnt-orange gems spill across his palm.

'They remind me of you,' he murmured, watching the light catch them. 'Light and colour and exuberance, but with innate integrity.' He looked up to find her wide gaze fixed not on the strands of gems but on him.

'Really?'

He nodded and moved behind her, drawing the ends carefully together around her throat. 'Absolutely.' Quickly he fastened the clasp and drew her across to a full-length mirror. 'They're pure summer, just like you.'

'What are the stones?' She sounded awed, as well she might. A frisson ran through him at how perfect they looked on her—how perfect she looked, wearing his gift.

'Imperial topaz, mined here in Brazil.'

Marisa lifted a hand to her throat then let it drop, her eyes wide as she stared at the necklace. From its wide topaz-and-diamond collar, separate strands of faceted topaz fell in an asymmetrical cluster to just above her cleavage. It was modern, sexy and ultra-feminine. Just like Marisa.

'You're the most beautiful woman I've ever seen.' At least he could admit that truthfully.

Predictably she opened her mouth as if to protest, but Damaso reached around her and pressed a finger to her siren's mouth.

'Put the earrings on.'

Silently she complied.

'And the bracelet.' A moment later diamonds and topaz encircled her slim arm and Damaso wrapped his arms around her and drew her back against his chest, watching their reflections in the long mirror.

'You like them? You're happy?'

Marisa nodded silently, but her eyes glowed.

He told himself that was enough for tonight. He'd been right to hold the ring back instead of proposing. But time was running out. He refused to wait much longer to claim her.

Marisa's cheeks ached from smiling. Ever since she and Damaso had stepped off the red carpet and into Silvio's soaring studio, she'd been accepting congratulations for her work and for the youngsters she'd been mentoring.

Silvio had been brilliant with the kids, letting them bask in the positive reception their work received without letting them be overwhelmed. One success, he'd warned them, didn't build a career. But hard work and application would.

Now, for the first time in what seemed hours, she found herself alone with Damaso amidst the buzzing, sophisticated crowd. His hand closed on hers and her heart took up a familiar, sultry beat as she looked into his gleaming eyes.

She was hyper-aware of the weight of his jewellery at her throat and wrist, a tangible proclamation of his ownership. That was one of the reasons she'd resisted accepting his gifts. He was a man who'd take a mile when offered an inch. She'd clung to her independence with the tenacity of a drowning man grabbing at flotsam as he went under for the last time.

Yet what was the point in pretending? It wasn't the jewellery that branded her as Damaso's but her feelings.

When he'd presented her with the exquisite pieces she'd been on tenterhooks, waiting for him to announce they were a symbol of what he felt for her. She'd hoped his feelings for her had matured miraculously through sexual attraction, admiration, liking and caring to…

A shiver rippled across her skin.

'Come on,' she urged before he could guess her thoughts. 'There's one piece you haven't seen, at least not blown up to this size.' Threading her fingers through his, she tugged him towards an inner room.

Damaso lowered his head, his mouth hovering near her ear, his breath warm on her skin. 'The portrait of me?'

Marisa nodded and kept walking, the jittery, excited feeling in her stomach telling her she was in danger of revealing too much to this perceptive man.

They stopped on the threshold of the room and, as luck would have it, the spectators parted so they had an unhindered view.

The tingling began somewhere in her chest and spread out in ever-widening ripples just as it did every time she saw it. The photographer in her saw composition and light, focus and angle. The woman saw Damaso.

Not the Damaso the world was used to—the fiercely focused businessman—but a man she'd only just discovered. The slanting light traced his features lovingly in the black and white shot, revealing the broad brow, strong nose, the angle of cheekbone and jaw and the tiny lines at the corner of his eyes. But it did more. It captured him in a rare, unguarded moment, hunkering down with a dark-haired little boy, bent over a battered toy truck.

The man in the photo leant protectively close to the tot, as if to shield him from the football game that was a blur of action on the uneven dirt behind them. His eyes were on the boy and his expression…

Marisa swallowed. How had she ever wondered if Damaso would make a good father? It was all there in his face: the intense focus on the child; the protectiveness; the pleasure lurking at the corners of his firm mouth as he solemnly helped the boy fill the back of the truck with dirt scooped from the earth at their feet.

Damaso would make a wonderful father; she knew it in her bones. Since being with him her doubts about her ability to be a good mother had receded too. His praise and his trust did so much for her. His steady presence had even helped her to find a purpose.

'Thank you for agreeing to let me hang this one.' Her voice was husky and she had to work to counter the urge to press her palm to the tiny swell where her belly sheltered their child.

Beside her, Damaso shrugged. 'You and Silvio were so adamant it had to be included. How could I refuse?'

'I—'

'How fortunate to find you here, princess.'

Marisa's head jerked around at the interruption, her hackles rising at the deliberate emphasis on her title. Her stomach dropped as she recognised the country's most notorious art critic, an older woman renowned for her venom rather than her eye for talent. They'd met at a high-profile event where they'd had opposing views on the merit of a young sculptor.

The woman's cold, hazel eyes told Marisa she hadn't forgotten, or forgiven.

'Damaso.' She turned. 'Have you met—?'

'I have indeed. How are you, Senhora Avila?'

'Senhor Pires.' The woman's toothy smile made Marisa shiver. 'You're admiring the princess's work?' Again that emphasis on her title. 'I hear Silvio is quite taken with his protégée.' Her gimlet gaze and arch tone said she couldn't see why. 'That he's even considering taking her on as an assistant!'

Fed up with being spoken about as if she wasn't there, Marisa simply pasted a smile on her face. If this vulture wanted details, let her pump Silvio. Knowing how Silvio despised the woman, she wouldn't get far.

When the silence lengthened the woman's face tightened. 'Of course, there are some who'd say social status is no replacement for real talent. But these days so much of the art scene is about crass commercialisation rather than true excellence. Anything novel sells.'

Her dismissive attitude scored at something dark inside Marisa. The belief that beneath her determined bravado her uncle had been right. That she had nothing of value to offer.

Dimly she was aware of Damaso squeezing her fingers.

She caught herself up. She'd let doubts undermine her too long. No more. She opened her mouth to respond but Damaso was quicker.

'Personally I think anyone with real discernment only has to see these works to recognise an amazing talent.' His tone was rich, dark chocolate coating a lethal blade. 'As for milking social status, I don't see any reference in the studio or the catalogue to the princess's royal status.'

Beside her he loomed somehow taller, though she hadn't seen him move. 'I suspect those who gripe about social status are only hung up on it because they're not happy with their own.'

Marisa bit back a gasp. It was the sort of thing she'd often longed to say but had never felt free to express.

'Well!' Senhora Avila stiffened as if she'd been slapped. Her eyes narrowed as she took in Damaso's challenging stance. Finally she looked away, her gaze sliding to the photo.

'I must say, Senhor Pires, this piece paints you in a new light. You look quite at home in that slum.' Her eyes darted back to him, glittering with malice. 'Could it be true, after all? The whisper that that's where you came from? No one seems to know for sure.'

Marisa stepped forward, instinctively moving to block the woman's venom. She knew how raw and real Damaso's past was to him, even now. His hand pulled her back to his side and she leaned into him as his arm circled her shoulders.

'I don't see why my birthplace is noteworthy to someone whose interest *purports* to be in art.' His tone lowered the temperature by several degrees. 'It's true I grew up in a *favela*. What of it? It wasn't an auspicious start but it taught me a lot.'

He leaned towards the woman and Marisa saw her eyes widen. 'I'm proud of what I've done with my life, Senhora Avila. What about you? Can you name something constructive you've done with yours?'

The critic mouthed something inarticulate and spun on her heel, scuttling away into the crowd beyond.

'You shouldn't have done that,' Marisa murmured. 'She'll blab to the whole world what she's learned.'

'Let her. I'm not ashamed of who I am.' He turned her towards him, his gaze piercing, as if the glamorous throng around them didn't exist. 'Are you all right?'

'Of course.' Marisa stood straighter, still shaken by the force of anger that had welled when the woman had turned on Damaso.

Because Marisa loved him.

There, she'd admitted it, if only silently. She'd fought so hard against the truth, acknowledging it was a relief. Marisa hugged the knowledge to herself, excitement fizzing through her veins.

She felt as if she could take on the world.

'You should have let me answer for myself. I'm not some dumb bimbo, you know.'

His mouth curled up at one corner. That smile should be outlawed for the way it made her insides melt.

'You? A bimbo?' He laughed and she had to fight the urge to lean closer. 'As if.' His expression sobered. 'But you can't ask me to stand by while that viper makes snide comments about the woman I intend to marry.'

Was it her imagination or did the crowd around her ripple in response to that low-voiced announcement?

'Not here, Damaso!' Suddenly she wanted more than anything to be alone with him. She longed for the privacy of his city penthouse or, even better, his island hideaway. 'Let's talk at home.'

The promise in his sultry stare sent her heart fluttering against her ribs. He looked like he wanted to devour her on the spot. Even his public assertion that he intended to marry her, something that would once have raised her ire, sent a thrill of excitement through her.

Yet it was another hour before they could leave, an hour of accolades that should have meant everything to her. Instead, Marisa was on edge, her mind reeling as she finally confronted her true feelings for Damaso. She wanted him…permanently.

The one thing she didn't know was what he felt for her. He'd publicly revealed his past to deflect that critic's spite. A past he'd once guarded jealously.

At last they were in the limo. Marisa couldn't sit still. Adrenalin streamed through her body, making it impossible to relax. She wanted to blurt out her feelings but what would that achieve? He famously didn't do relationships. Just marriage for the sake of his child.

But surely the way he'd stood up to that harpy meant something?

Something as impossible as him loving her?

The idea shimmered like a beacon in the distance, filling her heart with hope.

Even if he didn't love her, Marisa couldn't resist any

longer. She'd marry him anyway. She'd never meet a better man than Damaso, or a man she cared about more.

She wanted to spend her life with him.

A weight slid off her shoulders as doubt was banished. She wanted love, she'd fight to get it, but she'd start small if she had to. Surely she could make him love her in time?

She was so engrossed in her thoughts she barely noticed him talking on his phone until he spoke to her.

'It's bad news, Marisa. A fire in the new Caribbean eco-resort.'

'Is anyone hurt?'

'They're checking now. It's too early to say. But I need to go there tonight.'

Marisa reached out and wrapped her hands around his tight fist. She knew how much worker safety meant to him and this new complex, due to open in weeks, had been the focus of his attention for so long.

'Of course you should go. You've invested too much time and effort not to.'

'I'll be gone a week, probably more like two. You can come with me. I don't like leaving you alone.'

'I'll hardly be alone.' She shook her head. 'You'd get more done without me and I have lots of work to do too, remember? Silvio and the kids are relying on me.'

Besides, it struck her that she had other unfinished business.

She'd used Damaso's opposition as an excuse to stay away from her homeland. Yet increasingly she'd known she had to face her past just as Damaso had faced his.

Her past took the form of her uncle and the Bengarian court and press. Staying in Brazil, pretending the coronation wasn't happening, felt too much like hiding, as if she was ashamed of who she was and what she'd done.

If she didn't stand up to them, how could she hold her head high?

Marisa was determined to become the woman she wanted

so badly to be—not just for herself but for Damaso and their child. For Stefan too. She'd make them proud.

She wanted to be strong the way Damaso was. The past was part of her, but she had to prove to herself she wasn't cowed by it.

Besides, she had to be stronger now than ever before. Enough to take the chance and stay with a man who had never said he loved her and who might never say it.

Marisa swallowed hard, trying to ignore the fear crawling down her spine.

She'd go to the coronation, face her past and reconcile the two parts of her life. Maybe then she'd be the sort of woman Damaso could love.

'Marisa? What is it? You have the strangest expression.'

She turned, her emotions welling unstoppably. 'Don't worry about me,' she urged. 'Just go. I'll be fine while you're away. I'll be busy.'

She needed to do this alone.

CHAPTER FOURTEEN

His two weeks in the Caribbean had felt like two months.
More.

Damaso jabbed the button for the penthouse and shoved
his hand through his hair. He needed a haircut. He rubbed
his chin, feeling the rasp of stubble, and knew he should
have shaved on the plane. But he'd still been working frantically, trying to get everything organised so he could come
back a couple of days early.

He'd shave when he got to the apartment.

Except he knew once he saw Marisa his good intentions
of sparing her delicate skin would fly out of the window.
There would be no holding back.

He needed her *now*.

He needed her in ways he'd never needed a woman.
His arms felt empty without her. He missed her smile, her
sassy challenges, the sly way she teased him, the fearless
way she stood up to him. He missed having her nearby,
sharing the small stuff from their days he'd never thought
important before he met her.

The doors opened and he strode into the apartment.

'Marisa?'

Long strides took him past the vast sitting room to their
bedroom suite. She wasn't there. He headed back down
the corridor.

'Marisa?'

'Senhor Pires.' It was Beatriz, wiping her hands on an apron. 'I didn't expect you back yet.'

'I changed my plans.' He looked past her for Marisa. Surely she'd heard him by now. 'Where is the princess?'

Beatriz stilled, her brows lifting. 'She's gone, Senhor.' Damaso felt his blood turn sluggish, as if his heart had slowed. 'Back to Bengaria for the coronation.'

Damaso rocked on his feet, absorbing the smack of shock. He'd spoken to Marisa daily and she'd said nothing about leaving.

Because she feared he'd stop her?

It was the only explanation.

That last night at the exhibition he'd mentioned marriage and she'd tried to hustle him away. Because she'd decided to leave him?

'Senhor? Are you all right?'

Damaso shook his head, trying to stop the sick feeling surging through him. He reached out and splayed a hand against the wall, grateful for its solidity.

'Can I get you—?'

'Nothing,' he croaked. 'I don't need anything.'

Except Marisa. Hell! It felt like the world crumbled beneath his feet.

Heedless of Beatriz's concerned gaze, he stumbled back to the bedroom.

Fifteen minutes later Damaso slumped on the bed. He'd tried her phone but it was switched off. He'd checked his email—nothing. He'd even accessed her personal email, something he'd never before stooped to doing, and found nothing relevant.

There was no note, no message. Nothing except, in the drawer of her bedside table, a crumpled letter from her uncle. A letter demanding her presence for the coronation. A letter that spelled out the importance of Marisa returning to meet the man her uncle intended her to marry.

Bile rose in Damaso's throat as his gut knotted.

She'd left him and gone to her uncle, the man she abhorred.

Because she'd rather marry some blue-blooded aristocrat than Damaso, a man without a family tree to his name? A man whose only pretensions to respectability had been bought with his phenomenal success. A man who still bore scars from his slum background.

He'd have sworn that didn't matter to Marisa. But, if not that, then what?

Unless, like him, Marisa had doubts about his ability to be a father. To provide love.

How could you give what you've never known?

Fear gouged his belly, scraping at his deepest, most hidden self-doubt.

Something nudged his knee and he slanted his gaze down. That ragged mutt of Marisa's leaned against him, its chin resting on his leg, its eyes soulful in its ugly face.

The dog's coat felt surprisingly soft under his fingers. Its huge eyes narrowed to slits of pleasure as Damaso stroked one torn ear.

'You miss her too, don't you, Max?'

Strangely, it seemed completely natural to talk to the dog. It leaned close, its weight warm and comforting.

Surely she'd have taken the mutt if she'd intended leaving for good?

That shard of hope gave him strength.

'Don't fret.' Damaso straightened his spine. 'I'm going to get her back, whatever it takes.' He refused to dwell on whether he spoke to reassure the dog or himself.

The cathedral was huge and impressive. Damaso barely gave it a glance as he stalked up the red carpet, ignoring the usher frantically trying to catch his attention.

The atmosphere was expectant and the air smelt of massed blooms, expensive scent and incense. Baroque organ music swelled, lending pomp to the occasion.

Damaso slowed, surveying the crowd. He saw uniforms and dark suits on the packed seats, clerical robes and women in designer dresses. But the hats the women wore obscured profiles and made it impossible to identify the wearers till they turned and stared.

'Princess Marisa,' he barked to the usher. 'Where is she?'

'The princess?' The man's gaze flicked nervously up the centre aisle to the front seats. Instantly Damaso strode away, leaving the goggling man behind.

Heads whipped around as he passed but he looked neither right nor left as he scanned the front rows. Pale blue, lemon, ivory, that light shade of brown women insisted on giving names like 'beige' or 'taupe'. His stare rested on each woman then moved on, dismissing them in turn. White, pink, more pink, light grey. They were dressed expensively but sedately. Obviously there was a book of etiquette on what to wear for a coronation: expensive but subdued.

Damaso shifted his gaze to the other side of the aisle. Grey, black, and…deep sapphire-blue swirled with an orange so vivid it reminded him of the sun blazing on his island beach at sunset. He faltered, his heart pounding.

He'd found her.

Instead of a suit she wore a dress that left the golden skin of her arms bare. She looked like a ray of light amidst the sedate pastels. She moved her head and the jaunty concoction of orange on her golden hair caught the light. It looked saucy even from behind.

His pace lengthened till he stood at the end of the row and he caught the full impact of her outfit. Elegant, but subtly sexy in the way the fabric hugged her curves. At her throat she wore the magnificent topaz necklace and for a moment Damaso could only stare, wondering what it meant that she'd chosen to wear *his* gift to an event that would be televised to millions.

The murmurs became a ripple of sound around him. The usher had caught up and was whispering urgently about the correct seating.

Still Marisa didn't turn. Her attention was on the man sitting on her far side. A man with a chiselled jaw, wide brow and face so picture-book handsome he didn't look real. Or maybe that was because of the uniform he wore. His jacket was white with gold epaulets, a double row of golden buttons down the front, and he sported a broad sash of indigo that perfectly matched his eyes.

Damaso's fists curled. Was *this* the man she was supposed to marry?

Far from spurning him, she was in deep conversation with the guy. He said something and she leaned closer, her hand on his sleeve.

Something tore wide open inside Damaso. Cold rage drenched him as his fists tightened.

'Sir, really, if you come with me I'll just—'

'Not now.' His voice was low, almost inaudible, but it had the quality of an animal growl. The usher jumped back and heads whipped round.

'Damaso?' Marisa's eyes were wide and wondering.

She'd forgotten to remove her hand from Prince Charming's sleeve and Damaso felt a wave of roiling fury rise up inside him.

Marisa stared up at the man blocking the aisle. Despite his formal clothes, his perfectly cut hair and clean-shaven face, there was something untamed about him.

Emotion leapt. A thrill of excitement, of pure delight that Damaso was here.

'How did you get here?' Cyrill wouldn't have invited the father of her unborn child.

'Does it matter?' Damaso shrugged off a couple of ushers who were trying to lead him away. He looked broad and bold and impossibly dangerous, like a big jungle cat caged with a bunch of tabbies.

Silently she shook her head. No, it didn't matter. All she cared about was the fact he was here. Her heart tilted and beat faster.

He held out his arm, palm up. 'Come on.'

Marisa stared. 'But the coronation! It's due to begin in a couple of minutes.'

'I'm not here for the coronation. I'm here for you.'

Her pulse fluttered high in her throat at the command and possessiveness in his voice. She prized her independence but his proprietorial attitude spoke to a primitive yearning within.

Behind her, women leaned close, fanning themselves.

'Marisa?' Alex spoke beside her. 'Do you want me to deal with this?'

Before she could answer, Damaso stepped close, shoving aside an empty chair into the path of a uniformed man who'd reached to restrain him.

'Marisa can speak for herself. She doesn't need *you*.' She'd never heard Damaso sound so threatening. His eyes flashed pure heat and there was violence in his expression.

'Damaso. Please.'

'Please what? Go away?' Those hot eyes turned to her, scorching her skin and sending delicious chills rippling through her tummy. 'Not a chance, *querida*. You don't get rid of me so easily.'

'It's not a matter of getting rid—'

'We need to talk, Marisa, *now*.'

'After the ceremony.' She gestured to the fallen chair. 'I'm sure we could arrange for you…'

Damaso's eyes cut to Alex and his look was downright ugly. 'If you think I'm leaving you with him…' He shook his head. 'I know you don't want to be here, Marisa. Don't let them force you.'

Marisa frowned, trying to make sense of his attitude.

Then Alex surged to his feet and so did Marisa, arm out to separate him from Damaso.

'Stop this now,' she hissed. 'You're making a scene, both of you. Everyone's watching.' Yet part of her revelled in Damaso's single-mindedness.

'Are you coming with me?' His accent was thicker, enticing, like rich coffee laced with rum. It slid along her senses, beckoning.

'Damaso, I don't know what this is about but I—'

A swoop of movement caught the rest of the sentence in her throat. Next thing Marisa knew, she was in Damaso's arms, held high against his chest. On her peripheral vision, she saw a television camera turn to focus on them. A babble of sound erupted.

'Marisa.' Low, urgent, Alex's voice reached her. She turned her head and saw him just inches away, scowling, as if about to tackle Damaso. He had no idea she'd rather be in Damaso's arms than anywhere. She groped for Alex's hand, squeezing it quickly.

'It's okay, really,' she whispered. 'I'm fine.' And then his hand slipped from hers as Damaso swung round, stalking through the protesting crowd to turn back up the long aisle.

Perhaps the tabloids were right—she was lost to all propriety. Rather than being outraged by Damaso's scandalous behaviour, Marisa found herself thrilled at his masculine display of ownership. Hope rose.

He *must* care for her.

No man would behave so outrageously unless he cared. She was sure that was jealousy she'd seen glinting in the basilisk stare he'd given Alex.

'You could just have phoned,' she murmured, snuggling closer to his solid chest.

His firm stride faltered and he looked down at her. 'Your phone was off.' A ferocious scowl marred his brow and beneath it his eyes were shadowed by something that looked like doubt. 'You didn't tell me you were coming.'

Marisa frowned and lifted her hand to his face. His skin was tight and hot.

'I thought you'd follow me if I told you.'

His nostrils flared and his jaw set as he looked away and started moving again, shouldering his way through the clustering crowd. 'You wanted to be alone to meet the man your uncle has arranged for you to marry.'

'You know about that?' To her amazement, she still had the capacity to feel shock.

'Isn't that why you came? To get engaged to some pretty-boy aristocrat who doesn't give a damn who you really are? Who doesn't even care you're carrying another man's baby?'

Marisa heard the gasps around them but only had eyes for Damaso. What she read in his face outweighed any annoyance she might have felt for his careless words. She read *pain*. The sort of pain that tore at the heart and shredded pride.

She should know. She'd seen the symptoms in her own face when she'd faced a future loving a man who cared only for their baby.

How it hurt to see Damaso suffering too.

His big body hummed with tension. His jaw was set so hard she wondered how he'd ever unclench it.

'I won't let you do it. He's not the man for you, Marisa.'

'I know.' Her voice was so soft she thought at first he hadn't heard. Then he juddered to a halt, his head jerking round. The intensity of that midnight gaze transfixed her.

'You know?' His voice was muted roar. She'd never seen a man so close to the edge. Her heart clenched. Could it be true? Could the miracle she'd hoped for have happened?

'I'm not here to choose a fiancé.' She planted her palm on Damaso's chest, feeling the racing rhythm of his heart. 'I'm here because I'm a princess of Bengaria. I have a right to be at the coronation, as well as a duty. This is my country, even if I don't plan to live here full-time.'

'Where do you plan to live?' His low voice was barely audible, yet the echo of it rolled across her flesh, raising shivery goose bumps.

'Brazil looks nice.'

Marisa felt the jolt of shock hit him. His hands tightened as his head lowered to hers.

Dimly she was aware of a distant camera flash.

'You're not trying to leaving me then?'

She shook her head, her throat closing, as for the first time she saw right to his soul. Longing, pain and determination were there, plain for her to see.

'You'll marry me.' It was a statement, not a question, but Marisa nodded.

'Why?'

The question floored her. From the first, he'd been the one demanding marriage. Had he changed his mind? Her stomach swooped. 'I could ask you the same thing,' she whispered.

'Why do I want to marry you?'

She nodded again, aware that this wasn't the best place for this conversation. But nothing, not protocol or natural disaster, would have stopped her now. She had to know.

A slow movement started at the corner of his mouth, pulling it up in a crooked smile that grew till it carved a dimple down one cheek and broadened into a grin. It transformed Damaso's face from hard and determined to charismatically sexy. Marisa's heart missed a beat.

'Because I want to spend the rest of my days with you.' He lifted her in his arms till his words were an invisible caress on her parted lips. His dark gaze locked with hers, promising a gift far more precious than any regal entitlement. 'Because I love you.'

She blinked but still couldn't take it in. 'Say that again.'

This time Damaso lifted his head and when he spoke his words rang through the crowded cathedral for all to hear. 'I love you, Marisa, with all my heart and soul. I want to be your husband, because there's no woman in the world more perfect for me than you.'

He loved her?

Marisa felt the hot glaze of tears film her eyes as emotion welled from deep within. A sob rose, turning into a hiccup of desperate happiness. Never in her life had she felt like this.

'Now, *meu anjo,* tell my why you want to marry me.' His gaze dropped to her belly and she knew he was thinking of their child.

She shook her head. That wasn't the reason.

'Because I love you too, Damaso. I love you from the bottom of my heart and I couldn't bear to be with anyone else.'

Beyond them the sophisticated crowd went wild.

'I've been in love with you so long,' she whispered, drawing him closer, her words for his ears only. 'It feels like I've only come alive since I've been with you.'

Finally Damaso spoke, his voice uneven, his eyes glittering. 'Do you really want to stay for the ceremony, since you came all this way?'

'I'd rather be with you, Senhor Pires. Take me home.'

Marisa had thought his last smile potent but this one was enough to stop clocks. Two ladies-in-waiting swooned as Damaso tucked her against his heart and strode down the aisle.

'And they accuse *me* of being scandalous! Your behaviour was outrageous.'

Damaso smiled at the lush, lovely woman sitting in the jet's private lounge, sipping sparkling water.

Marisa was his. Incontrovertibly, absolutely *his*.

Something smacked him hard in the chest. Relief? Triumph? Joy? He didn't give a damn what name it went by. It was the best feeling in the world. He felt like he might burst with happiness.

'Your uncle will get over it,' he murmured, sitting down beside her, one hand on her thigh. The whisper-thin silk of her dress was warm from her flesh, inviting further exploration.

'I doubt it. The look on Cyrill's face when you told him I couldn't stay for the ceremony because I had another engagement! I thought he was going to have a seizure.' She shook her head. 'Upstaging him at his own coronation! Such lack of decorum.'

Marisa looked down as his hand slipped higher up her leg but did nothing to stop him. 'At least that will have dashed any plans he had to marry me off.'

'You wouldn't have been happy with that pretty-boy aristocrat.' Only he could give her what she needed, for he was the one she loved. He'd never known love. It took some getting used to.

'Of course not.' She leaned forward and he was momentarily distracted by a glimpse of delicious cleavage.

'He didn't even have the gumption to stop me.' Satisfied, he ran his fingers lightly up to her hip, feeling her shiver under his touch.

His.

'You mean Alex?' Her brow puckered. 'He's not the man Cyrill wanted me to marry. He's a friend.'

'I thought you didn't have any friends in Bengaria.' Despite everything, jealousy stirred. Just how close a friend was this Alex?

She shrugged. 'Okay, more Stefan's friend than mine. I haven't seen him for years. He's been away. And, no.' She paused, studying his face. 'He's not the man for me.'

'But I am.' He intended to make sure she remembered it, and rejoiced in it, every day for the rest of her life.

'You definitely are.' She lifted her hand to his cheek and an incredible peace descended as she feathered a touch across his skin. 'I'm a better person with you, Damaso. I feel...proud of what I've done and what I'm doing. Confident about the future. You gave me the strength to face what I'd been running from.'

'You were strong before you met me, Marisa.' He'd never known a woman more feisty and independent.

She shook her head. 'It was only when I saw how you'd faced your past and got on with your life that I realised I'd been a coward, letting Cyrill and the press drive me from my home. That's why I had to go back. To prove to them, and to myself, that I'm happy with who I am. I mightn't fit their mould but that doesn't matter.'

'You're perfect just the way you are.' His hand strayed to her abdomen and the baby bulge that had popped out in the two weeks since he'd seen her. His palm closed protectively over it. His woman. His child.

Marisa shifted, her eyes skimming away from his. She took a swift sip from her glass.

'What is it?' Instantly he sensed her discomfort. 'What's wrong?'

She lifted one shoulder. 'Nothing. Everything's perfect.'

Yet her smile wasn't quite as radiant as it had been. Damaso tilted her head around till she had no choice but to meet his scrutiny. 'Something's bothering you. Tell me.'

One slim shoulder lifted. 'No, really, I—'

'Don't, Marisa. You've never lied before. Your honesty is one of the qualities I admire most. Tell me the truth. If there's anything wrong, we need to work it out together.'

Eyes of bright azure locked with his, her regard so searching it was as if she looked deep into him.

Damaso looked right back. He had no secrets from Marisa.

'I *like* that you're so eager to be a father.' She paused, giving him time to process the doubt in her voice.

'But...?'

A flush coloured her cheeks. 'But...' She bit her lip, reminding him of the early days on his island estate when she'd refused his offer of marriage. She hadn't thought a child sufficient reason to marry.

'But you're afraid it's our baby I want,' he murmured. 'Rather than you.'

She opened her mouth to answer but his finger on her lips forestalled her.

'I love our child already, *meu anjo,* and I'll work hard to learn to be a good father.' He swallowed hard, knowing that would be a bigger challenge than any corporate dealings. 'But, even if there was no child, even if there could never *be* a child, I would love you with my whole heart.'

Marisa's eyes shone brilliantly as she looked up at him. He took the glass from her hand and set it down, then gathered both her hands in his. They trembled. Or perhaps it was he who shook.

'You are my sun and stars and moon, Marisa. You've taught me how to care about more than a balance sheet. That it's not my corporate empire that defines who I am. It's who I love.'

He raised her hand and kissed it, revelling in the fresh apple and sunshine scent of her skin, knowing it would always be his favourite perfume.

'I didn't know I *could* love till until you came into my life.'

Her eyes glittered with tears but her smile was the most wonderful thing he'd ever seen.

Damaso dropped to his knees in front of her. 'Will you be mine? We don't need to marry if you—'

This time it was Marisa's finger on his mouth.

'I'll marry you, Damaso. I want everyone to know you're mine.' Her smile was incandescent. Damaso felt its warmth in every cell of her body. 'Besides, for a scandalous princess, I have a hankering for respectability, so long as it's with you.'

'Ah.' Damaso rose and lifted her into his arms, turning towards the luxuriously appointed bedroom. 'That's a shame. I was rather hoping for a little scandalous behaviour now and then.'

Marisa reached out and with one quick tug undid his bow tie and tossed it over his shoulder. Her smile was pure seduction. 'I'm sure that could be arranged, Senhor Pires.'

* * * * *

ALEJANDRO'S REVENGE

ANNE MATHER

CHAPTER ONE

THE car radio was droning on and on about the temperature in Miami, the highs and lows, the relative humidity. But actually Abby was finding it anything but relative. And heat, or the lack of it, was a subjective thing anyway.

When she'd stepped out of the shadows of the airport buildings half an hour ago she'd been dazzled by the sunlight. Perspiration had soon been trickling down her spine and between her breasts. Now, in the air-conditioned luxury of the limousine, she was practically freezing, and all she really wanted to do was reach her destination and lie down until the throbbing in her head subsided.

But that wasn't going to happen. Not any time soon anyway. The arrival of the limousine, which surely couldn't be Edward's property, seemed to prove that. Instead of Lauren being there to meet her she'd been faced with a blank-faced chauffeur who, apart from the necessary introductions, seemed unable—or unwilling—to indulge in polite conversation.

At first she hadn't been concerned. The roads leading away from the airport had been jammed with traffic, and when her swarthy driver had turned off the main thoroughfare to thread his way through a maze of streets only a native of Miami would recognise she'd assumed he was taking a short cut to the hospital.

Which just went to show that you shouldn't take anything for granted, she thought uneasily. Although they'd rejoined the freeway, she was fairly sure they were heading away from the city and South Dade Memorial Hospital where her brother was lying, injured, waiting for her to rush to his bedside. What little she recalled of her first and only other visit to the area was convincing her that they were heading into Coral Gables.

And the only people she knew who lived in Coral Gables were Lauren's parents.

And Alejandro Varga, her treacherous memory reminded her unkindly, but she ignored it.

Still, if they were going to the Esquivals' home then she would just have to put up with it. And at least they'd be able to tell her how serious Edward's injuries were. Perhaps Lauren was staying with them while her husband was in hospital. She hadn't thought to ask any questions when Edward had called her.

Concentrating her attention on her surroundings, she looked through tinted windows at a scene straight out of a travel ad. The broad tree-lined avenue they were driving along ran parallel with the glistening waters of Biscayne Bay, and yachts and other pleasure craft were taking advantage of the late afternoon sunshine. This area, south of Miami, was known for the beauty of its scenery, for the lushness of its vegetation. Palmetto palms and other exotic trees were commonplace here, and the richness and colour of plants and flowering shrubs gave the place a decidedly tropical feel.

Coral Gables, she knew, possessed some of the oldest buildings in Miami, and the architecture showed an innately Spanish influence. There were squares and plazas, pools and tumbling fountains. It was also one of the wealthiest parts of the country: Edward's in-laws had taken some pains to impress that upon her, too.

Thinking about Lauren's parents brought her mind back to the reason she was here, and she wished one of them could have come to meet her if their daughter couldn't. They must have known she'd be worried about her brother. Had something happened? Had something gone wrong? Was that why they were bringing her here?

Perhaps he was dead!

The horrifying thought came out of nowhere. It couldn't be true, she told herself fiercely. Dear God, she'd only spoken to him two days ago, and, although he hadn't spared her the details of the car smash that had resulted in him being hospitalised, at no time had he given her the impression that his condition was critical. He'd been upset, yes; resentful, even. But she'd understood that that was because he still felt like a stranger, hospitalised in a strange country.

Though that was a little ridiculous, too. Technically, Edward was a US citizen. He'd lived in Florida for over three years, and for the last two of those years he'd been married to Lauren Esquival. Well, she'd changed her name to Lauren Leighton when she'd married Edward, of course, Abby corrected herself. Even if it had always been hard to attribute such an Anglo-Saxon surname to her essentially Hispanic sister-in-law.

Abby heaved a sigh.

Something told her this was not going to be an uneventful visit. And, remembering Ross's reaction when she'd told him what she planned to do, going home was not going to be without incident either. Her fiancé—it was still hard to think of him in those terms—had never been one to pull his punches. In his opinion it was high time Edward grew up and started taking responsibility for his own actions, instead of calling on his sister every time he had a problem.

Which wasn't entirely fair, thought Abby a little defensively. All right, when he was younger Edward had been something of a tearaway, and he had relied on his sister to get him out of many of the scrapes he'd got himself into. Nothing too serious, of course. Lots of youths his age had spent money they didn't have. He wasn't a criminal. Nevertheless Abby had spent a goodly portion of her teens and early twenties paying his debts.

Then, when he was nineteen, he'd had what to him had seemed the brilliant idea of going to work in the United States. He'd been studying for a catering diploma at the time, and although Abby had had her doubts when he'd started the course he'd definitely shown an aptitude for the work.

Or perhaps his diligence had been due in part to his infatuation with one of his fellow students, Abby reflected a little cynically now. Whatever, when Selina Steward had taken off for Florida Edward had wasted no time in getting the necessary paperwork and following her.

Abby had been twenty-four then and, although she'd never have admitted as much to Edward, she'd been desolated by his departure. For so long he'd been an integral part of her life. She'd shunned any lasting relationships to be the mother he hardly remembered, and when he'd left she'd had only her career as a teacher to console her.

Still, she'd survived, she conceded ruefully. And she'd been glad when Edward had adapted well to his new surroundings. She'd even convinced herself that it would work out when he'd phoned to say he was going to marry the daughter of the man who owned the Coconut Grove restaurant where he worked. The fact that he and Lauren had only known one another for a matter of months wasn't important, he'd insisted. And, what was more, Abby had to come over for the wedding...

But she was digressing. The wedding and its painful aftermath were long over, and she had to focus on why she was here now. But even the sight of acres of manicured turf— courtesy, so the sign read, of the Alhambra Country Club— and the sunlit plaza that adjoined it couldn't compensate for the feelings of anxiety that were growing inside her. If only she knew what was going on. If only she knew how Edward was, *where* he was...

He had to be all right, she told herself fiercely. She'd never forgive herself if anything had happened to him. All right, as Ross had so painstakingly pointed out, she couldn't hold herself responsible for Edward's decision to move to Florida, and at twenty-two he was surely old enough to look after himself. But Edward would always be her little brother, and Abby supposed it was her own thwarted maternal instinct that made her so protective of him still.

But that was something else she didn't want to get into now. Looking down, she massaged her finger where Ross's diamond sparkled with a cold light. They'd been engaged since Christmas, after knowing one another since before Edward had left for the States. But it was only in recent months that they'd become close.

And now Edward was causing a rift between them. Ross considered her decision to come rushing out here at her brother's behest nothing short of foolhardy. They were planning to get married in six months, for heaven's sake, he'd protested. Wasting money on airfares to Florida, when she had no real proof that her brother was in any danger, was downright stupid.

Well, Ross hadn't exactly said she was stupid. He was far too prudent for that. But he had maintained that after they were married things would be different. She would have to stop behaving as if Edward still needed her to hold his hand.

Abby grimaced. When they were married. Somehow the words had even less conviction here than they'd had back in London. It wasn't that she didn't care for Ross, she told herself. She did. Perhaps she'd just been single too long. Why did she find it so hard to contemplate putting her future in any man's hands?

Or had Alejandro Varga…?

But once again she steered her thoughts away from that disastrous memory. Like her mother's desertion, and her father's subsequent death from alcohol poisoning, it was all water under the bridge now. It had no bearing on the present. She was here to support Edward and nothing else.

Unless Alejandro visited his cousin while she was here.

But that wouldn't happen, she assured herself. His association with Lauren's parents had seemed tenuous at best. As far as she remembered Alejandro was a distant cousin of Mrs Esquival, and his presence in their home had been because of the wedding. Besides, he had a wife. And somehow Abby didn't think he'd want to introduce them.

Her throat tightened in spite of herself, and she was glad that the sudden slowing of the car brought her quickly back to the present. For a few moments she'd been lost in thought, but now she saw that they had entered the residential district where she knew the Esquivals had their estate.

It wasn't an estate such as was meant by the word back in England, of course. The Esquivals' property comprised a rather large villa set in cultivated grounds. There was no parkland surrounding it, no gatehouse. Just a high stone wall protecting it from public view.

The names of the various streets they passed were appealing, and Abby forced herself to look for South Cutler Road, where Lauren's parents lived. Fortunately it was nowhere near Old Okra Road, where Alejandro had his house. She'd have been far more apprehensive if it was.

Abby was just admiring the Renaissance façade of the newly refurbished Gables Hotel when the chauffeur turned his head and spoke to her over his shoulder. 'I guess this is your first visit to Florida, ma'am,' he said, albeit with a heavy Spanish accent, and Abby was so taken aback that for a moment she could only stare at him.

'I—my second,' she got out at last, trying not to feel aggrieved that he'd waited so long before speaking to her. Also, being addressed as 'ma'am' took some getting used to, as well. She touched her hair defensively. Did she really look that old?

'So you've been to the Esquivals' house before?' he went on, and she swallowed.

'Is that where we're going?' she asked, gathering her composure with an effort. 'What about my brother? Do you know how he is?'

'No one told me anything about that, ma'am,' responded the chauffeur annoyingly. 'But as he's staying with the Esquivals right now I guess you'll soon find out.'

Abby's jaw dropped. 'He's staying with the Esquivals?' she echoed disbelievingly. 'But—I understood he was in hospital.'

'Guess he's recovered,' the man remarked laconically. 'Like I say, you'll soon see him for yourself.'

Abby realised she must look as stunned as she felt, and hastily pulled herself together. But all Ross's misgivings were coming home to roost. She should have insisted on speaking to Edward's doctor before she left England. She just hoped her brother hadn't brought her here on a wild-goose chase.

Any further speculation was balked by the realisation that the chauffeur had halted the impressive limousine outside tall electrically operated gates. He barely had time to roll down his window and identify himself to the security cameras before the heavy gates started to open, and they drove up the curving driveway to the Esquivals' sprawling residence.

Not surprisingly now, Abby was anxious, and she found herself moving to the edge of her seat. It was as if she hoped she could precipitate her arrival. For the moment all she could think about was seeing her brother again, and she barely looked at the beautiful Spanish-style house with its ornamental pillars and trailing vines.

The car braked before double-panelled doors, and almost immediately they opened to allow a uniformed maid to run down the shallow steps to meet them. Small and foreign in appearance, she seemed unusually eager to please, opening the door of the limousine, inviting Abby to step out.

'Thanks.'

Abby did so, brushing down the slightly creased legs of her khaki pants. In fact, she was sure she must look distinctly travel-worn, and she wished she'd thought about taking a change of clothes onto the plane.

The khaki pants and cream shirt would have to do, though she thought about taking her jacket out of her haversack. But now that she was out in the sunlight again the heat was almost palpable. She certainly didn't need a jacket. And it was only March.

'Welcome to Miami, *señora*,' the maid greeted her politely as the chauffeur got out to heft Abby's suitcase from the boot. Then, with a distinctly flirtatious air, she added, '*Hola, Carlos. Como esta?*' How are you?

As Abby digested the fact that she now knew the chauffeur's name, he responded to the maid's greeting with rather less enthusiasm. '*Bien, gracias,*' he said, which Abby knew was usually followed by *Y usted?* but wasn't in this case. Then, to Abby, 'I'll leave this here, ma'am.' He put down the heavy case. 'And I hope all goes well with your brother.'

'Oh—thank you.' Abby blinked, wondering if the house was off-limits to the other staff. But when he got back into the limousine and drove away she revised her opinion. She had probably taken him away from his usual work.

To her chagrin, the maid took charge of her case. Lifting the strap, she tugged it on its wheels up the steps, waiting rather impatiently now for Abby to join her.

'Come,' she said, leading the way into the wide entrance hall. It was cooler inside, and a huge urn of flowers spilled scarlet blossoms over the marble surface of a stone table.

Air-conditioning cooled the heat that had beaded on Abby's forehead, and she ran a nervous hand over her hair, feeling the damp strands clinging to her cheeks. She probably looked as flushed and harassed as she felt.

Looking about her, she had to admit she'd forgotten exactly how beautiful the Esquivals' home was. Cool and spacious, it epitomised all that was good about Spanish architecture. Long windows looked out onto an inner courtyard and hanging baskets edged an arching colonnade.

'Mees Leighton—Abigail!' The voice that accosted her was soft and feminine, and Abby turned to find Lauren's mother emerging from the salon that adjoined the reception hall. Small and plump, but exquisitely dressed, Dolores Esquival matched her surroundings, her sleek chignon of dark hair putting Abby's explosion of crinkled red curls to shame. 'Welcome to Florida,' she added, her high heels tapping across the polished floor as she came to meet her guest. Air kisses whispered at either side of Abby's head as she continued, 'I hope you had a good journey, *cara*.'

'I—yes. Thank you.' Abby felt a little bemused as she returned the greeting. Lauren's mother was behaving as if she was here for a holiday instead of flying out to be at her brother's bedside. 'It's very—kind of you to ask.'

'Not so, *querida*.' Was Abby mistaken or did Dolores's mouth tighten a little. 'We are very happy to have you here.'

'Yes, but—'

Ignoring her now, Lauren's mother switched her attention

to the maid, who was hovering in the background, directing her to take their guest's suitcase upstairs. At least that was what Abby thought she was doing. Her imperious signal towards the curving staircase seemed to indicate it was.

'Oh, but—' Abby began, eager to explain that she had no intention of presuming on the Esquivals' hospitality, but Lauren's mother turned to her again.

'This way,' she said, apparently deaf to Abby's protests. 'I am sure you are eager to see your brother,' she added, heading into the salon. 'Everyone is through here.'

Afterwards, when she was unwillingly installed in the first-floor suite she had occupied on her first visit to Florida, Abby marvelled that she had had no suspicion that Alejandro might be there.

Yet how could she have? she asked herself defensively. She'd believed that he was just a distant relative, invited to the wedding because family politics dictated as much. She'd had no idea that he was such a close friend of the Esquivals, nor that Lauren seemed to regard him with a distinctly possessive affection.

Still, when she'd followed Dolores into the enormous salon that seemed to stretch right across the back of the house, she'd had eyes only for her brother. Besides, she'd still been slightly dazzled by the change from sun to shadow. With spots of brilliance dancing before her pupils, she'd been in no condition to instantly register all the people in the room.

Edward was there, she'd seen with some relief, apparently confined to the cushioned divan where he was reclining. With one leg encased in plaster from hip to knee, he had apparently been incapable of coming to greet her. She had hesitated only a moment before hurrying to his side.

'Oh, Eddie,' she exclaimed huskily, suddenly inexplicably near to tears. 'What on earth have you been doing to yourself?'

She bent to kiss his cheek and Edward captured one of her hands and held onto it. 'Hey, Abbs,' he greeted her urgently. Then, in an undertone, 'Thank God you've come!'

Abby's eyes widened at his unexpected words. But before she could say or do anything rash, another hand touched her sleeve.

'Abigail,' declared a vaguely familiar voice. 'How—good it is to see you again.'

Abby turned, straightening, to find Luis Esquival standing right behind her. Lauren's father was only slightly taller than his wife, with a broad dark-skinned face and luxuriant moustaches. He extended his hand towards her. 'Did you have a pleasant journey?'

Abby was confused, as much by her brother's words as by the fairly obvious conclusion that there was nothing seriously wrong with him. He had let her believe that he'd be in hospital for some time, whereas now it appeared that apart from a probable fracture he was okay. Heavens, she thought ruefully, Ross was going to love this.

But Lauren's father was waiting for an answer and, summoning her composure, she managed a polite smile. 'It was— tiring,' she admitted. Plane journeys were not her thing, and she'd had the doubtful privilege of being seated next to the toilets. 'Thank you.'

She glanced round then, expecting to see Lauren, but her sister-in-law wasn't in the room. Instead she saw an elderly woman seated by an arrangement of potted palms, and behind her, standing in the shadows near the ornate brick fireplace, was a tall man dressed all in black.

It was strange, but even then she had no inkling that she might know him. So far as she was concerned the only other person she was eager to speak to was Lauren herself. She wanted to find out what was behind Edward's desperate words. She wanted to know why he'd felt the need to send for her.

But once again Luis Esquival demanded her attention. 'We were most surprised when Edward told us you intended paying us a visit,' he said silkily. 'As you can see, your brother is recovering very well.'

Abby was nonplussed. Her eyes sought Edward's, but he was suddenly intensely interested in the cast on his leg. Below the hem of his navy shorts the plaster looked extremely white against his bare skin, and as she watched he shifted a little uneasily in his seat.

'I—I thought—' she was beginning, when the man beside the fireplace suddenly moved into the shaft of sunlight slicing through the half-drawn blinds.

'I am sure—Abigail—was concerned when she heard about her brother's accident,' he drawled in the low, seductively sensual tone that Abby remembered not just in her mind but in her bones. And as she swung round, hardly daring to believe he'd have the nerve to come here and face her, Alejandro Varga acknowledged her dismay with an ironic little smile. 'Abigail.' He inclined his head towards her with all his old arrogance. 'What an unexpected pleasure!'

CHAPTER TWO

YOU smug bastard!

For a moment Abby was half afraid she'd said the words out loud. But when she glanced apprehensively about her she saw no look of horror on anyone's face, no embarrassed apology trembling on anyone's lips. On the contrary, everyone—excluding Edward—was looking at Alejandro with undisguised approval, and Abby wanted to sink into the floor at the realisation that she was expected to acknowledge him, too.

'Mr Varga,' she said tightly, allowing her eyes to drift only briefly over his dark face. She was sure he must know exactly how she was feeling, and the hot colour that she had never been able to control spread revealingly into her throat.

The fact that she was instantly aware of everything about him, from the sleek smoothness of the hair that brushed his collar at the back of his head to the lean, aristocratic hollows beneath his cheekbones, was irritating. But that was her problem. It would have been difficult to pretend, to herself at least, that his image hadn't been indelibly printed on her memory for the past two years. Just because she hated and despised him it hadn't disappeared. She doubted it ever would.

Narrow arching brows framed eyes so dark she'd once believed they were black. But they weren't. Close inspection had revealed that they were merely dark brown, albeit shadowed by black lashes that any woman would envy.

But that was the only feminine thing about Alejandro Varga. Tall for a man whose appearance proclaimed his Cuban heritage, he had evidently inherited his American mother's genes, too. They were visible in his lean, athletic body, and his long powerful legs. In an impeccably cut suit—Abby guessed it was probably Italian in design—his tie his only concession to col-

16

our, he looked strong and invincible, and so painfully familiar that Abby's heart ached.

God, she had been such a fool, she thought raggedly. It was obvious that as far as he was concerned he had no regrets about the past. And why should he have? To him she had been merely a novelty, a diversion. Edward's older sister, who should have known better than to get involved with a man like him.

Now he was holding out his hand towards her and she was obliged to take it. Anything else would have been taken as an insult to the Esquivals, and she had no quarrel with them.

Nevertheless, when Alejandro's cool fingers closed about hers, she couldn't prevent the shiver that rippled down her spine at his touch. Even in the cool tranquillity of the Esquivals' living room, the memory of those strong brown hands upon her body was unavoidable. Awareness, hot and palpable, spread from his fingers to hers, and whereas before she had been chilled, now she was suddenly engulfed with heat.

Snatching her hand back, she pressed it to her midriff, hoping no one else had noticed her reaction. It would be embarrassing if the Esquivals imagined she was harbouring some abortive feelings for the man. Which she wasn't. But, to divert any suspicion, she added stiffly, 'I didn't expect to see you here.'

'Oh, but Alejandro considers this his second home,' declared Dolores warmly, moving towards him, preventing any rejoinder he might have made. She slipped her hand through his arm. 'Is that not so, *caro*?'

'Thanks to your gracious hospitality,' Alejandro told her gallantly, and Abby, looking away from the tableau they presented, saw her brother's lip curl in undisguised disgust.

No love lost there, then, she reflected curiously, wondering what Edward had against the man. He knew little of her dealings with Alejandro, and as he was apparently a close friend of Edward's in-laws surely it would have been in her brother's interests to try and get along with him. After all, whatever his faults, there was no doubt that he was a powerful man in Miami.

But once again she was allowing Alejandro to figure far too strongly in her thoughts. She hadn't flown several thousand miles to fret about his relationship with her brother. It was Edward she was concerned about; Edward whose strange behaviour was definitely a cause for concern.

However, before she could speak to him, she heard the sound of light footsteps crossing the hall. Everyone glanced towards the door so that when the young woman whose footsteps they'd heard paused on the threshold, she was instantly the cynosure of all eyes.

Abby supposed that that was what was meant by making an entrance. Lauren—for she saw at once that it was her sister-in-law—gazed about her for a moment before stepping delicately into the room. Small, like her parents, but enviably slender, Lauren was wearing a gauzy floral dress that swished about her calves. Her ankles looked absurdly narrow above perilously high-heeled sandals, and Abby was sure she wouldn't have been able to stand in them, let alone walk.

The younger girl's eyes lingered longest on Alejandro, but she was too well bred to allow her parents to suspect her smile of welcome was for anyone other than her sister-in-law. With a little cry of delight she launched herself towards Abby, enveloping her in a perfumed embrace.

'Abigail,' she exclaimed. 'I did not realise you were already here.' The slight lisp she favoured added a breathy sibilation to the words.

Abby managed a warm word of greeting, but she was intensely conscious of the differences between them, and of how obvious they must appear to everyone else. To Alejandro, she admitted honestly. He must have noticed she was at least six inches taller than her sister-in-law, and infinitely more generously endowed.

Her duty done, Lauren drew back again and turned to smile at their other guest. 'Alejandro,' she said, and even the way she said his name was revealing. 'Why did you not let me know you were coming?'

'You mean he didn't?' muttered Edward in an undertone which Abby was fairly sure only she could hear. But her brows drew together in some concern. Surely Edward wasn't jealous of Alejandro Varga. For heaven's sake, the man was married. Though she had to concede that hadn't stopped him before. Even so...

'I did not intend to be here,' Alejandro was saying as Lauren captured his hands and gazed up at him in youthful reproach. 'I had some business I wanted to discuss with your father, that is all. And when I heard that Abigail was expected...' His eyes moved beyond her to where Abby was standing, his brows lifting consideringly. 'How could I leave without first renewing our acquaintance?'

'What a prince!' grunted Edward rudely, but once again only Abby was close enough to hear him. Besides, Dolores was moving forward, eager to make her own contribution.

'Alejandro insisted on sending his chauffeur to the airport to meet Abigail,' she declared, suddenly explaining why Carlos hadn't hung around after dropping her off. And, as Lauren was obliged to relinquish her hold on his hands and turn to her husband, Abby realised that she was now in the ignominious position of being beholden to him, too.

'He's all heart,' said Edward, before she could speak, this time making no attempt to lower his voice. And, although Abby was diverted from having to make a response, she was uncomfortably aware that the Esquivals did not approve of their son-in-law's levity.

'You must forgive Edward,' declared Luis, taking the initiative, his dark eyes hot with anger. 'I fear the accident has not improved his temper, *mi amigo*.' Then, summoning a smile, he turned to Abby again. 'Come, Abigail, let me introduce you to my aunt.'

He drew her across the room to where the elderly woman was sitting. She was nodding in the sunlight that filtered through the long blinds, and he touched her shoulder with a

gentle hand. 'Tia Elena,' he said, his tone softening percepti-
bly, 'do you know Edward's sister? She has come to spend a
few days with us.'

Tia Elena was very old. Her face was a network of lines
and creases, her gnarled hands plucking almost absently at the
embroidery silks in her lap. But her eyes were surprisingly
bright when they opened to Luis's words, her gaze turning up
to Abby's face with undisguised interest

'*Por supuesto,*' she said. Of course. She held out her hand
towards the young woman. 'It is Abigail, *no*?' She paused.
'Edward told me you are escaping from the English winter,
sí?'

No!

Once again Abby had to bite her tongue to prevent herself
from protesting her innocence. Instead, she shook the old
woman's dry hand and managed a faint smile. 'Who wouldn't
want to escape here?' she said, deciding there was no point in
making an issue of it with the old lady. 'Everything is so—
beautiful.'

'You are saying all the right things,' observed Tia Elena
approvingly. 'Luis, we should hire this young woman to promote your new leisure complex, *no*?'

'You could be right,' responded Luis politely, but Abby had
the impression that he was still finding it difficult to control
his anger. 'Abigail is always welcome here. She knows that.'

Did she? Abigail was getting the distinct impression that the
Esquivals were not exactly overjoyed that she had arrived.
And why not? Edward was obviously in no danger. It looked
very much as if he had got her out here for his own purposes.
But what those purposes were she had yet to find out.

Now Abby abandoned her thoughts and stepped out onto her
balcony. It was good to feel the warmth of the sun reversing
the chill of apprehension on her skin. She already felt like an
interloper and it wasn't pleasant. Particularly as she hadn't
wanted to come.

Yet why did she feel this way? She couldn't fault the

Esquivals' hospitality. Despite Edward's rudeness, a maid had been summoned and iced tea had been served before Abby had been escorted to her room. And, thanks to Tia Elena's attentions, she'd managed to avoid having to say anything to either Alejandro or her brother. She'd perched instead on the edge of a bright yellow sofa and replied to the old lady's questions about her journey.

But why had Edward brought her out here? she wondered restlessly, plucking at the petals of the flowering vine that rioted over the iron railings of the balcony. What possible purpose could he have had? When she'd left England she'd imagined the worst, afraid that there must be something about his injuries he wasn't telling her. Now she was sure there was something Edward hadn't told her—but it wasn't about his accident.

The sound of voices came from below and her scalp prickled. Although she couldn't understand what he was saying, she thought she would have recognised that voice anywhere. It was Alejandro. He was leaving. And all three members of the Esquival family had come out to bid him farewell.

Abby glanced down almost nervously. Her balcony overlooked the formal gardens that lay to the right of the long drive, and by turning her head she could easily see the entrance portico and the four people who had emerged onto the shallow steps.

She knew she should draw back, that even by standing here, watching them, she was invading their privacy, but she stayed where she was. She wished she knew what her sister-in-law was talking about. Lauren's dark excitable posturing intrigued her. It was obvious that they all deferred to the man Abby had never expected to encounter here, and her heart twisted painfully at the way they fawned around him.

Alejandro seemed calm and unruffled. His lazy smile split the dark contours of his face. He gave a polite wave before walking towards the sleek black vehicle that Abby now saw was parked to one side of the forecourt. A click of the key-fob and then he was swinging the door open, coiling his long length behind the wheel.

No wonder the chauffeur hadn't hung around, Abby reflected, reluctantly admiring the lines of the expensive sports saloon. Clearly Alejandro preferred to drive himself.

The Esquivals clustered around the car, reluctant to let him go, but evidently he had had enough. His firing of the ignition signalled his eagerness to be on his way. And, although Abby told herself she was relieved that he would apparently not be joining them for dinner, she couldn't prevent the unexpected frisson of nostalgia she felt as he swung the wheel towards the gates.

Crushing the emotion, she turned and went back into the bedroom behind her. Perhaps she ought to be thinking of leaving, too, she reflected. There was a flight to London tomorrow afternoon at about this time, and if she had any sense she'd arrange to be on it. She owed it to Ross, and to her local education authority, not to take advantage of their good nature. And now that it appeared that all Edward needed was someone to complain to she had no excuse for staying on.

But for tonight at least she had to make the best of the situation. The suite, which comprised this room, a small sitting area, a dressing room and bathroom, was very comfortable. Okay, maybe the rather heavy and ornate furniture was not to her taste, but so what? It suited the house.

Nevertheless, she decided not to take everything out of the case the maid had deposited on the carved chest at the foot of the bed. Fortunately, she'd packed a couple of dresses near the top of the case that she'd hoped would be suitable for both day and evening wear, and that was all she'd need. Oh, and a pair of heels, of course. She couldn't wait to get out of the khaki pants and into something cool and feminine.

Say *what*?

Abby's lips twisted. What was she thinking of? Just because Lauren and her mother chose to wear extremely feminine clothes that was no reason for her to feel she had to do the same. For heaven's sake, she'd always been more at home in jeans and sweaters, or in warmer weather shorts and tees. She was no fashion plate. She never had been. She'd never get away with the kind of fussy flowing outfits Edward's in-laws favoured.

She heaved a sigh. This whole trip was going to be a disaster. She just knew it. She could willingly strangle Edward for getting her into this situation.

A knock at her door brought a momentary halt to her soul-searching. Throwing the two dresses she'd taken from the suitcase onto the bed, she walked resignedly across the sitting area to the door.

Edward was waiting outside. He could evidently get around with the help of the crutches he had propped beneath his arms. He looked a little shamefaced, however, and Abby only hesitated a second before stepping back to let him in.

Closing the door, she leant back against it for a moment. Then, still without saying anything, she walked past him and into the bedroom, returning to the examination of her clothes she'd been making before he'd interrupted her. But her heart wasn't in it, and when her brother limped to stand in the archway, watching her, she was forced to meet his pleading gaze.

'Are you mad at me?' he asked, giving her an appealing look, and she took a calming breath before replying.

'Can you blame me?' she demanded. Then, after a pause, 'You let me think you were seriously injured, Eddie. I was really worried about you. And now I find there's nothing wrong with you that a few weeks' rest won't cure.'

Edward looked injured. 'I wouldn't say that.'

Abby gave him a forbearing look. 'Comparatively speaking,' she retorted shortly. 'What have you got? A fractured femur? Cuts and bruises? Life-threatening? I don't think so.'

Edward limped to the armchair by the open balcony doors and eased himself into it. 'So what are you saying?' he asked. 'That I have to be at death's door before you'd make the effort to come and see me?'

Abby sighed. 'That's not what I meant and you know it.'

'Do I?' Edward was on the offensive now. 'It sounds suspiciously like it to me.'

'Well, that's because you're choosing to take it that way,' replied Abby, catching on fast. 'And you're not going to make me feel guilty, Eddie. I know you too well. What's really going on here? You might as well tell me. I haven't got the time to waste trying to second-guess you.'

Edward's mouth took on a resentful curve. 'It sounds as if you don't care what happens to me any more.'

'Oh, Eddie!' Abby flopped down onto the side of the bed, feeling as if she wanted to scream. It was bad enough that he'd got her out here in the first place. She could do without his self-pity now she was here. 'Stop twisting my words. I'm pleased to see you again. Of course I am. But you have to understand, this is not a holiday for me.'

'It's not a holiday for me either,' muttered Edward peevishly, and Abby shook her head.

'You know what I mean. I've had to take leave of absence from school, and now that Ross and I are—'

'Oh, I wondered when Kenyon would come into it,' Edward interrupted her harshly, and Abby remembered belatedly that he didn't care for Ross any more than her fiancé cared for him.

They'd all met last year, when Edward had brought Lauren to see where he'd used to live in England, and Abby recalled how she'd hoped that the two men would hit it off. Her relationship with Ross had still been in its initial stages at that time, and it had seemed a good idea to get the two men together.

It hadn't worked. Ross had considered Edward selfish and immature, and her brother had resented the occasionally patronising attitude Ross had adopted. She'd tried to explain that Ross was used to dealing with recalcitrant teenagers, but that had only exacerbated the situation. Edward had accused her of implying that he was no better than one of Ross's students, and in her efforts to placate him she'd inadvertently offended

Ross, too. The whole affair had been a nightmare, and she should have known better than to mention her fiancé now.

However, before she could think of some way of defusing the situation, Edward spoke again. Scuffing the toe of his canvas shoe against the polished floor, he lifted one shoulder in a conciliatory gesture.

'Anyway,' he mumbled, barely audibly, 'you're right. I didn't ask you to come out here just because of the accident.'

Abby's brows, which were considerably darker than her hair, drew rather warily together. 'You didn't?' she asked carefully, as if she hadn't been implying as much for the past few minutes. 'So why did you ask me to come?'

Edward blew out a breath. 'I—well, I needed to talk to you about Lauren. I think she's having an affair.'

CHAPTER THREE

ABBY was stunned. 'You're not serious!'

'Why not?' Edward, who had been staring moodily at the rug he had displaced with his toe, now looked up. 'Don't you think any man would want to have an affair with her?'

'Don't be silly.' Sometimes Abby was inclined to agree with Ross's assessment of the younger man. 'That has nothing to do with it.' She hesitated. 'What I mean is, I can't imagine why you would think such a thing.'

Or could she? Unwillingly Abby remembered how Lauren had behaved towards Alejandro Varga. Even if their relationship allowed for some familiarity, Abby had noticed that she'd been inordinately pleased to see him.

Edward scowled now, his next words shocking her out of any lingering sense of complacency. 'What am I supposed to think when she takes every chance she gets to spend time with Varga?' he demanded. 'And now that I'm half crippled with this leg, I don't even know where she is half the time.'

Abby's jaw had dropped as he spoke, but now she hurriedly rescued it. 'You're not implying she's having an affair with—with Alejandro?' she exclaimed disbelievingly.

'Why not?' Edward's pale eyes challenged hers.

'Well, because—because he's married?'

'Not any more.'

'Not any more?' Abby blinked. 'You mean, he's—divorced?'

'It happens,' said Edward bitterly. 'I always knew Maria was too good for him.'

Abby didn't know what to say. The last thing she wanted was for Edward to imagine she was still interested in Alejandro. All the same...

'Are you saying that Lauren had something to do with him getting a divorce?' she ventured incredulously, and Edward hunched his shoulders.

'No.' He was impatient. 'That happened a while ago. He and Maria were having problems before we even got married.'

'They were?'

Abby tried to hide her reaction from him. She clearly remembered Edward giving her the impression that Alejandro and his wife were happy together. That Dolores had been devastated when Maria had suffered a family emergency and hadn't been able to attend the wedding.

What emergency had that been? Her impending divorce?

Aware that Edward was watching her rather suspiciously, Abby realised that her face was far too expressive. Raising defensive eyebrows at him, she opted for a casual enquiry. 'What?'

'You tell me,' he said. 'Why are you looking at me like that?'

'Like what?'

'Don't pretend you don't know.' Edward was resentful now. 'I bet you were thinking that that wasn't what I said before.'

Abby chose to be obtuse. '*What* wasn't what you said before?' she asked, refusing to make it easy for him.

'That Varga and his wife were having problems,' he retorted. 'Okay, I admit it. I wanted to put you off him. I could see you were attracted to him, and I didn't want someone like him involved with my sister.'

Abby stared at him. 'So, what are you saying? That you told lies about him?'

'Not lies, no.' Edward was defensive. 'I just exaggerated the truth a little, that's all. No big deal.'

Abby shook her head in disbelief. 'And what gave you the right to interfere in my life?'

'Oh, let's not get carried away here,' protested Edward insensitively. 'The chances of you and Varga getting it together weren't exactly likely, were they? I mean, I know you were flattered when he offered to take you sightseeing and all, but you have to understand that's what these guys are like. Coming on to a woman—any woman—is second nature to them, and Varga more than most. I never liked him. I hoped that when the wedding was over he'd crawl back under his stone.' He scoffed. 'Some chance!'

'Edward!'

'Well…' He was unrepentant. 'I assumed he was just a distant relative. I had no idea he'd become such a constant presence in our lives. Do you know, he's a major shareholder in Luis's company? This new leisure complex they're hoping to open next Christmas is being financed by Varga. He and Luis are partners. Partners! How do you think that makes me feel? I'm Luis's son-in-law, not Alejandro.'

Abby was stunned—as much by the fact that Edward had lied to her as by his obvious envy of the other man. She didn't know what she thought of his suspicions about Alejandro and Lauren. She would reserve judgement. But after what he'd told her, how dependable was anything he said?

She was so glad now that she'd never confided her own feelings to Edward. Though perhaps it would have been easier if she had. Surely then he would have thought twice about involving her in his present problems. Yet, knowing Edward as she did there were no guarantees.

Feeling her way, she said cautiously, 'I still don't see what you're saying. All right. I accept that—that Alejandro is a regular visitor to the house. But you and Lauren don't live here. You have your own apartment, don't you? In Coconut Grove.'

Edward gave her an exasperated look. 'You don't know much about Cuban families, do you?' he snorted. 'Well, let me tell you, they stick together. Like, living in each other's pockets, if you know what I mean? Sure, we have our own place, but Lauren's hardly ever there. When I'm at work she's more often here. Or somewhere else, if you get my drift?'

'Somewhere else?' Abby suspected she knew what he was getting at but she decided to let him go on.

'Yeah.' Edward scowled. 'Making nice with—Alejandro.'

He pronounced the other man's name just as Lauren did, and Abby's stomach tightened unpleasantly. 'But he's her cousin,' she protested. 'Cousins don't get involved with one another in this country. I read it somewhere. It's considered too close a relationship.'

'Tell that to my wife,' retorted Edward dourly. 'In any case, he's not her cousin. Not exactly. He's a distant relation of her mother's.'

Abby sighed. 'Even so—'

'Even so, I know what I'm talking about,' snapped Edward irritably. 'I might have known you wouldn't believe me. It's Kenyon, isn't it? He's poisoned your mind against me.'

'Don't be so ridiculous!' Abby gasped. 'Ross couldn't do such a thing. I just—' She paused. 'What proof do you have?'

'What more proof do I need? You saw them together. Can you honestly tell me that you didn't think they seemed pretty close for distant cousins?'

Abby pushed herself up from the bed, feeling incredibly weary suddenly. It had been a long day. It might only be early evening in Miami, but it was after eleven o'clock back home. And, after all the upheaval, she'd forgotten to phone her fiancé as she'd promised. Would he understand that she'd had other things on her mind?

But breaking a promise to Ross was the least of her worries, she thought heavily. When she'd agreed to come here she'd hoped to avoid any mention of the man who'd caused such anguish in her life. Now it seemed he was an integral part of Edward's reasons for contacting her. And she so much didn't want to have to think about Alejandro again.

She'd done all her thinking and regretting two years ago, she thought bitterly. Even if, as it appeared now, he hadn't been as black as she'd painted him in her own mind. But he'd still behaved quite heartlessly. She didn't think she'd ever forgive him for that.

'Abbs?'

Edward was gazing up at her with a look of hopeful expectation on his face and she guessed he wasn't thinking about her. Had it ever occurred to him that she might have a life of her own? she wondered. As far as Edward was concerned, she'd only ever been there for him.

'I'm tired,' she told him now, glancing longingly towards the large colonial bed. But as that evidently wasn't the right answer, judging by his sulky face, she tried again. 'I just don't know what you want from me, Eddie. I'm only going to be here for a couple of days. If you're expecting me to spy on your wife for you, then—'

'Hey, I didn't ask you here to act like some kind of private eye,' exclaimed Edward impatiently. 'I doubt if you'd be any good at it anyway.' He grimaced. You're not exactly the inconspicuous type!'

Abby caught her breath. 'You know,' she said tensely, 'I've a good mind to phone the airport here and now and ask how soon I can get a flight home. I realise you're upset about Lauren, but that doesn't give you the right to insult me.'

'I'm not insulting you,' Edward snorted angrily 'Dammit, you couldn't be further from the truth. Okay, maybe I'm no good at choosing the right words. I'm not an English graduate, am I?' he taunted. 'What I'm trying to say is, people notice you. Hell, they'd notice any tall redhead around here. You may have noticed. They're not exactly thick on the ground.'

Abby expelled a resigned breath. 'If you say so.'

'I do say so.' Edward tried to reach out and grasp her hand but she evaded him. 'Come on, Abbs. Lighten up. You could at least say it's good to see me again.'

Abby shook her head. 'I'd just like to know why you've brought me here,' she said. 'I mean, I am glad to see you again, but if it's just my advice you want you could have had that over the phone.'

Edward's hand dropped onto his thigh. 'Well, that's telling me straight, isn't it?'

'Eddie!'

'Oh, all right.' He levered himself up from the chair and, using the crutches, made his way out onto the balcony. 'I want your help.'

'My help?' Abby followed him to the doorway, watching as he turned and propped his back against the railings. 'How am I supposed to help you? Do you want to come back to England? Is that it? Do you need my support to get started again over there?'

'As if!' Edward looked incredulous now. 'Abby, nothing could persuade me to come back to England again. I like it here. It's my home. Not this house, of course, although with a bit of luck it will be mine one day.' He grinned momentarily, and then, realising his sister was watching him with appalled eyes, he sobered. 'No, what I mean is, I've got a good job at the restaurant. I'd be a fool to even think about leaving Florida and starting again.'

'Then—?'

'Give me time,' he protested. 'I'm getting there. But this isn't easy for me, Abbs. I don't want you to think I haven't thought this through.'

'Thought what through?' Abby could feel herself getting edgy. 'Eddie, if you expect me to try and persuade Lauren—'

'Lauren?' He pushed himself away from the railings and came back to where she was standing. 'Lauren wouldn't listen to anything you had to say.' He pulled a face. 'She's blind and deaf to any criticism where Varga is concerned.'

'Well, that's good, because I was going to say I wouldn't do it,' retorted Abby shortly. 'Come on, Eddie, get to the point.'

Edward hung his head, staring down at the plaster that encased his leg as if he hoped it would provide him with some inspiration. Then, when she was on the point of yelling at him, he said, 'As a matter of fact I don't want to you to *talk* to anyone.' He paused. 'I want you to use any means necessary to get Varga off my back.'

It was barely light when Abby opened her eyes. Her body clock was still working on British time, and even though she'd found it incredibly difficult to get to sleep the night before, she had no desire to stay in bed now.

Being tired didn't stop her brain from working. It just added to the chaos in her head. She couldn't wait to escape the turmoil of uncertainty that was gripping her. Dear God, what was she going to do?

Although it was almost twelve hours since Edward had exploded his bombshell, she still felt numb. No, that wasn't true. If she'd still felt numb she wouldn't be suffering such a sense of betrayal. Wouldn't be wondering if she'd ever trust her brother again.

Had he actually asked her to try and use her influence on Alejandro? Did he really believe that the other man would care about anything she had to say? It was two years since she'd spoken to the Cuban; two years and many hours of heartache she couldn't bear to go through again.

Besides, speaking to Alejandro was only a part of what he wanted. As Edward had implied when he was talking about his wife, words wouldn't accomplish anything at all. What he really needed was for her to try and rekindle whatever interest Alejandro had had in her. He was asking her to jerk Alejandro's chain. To do whatever was necessary to distract the other man's attentions from his wife.

In other words to seduce him, if she could.

And what kind of a brother would ask his sister to do something like that?

Throwing back the covers, Abby thrust her feet out of bed. She had the distinct feeling she was dreaming all this. But when she accidentally stood on an earring that she'd dropped the night before, and it dug into the pad of her foot, she realised it was no dream.

A nightmare, maybe, she thought, bending to pick up the circle of gold and automatically threading it through her ear. Certainly last night's dinner hadn't been exactly what she'd expected, and it had been apparent from the Esquivals' behaviour that they thought she'd invited herself here.

'How long can you stay?' Dolores had asked politely, passing her a bowl of rice and beans so that she could serve herself. 'Edward couldn't tell us what your plans were.'

I bet he couldn't, Abby had fumed silently, noticing that once again Edward was avoiding her eyes. But, 'I'm not sure,' she'd responded, deciding he shouldn't have it all his own way. 'When Edward told me about his accident I felt I ought to come and see how he was for myself. I hope you don't mind.'

'Of course we don't mind,' Luis Esquival had assured her smoothly, his innate courtesy not allowing him to make any other response. 'You are Edward's sister, Abigail. You are welcome here at any time. I hope your brother assured you of that.'

Abby had managed a smile, but she felt uneasy at accepting their hospitality under false pretences. She'd hardly been able to swallow any of the rather spicy rice and fried beef, which Dolores had told her was a Cuban speciality, and when the meal was over she'd pleaded tiredness and retired to her room.

She'd hardly exchanged two words with her sister-in-law all evening. Lauren had seemed singularly reticent to get involved in what little conversation there was, and Abby wondered if she suspected why she was here. Surely not. Edward wouldn't have told her. Though in retrospect Abby had to admit that Lauren had said very little to her husband either.

So what was she to gauge from that? Did Edward have some justification for his suspicions? He'd left her in no doubt that he believed his happiness was at stake. He'd even told her that he didn't know how he would go on if Lauren left him. And, while Abby was sure that was an exaggeration, nothing could alter the fact that he was distraught.

She shook her head. The whole situation was unbelievable. Could he really have invited her here because of some fleeting interest he thought Alejandro had shown in her two years ago? How was she supposed to get a man who was virtually a stranger to her, despite their torrid history, to choose her company over that of his cousin? It was ludicrous. She was engaged to Ross, for heaven's sake. Just because Edward didn't like him that didn't mean she could ignore her fiancé's feelings and act like a—a tart!

Picking up the matching earring from the table beside the bed, she padded across the floor to the windows, securing it to her ear as she went. Then, drawing the blinds aside, she unlatched the balcony doors and stepped out into the comparative coolness of early morning.

A sliver of brightness on the horizon heralded the imminent arrival of the sun, but for the moment the garden below was shrouded in shadow. Yet already she could hear the sound of running water and guessed someone was tending to the plants. The lawns didn't get to be so green by accident, she mused, and, unwilling to be observed in just her nightshirt, she turned and went back into her room.

Deciding a shower would serve the dual purpose of filling time and helping to clear her head, Abby walked into the bathroom. It was such a treat, she thought wryly. When she stayed at Ross's house she had to compete with him for the shower, and her fiancé tended to ignore the fact that the hot water wasn't unlimited. He often left it running needlessly, so that when Abby went for her shower the water was cold.

She didn't have that problem this morning. But it did remind her that she had to ring Ross before she did anything else. Knowing him, she was sure he'd have checked that her flight had arrived safely, but she still needed to explain what was going on.

Or not.

Heaving a sigh, she adjusted the shower, wondering what on earth she was going to tell her fiancé when she made her call. If she told him that Edward wasn't seriously hurt he'd expect her to return home almost immediately. And that was what she should do, she chided herself fiercely. If she just pretended that she'd made a mistake Ross need never know what Edward had asked of her.

Stepping into the pulsating stream of water, she wondered why she was even hesitating. Delaying her return was just giving her brother false hope. All right, she was prepared to accept that he and Lauren might be going through a bad patch. These things happened. But nothing she did was going to change things. It was up to him to make an effort, to do everything in his power to rekindle whatever it was that had attracted her to him in the first place.

There were bottles of shower gel and shampoo on a glass shelf to one side of the shower, and Abby chose a lemon-scented mousse to wash her hair. It was good to massage her scalp, to feel the cleansing fragrance refreshing her completely. She emerged feeling infinitely brighter, if no less certain of what she was going to do.

The long mirrors that lined the walls of the bathroom were barely steamed when she stepped out. Reaching for a towel from the rack, she dried herself quickly and then used the towel to rub the condensation from the mirror nearest to her. Surveying her appearance with a critical eye, she wondered why on earth Edward thought that Alejandro might prefer her to Lauren. It just wasn't realistic, however she might feel about it.

She shook her head and the tumbled tangle of dark red curls sprayed water all over her dry shoulders. Reaching for the towel, she dabbed herself dry again, aware as she did so that her nipples were suddenly tight and hard. It was because she'd shivered, she assured herself, turning away from the mirror. But not before her eyes had made a swift appraisal of her narrow waist and rounded hips.

The realisation that what she was really doing was trying to see herself with Alejandro's eyes irritated her. Did she really care what he thought of her now? Or was she naïve enough to believe Edward's assessment of her appearance? A final glance at her backside convinced her. Her brother was desperate, and he'd say anything to get his own way.

CHAPTER FOUR

SHE decided to ring Ross before drying her hair.

With the balcony doors open, heat was spreading into the room from outside, and she turned the thermostat down to warm the room. Then, wrapping the folds of the towelling robe she had found behind the bathroom door more closely about her, she seated herself in the chair Edward had used the night before and picked up the phone.

Discovering she had an outside line, she dialled the school where they were both employed. It was still early, but Ross should be taking his lunch at this time. One of the school secretaries put her through to the staff room and she was relieved when Ross himself answered the call.

'Abby!' he exclaimed, after she'd identified herself. 'I thought you were going to ring me last night. I waited up until after midnight, hoping you wouldn't forget.'

'I know. I'm sorry.' Abby wished he hadn't had to begin with a complaint. 'And I didn't forget. Not exactly. It's just—well, I'm staying with Eddie's in-laws at the moment, and it's a little—complicated.'

'What's a little complicated? Your brother's injuries?' Ross immediately leapt to the wrong conclusion and Abby sighed.

'No,' she said, knowing that he deserved a straight answer. 'Eddie's injuries aren't complicated, but—'

'But it's going to take more than a couple of days to get him home again, is that it?'

Ross's attempts to second-guess her were annoying and Abby wished he'd just listen to what she had to say instead of jumping in every few seconds with his own version of events.

'I—Eddie's out of hospital,' she persisted, trying to explain

36

that he was staying with the Esquivals, too. But Ross seemed determined to put his own interpretation on her words.

'Oh, I see,' he said, when he obviously didn't see at all. 'He's back at the flat. I suppose Lauren's looking after him. But that's only a small place, isn't it? Is that why you're staying with her parents?'

Abby blew out an exasperated breath. 'No,' she said shortly. 'Neither of them are at the—apartment.' She deliberately used the alternative term. 'They're staying here.'

'They are?' For the first time her fiancé sounded less sure of himself. Then, almost as an afterthought, 'So, how is Edward? Have you found out what happened?'

'I know what happened,' said Abby, trying not to be impatient. 'A drunk driver slammed into his car. He was lucky he was hit on the nearside and that he wasn't carrying any passengers. He could have been killed.'

'Well, he evidently wasn't very badly hurt if they've discharged him from hospital already,' said Ross practically. 'I thought as much. So when are you coming home?'

Until that moment Abby had been thinking about going home. She'd all but abandoned any thought of taking what Edward had said seriously, and, although she was worried about the problems he and Lauren were having, she'd had no intention of interfering in their lives.

But Ross's casual assumption that if Edward wasn't in any danger she'd be catching the next flight back to London caught her on the raw. He might show some concern for the man he was planning to make his brother-in-law. His annoying habit of always having to be right infuriated her.

'I don't know,' she said now, deciding it served him right for being so unfeeling. 'I may stay on for a few days.'

'But why?' Ross seemed insensible to the fact that he was treading on dangerous ground. 'Surely he doesn't need you to hold his hand. He's got a wife, Abby. I doubt if she appreciates you turning up out of the blue.'

'I didn't come here because of Lauren,' retorted his fiancée tersely. 'You don't seem to realise the emotional stress an accident can cause.'

But as she said the words Abby wondered who she was kidding. For heaven's sake, if Edward was stressed it wasn't because of the accident. She knew that.

'Oh, right.' Ross sounded irritated now. 'I'd forgotten what a sensitive flower Edward is.' He made a sound of derision. 'Get real, Abby. Edward doesn't need you. He's just using this to get back at me. I bet it really ticked him off when you told him we were engaged.'

'Is that what you really think?' Abby was appalled at his hostility. 'For heaven's sake, Ross, I didn't ring you to get a lecture about my brother's character. He's had a bad shock, okay? Is it any wonder if he needs some moral support?'

'Moral support!' Ross snorted. 'Sometimes I wonder about you, I really do. You're so easily duped. No wonder Edward can run rings around you. Well, after we're married things are going to change. I'm going to let him know he can't come running to you every time he needs a shoulder to cry on.'

Abby caught her breath. 'We may not be getting married at this rate,' she said, wishing she'd never made this call. 'I've got to go, Ross. I'll speak to you later.'

'Well, where—?'

But Abby didn't wait to hear any more. With a feeling of revulsion she put down the phone, staring at it blindly for a few seconds before getting up and moving away. She was glad he couldn't call her back, she thought tensely. Although he knew Edward's number, he didn't know this one. He could be so unpleasant at times. He hadn't even asked her about her journey. He didn't seem to care about anything except when she was going back.

Surely he should sense how she was feeling. Why couldn't he have been sympathetic, understanding? If he had been, she'd probably have been packing her bags right now. As it was, she'd committed herself to staying on for several more days when she hadn't intended to. Either that or run the risk of Ross believing he'd got his own way again.

A glance at her watch reminded her that it was almost eight o'clock. She didn't know where, or even if, the Esquivals had breakfast, but she was desperate now to get out of her room. She'd go downstairs, she decided. Maybe Lauren would join her. She'd welcome the chance to speak to the other girl. Anything was better than staying here at the mercy of her thoughts.

It was already hot. She could feel the heat pouring into the room from outside now, and after closing the balcony doors she turned the air-conditioning up again. Immediately a draught of deliciously cool air swept over her shoulders as she shed the robe and rummaged in her suitcase for something to wear.

By the time she'd found a sleeveless shirt and denim shorts her hair was practically dry. But it was unruly, and snatching up her brush, she quickly plaited the damp curling strands into a single braid. It wasn't very long. It barely reached to the top of her shoulderblades. But at least it was tidy, even if a few wispy curls persisted in escaping to cling to her flushed cheeks.

She didn't bother with make-up. In this heat it wouldn't last, and her face was glowing as it was. Probably due to her rising temperature, she reflected. Unlike many redheads, she did tan, so her skin still retained some of the colour she'd acquired in southern Italy the summer before. Perhaps no one would notice, she hoped optimistically. At least she didn't look as anaemic as she felt.

Her legs looked very pale, though, she conceded, as she went out onto the gallery that circled the hall below. But it was still winter back home and she wasn't used to exposing them. Nevertheless, they were long and slim, even if Edward was fooling himself if he thought any man would notice her while his wife was around.

There was no one about when she reached the ground floor, and after getting her bearings she walked along the wide passageway that led to the back of the house. A sunlit terrace, enclosed by long screens, gave access to an inner courtyard, and the mingled scents of a dozen exotic blooms assaulted her senses.

Stepping out of the shadows of a colonnade that ran along two sides of the courtyard, Abby saw the glinting waters of the swimming pool ahead of her. She wondered if anyone used it these days. When she'd been here two years ago none of the Esquivals had ever been tempted to swim in its lucid depths. As far as they were concerned it was an ornament, a status symbol. As necessary to their lives as the gymnasium in the basement which no one used either.

Pushing her hands into the pockets of her shorts, Abby walked down the two shallow steps that divided the pool deck from the courtyard above. She wasn't thinking about anything at that moment except how delightful it would be to have the freedom to immerse herself in the cool water, and she was shocked when a tall, dark-clad figure rose up from beside the pool.

It was Alejandro. Wearing a black tee shirt and black trousers, he had evidently been sitting on one of the shaded loungers that stood in a regimented row beneath a hedge of flowering bougainvillaea. Lean and imposing, he was looking at her with dark enigmatic eyes, and Abby's mouth dried at the realisation that she didn't know what she was going to say to him.

'Abigail,' he greeted her, inclining his head politely. 'I am sorry if I startled you. I thought perhaps you had seen me.'

And come down here to speak to you? contributed Abby silently. As if she would! The truth was, if she'd seen him first she'd probably have turned tail and gone back into the house.

And how mature was that?

'I—no,' she answered now, glancing back over her shoulder, hoping for deliverance. 'You're an early caller. Are you waiting for Luis?'

'No.' Alejandro's mouth compressed for a moment. 'As a matter of fact, none of the family knows I am here. Except for yourself, *por supuesto*.' He paused. 'Does that bother you?'

'Why should it bother me?' she retorted, stung for a moment into revealing her true feelings. But then, realising that was hardly the image Edward would want her to promote, she added, 'Not at all.'

'Good.' Alejandro turned and indicated the row of loungers behind him. 'Perhaps you will join me?'

Abby saw now that there was a tray residing on the glass-topped table beside the chair he had been occupying. A jug of freshly squeezed orange juice and two glasses, a pot of coffee, and two cups. He had evidently been expecting company, whatever he said, and she wondered with a momentary frisson of distaste if Lauren had stood him up.

But, no. That was pandering to Edward's paranoia, and she had no reason to assume the worst. One of the maids had made an error, had provided breakfast for two instead of one.

'I'm—not sure that would be a good idea,' she said at last, even if this was an opportunity to find out what she wanted to know. 'I was looking for Lauren. Do you know if she's about?'

'If I know my cousin, she is unlikely to appear much before noon,' Alejandro said smoothly. 'I am sorry I cannot help you there. Perhaps you will reconsider my invitation instead.'

He had taken a step towards her and Abby had to steel herself not to retreat before his potent masculinity. Her skin prickled in anticipation of his touch, however, and although she might deny it to herself he could still set her pulses racing just by standing close to her.

'I—don't know,' she said unevenly, wishing she could put her emotions aside and deal with him as casually as he was dealing with her. What was wrong with her, for heaven's sake? It wasn't as if she still believed in hearts and flowers, after all. After her brief encounter with this man she'd been very careful not to trust too much again.

'I do not think there would be any harm in us sharing a pot of coffee,' Alejandro said now, and for a moment she thought he was going to take her arm and guide her to a chair. 'Do not be alarmed, Abigail. I only wish to speak with you. That is all.'

Was she supposed to be grateful for that? Abigail wondered what he was really thinking behind that cool, disturbing mask. 'Well—all right,' she submitted at last, a little breathily. If she wanted him to believe she'd forgotten what had happened two years ago, she would have to do better than this. 'Where do you want me to sit?'

Alejandro drew back to indicate a chair at right angles to the table. 'I think you would be most comfortable there, in the shade,' he replied, and she sucked in her breath as she circled round him, desperate to avoid any contact between them. He waited until she was seated before taking the chair opposite, sitting sideways on the recliner, legs spread to accommodate the table. 'Which would you prefer? Orange juice or coffee?'

In actual fact, Abby would have preferred orange juice, but she needed the caffeine so she chose coffee instead. To her surprise, Alejandro lifted the pot himself, asking her preference for milk and sugar before passing a cup to her.

She was tempted to say *Isn't this cosy?* but she restrained herself. It was just the bubble of hysteria in her stomach that was putting such ideas into her head. Still, the thought of her sitting here, drinking coffee with the man who had seduced her after her brother's wedding and then allowed her to return to England without once attempting to find out if she was all right was quite incredible. Did he have no shame? When was he going to mention that he'd forgotten to tell her that he had had a wife?

But that was all in the past, she reminded herself. Concentrating on the swirling coffee in her cup, she forced herself to put such memories aside. What she ought to be asking herself was why he'd invited her to join him. Why would he want to spend any time with her? The fleeting attraction he'd felt for her was dead and buried. She was right to be suspicious about his motives now.

Nevertheless, she remembered unwillingly, he had wanted

her once. Had wanted to have sex with her, at least. Well, he'd achieved his aim, she thought, an angry sob rising in her throat. So what now? A belated apology for past sins? Her lips twisted. More likely a plea that she wouldn't spoil his current plans by denouncing him to his family.

She noticed that although Alejandro had poured himself a cup of strong black coffee he didn't touch it. Instead, he played with the gold signet ring on his smallest finger, causing it to glint hypnotically in the sunlight. His hands hung between his thighs and Abby had to force herself not to watch him—had to force her eyes not be to be drawn to the taut seam of his pants between his legs.

'You are looking good, Abigail,' he said abruptly, and she set her cup down in its saucer rather harder than she'd intended. This was not what she'd expected at all. 'How are you? I understand you are still teaching. You are quite happy to pursue your career?'

'I have to earn a living, if that's what you mean,' she responded tersely, wondering why he'd be interested enough to find out, and Alejandro inclined his head.

'*Por supuesto.* Of course.' A half-smile touched his lips. 'Edward would have told me if your circumstances had changed.'

Would he? Abby doubted that very much. Why would Edward tell him anything? What he meant was that Edward would have mentioned it to his in-laws and it might then have found its way to his ears.

'Do you see much of Edward?' she asked, deciding this was as good a way as any of finding out what Alejandro thought of her brother, and the dark man gave her a level look.

'Did he not tell you?' he countered surprisingly, and once again she gave him a wary look.

'I—I believe you and—and Luis are working together these days,' she said obliquely, reminding herself to keep her tone impartial. 'Do you—er—do you spend a lot of time here?'

Alejandro studied her expression for a moment, before responding drily, 'Is that a polite way of finding out if I am likely to be—what is it you say?—under your feet?'

'No!' Abby's face was suddenly suffused with hot colour. 'What you do is nothing to do with me, Mr Varga. I was just wondering why—why you are here so early, that's all.'

'And I thought I had made that clear.' Alejandro arched a dark brow. 'And—*Mr* Varga? Do you honestly think we can behave as if there was never anything between us?'

Oh, God!

Abby had been about to pick up her coffee cup again, but now she pressed her hands together in her lap. She'd never dreamt that he might confront her with what had happened two years ago. Had he no shame? Or did he just enjoy making her squirm?

'I'd prefer not to talk about it,' she said at last, though she balked at addressing him as *Mr* Varga again. She didn't want to anger him. That would be foolish. 'It was a mistake I'd just as soon forget.'

Alejandro's mouth compressed. 'You think?' he said, regarding her flushed face for several long nerve-racking seconds. His eyes dropped to the ring on her finger. 'Edward told me there was a new man in your life.'

A new man?

Abby didn't know what he meant by that, but she had no intention of entering into a discussion about her private life. It was hard enough to believe Edward would have told him anything. And that rekindled all the suspicions about Lauren her brother had raised.

'Look,' she said, trying not to sound concerned, 'what is this all about? And please don't tell me you're interested in what I've been doing. It's a little late to find your conscience now.'

'My conscience?' He seemed amazed by her directness. 'I am sure your brother has told you I do not have such a thing. But you, Abigail—you are different from Edward. And I still find you attractive. Please have no doubts about that.'

Abby was stunned into silence. Had he guessed why

Edward had tricked her into coming here? But, if so, did that mean there was some truth in what Edward had been saying? Were he and Lauren really involved in an affair?

'I—my brother has had an accident,' she said unevenly. 'That's the only reason why I'm here.'

'If you say so,' he said, his eyes dark and guarded. 'But your brother has another agenda, I think.'

Abby swallowed. 'I don't know what you mean,' she said, not sure now she even wanted to know.

'Edward has a hairline fracture to his leg,' he said, his tone dismissive. 'Hardly life-threatening, I think you will agree.'

The fact that Abby herself had said much the same when she'd found out was not an issue. 'He's had a terrible shock,' she insisted tensely. 'He could have been killed—'

'But he was not,' inserted Alejandro unfeelingly, much like her fiancé. 'Forgive me, Abigail, but your brother leads far too charmed a life to have it taken away by a drunken driver. The accident was unfortunate, but not serious. The car was damaged, *sí*, but it was not a write-off.'

Abby pushed back her chair and got to her feet. Whatever Edward expected of her, she couldn't stand any more of this. Did Alejandro know why Edward had brought her here, or was he only guessing? And why, when he insisted he was still interested in her, did she feel so aggrieved when this was exactly what her brother had hoped?

'If you'll excuse me…' she said, not really caring whether he did or not. But Alejandro wasn't finished with her.

When she would have circled the table and hurried up the steps to the terrace, he moved into her path. 'You are not leaving already,' he said, and although it was said innocently enough Abby thought it sounded like a warning. 'We have not finished our discussion, Abigail. Edward is not going to like it if you don't get a favourable result.'

'How dare you?'

Abby was so incensed her hand moved automatically towards his face. But Alejandro's hand was quicker, trapping her wrist in mid-flight, holding it effortlessly away from harm.

'I think not,' he said softly, his warm breath lifting the unruly strands of hair from her cheek. 'If your brother wants my help, you will have to do better than this, *cara*. I regret the need to use these methods, Abigail, but I did not make the rules.'

CHAPTER FIVE

LOOKING back, Abby didn't quite know how she'd managed to get away from Alejandro with her dignity still intact.

Her first impulse had been to drag her wrist out of his grasp and run, kicking and screaming her frustration, into the house.

Not, she acknowledged later, that she'd have got away from him without his co-operation. Whatever else, Alejandro was infinitely stronger than she was, and indulging in a childish tug-of-war, with her arm as the rope, would have been downright stupid.

Not to mention embarrassing.

And painful.

But, with her lungs constricting in her chest and her panic only lightly controlled, she'd found the guts to stand up to him. And when it had become apparent that she wasn't going to answer him Alejandro had opened his fingers and released her.

It wasn't over. She knew that. Even though he'd let her go without another word, she knew it as surely as if he'd voiced his desire for retribution. Something was going on here, something she knew nothing about, and she couldn't wait to speak to Edward and find out what the hell it was.

In that, however, she had not been successful. Whether her brother knew of her encounter with Alejandro that morning or not, she didn't know, but he had proved suspiciously elusive since then.

Abby, herself, would have preferred to spend the rest of the morning in her room. But, after sluicing her hot face in the basin in her bathroom, she'd known that would achieve nothing. Even if Alejandro joined the family for breakfast she had to show her face. Besides, how else was she going to corner her brother when she had no idea where his suite of rooms was?

In any case, she could hardly confront her brother in front of his wife. According to Edward, it was because of Lauren that he'd brought her here. And, although she suspected there was more to it than that, she couldn't dismiss his fears out of hand. Alejandro had virtually admitted that something was going on. But she had no idea what it was.

She had breakfast alone.

When she eventually summoned up the courage to go downstairs again, it was to find that no one else was about. The maid directed her to a rattan table and chairs set in the shade of the colonnade and explained that Mr Esquival had already left for his office. Apparently Mrs Esquival didn't eat breakfast, and Abby, who had steeled herself to face a family breakfast similar to the dinner she'd faced the night before, didn't know whether to be glad or sorry.

There was no sign of Alejandro either, which was a relief. When she asked about her brother and his wife she was told that he and *Mees* Lauren usually had breakfast in their rooms. Abby thought that Edward at least might have made an exception in these circumstances. But he was obviously in no hurry to explain himself.

Instead, she had to make the best of it, accepting a serving of scrambled eggs and bacon when the maid offered them against her better judgment. Despite her fears—or perhaps because of them—she was starving, and she consoled herself with the thought that it was after midday back home.

But, with the meal over, the rest of the morning stretched emptily ahead of her. On edge, as she was, she had no interest in the pool. Even the idea of sunbathing on the pool deck reminded her too strongly of what had happened there just a couple of hours earlier. Until Edward decided to show his face she could only wait impatiently for him to appear.

Going up to her room again, she decided to unpack her suitcase, realising that, however much she might want to leave, it wasn't going to happen today. Leaving her clothes in the case would only add to the creases they'd gained on the journey across the Atlantic. And in her present position she didn't want to add to her feelings of inadequacy by looking unkempt.

An hour later she was downstairs again, pacing up and down the terrace, wondering when Edward was going to grace her with his presence, when Dolores Esquival joined her. She paused in the doorway to the salon, looking at Abby a little uncertainly, as if she didn't quite know what she was going to do with her. Abby noticed she was quite clearly dressed to go out.

'Good morning,' Abby greeted her politely, once again cursing her brother for putting her in this position. 'It's a beautiful day.'

'Yes, isn't it?' Dolores hardly glanced up at the cloudless blue sky overhead. Then, linking her hands together at her waist, she added pleasantly, 'Is everything all right?'

As all right as anything could be in the circumstances, thought Abby drily, but she managed a matching response. 'It's fine—everything's fine,' she assured the older woman. Then, because she felt she had to say something more, 'I hope you don't think I was presumptuous in coming here, Mrs Esquival. I really was—worried about my brother.'

Dolores shook her head. 'I am sure you were,' she said, with the first evidence of warmth she'd shown. 'We were worried about him, too. But, happily, he seems to be making a good recovery. We are all hoping his leg heals very soon.'

'Yes.' Abby was grateful for her understanding. 'I—er—I was just waiting for him.'

'Oh, but he is not here,' exclaimed her hostess in surprise. 'I thought you knew. Lauren and Edward's apartment in Coconut Grove was broken into last night. They've gone to accompany the police on an inspection of the property.'

'Oh, no!' Abby immediately felt ashamed of herself for blaming her brother for neglecting her. She frowned. 'Was anything taken? Was anyone hurt?'

'There was no one there, fortunately, and I imagine the police are hoping Lauren and Edward can tell them if anything is missing,' declared Dolores practically. 'Electrical goods are always attractive to thieves, as you probably know, and Edward had—may still have—a very sophisticated entertainment system in the bedroom.'

Abby shook her head. 'Is there anything I can do?'

'I don't think so.' Dolores pulled a wry face. 'If there is any vandalism Luis will arrange to have it dealt with, you can be sure. But of course we will have to decide whether we consider it safe for Lauren to go back there. We will think about that when Edward is on his feet again.'

Abby noticed Dolores was more concerned about Lauren than her brother. But that was only natural. Lauren was an only child, and she was very precious to them.

'I wonder when they'll be back,' she murmured, more to herself than to the other woman. But Lauren's mother had evidently heard her.

'I have no idea,' she said, looking thoughtful. It was as if she'd just realised she couldn't abandon her guest. 'Perhaps you'd better come with me, Abigail,' she decided abruptly. 'I have an appointment at my dress designer's at twelve-thirty, but afterwards we could have lunch together. There is a Cuban restaurant close by that serves the most delicious stone crab claws.' She kissed the tips of her fingers in anticipation, her eyes drifting assessingly over Abby's shirt and shorts as she spoke. 'You would have to change, *no,* but...' She shrugged. 'Would you like to see a little of our city?'

Abby wanted to refuse. She desperately needed to talk to Edward, and it had never been part of her plan to make herself anyone else's responsibility. But Dolores evidently expected her to jump at the chance of some sightseeing and, short of pleading tiredness, she couldn't think of a single reason why not.

'I—you don't have to worry about me,' she protested, making a final attempt to avoid the outing, but Dolores was adamant.

'It will be my pleasure,' she insisted, even if she did cast another doubtful look at Abby's appearance. 'Shall we say—twenty minutes? Will that be enough?'

Not nearly, thought Abby a few moments later, riffling through the clothes she'd hung out earlier. Whatever she wore, she was going to look tall and ungainly beside the petite—if plump—Dolores. Why hadn't she pretended to have a headache? Surely no one could have argued with that?

But she hadn't, and she had only fifteen minutes left to make herself presentable. On her own, she would have stuck with the shorts. But it was obvious Dolores didn't think they were suitable for a trip to town.

Which left—what? A dress with spaghetti straps that Dolores would probably consider equally unsuitable? Or pants and a vest teamed with a cream suede jacket she'd brought along because it was her favourite?

The pants and jacket won out, and, deciding the plait she'd made of her hair would have to go, she brushed the tangles out, leaving it loose about her shoulders.

She gave one final glance at her reflection before leaving her bedroom. The purple vest was taut across her full breasts, and the beige cotton pants hugged her behind, but she couldn't help that. Thankfully the suede jacket hid a multitude of sins, she thought, even if she was going to feel incredibly hot when she was out in the open air.

The look Dolores gave her when she rejoined the older woman in the reception hall was hardly encouraging, but she ignored it and forced a smile.

'Ready,' she said, realising that Dolores's sky-blue tussore suit had probably cost more than her whole wardrobe put together. 'You look—wonderful.'

'Why, thank you, *cara*.' Dolores evidently appreciated the compliment, though she didn't return it. 'Shall we go?'

They drove to an exclusive little shopping mall in Dolores's car. Dolores herself took the wheel, and Abby was alarmed at the number of near misses they had on the comparatively short journey. Lauren's mother's fingers were never far from the horn, and although some of the almost-accidents were not her

fault, Dolores switched lanes indiscriminately, showing little
respect for other drivers.

Abby was relieved when they reached their destination. She
got out of the car in the busy lot adjoining the mall feeling as
if she was lucky to be alive. Even the exhaust fumes that
lingered in the sultry air were preferable to the heated atmosphere Dolores had generated and, deciding she was too hot
to worry about appearances, Abby slipped off her jacket.

She noticed Dolores gave her bare arms a doubtful look as
they crossed the lot to the glass doors that led into the mall.
But Abby ignored it. She didn't want to offend her, but she
simply wasn't used to the heat.

The doors into the mall were attended by a uniformed security guard, who welcomed them with an obsequious smile.
If he wondered who the tall redheaded woman was, he contained his curiosity, greeting Dolores with, '*Señora Esquival!
Que tal?*' How are you? Almost falling over himself in his
eagerness to open the doors.

'*Bien, gracias, Tomas,*' Dolores responded, sailing past him
with barely an acknowledgement of his assistance. She seemed
more intent on ridding herself of Abby's presence, saying in
a careless tone, 'I am sure you can entertain yourself while I
go to the salon, can't you, Abigail?'

Abby expelled a breath. 'Of course,' she said, as relieved
as the other woman to have a little time to herself. 'I can meet
you back at the car, if you'd rather. You don't have to take
me to lunch. I'd be quite happy to go back to the house.'

And see Edward, she added, though only to herself.

Dolores considered for a moment, but, although she might
have been attracted by Abby's suggestion, courtesy won out.
'Nonsense,' she said firmly. 'I'm looking forward to it.' Which
patently wasn't true. 'The restaurant is at the end of the mall.'
She pointed. 'It's called La Terraza. Why don't we meet there
in—say, thirty minutes, okay?'

'All right.'

Abby could hardly refuse if Dolores was prepared to put
herself out on her behalf. But after the little woman had

walked quickly away, swaying a little precariously on her high heels, she wondered how she was going to fill in the next half-hour here. The mall seemed full of designer shops, selling everything from *haute couture* to sports equipment. But everything had a label and the corresponding price tag was out of her reach.

Deciding she could always window-shop, Abby sauntered along the arcade, stopping every now and then to admire a piece of jewellery or a particularly attractive display of evening wear. If you need to ask the price, you can't afford it, she reminded herself drily. Her lips twitched. Evidently her fellow shoppers were far more wealthy than they appeared.

A bookshop offered a welcome escape from the material world. Books, at least, were affordable, and it was interesting to see what novels had made it to the top ten. There were lots of authors she didn't recognise, and she spent quite some time examining the shelves containing crime novels and thrillers. She was wondering if she could buy a couple of books to take home for Ross to read when she glanced at her watch and saw that she was already running out of time.

Dammit! Putting down the books she'd been considering, she hurried out of the store. She had still to find the restaurant, she thought crossly. What had Dolores told her? That it was at the end of the mall?

To her relief, she found the place without difficulty. Fate must have been smiling on her for once, she thought, pausing outside, not sure where Dolores would expect them to meet. She was only seven minutes late, and there was no sign of the other woman. With a bit of luck she might not have arrived yet.

The restaurant itself looked exclusive. But then, she'd expected that. She already knew that Dolores put a lot of stock in appearances. Perhaps she should put her jacket on again, if only to please her.

She was wishing she'd also taken the time to visit the restroom when she became aware that someone was watching her. A man who had been passing the smoked glass doors of the restaurant had paused and was looking at her. And when she turned her head, prepared to give him a cool put-down, she discovered that for the second time that day Alejandro had caught her unawares.

Immediately her pulse went into overdrive, and the dampness she had been feeling at the back of her neck now spread to her hairline. Every pore in her body felt as if it was oozing moisture, and she rubbed a furtive finger over her top lip as he strolled towards her.

'Abigail.' His greeting was polite enough, but she guessed he was remembering their earlier encounter and enjoying her discomfort. 'We meet again.'

Not through choice, I can assure you. Abby bit back the ready retort that sprang to her lips and gave him a thin smile. 'So it seems,' she said tightly, wondering where Dolores was. The other woman had said they should meet *outside* the restaurant, hadn't she? Surely she hadn't sent Alejandro in her place.

Alejandro's dark brows drew together. 'Forgive me,' he said softly, 'but are you waiting for somebody? Edward, perhaps?'

Abby looked up at him and then wished she hadn't. His dark gaze was far too disturbing and she was instantly aware of her own vulnerability where he was concerned. She might hate him, she might despise him for the way he'd treated her, but she could never ignore him. And he knew that, damn him. She could see the awareness glinting in his eyes.

'I—not Edward, no,' she said shortly, wishing he would just go away and leave her. She'd rather attract a stranger's unwelcome attentions, she told herself rashly, than his mocking stare.

'Who then?' he persisted, obviously amused by her red face. '*Que te pasa,* Abigail? What's going on? Surely you are not afraid to tell me?'

'Afraid?' She looked at him again, angry that he should even think such a thing. 'No, of course I'm not afraid, Mr Varga. I just wish you would leave me alone. I'm not Lauren. Nor am I flattered by your attentions. Or the attentions of any

man who thinks his wealth gives him the right to have anything he wants!'

Alejandro's face darkened. '*Por Dios*, Abigail, that is unforgivable.'

'Is it?'

Abby was unhappily aware that she had probably gone too
far. Edward expected her to be polite to this man, to persuade
him to leave Lauren alone, if that was at all credible. Instead
of which she was going out of her way to make an enemy of
him.

Alejandro took a deep breath now. 'It seems you are determined to believe the worst of me,' he said, flicking back the
cuff of his sleeve and glancing at his watch. 'It is almost one-
fifteen.' He looked up. 'I suggest you allow me to seat you at
my table until your—companion—shows up.'

Abby pressed her lips together, thinking it was a surprisingly conservative watch for someone like him. Slim and gold,
perhaps, but it wasn't flashy. Unlike the one Ross wore on his
wrist.

'Why should you want to do that?' she asked, unhappy at
the turn of her thoughts. Aware, too, of a trickle of moisture
sliding down between her breasts. Her nipples felt tight and
sensitive and she was sure he must have noticed. Her bra was
damp and she might as well have left it at home.

'It is not wise for a woman like you to stand alone in a
public shopping mall,' he said now, his dark eyes enigmatic.
'If you were my sister I would not be happy that you are alone.
Call it courtesy, if you will. I am merely trying to help you.
I would expect your brother to do the same for me.'

Abby made a helpless gesture. 'I'm not waiting for
Edward,' she protested.

'No. So you said.' Alejandro's eyes lingered almost palpa-
bly on her mouth before moving away. '*No obstante,* my invitation still stands.'

Abby hesitated. Then she said quickly, 'I'm waiting for Mrs
Esquival—Dolores. She should be here any minute.'

Alejandro's lean mouth took on a sardonic slant. 'What is

it they say? You should not hold your breath, *no*?' He glanced towards the entrance of the restaurant as the doors opened and a dark-clad man hovered on the threshold. 'Ah, here is Miguel de Brazos. He is the *maître d'* of La Terraza. Allow me to introduce you to your host.'

Abby blew out a breath. 'I don't think—' she began awkwardly, but Alejandro's fingers had slipped about her upper arm, just above her elbow. They were cool against her warm flesh, and unbearably sensual, and she couldn't pull away. In her condition any contact between them would have been sensual, she acknowledged, feeling a little dizzy when Alejandro drew her towards the other man.

He and de Brazos evidently knew one another well, and their rapid exchange in their own language was too swift for Abby to comprehend. Her grasp of Spanish was very limited and Alejandro knew that. She was very relieved when the man stepped forward to greet her in English.

'*Señora,*' he said, with a polite bow. 'You are most welcome. Come.' He gestured eloquently. 'You are waiting for Señora Esquival, are you not? I will have a member of my staff look out for her. It is much more pleasant to wait inside.'

Abby's eyes turned to Alejandro's, but this time he was not looking at her and she was obliged to speak for herself. 'I— that's very kind of you—' she started, grateful for his understanding. But she felt an unwilling pang when Alejandro's hand dropped away from her arm.

'The pleasure is all mine,' de Brazos insisted, taking her answer to mean that she accepted his invitation. Without further ado, he led the way into the restaurant.

Abby glanced back once, but there was still no sign of Dolores. Only Alejandro was behind her, and his expression was inscrutable once more. What was he thinking? she wondered, as the smoky glass doors enclosed them in the cool environs of a palm-shaded lobby. That de Brazos had succeeded where he had failed? Or had this been his intention all along?

The *maître d'* led them to a table at the far side of the

elegantly appointed restaurant. They were seated overlooking a pretty inner courtyard where a fountain played into an ornamental basin. Flowers grew in profusion about the rim, their colours muted by the tinted glass of the windows. But the courtyard was open to the air and birds came to drink from the pool.

It was obviously a favoured spot, and Abby was aware of several pairs of eyes turning in their direction when Alejandro joined her. And, although she told herself that he was completely without shame, she couldn't help but be grateful that he hadn't abandoned her. It would have been rather daunting to wait alone.

'*Que le apetece, señora?* What can I offer you?' de Brazos asked, obviously intending to serve them himself, and Abby drew her upper lip between her teeth as she considered.

'Um—just iced tea for me, please,' she said at last, not trusting herself to drink anything alcoholic in Alejandro's presence. The *maître d'* tutted and pulled a long face.

'Are you sure I cannot tempt you with a margarita, *señora*?' he protested. 'They are the house speciality. I can recommend them.'

Abby shook her head. 'I don't think so, thank you.'

The man arched his eyebrows and turned to her companion. 'And you, *señor*,' he said. 'Will you indulge me?'

'*No lo creo, Miguel,*' Alejandro responded. 'I have work to do this afternoon. I will have iced tea also, *por favor.*'

Miguel spread his hands expressively, but he didn't attempt to try and change Alejandro's mind. He merely inclined his head politely and bustled away, issuing orders to other members of his staff as he went.

There was silence for a few moments after he'd gone, but then, feeling obliged to say something, Abby murmured quietly, 'This is a beautiful restaurant. And this must be the best table in the house.'

Alejandro shrugged. 'I am glad you like it.'

'Who wouldn't?' Abby was feeling a little light-headed now, but she assured herself it was only jet lag, or tiredness, or a combination of both. She studied her jacket uncertainly. 'Do you think I should put this on?'

'*Por que?* Why?' Alejandro regarded her intently. 'Are you cold?'

'No.' Abby glanced expressively around the room, observing the expensively clad patrons with an uneasy eye. Then, speaking almost absently, she added, 'I'm surprised Dolores wanted to bring me here.'

Alejandro's eyebrows ascended. 'And that would be because…?'

'Oh, come on.' Abby forgot who she was speaking to for a moment. 'Haven't you noticed all the diamond bracelets, the strings of pearls, the ruby rings? I'm wearing one ring, one gold chain, and some hoop earrings. I bet your friend Miguel knows their value down to the last cent!'

Alejandro shook his head. 'Perhaps he realises that you do not need diamond bracelets and pearl chokers to accent your beauty,' he responded softly. 'And I do not need to be reminded that you are wearing another man's ring. What do you want me to say, Abigail? That you are still the most attractive woman I have ever known?'

'No!' Abby's face flamed. 'You know I didn't mean anything like that.' Then, aware that her voice had risen and people were looking at them again, she whispered hotly, 'Don't say things like that to me. We both know how insincere your compliments are.'

'Are they?' Alejandro rested his elbows on the table and leaned towards her. 'Would it not please Edward to believe I am still attracted to you? You are very good to look at, *cara*. When Miguel speaks of indulgence, I think of only one thing.'

Abby caught her breath. 'You don't know what Edward wants,' she told him fiercely, choosing the least provocative comment he had made. She cupped her hot face between her palms, wondering why she'd agreed to come here. Where was Dolores? She'd never thought she'd be so eager to see her brother's mother-in-law—but she was.

'I know he did not send for his so-protective older sister to sit beside his sickbed,' responded Alejandro drily, and Abby gave a helpless little moan.

'Then you know more than me,' she retorted, casting another glance towards the entrance. What was Dolores doing? How long did it take to try on a dress?

'You do not make a very convincing liar, *cara*,' murmured Alejandro, relieving her a little by leaning back in his seat. He unbuttoned the jacket of his charcoal suit and hooked a negligent arm over the back of his chair. 'But we will not waste time arguing over your brother.' Absurdly long lashes shaded his eyes as he baited her. 'Tell me about yourself, Abigail. Or tell me why you are lunching with Dolores. I did not realise you were such close friends.'

'We're not.' The words were out before she could stop them, and she hurried to explain what she'd meant. 'That is— Dolores took pity on me. She thought I'd prefer lunching with her rather than just—waiting around at the house for Edward. She'll be here soon. She'll probably tell you the same herself.'

Alejandro frowned. 'Waiting around for Edward?' he said, immediately latching on to the anomaly. 'And why was your brother neglecting you today?'

Abby sighed. 'He wasn't there,' she admitted reluctantly, not really wanting to confide in him. 'He—er—he and Lauren had apparently gone out.'

'Gone out?' Alejandro echoed her words again, and then made an apologetic gesture. 'Forgive me, I thought he could not walk?'

Abby blew out a breath. 'He can't. Not far, anyway.'

Alejandro didn't say anything and, realising she couldn't avoid the inevitable, she said shortly. 'Their apartment has been broken into, if you must know. They've gone to meet the police to assess the damage.'

Alejandro looked less indolent now. 'And when did this— break-in occur?' he asked sharply, and Abby gave him an indignant look.

'Last night, I suppose.' She pretended to be busy folding

her jacket over her lap. 'Why?' She paused, and then added provocatively, 'Do you know anything about it?'

She'd expected an angry denial, but his answer startled her. 'Perhaps,' he said, smoothing his hand over the pearl-grey silk tie which perfectly matched his shirt. 'Perhaps.'

Abby was glad of the distraction of watching that brown long-fingered hand as it moved caressingly against the pale fabric. She was sure if she looked into his eyes he'd see the accusation in hers. Nevertheless, she had to say something, and she was relieved to see the waiter heading towards them. 'I think these are our drinks,' she said, knowing she'd be glad of the refreshment. Her mouth felt suddenly as dry as snuff.

The waiter delivered the two glasses of iced tea with a flourish and then turned to Alejandro to ask if he would like to see the menu.

'*Mas tarde. Later.*' Alejandro inclined his head. '*Gracias.*'

'*Gracias, señor.*'

The waiter bowed and left them and Abby immediately lifted her glass. The ice-cold liquid was both crisp and invigorating, and she closed her eyes for a moment, responding to its delightful flavour. She felt better already, she thought, opening her eyes again. Only to revise her opinion when she found Alejandro was watching her.

'You were thirsty,' he remarked, and she almost jumped out of her skin when he leaned forward and wiped a drop of moisture from the corner of her mouth with his thumb. She was even more disturbed when he brought his thumb to his lips and licked the moisture from it, adding swiftly, 'Have you ever drunk wine from a lover's lips?'

'It—it's not wine,' she stammered, too shaken to realise what she was saying, and his thin lips parted in a sensual smile.

'A pleasure I will save for later,' he told her huskily. 'Perhaps you will allow me to buy you dinner tomorrow evening. We can continue this discussion then.'

Abby swallowed convulsively. 'I—don't think so.'

'Why not?'

'I—I don't want to,' she said. 'Besides, I don't think my fiancé would approve.'

'As I recall, it did not bother you before,' declared Alejandro obscurely, but before she could take him up on that, or on what he'd meant about the break-in, she heard the sound of hurried footsteps crossing the floor. Abby turned her head. It was Dolores. Of course, she thought defeatedly. Who else would it be?

She stifled a sigh as Alejandro rose to greet his cousin.

'*Querida,*' Dolores exclaimed, capturing his hands and reaching up to bestow air kisses beside his cheeks. 'What are you doing here?' She cast a faintly accusing glance in Abby's direction. 'When Miguel told me you were keeping my guest company, I couldn't believe it. I thought you told me you were always too busy to stop for lunch.'

'Surely you would not have had me leave Abigail standing outside the restaurant, Dolores?' he chided her suavely. 'She looked—lost,' he added, his dark eyes meeting Abby's frustrated gaze with undisguised intent. 'What could I do but offer her myself as a very poor substitute? We have both been waiting anxiously for you to arrive.'

'Oh, Alejandro!' However irritated Dolores might have been at finding them together, his words had successfully diluted any resentment she felt. 'You are so generous! I hope Abigail appreciates your kindness.'

'Oh, I am sure she does,' replied Alejandro, once again looking at Abby with mocking eyes. Then, turning back to his cousin, he added, 'But tell me, *cara*, what is this I hear about your daughter's apartment being broken into? I was most concerned when Abigail told me. Have you heard anything more?'

Dolores immediately lapsed into a torrent of Spanish from which Abby could only distinguish the names of Luis Esquival and her brother and his wife. Whatever Dolores was saying, she evidently didn't want the English girl to interrupt them. It was this as much as anything that caused Abby to remark with contrived innocence, 'Actually, Mr Varga said he might know something about it himself.'

At once Dolores broke off what she was saying to stare at the younger woman. *'Que?'* she said blankly, and Abby was absurdly pleased to see the brief look of irritation that crossed Alejandro's face.

'Mr Varga said he might know something about the robbery,' Abby repeated, widening her eyes. 'That is what you said, isn't it, Mr Varga? I'm sure we're both dying to know what you meant.'

'I believe I said that there might be something I could do to help, *cara*,' he replied smoothly, turning back to Dolores with a reassuring smile. 'Abigail must have misunderstood my desire to be of some assistance.' He cast the culprit a challenging look. 'She knows how fond I am of Lauren—and Edward, too.'

CHAPTER SIX

EDWARD was waiting for Abby when she got back to the house. He was sitting on the terrace, in the shade of the colonnade, his injured leg propped on a cushioned stool. He looked up at his sister belligerently when she came out of the house to tell him she was back.

'Where the hell have you been?' he demanded at once, before Abby could say anything, and her lips parted disbelievingly at the accusation in his voice.

'I've been out to lunch,' she said at last, keeping her tone even with an effort. 'Your mother-in-law took pity on me. It was either that or spend the morning here, on my own.'

'And that would have been a tragedy, would it?' Edward demanded, the freckles on his face standing out against his fair skin. Unlike Abby, he didn't tan, and he looked very pale in these surroundings. 'You didn't come here to go swanning off with Dolores, Abby. As you reminded me last night, this isn't supposed to be a holiday.'

Abby stared at him indignantly. 'Do you honestly think I was eager to go out with Dolores?' she exclaimed. She glanced swiftly behind her, half afraid she might have been overheard, and lowered her voice. 'You didn't tell me where you were going, Eddie. In fact, I got the feeling you were keeping out of my way.'

Was it only her imagination or did Edward look a little shame-faced now? 'Why would I do that?' he asked, making a play of adjusting the cushion that was supporting his leg. 'What has Dolores been saying? She's never liked me, you know. As far as the Esquivals are concerned, I've never been good enough for their daughter.'

Abby shook her head. 'Dolores hardly mentioned you,' she

said shortly, irritated that he would try to gain her sympathy again. 'And after what you asked me to do last night I wasn't surprised that you'd want to avoid me. But don't think you're deceiving Alejandro. He knows what you're trying to do.'

Now there was no doubt about Edward's agitation. 'He knows?' he echoed faintly. 'How do you know that?' He pushed himself up in his seat, almost overbalancing the stool in the process. 'Have you seen him?'

'Yes—'

Abby had been about to explain that he'd come to the house earlier that morning, but Edward didn't allow her to go on.

'Where did you see him? Was Dolores there when he mentioned me?' A sheen of sweat stood out on his forehead. 'Oh, God, if the Esquivals find out what's going on, I'm dead!'

Abby was confused, and it showed. Surely if Lauren was having an affair it was she who should deserve her parents' censure, not Edward.

Unless…

Studying her brother's anxious face, Abby had the sudden premonition that he wasn't being honest with her. But what was it that he wasn't telling her? What did Alejandro know that he thought might cause the Esquivals to turn against him?

Deciding this was not the time to get into that, she pulled out a nearby chair and sat down beside him. 'Anyway,' she said, trying to be upbeat, 'tell me about your morning. Dolores said your apartment was broken into. Was there much damage? What did they take?'

Edward made an offhanded gesture. 'What do they usually take?' he asked dismissively. 'Break-ins happen. You know that. It was probably some druggie, looking for something he could sell for a fix.'

'Is that what the police think?'

'How should I know what they think?' Edward didn't seem interested. 'No one tells me anything.'

Abby refused to answer that. Taking another tack, she said, 'Ross's house was broken into last year. They never did find who did it. Like you say—'

'Like I'm interested in your boyfriend's problems,' muttered Edward rudely. 'Let's get back to Varga. Are you going to explain how you came to be talking to him? Did he invite himself for lunch with you and my so-delightful mother-in-law?'

Abby shook her head. She had thought she'd deflected any discussion of Alejandro, but she should have known better. And why was Edward so worried about what the other man might have said?

She knew Alejandro wasn't to be trusted. Look how he'd deflected her accusation at lunchtime. Dolores had virtually apologised to him for what he'd implied was Abby's mistake. Only it hadn't been a mistake. She would swear it. Alejandro had intimated that he might know something about the robbery at Edward's apartment. But what? *What?*

'He—met us outside the restaurant,' she replied at last, deciding not to mention his earlier visit. 'He joined us for a drink, that's all.' She paused. 'What is this all about, Eddie? If Lauren is having an affair with Alejandro, why are you so upset about what her parents might think? It's not your fault.'

Edward's head jerked towards her. 'Is she having an affair with Varga?' he exclaimed, clutching her hand with sweating fingers.

'I don't know.' Abby pulled her hand away with a feeling of distaste. 'It was you who said she was.' She sighed. 'Perhaps you'd better start being honest with me, Eddie. Why are you so afraid of Alejandro? It's not just because of Lauren, is it?'

'What else could it be?' Edward had stiffened at her words and now he glared at her with angry eyes. 'And I'm not afraid of Varga.' He paused. 'Only of what he might—do.'

'To your marriage?'

'What else?' Edward was defiant. 'Anyway, why did you say he knows what I'm doing? What did he say to give you that impression?'

Abby shrugged. 'I don't remember,' she said, deciding if Edward could be evasive, so could she. But that didn't stop her from wishing she'd never started this conversation. Edward was lying to her. She was almost sure of it now. Perhaps she ought to speak to Alejandro himself.

Edward was looking infuriated now, but Abby was not inclined to humour him. 'We'll talk later,' she said, getting to her feet. 'I need to change. I'll see you in a little while.'

'Wait!'

Edward tried to catch her hand, but she was too quick for him. Wrapping her arms about her waist, she hurried into the house, running up the stairs to her room with a feeling of total isolation.

Abby rang Ross before going down for dinner.

She'd spent the remainder of the afternoon in her room, going over both what Alejandro had said and her brother's reaction to it. But she was no further forward. Alejandro's attitude had been enigmatic; Edward's had been downright defensive. Or should that be apprehensive? There was no doubt that he'd been alarmed when she'd told him Alejandro had joined her and Dolores for a drink.

She shook her head. She hardly remembered what Alejandro had said now. Only that there had been a definite air of menace in his words. Why would he presume that Edward needed his assistance? The two men obviously despised one another. What could there possibly be between them to have caused such an unlikely alliance?

Herself? No! Edward knew nothing of what had happened after she'd returned to England. Lauren? She was unwilling to accept that either. Yet why? Didn't she want to believe Alejandro was capable of having an affair with her sister-in-law? Was she jealous, perhaps? Even after all this time did she still harbour feelings for him herself?

No!

Staring at her reflection in the mirror above the vanity unit, Abby dismissed the suggestion out of hand. Edward might dislike Alejandro; she *hated* him. She'd hoped she'd never have to lay eyes on him again.

Nevertheless, it was thinking about Alejandro that persuaded her to ring her fiancé again. She needed Ross's advice, she thought eagerly. She needed his cool voice of reason to still the chaotic turmoil in her head.

To her relief, he answered the phone at the first ring. Which meant he was probably sitting at his desk in his study, she reflected, marking papers that he'd brought home from school.

What she'd give to be back there with him, she thought. She might even revise her decision not to move in with him until after they were married. Continuing to live in her own apartment when she spent so much time at Ross's house seemed foolish from this distance. She had to learn to trust him. He was going to be her husband, for goodness' sake.

'It's me, Ross,' she said brightly, after he had identified himself. 'I hope you don't mind me ringing so late.'

'It's only eleven o'clock, Abby,' he retorted, his tone hardly boding well in the circumstances. 'I was expecting you to ring, actually. I knew you'd want to apologise for the way you spoke to me this morning.'

Abby blew out a breath. Until that moment she'd forgotten the argument they'd had earlier. She'd been so wrapped up in Edward's problems she'd ignored the fact that she'd probably offended her fiancé.

But she should have known he wouldn't forget, and it was easier to give in than risk more hostility. 'Yes,' she said ruefully, somehow managing to keep the resignation out of her voice. 'I shouldn't have said what I did. I'm sorry. But I have been worried about Eddie, you know.'

'Mmm.' Ross didn't sound as if he thought that was any excuse. 'So, what's going on? Have you made any arrangements yet for coming home? Or is that asking too much?'

'It is, rather.' Abby wished he could be more understanding. She needed his support, not his censure. 'There have been—more complications.'

Ross snorted. 'Let me guess: Edward's had an emotional relapse?'

'No.' Abby kept her temper in check with an effort. 'His

apartment—the apartment he shares with Lauren—was broken into. Last night, I think. It's just not what he needs when he's practically incapable of doing anything for himself.'

'I don't believe it.' Ross was impatient. 'That man is a walking disaster, Abby. Or in this case an *un*walking one.'

'That isn't funny, Ross. Couldn't you try and show a little sympathy? Remember how you felt when your house was vandalised last year.'

'That was different.'

'How was it different?'

'Oh, Abby...' Ross sighed. 'I have some valuable things here—things that are precious to me, that were my mother's. I doubt if your brother owns anything he couldn't replace at the nearest supermarket.'

Abby gasped. 'That's a horrible thing to say,' she exclaimed, although she was uneasily aware that he might be right. Edward had seemed decidedly blasé about the robbery. He'd dismissed it in a few words, she remembered, more concerned about Alejandro than anything else.

'I'm only trying to be practical,' said Ross, and Abby had to admit that that was why she'd called. She'd wanted Ross's practicality. It was a pity it seemed so cold when it was put into words.

'Even so...'

But Abby sounded defensive, and, as if sensing her weakness, Ross changed his tack. 'I'm only thinking of you, sweetheart,' he said, his voice softening. 'I'm sure the authorities have the situation under control. And you have to remember Edward has a wife and in-laws to support him. I need you here, Abby. I miss you. I really do.'

'I miss you, too,' said Abby automatically, yet in truth she'd had too much else on her mind. 'But I can't leave yet, Ross. I can't. Not until I'm sure Eddie can cope.'

'Can cope with what?'

Ross's voice had risen and Abby knew there was no way she could justify her reasons for staying on to him. He didn't know Alejandro. He didn't know anything about what had happened the last time she'd visited her brother. All he knew was that she'd been ill after she'd got back from Edward's wedding. So ill that she'd been away from school for several weeks after her return from Florida.

She sighed now. 'Just give me a few more days, Ross,' she pleaded. 'I've hardly spoken to Lauren yet. Things have been so hectic today that we haven't found time to talk.'

'To talk!' Ross sounded incredulous. 'You're not trying to tell me you want to stay on because you and your sister-in-law haven't had the time to exchange all the latest gossip?'

'No, of course not.'

'It sounds that way.'

'Well, I'm sorry for how it sounds,' said Abby tiredly. 'In any case, I'm staying on until after the weekend at least. I'll ring you tomorrow if I have any more news.'

Ross was silent, and she thought at first he wasn't going to say anything else. But then he expelled a weary breath. 'I hope you know what you're doing, Abby,' he said heavily. 'Letting Edward think he can call on you every time things don't go his way doesn't seem very sensible to me.'

And it wasn't, thought Abby unhappily, after she'd ended the call. She'd always been a push-over where her brother was concerned and he knew it. But this time she was really worried about him. Even the injuries he'd received in the car accident seemed incidental compared to all the rest.

She'd undressed and was about to get in the shower when the phone rang again.

Ross, she guessed wearily. She'd had to give him this number and he was probably ringing to reinforce his contention that she ought to return home. Couldn't he just cut her some slack, here? She groaned, clutching a towel about her. She was tired and anxious and his constant carping wasn't helping at all.

'Okay, it's me,' she said, after picking up the receiver, and then nearly dropped the thing when an unexpected voice spoke in her ear.

'Am I supposed to be flattered that you anticipated my call?'

Alejandro enquired softly, and Abby despised the sudden quiver of excitement that feathered down her spine at his words.

She swallowed. 'Ale—Mr Varga!'

'As I do not believe you were about to say alleluia, Alejandro will do,' he told her drily. 'That is obviously how you think of me. And why not? We know one another rather too well to stand on ceremony.'

Abby sucked in some air. 'What do you want, Alejandro?' she demanded shortly and she heard his small sigh of regret.

'So cold, *cara*,' he murmured. 'Is this what your English men have done to you? You used to have such a lust for life.'

'Whereas you—' Abby broke off before she said something unforgivable. Then, determinedly, 'Why did you ring, Alejandro? Aren't you afraid that the Esquivals might be curious about why you're contacting me?'

'Why should I care what my cousins think?' he replied carelessly. 'I do not have to ask their permission to speak to an old friend.'

'We were never friends, Alejandro,' Abby blurted, too tired to be tactful, and then shivered uncontrollably when he gave a soft laugh.

'I am glad you agree,' he said. 'We were not friends, we were lovers. Like me, I think, you cannot forget what we shared.'

'We didn't share anything,' Abby broke in desperately. 'I don't know why you're doing this, Alejandro, but I wish you'd just leave me alone.'

'Do you?' Alejandro hesitated. 'Is that what your brother wishes also?'

Abby gasped. 'Leave Edward out of this.'

'Unfortunately, I cannot.' Alejandro gave a regretful sigh. 'Is that not why he sent for you? Because he hopes you may succeed where he has failed?'

Abby stiffened. 'Failed?' she echoed. What was he admitting? 'Failed at what?'

'Ah...' Alejandro sounded as if her confusion had pleased him. 'You do not know. I thought that must be true.'

'Know what?'

'That is for me to know and you to find out,' declared Alejandro tormentingly. 'So—you will have dinner with me tomorrow evening. We will continue this discussion then, *no*?'

'No!'

'Oh, I think you will, *cara*,' he told her softly, and again she felt that little twinge of menace she'd felt that morning by the pool. 'Do not make me angry, Abigail. Your brother would not like it. After all, he wants us to be—friends.'

Abby's hands trembled and she badly wanted to slam down the phone. She was no match for a man like Alejandro. She didn't know what he was or what he was capable of. He was Edward's problem, not hers. She was getting too far out of her depth.

'Please,' she said, and she despised the beseeching note she could hear in her voice, 'tell me what this is all about.'

'Tomorrow evening,' said Alejandro inexorably, and she didn't know whether it was a threat or a promise. 'I will tell Luis and Dolores that we were discussing sailing at lunch today and that I have offered to show you my boat, *sí*? They may be—surprised, but that is not your concern.'

Abby blew out a breath. 'I'm their guest,' she protested. 'I can't just have dinner with you. What will they think?'

'At least you are no longer refusing to consider my proposition,' remarked Alejandro sardonically. 'Leave the details to me, *cara*. I will see you tomorrow. *Adios*.'

CHAPTER SEVEN

DINNER that evening was a more relaxed affair.

The robbery at the Coconut Grove apartment was the main topic of conversation, and although Edward had been dismissive of it earlier he now appeared to be as willing to talk about it as everyone else.

Or perhaps that was just because Lauren and his in-laws expected that of him, reflected Abby broodingly, aware that she was getting very cynical about her brother's motives for anything. It didn't help to see him sitting there, looking as if he was innocent of any wrongdoing, when he must know that the Esquivals believed Abby had invited herself here.

'At least they didn't trash the place,' said Lauren fervently. She turned to her sister-in-law. 'Perhaps you'd like to come and see it tomorrow. The music centre and the TV are missing, of course, but the rest of the apartment is okay.'

'Which proves they were only after items they could easily sell,' observed her father, before Abby could respond. 'Like Edward said earlier, they were most probably kids looking for ways to make money to buy drugs.'

'I don't think they were kids,' Lauren insisted, glancing at her husband almost defensively. 'Kids couldn't have got in without setting off the alarm.'

'So what do you think it was?' Edward asked scornfully. 'A professional hit?'

'It could be.'

Lauren wasn't deterred, and Abby sensed that she had doubts about the break-in. Edward, meanwhile, was avoiding his sister's eyes, and she wished she didn't have the feeling that he had his own reasons for not pursuing that line of thought.

'*No obstante*, I am not at all happy about Lauren returning to the apartment,' declared her mother staunchly. 'Do you not agree, Luis? If these—thieves—can get in once, they may get in again.'

'*Es verdad.* That's true,' agreed her husband sagely. 'What do you think, Abigail? Have you heard that villains often return to the scene of the crime? Particularly if they think the insurance company has paid for the stolen items to be replaced, *no*?'

Abby wasn't at all happy about being put on the spot, particularly as she suspected her brother had his own reasons for wanting to return home. But Luis was waiting for her answer and she shrugged. 'I've heard that, too,' she admitted, giving Lauren a sympathetic look. 'But perhaps if you fitted a new alarm—'

'That's a good idea, Papá,' said Lauren at once. 'And if it was teenagers, as Edward thinks, they probably won't bother us again.'

'That's what I think,' said Edward, and Abby wondered why he seemed so keen to play the incident down. Did he have something to hide? Surely he hadn't arranged to have the apartment burglarised himself.

But, no. As Abby determinedly put such thoughts aside, Luis's aunt chose to make her own contribution. 'Why do we not all wait and see what *la policia* come up with?' she remarked mildly. 'I am sure Abigail does not wish to spend her holiday discussing our little problems.' She paused. 'How are you enjoying your stay, *pequeña*? Dolores tells me you and she had lunch together at La Terraza. Did you know that I used to work at La Terraza? When I was a much younger woman, *naturalmente*.' She smiled.

'What Tia Elena means is that her husband's family used to own La Terraza,' Dolores explained shortly, clearly eager that Abby shouldn't get the wrong impression. She gave the old woman a reproving look. 'It is a great pity that they decided to sell. These days it is making a fortune, *no*?'

'Money is not everything, Dolores,' returned the old lady, undaunted. 'I think you forget that sometimes.'

'I forget nothing, Tia,' retorted Dolores quellingly. She lifted the bell beside her plate and rang it imperiously, speaking in rapid Spanish to the maid when she arrived. Then, after the girl had cleared their plates, she said, 'Shall we go into the salon? I have asked Anita to serve coffee in there.'

Abby got the chance to talk to Lauren after they'd all adjourned to the salon. The younger girl had settled herself on a hide-covered sofa set at right angles to the huge fireplace and Abby hesitated only a second before taking the seat beside her.

She noticed that Edward didn't look particularly pleased that she'd chosen to join his wife, but that couldn't be helped. He shouldn't have told her Lauren was having an affair with Alejandro Varga if he'd wanted to keep it a secret. Besides, Abby had no intention of asking her about that. She just wanted the opportunity to gauge for herself exactly what was going on in her brother's marriage.

Lauren herself looked slightly surprised when Abby sat down, but she was too polite to offer any objection. On the contrary, she immediately struck up a conversation, asking Abby about her engagement, admiring her ring and proffering the suggestion that she and Ross ought to consider returning to Florida for their honeymoon.

Abby, knowing full well that Ross would never agree to such a thing, made some neutral rejoinder before saying lightly, 'It seems no time since we were discussing your honeymoon, Lauren. But I suppose you and Edward are quite used to being married now.'

'Y—e—s.' Lauren drew out the word in such a way that Abby was hardly reassured. 'We are happy enough, I suppose. Though this has not been an easy year for us.'

'No.' Abby nodded understandingly. 'I suppose the accident was quite a shock.'

'It was.' Lauren accepted a cup of coffee from the maid before continuing. 'But that isn't what I meant.'

'It's not?' Abby was aware that her brother was watching them with a lowering expression. She moistened her lips. 'I'm sorry. I didn't mean to pry.'

'It's not your fault.' Lauren hesitated. 'Oh, I suppose I should not say anything to you. But you are Edward's sister. You have a right to know.'

Abby wondered if she did. And if this was about Alejandro she didn't think she wanted to know. Though how else was she to learn the truth? She had the feeling Lauren wouldn't lie.

'Has he said anything to you?' the younger woman persisted, and Abby had no idea how to answer her.

'I—Edward and I haven't had a lot of time to talk about anything,' she murmured evasively. 'What with the break-in and all.'

'Por supuesto.' Of course. Lauren circled the rim of her cup with a nervous finger. 'And I suppose it is not an easy thing for him to tell you.'

This was getting worse and worse. Abby, glancing at her brother, was uneasily aware that she might have misjudged him all along. It sounded very much as if Lauren was trying to break it to her gently. Had Lauren been having an affair? And, if so, with whom?

'You—er—you don't have to tell me if you don't want to,' Abby said quickly. 'Honestly, I—'

'But I want to tell you,' said Lauren firmly. 'Perhaps you will understand my feelings better than your brother. Now that you are going to be married yourself.'

Abby wanted to say *Don't hold your breath*, but her mouth was too dry to allow more than a strangled gulp to escape her.

Lauren seemed to take her silence as acquiescence, however. Setting her cup on the low table in front of them, she said quietly, 'You see, Edward and I have been having some—personal—problems.'

Oh, no! Abby was convinced now that she didn't want to hear this. 'Really…' she began again, recovering her voice. 'I don't think I am the person you need to talk to.'

Lauren gave her a thoughtful little look. 'Perhaps that is so,' she conceded softly. 'I forget—things are different in your country, are they not?'

Abby didn't quite know what she meant by that, but she thought it was wiser not to probe. Obviously Lauren couldn't talk about this to her mother and father. Still, why she should think her sister-in-law might view her behaviour more sympathetically, Abby didn't know.

Or want to, she assured herself. It was bad enough having Edward unloading all his troubles onto her shoulders. She couldn't take on Lauren's as well.

'Did I tell you Alejandro joined your mother and Abby for a drink at lunchtime?' Edward asked suddenly. He had propelled himself across the room to where they were sitting and now perched on the arm of the sofa at his wife's side. 'He's very fond of Abby. They met at our wedding, you know.'

His wife looked up at him with narrowed eyes. 'No, you did not tell me,' she said, a wary note entering her voice. She turned back to Abby. 'I did not realise you knew Alejandro so well.'

'I don't,' said Abby shortly, wondering what her brother was playing at now. 'Edward's exaggerating.'

'I don't think so,' he said annoyingly. 'He was certainly delighted to renew your acquaintance yesterday, as I recall.'

Abby's eyes bored into his. 'Mr Varga was simply being polite, that's all,' she said tersely. And then, remembering that she was supposed to be having dinner with Alejandro the following evening, she cursed Edward anew for getting her into this situation. She clenched her fists. 'You know him better than I do.'

Edward was undaunted. 'Do I?' he challenged. 'I wouldn't say that. I shouldn't be at all surprised if he wants to see you again before you leave.'

Abby's face burned with embarrassment. Was he only guessing that Alejandro had been in touch with her? She could tell little from his expression, and she didn't know whether to be glad or sorry when Dolores chose that moment to stroll across the room to join them.

'Who wants to see you, *cara*?' she asked, touching her daughter's shoulder with a gentle hand, and Lauren looked up at her mother with some misgivings.

'Not me, Mamá,' she said tautly. 'Abigail. Edward has just been telling me that Alejandro had a drink with you both at lunchtime.'

'Well, yes. He did. But I do not understand.' Dolores frowned. 'What are you saying?'

Abby stifled a groan. In spite of the fact that her brother had presented her with the perfect opportunity to tell them all about Alejandro's invitation, she couldn't speak. Not after what Lauren had just told her. Not after she had virtually admitted that she was involved with another man.

'I was just saying that it was possible that—Alejandro—' and, although Abby was dismayed at his audacity, she sensed the effort it took for Edward to use his name '—that he might like to see Abby again before she leaves,' he continued, his words dropping into the sudden silence like pebbles into a still pool. 'What do you think, sweetheart?' He laid a possessive hand on his wife's arm, as if challenging her mother's protection. 'Didn't you get the feeling that he was unusually pleased to see her the other day?'

'But Abigail hardly knows Alejandro,' protested Dolores, before her daughter could speak.

'They spent some time together when Abby came over for the wedding,' Edward countered, despite the look his sister cast his way. 'And now that he's divorced the situation is different. There's no reason why they shouldn't be friends.'

Dolores was not pleased. 'Alejandro is a busy man,' she said tightly. 'Abigail should not be deceived by his very obvious charm.' She turned to Abby. 'I'm sorry if this sounds unfeeling, Abigail. But Alejandro can't help flirting with the ladies.' She forced a smile to soften her words. 'He's very naughty sometimes, but I'm afraid he treats us all the same.'

'Not all of us, Mamá,' Lauren contradicted, glancing up at

her husband, and Abby wondered if that was a tacit admission of her own guilt or something else. 'And we don't know what Alejandro thinks of Abigail. We are not in his confidence.' She turned her dark eyes on her sister-in-law now. 'Perhaps we should ask her.'

Abby hadn't expected this. 'I'm not in his confidence either,' she averred quickly. 'Like your mother says, I hardly know him.' *And what I do know, I don't like,* she finished silently, wishing Edward would stop embarrassing her. 'Um— would you mind if I said goodnight now? It's been a long day and I'm afraid my body's still working on London time.'

Abby spent the following morning with Lauren and her mother, visiting the Coconut Grove apartment.

The two women seemed to think last night's discussion about Alejandro required no further explanation, and Abby couldn't help a certain frisson of resentment that they had dismissed any connection between her and Alejandro out of hand.

Not that she wanted them to think that she was attracted to him, she assured herself firmly. She had quite enough to deal with as it was.

She would have found Coconut Grove itself delightful if she'd been more in the mood to appreciate it. The district was one of Miami's oldest, with lots of fabulous shops and boutiques and restaurants crammed into a comparatively small area. She guessed it would really come alive after nightfall, when the old-fashioned streetlamps were lit and the music swelling out of its bars and cafés took on a darker rhythm. But even in daylight it possessed a warmth and character that was different from even its closest neighbours.

Edward and Lauren's apartment was part of a restored complex surrounding a central open-air mall. Although the old buildings had been extensively modernised inside, outside they maintained their essentially Spanish appearance. Stucco-washed walls and tiles in different colours; palm trees growing in pots in the courtyard; narrow wooden balconies with white-painted rails.

If you could overlook the evidence that the place had been dusted for fingerprints, the apartment itself was cool and attractive. A large living area opened onto one of the balconies Abby had seen from below, and Lauren was quick to point out that they could see the tropical gardens and the marina from their windows. Adjoining the living room was a small kitchen, with every conceivable domestic appliance, but Abby guessed from its appearance that her brother and his wife seldom cooked at home.

Lauren proved to be surprisingly enthusiastic about returning to the apartment. 'It is our home,' she said, showing Abby into the master bedroom with its impressive king-sized divan. She pointed out the damage that had been done when the entertainment centre had been ripped from the fitted armoire at the foot of the bed. 'This can easily be repaired,' she added, paling a little at the sight of such blatant savagery. Then, determinedly, 'And I know Edward does not like living at my parents' estate.'

Abby agreed with her, although she could quite see why Lauren's mother felt so apprehensive about their return. And Dolores, bustling into the room at that moment, clicked her tongue at the shattered cabinet and splintered wood lying about the floor.

'You cannot think of coming back here, Lauren,' she exclaimed fiercely. 'Imagine what might have happened if you had been here alone when these men broke in. You could have been murdered in your bed!'

'They might not have attempted the break-in if we had been here,' declared her daughter practically. 'It probably only happened because the apartment was unoccupied. You never know, someone at the restaurant may have mentioned that Edward had had an accident and that for the time being we were staying with you and Papá.'

Dolores widened her eyes impatiently and then looked at Abby, almost as if she blamed her for her daughter's words.

'Well, I think your *Papá* should find you another apartment,' she stated tersely. 'Somewhere in Coral Gables, nearer to where we live.'

'I am not a child, Mamá.' Lauren drifted back into the living room, running a possessive hand over the back of a printed silk sofa. 'Besides, apart from a few dirty footmarks, the rest of the apartment is hardly touched. It's obvious they were in a hurry and only took what they could easily sell.'

Abby had been inclined to agree with her—until she saw the expensive laptop lying on a shelf beside the long windows. A thief surely would not have left the portable computer behind. Unless it had been overlooked. She supposed that was possible. But it was curious, and she intended to ask Edward what the police had said about it.

'I do not think we should talk about this right now,' said Dolores shortly, following them back into the living room. 'It's much too soon to be making any plans. Edward is unlikely to be able to walk unaided for several weeks yet.' She turned to Abby, evidently expecting her support. 'A man needs to be fit enough to defend himself and his family. Especially after what has happened. Do you not agree?'

Abby looked at her sister-in-law and then made a helpless gesture. 'I suppose,' she said awkwardly. 'But it's up to Edward and Lauren to decide when they want to return home. I understand your concerns. But if the police are satisfied…'

'The *policia* know no more than we do,' retorted Lauren's mother impatiently. 'It may be that someone is conducting a vendetta against Edward. How do we know?'

Abby felt a chill run down her spine at these words. And almost without her volition the memory of Alejandro's taunting arrogance caused a prickling to feather her skin. Was he behind this? Did he have some hold over her brother? Oh, God, she was going to have to have dinner with him, whatever her feelings. She had find out once and for all what was going on.

CHAPTER EIGHT

To ABBY's dismay, Alejandro was waiting for them when they got back to the villa.

He and Luis were sitting on the terrace, enjoying a cold beer, and both men rose politely to their feet when the three women appeared.

Lauren and her mother greeted Alejandro with great enthusiasm, a circumstance Abby was getting used to. And if they, like she, noticed that Edward was absent, they were too busy welcoming their guest to comment.

'Are you staying for lunch?' asked Lauren eagerly, clearly reluctant to let go of his hands, and, meeting Alejandro's gaze over the younger woman's shoulder, Abby saw the familiar mockery glinting in his eyes. Why was he here? she wondered. Was it just because he and Luis had business to discuss? Or had he some other motive? Making sure she didn't turn down his invitation, perhaps?

'Regrettably, no,' he replied now, using the ruse of ushering her into the chair he had been occupying to release himself. Reaching for his beer, he emptied the bottle in one swift swallow and set it back on the table. 'As a matter of fact I came to ask Abigail if she would care to come and see my boat this evening. It cannot have been much fun for her to learn that her brother had been injured. And now, with the break-in and all, I thought she might appreciate a diversion.'

Abby's lips compressed, and she was aware that both Dolores and her daughter had turned to give her a considering look. What were they thinking? she wondered. That they would all appreciate a diversion? And why had she ever thought that Alejandro might leave the decision of whether she accepted his invitation or not to her? He was a determined man. She knew that already. And an unscrupulous one, she added tensely. But the most frustrating thing of all was that she didn't dare refuse.

'Well, I—' she began, groping for words. Lauren interrupted her. 'I think we'd all enjoy an evening on the water,' she said, voicing the thought Abby had had. 'I assume we are invited, too. I don't know about my husband, but I'd certainly like to go.'

'You forget, *cara*, we are already committed to staying in this evening,' remarked Edward suddenly.

Abby swung round to find her brother propped against one of the vine-covered pillars that supported the colonnade. He was evidently enjoying their surprise, and he smiled at his wife disarmingly. Then, hooking the crutches beneath his arms, he moved jerkily towards them.

With a sideways glance at Abby, he went on smoothly, 'I believe your mother told me that your aunt and uncle are joining us for dinner, Lauren. I know Tia Rosa would be terribly upset if her favourite niece was absent.'

Lauren's mouth pursed. 'I had forgotten that,' she said, looking disappointed. She turned to her mother. 'Couldn't we possibly postpone Tia Rosa and Tio Ernesto's visit? After all, Abigail will be leaving soon. It seems a shame to deprive her of this opportunity to see Alejandro's yacht.'

'I'm sure Alejandro can be trusted to look after my sister without a chaperon,' said Edward at once, and Abby wished she had the nerve to tell him to butt out of her affairs. The trouble was, she knew she had to go. She had to find out what Alejandro wanted. She had to know what was really going on.

'Perhaps Abigail would prefer to spend the evening with the family,' put in Dolores, making her sympathies known, but Luis chose to come down on Edward's side.

'We were not invited, *cara*,' he said, the smile he gave Alejandro salving any offence. 'I am sure my friend would prefer it if Abigail was allowed to make her own decision.'

Abby wished she didn't have to make any choice at all, but that was not an option. 'I—it sounds delightful,' she said, hoping both Alejandro and Edward could hear the irony in her voice.

'It will be; I can assure you,' murmured the Cuban suavely. 'Shall we say—seven o'clock this evening? I will send a car to pick you up.'

Abby spent ages trying to decide what to wear. She wished now that she'd taken advantage of her trip to the mall with Dolores to buy something suitable for herself. But then she hadn't known Alejandro was going to take her sailing. Was she a good sailor? Her experiences with boats had been confined to pleasure steamers and cross-channel ferries.

She would have preferred to wear one of the two dresses she'd brought with her. But they were hardly appropriate for climbing on and off a yacht. The last thing she wanted was for him to think she'd chosen glamour over practicality, even if deep down inside her she wanted to look good.

Telling herself it didn't matter what he thought of her, she chose her one remaining pair of shorts. She'd bought them the previous summer in Rimini, and although when she'd got them she'd doubted she'd ever get the chance to wear them, they seemed appropriate tonight.

They had been extremely expensive, she remembered, and Ross had balked a little at her extravagance. Made of a rich emerald-green silk, with a gold-plated chain belt to hang loosely about her hips, they were obviously far too formal for casual wear. But probably ideal for what she wanted tonight.

Teamed with a black crêpe halter-top, she couldn't deny they suited her. She looked pretty good, she thought, turning sideways in front of the long mirrors, trying to see herself from behind. Too good, in fact, for going out with a man she purported to despise, she conceded. Her mouth compressed into a thin line. What was she thinking of?

She was crazy, she thought. Worse than that, she was betraying everything she had ever believed about herself. Not to mention her fiancé. Dear Lord, she could imagine how he'd react if he could see her now.

With an exclamation of distaste, she took hold of the two sides of the halter, ready to pull it over her head again when someone knocked at her door. She faltered. What now? It was barely a quarter to seven. She still had to apply her lipstick and put the finishing touches to her hair.

'Who is it?' she called, standing irresolutely in front of the mirror. Then closed her eyes in frustration when the maid opened the door.

'Carlos is waiting, *señora*,' she said, her eyes widening in both surprise and admiration. '*Por favor*, will you come?'

Abby expelled a resigned sigh. 'Just give me a couple of minutes,' she replied, realising there was no time to change her clothes now. 'I won't be long.'

'*Sí, señora.*'

With another lingering stare, the maid departed, and Abby turned back to the vanity, stifling a curse. Well, she was committed now. For her sins, she had to accept her fate.

Predictably, Edward was in the hall when she went downstairs. Probably ensuring that she didn't duck out of the date, she thought irritably. She just wished she could have been wearing jeans and a tee shirt, or something equally casual. Instead of which she could practically feel the satisfaction oozing out of his pores.

'Hey, way to go, Abbs!' he exclaimed approvingly. 'Varga's not going to know what's hit him.'

'Oh, grow up, Eddie,' retorted Abby, in no mood to humour him. 'I just hope there's not more to this than you've told me.'

Edward scowled. 'I don't know what you mean,' he said defensively. 'All I came to say was that I hoped you'd have a pleasant evening. I'm sure you will. If there's one thing Varga's good at, it's giving a woman a good time.'

'And you'd know all about that, would you?' Abby arched her brows sardonically. 'Just don't say anything else, Eddie. I may just decide to develop a migraine instead.'

Of course, she knew she wouldn't. She couldn't. And he knew that, too. But that didn't stop her from enjoying his uncertainty and the automatic look of anxiety that crossed his face.

She was glad none of the Esquivals appeared as she crossed the hall to the open doors. She'd had to wear her sandals again, in the absence of any alternative, and her high heels clattered on the marble floor. But, happily, no one seemed to notice. She was able to descend the steps without attracting attention.

Outside, the air was like a moist blanket. Heat, soft and palpable, coated her bare arms, and the scents of a dozen flowering shrubs filled the night with promise. If only she'd been going out with Ross, or even Edward, she thought ruefully. She would have enjoyed this so much more.

Or would she?

The traitorous thought was quickly squashed as she greeted Carlos, who was standing holding the door of the limousine. 'Evenin', ma'am,' he responded politely, his expression impassive. Then, after closing the rear door behind her and sliding in behind the wheel, 'You okay?'

'As I'll ever be,' murmured Abby to herself, before saying brightly, 'Yes, thanks. Are you?'

'Hey, I'm always okay,' said Carlos good-humouredly. He met her eyes in the rearview mirror and grinned. 'You sure look good tonight, Ms Leighton.'

Abby couldn't help feeling pleased. Even if he was confirming her fears that Alejandro would think she'd gone to all this trouble for him. Which she supposed she had, she admitted unwillingly. But there were limits to what even a designer outfit could do.

'Um—I hope my outfit is suitable for sailing,' she ventured, aware that it probably wasn't wise to question the chauffeur. 'I understand Mr Varga owns—a boat.'

'That he does, ma'am,' Carlos agreed. 'His daddy was into shipping in quite a big way. Mr Varga—he's into all sorts of things. But I expect you know that for yourself.'

Abby sighed, not prepared to admit how little she did know. 'So where are we going?' she asked, glancing out of the windows. At night everything looked different, and she had no idea where they were now.

'Well, not to the shipyard, ma'am,' he drawled wryly. 'Mr Varga, he wants me to bring you to his house. 'Course, he does have a cruiser in his backyard,' he added thoughtfully. 'I'd say that's what he has in mind.'

Abby hardly heard a word beyond the fact that they were on their way to Alejandro's house. She sank back in the seat and blew out an indignant breath. How dared he? she asked herself furiously. He must know what going to his house would mean to her. But then, when had he ever considered her feelings? She should have known better than to put herself into his hands.

But then something else Carlos had said impinged on her consciousness. 'What did you mean about him having a cruiser in his backyard?'

Carlos's eyes moved briefly to the mirror. 'I guess you've never been to Mr Varga's house,' he drawled easily. 'It's on the water. He keeps the cruiser at his dock.'

Abby blinked. 'But I thought—' She stopped herself and began again, 'Isn't his house on Old Okra Road?'

'No way. Mr Varga's daddy used to have a house on Old Okra, but he moved into a retirement community a couple years ago. I guess that's how you got the wrong address.'

'I guess it is.'

Abby frowned, not sure whether she was glad or sorry. Either way, Alejandro hadn't mentioned dining at his house.

She realised now that they were driving south of the city. Away to her left she could see the lights of Key Biscayne, and she seemed to remember Edward telling her that this road ran all the way to the Keys. Surely that wasn't where they were heading? There were over a hundred miles of causeway between the mainland and Key West, which was geographically closer to Havana than Miami. But then, Alejandro's origins did lie with the Cuban community, too. Perhaps he felt more at home with his father's people.

But before she could begin to panic Carlos turned off the

main highway into the quieter streets of the suburbs. They crossed Old Cutler Road, bypassed the tropical gardens, and headed towards the coast. Carlos opened his window a crack and she smelled the tang of the ocean. The breeze that invaded the car was refreshingly cool.

Alejandro's house was at the end of a narrow lane, where palms and rioting hibiscus hung over every wall. Unlike at the Esquivals' estate, the iron gates that led into the property stood wide, and in the lights of the car's headlights Abby saw that only a pair of stone griffins guarded the entrance.

Carlos turned skilfully between the gates and brought the big car to a halt before a rambling two-storeyed residence that was almost completely covered with flowering vines. It was evidently a much older property than the house on Old Okra Road, with a slightly Twenties appearance. It reminded Abby of Norma Desmond's house in *Sunset Boulevard*, and she wouldn't have been at all surprised to see a vintage Studebaker parked in the shade of the ancient oaks that cast their shadows over the already sombre driveway.

It wasn't at all what she'd expected. The other house had had a much grander appearance, with a soaring roofline and glass everywhere. This house was totally different, and although carriage lamps provided some illumination, its appeal lay in the air of mystery that surrounded it like a cloak.

Carlos barely had time to get out of the car and swing open her door before the porch door opened and a shaft of golden light speared out from within. Alejandro stood in its brilliance, his expression hidden by the halo of light behind him. But in a wide-sleeved white shirt and tight-fitting black pants, his open collar just hinting at the darkness of the flesh beneath, his identity was unmistakeable.

Abby quivered. She couldn't help it. This was so much the way she remembered him. She had to fight back the urge she had to step out of the car and walk into his arms.

But that was crazy; *she* was crazy. Whatever Alejandro wanted, it wasn't her body. He had invited her here to talk about Edward and perhaps about Lauren. He was obviously as fond of his cousin as she was of him. So why was she sitting here wishing things—wishing life—could have been different? *Get over it, Abby,* she told herself. *Alejandro Varga was never meant for you.*

With a feeling of sudden helplessness she moved across the seat and thrust her foot out onto the crushed shell drive. Her sandal sank into the surprisingly soft surface, and she guessed the humidity seldom dried out here. Then Alejandro stepped forward and took her hand, and she was powerless to stop him from raising it to his lips.

His mouth was moist, too, his breath—or was it his tongue?—dampening her skin, and she shivered again. She should never have agreed to this, she thought unsteadily. Never have come here. Talk about walking into the lion's den.

'Bienvenido,' he greeted her softly. 'Welcome to my home. It is good to see you again, *cara.* I have been waiting for this moment for so long. Please.' He gestured behind him. 'Come in.'

'You didn't say we'd be having dinner at your house,' whispered Abby accusingly, but Alejandro only lifted enquiring eyes to the chauffeur, who was still waiting by the car.

'You can go, Carlos,' he said without inflection. 'I will call you if your services are required later. *Adios, amigo.* Have a good evening.'

'Gracias, señor.'

Abby was aware that the man looked at her before leaving. What was he thinking? she wondered. Did he have any sympathy for her plight? Had he any idea how much she longed to be leaving with him? That even returning to the Esquivals would be better than this?

Safer, certainly. But it was too late to be having second thoughts. Alejandro's fingers had fastened about her upper arm and he was guiding her across the forecourt and up the steps to the porch. Leading her, irresistibly, into his house.

A polished brass chandelier cast its light over the amber and black tiles of the entry, and beyond silk rugs in jewelled shades complemented dark wood panelling and rich satin drapes. The house was cool, but not excessively so, and Abby's skin cooled rapidly. The mingled scents of a dozen tropical blooms gave the air a heady fragrance.

A staircase wound to the upper floor of the house, but Abby averted her eyes quickly. Before she started to wonder whether Alejandro's bedroom was anything like the one in his father's house. In any case, he was guiding her into a spacious living room, and she forced herself to pay attention to that instead.

Three velvet sofas surrounded a flower-filled hearth that was richly patterned. Carved oak cabinets contained a veritable fortune in *objets d'art*. Trumpet-shaped orchids and delicate magnolias spilled from porcelain bowls and crystal vases that matched the chandelier sparkling above her head.

There were high-back chairs set against the walls, and lots of paintings, and an ornate bureau that was obviously an antique. Once again, the colours were vivid, but subtle, and Abby was reminded of her earlier notion. It was evident that the house was even older than she had thought.

But it wasn't sensible to allow herself to be overwhelmed by her surroundings, however beautiful they undoubtedly were. Alejandro hadn't brought her here to admire his house or his possessions. He'd brought her here for his own reasons, and she'd be wise to remember that.

To distract herself, she pulled away from Alejandro and moved to the long windows at the far side of the room. The sliding doors that led out to the deck were closed, but tall iron lamps set amongst the surrounding foliage illuminated the scene. The lights winked between the moving fronds of palm trees and added radiance to the bougainvillaea that tumbled from the balcony above.

There was a lizard, too, on the wooden railing. It seemed mesmerised by the light that came from the house. It waited, motionless, hoping to blend in with the vegetation, its little pulse beating rapidly in its throat.

Alejandro's shadowy reflection showed that he'd come to stand behind her, and she was as instantly aware of him as of the faint draught of cool air from the vent above her head. At once the encroaching greenery beyond the windows seemed to trap her, between its rampant vegetation and the subtle menace of the man at her back.

CHAPTER NINE

BECAUSE she needed to say something, anything, to break the spell he seemed to cast so effortlessly over her, Abby hurried into speech. 'Carlos said this house is on the water,' she said, keeping her eyes on the lizard, with whom she felt a certain affinity. 'Is—is the ocean visible from here?'

She could hear the mild amusement in his voice as he answered her. 'No,' he said indulgently. 'This whole coastline is honeycombed with small bays and waterways. My dock is on Turtle Creek. Biscayne Bay is about half a mile away.'

'Oh.'

Abby was trying desperately to think of something else to say when he murmured, 'And to answer your accusation earlier: I do not recall telling you where we were going to have dinner.'

'No, but—' She'd turned before realising how unwise that was, and she was forced to take a backward step to keep a sensible space between them. Even so, she was intensely conscious of his nearness, and of how dark his skin looked against the whiteness of his shirt. 'That is—you must have known what I would think when—when Carlos told me where we were going.'

'No.' Alejandro was deliberately obtuse. 'Why do you not tell me?'

Abby shook her head. 'Don't play games, Alejandro. You knew I'd think we were going to the house on Old Okra Road.'

'But the house on Old Okra Road is not my house.'

'I know that now.' Abby was infuriated by his ability to behave as if he was incapable of any deceit when she knew

91

only too well he was. 'But you didn't tell me it wasn't your house. Carlos did.'

Alejandro pushed his hands into the back pockets of his trousers. 'Good old Carlos,' he said drily. 'Tell me, *cara*, is this going somewhere?'

Abby pressed her lips together for a moment, controlling her impatience. 'As I said before, you like playing games, Alejandro. But I don't.'

'Which means…?'

'It means you deliberately let me think the house on Old Okra Road was your house,' she retorted tensely. 'But of course you couldn't take me to your house, could you? Your wife wouldn't have liked it. And that was something else you forgot to tell me.'

Alejandro's nostrils flared, and for a moment his dark features looked almost sinister. 'I suppose Edward told you,' he said harshly. 'Your dear brother, who is as culpable for keeping secrets as I am, it seems.'

Abby met his challenging gaze only briefly. It was hard to sustain her composure in the face of such blatant hostility, and she was uneasily aware of how vulnerable she was here. This was Alejandro's house, Alejandro's territory. He could say— and do—what he liked.

'Edward did tell me you were married,' she admitted at last. 'Do you blame him? I am his sister, after all. He was only looking out for me.'

'That must be a first,' remarked Alejandro, swaying back on his heels before turning and walking away from her. And before she could think of a suitable retort he stopped beside a cabinet and swung open the doors to reveal a comprehensive wet bar. 'What will you have to drink? And please do not say iced tea because I do not have any. Wine, perhaps, or a cocktail? You choose.'

Abby caught her upper lip between her teeth. Then, realising she wasn't going to get anywhere if she behaved sullenly, she shrugged. 'Do you have a spritzer?'

Alejandro gave her a resigned look. 'No.'

'Wine, then,' she said tightly. 'White wine, if you have it. Just a small glass.'

'I was not about to give you a tumbler,' he responded drily. 'And, yes, we have white wine. Is a Californian Chardonnay all right?'

As Abby was seldom able to tell one white wine from another, she could hardly object. But because he had been so sarcastic she said, 'I suppose so,' and had the satisfaction of seeing the way his mouth tightened at her words.

The appearance of a white-clad steward provided a welcome diversion. The man spoke to his employer in Spanish, and because he was obliged to deal with the enquiry Abby was able to take her glass from Alejandro's outstretched hand without worrying too much about whether their fingers touched or not.

In fact, they didn't, but that didn't prevent her from feeling grateful for the interruption. The atmosphere had been getting increasingly intense and it was good to breathe normally again.

Deciding she might feel safer if she was sitting down, Abby took the initiative and seated herself in a tapestry-covered armchair. She chose the chair deliberately rather than one of the sofas. Sitting on a sofa was an invitation for him to join her, and despite her efforts to keep their association on an impersonal level Alejandro seemed determined to thwart her.

'Your drink is all right?'

She realised abruptly that while she'd been lost in thought the servant had gone away again and Alejandro was now standing right in front of her. Unfortunately, as well as intimidating her, it put her eyes on a level with the impressive bulge of his manhood. Averting her eyes again, she took an unwary gulp of the wine in her glass and almost choked as it went down the wrong way.

Red-faced and embarrassed, she was obliged to take the napkin Alejandro offered her, and was frustratedly aware that he'd probably stood over her deliberately, knowing exactly how on edge she'd feel.

But just as she was considering how best to deal with the

threat he posed he seemed to take pity on her. Crossing the room, he sat down on one of the dark red velvet sofas she'd admired earlier. Hooking one deck-shoed foot across his knee—she noticed inconsequently that he wasn't wearing any socks—he draped one arm along the back of the sofa before raising the glass he was carrying to his lips. It was a tumbler, and she wondered if the colourless liquid in the glass was water or something stronger. Either way, it was obvious that he was perfectly at ease with himself, and it infuriated her anew that she should be such an easy mark. All the same, she was grateful for the respite that the distance gave.

'Feeling better?' he asked now, his deep voice with its distinctive Cuban accent scraping across her raw nerves. She was instantly aware that she was achieving nothing by putting off the inevitable. She had to talk to this man; she had to find out what he wanted. But most of all she had to stop making it so easy for him to control the conversation.

'Yes, thank you,' she answered, taking another sip of her wine just to prove that she could. Then, setting her glass down on the coaster he'd placed on a nearby table, she forced herself to look at him. 'Have you lived here long?'

His mouth compressed, as if he knew exactly what she was thinking, but he was coolly indulgent when he replied. 'The house used to belong to my aunt. When she died, it came to me.'

Abby hesitated. 'Was that before or after you got your divorce?' she asked crisply, and had the satisfaction of seeing his eyes darken with an irritation he couldn't hide.

'After,' he said eventually. 'My ex-wife never lived here, if that's what you want to know.' Then, with equal audacity, 'When did you break your engagement? Was that before or after you got back from the wedding?'

Abby blinked. 'I—' She was nonplussed. 'Who told you I'd broken my engagement?'

'Guess,' he said drily, and her brows drew together in total confusion.

'But—I only got engaged two months ago,' she protested. 'Why would I—?'

But she didn't complete the sentence. Suddenly something else he'd said came back to her, and she stared at him uncomprehendingly. 'What wedding are you talking about?'

Alejandro's lips twisted. 'How many weddings have you and I attended?'

'Edward's wedding!' she said incredulously. And, at his curt nod, 'I wasn't engaged when Eddie got married.'

'So it was before,' said Alejandro harshly. 'I should have known your brother wouldn't tell the truth.'

Abby gazed at him. 'I don't know what you're talking about,' she declared coldly. Then, holding up her head, she added, 'In any case, I didn't come here to talk about me. I came to talk about Eddie. I'd like to know why you persist in accusing him of—of God knows what when—when you're the—the—'

'Villain?' he supplied mockingly, but she ignored him.

'—the transgressor here?' she finished primly. 'I'm glad you're not denying it.'

Alejandro's expression softened. 'You really do not know, do you, *cara*?' he mused. 'What has he told you, I wonder? What explanation has he given you for his—what shall I call it?—his hostility towards me?'

'Don't pretend you don't know,' she exclaimed at once. 'You—you can't keep your hands off his wife. Why wouldn't he be hostile towards you when you're trying to destroy his marriage?'

Alejandro made a strangled sound and she thought for a moment he was choking. But he wasn't. She quickly realised he was fighting the desire to laugh, and it infuriated her that he could find it funny. This wasn't a game. This was her brother's life, his future. But then, what could she expect from a man who'd betrayed his own wife?

Abby wanted to get up and walk out of there. But she didn't. She couldn't. Now that it was out in the open, she owed it to Edward to try and put things right. Whatever hold the Cuban had over him, surely it could not withstand the exposure of Alejandro's treachery? He'd had it all his own way for far too long. It was up to her to level the score.

But to her dismay Alejandro had put down his glass now and got to his feet again. She steeled herself for a confrontation, but instead of coming towards her he went to stand by the windows, looking out onto the floodlit deck as she had done earlier.

'*Bien,*' he said softly. 'So that is what he has told you. And you believed him. I do not know whether to be flattered or insulted, *cara*. What do you think?'

Abby swallowed, aware that he had turned his head and was looking at her now, but she couldn't back down. 'I think you should be ashamed,' she said tensely. 'I would be, in your shoes. Lauren—Lauren must be young enough to be your daughter.'

'Or my niece,' agreed Alejandro, without expression. He shook his head incredulously. 'I would have to be very desperate or very stupid to regard my good friend's daughter in that way.'

Abby turned her head now. 'Are you denying that you're having an affair with her?'

'Denying it?' Alejandro echoed the words disbelievingly. '*En que piensas*! What are you thinking! The question is not a serious one. I am not interested in Lauren Esquival.'

'It's Lauren Leighton,' put in Abby quickly, and he sighed.

'Lauren Leighten, *sí*,' he amended flatly. '*Por Dios*, Abigail, she is a child. A trying child at times, *a lo mejor*. But a child, *no obstante*.'

Abby got unsteadily to her feet. 'Of course, you would say that.'

'Yes, I would.' He turned right round now, and suddenly the space between them didn't seem half as safe. '*Cristo*, are you listening to me, Abigail? Lauren is charming—amusing, even. But I have never touched her. I treat her as I would a younger sister. I have never been attracted to her.'

Abby swallowed, trying to concentrate her attention on the

brown flesh rising from the unbuttoned neckline of his shirt. 'I—I hear what you say,' she said, noticing the pulse that was beating in his throat. His heart appeared to be racing just as hers was. But in his case it was probably frustration, whereas she was fighting an awareness that was rapidly overwhelming her good sense.

Alejandro stared at her for a long moment and then, just as she'd feared, he strolled back to where she was standing. 'Pobrecita,' he said huskily. 'You hear my words but you do not believe me. You know in your heart it is the truth, but for your brother's sake you tell yourself you are not convinced.'

'Do you blame me?' She expelled a nervous breath. 'And if you're trying to intimidate me, Alejandro, you're succeeding.'

'Hijo de puta!' he swore softly. 'I am not trying to intimidate you, cara. I am trying to make you understand that there is more going on here than you think.'

Abby pressed her lips together. 'I've known Eddie all his life—'

'Which means what, exactly?'

Abby shook her head. 'I—I would know if he was lying to me.'

'Muy bien.' Alejandro shrugged. 'And what if I told you he is afraid to tell the truth? What then?'

Abby swallowed. 'Eddie's not afraid of you,' she exclaimed unsteadily, but her words sounded hollow even to her own ears.

'I did not say he was afraid of me,' said Alejandro softly, lifting his hand almost involuntarily and drawing his knuckles along the stiff line of her jawline. 'Must I say it again, cara? I am not Edward's enemy. Whatever he may have told you, it is not true.'

She jerked back from his touch, but, as if her action had achieved the opposite of what she'd intended, he didn't withdraw his hand. Instead, he allowed his fingers to trail over her throat to the low vee of her halter, sliding beneath the cloth, his nails gently scoring her skin.

Abby felt weak. In spite of everything that had happened, she was suddenly overwhelmed by needs she'd assured herself were consigned to oblivion. Memories of the night he'd made love to her came flooding into her consciousness, and his touch was unbearably real, unbearably familiar. His nearness, the warmth of his breath, his hands, were stripping away her defences, and she knew if she didn't move soon she wouldn't be able to move at all.

'I think you'd better let me go,' she said, hearing the underlying panic in her voice and praying that he couldn't detect it. 'This isn't going to work.'

His smile was enigmatic, but she guessed he knew exactly how feeble her boast was. The truth was, it was succeeding all too well, and when she put out her hand to ward him off she found her fingers caught in his tormenting grasp.

'I fear Edward knows how wrong you are,' he breathed, and to her dismay he brought her hand to his lips. His tongue brushed her palm and she felt its sensual caress in every quivering nerve of her body. Hot and dark, his sexuality poured over her, and when he spoke again she had to concentrate hard to understand what he was saying. 'He knows I still want you, does he not?' he murmured thickly. 'That is what he has told you. That I would—how would he say it?—ditch Lauren, *no*, if I thought I could have you?'

'Don't be so ridiculous!'

Abby dragged her hand away from his, scrubbing it violently against her hip. Yet she could still feel his tongue, still feel his heat enveloping her. Oh, God, she thought unsteadily. Why had she ever thought she could do this? Why had she let Edward persuade her that Alejandro would listen to her?

To her relief, however, Alejandro didn't pursue it. She didn't believe he'd accepted defeat. That was unlikely to be his way. He was probably only saving himself for a future confrontation. He knew as well as she did that she wasn't going anywhere right now.

'Come,' he said abruptly, turning back to the windows. He

offered her his hand, but this time Abby knew better than to take it.

'Where are we going?' she asked, trying to keep the tremor out of her voice, and he smiled.

'To the dock, of course,' he said, unlatching the sliding doors and stepping aside to allow her to precede him. 'I want to show you my boat.'

His boat! Abby took a calming breath. She'd forgotten why he'd invited her here. And she so much didn't want to leave the comparative safety of his house.

'I—don't know,' she said, making no move to join him. 'I'm not a very good sailor.'

'You will not have to be,' he told her firmly. And she wondered if he thought that anything he said would reassure her.

'Alejandro—'

'Come,' he said again, with just a trace of impatience in his voice. 'Would you disappoint your brother? He wishes for me to be so infatuated with you that I will do whatever he wants.'

CHAPTER TEN

ALEJANDRO'S boat was both more and less than Abby had anticipated.

It was smaller, certainly: a forty-foot vessel, with two masts gracing its shining teak deck. There were living quarters below that were both conservative and comfortable. But it wasn't the gleaming steel yacht Abby had expected. Like his house, it possessed charm and character instead.

They'd reached the dock by walking through a lush paradise of ferns and palms and creepers. Delicate orchids with trumpet-shaped petals had brushed her cheeks and waxy magnolias and vivid hibiscus grew in wild profusion, their scents alone heady and overpowering. Abby had been almost glad when Alejandro placed a firm hand in the small of her back to guide her over a particularly uneven patch of ground. Her head had been spinning, and it wasn't just the intoxication of the flowers.

She'd been intensely aware of his nearness. Of how easily he had overpowered her. But she had also been aware that the tropical undergrowth might hide other exotic specimens that were less attractive. Snakes and spiders, for example, although she doubted she was in any danger here.

Nevertheless, she'd been relieved when they had stepped onto the ribbed planking of the dock and she'd been able to free herself both from Alejandro's hold and the fears that had pursued her from the house. Yet now, when Alejandro went past her to check on the mooring lines, she found herself watching him again, admiring the tight curve of his buttocks as he bent to pull on the ropes. All his movements were lithe and sensual, she admitted. He seemed to possess a dark power she was unable to resist.

Dear Lord!

She dragged her eyes away from temptation and found herself gazing instead into two eyes staring at her from the darkness of the creek. They seemed to float just above the surface of the water, their appraisal heavy-lidded and intent.

A little squeak of alarm escaped her. She was sure it was an alligator, and she glanced in panic around the dock. Fortunately, it was built well above the water, to accommodate Alejandro's boat, but she could easily imagine the reptile crawling up the bank towards them.

Alejandro straightened at the sound of her cry. He turned quickly towards her and she realised she was probably making a fool of herself again. The creature, whatever it was, had disappeared beneath the surface of the water, and there was no way anyone could identify it in the creek's murky depths.

'Is something wrong?'

Alejandro came towards her, and despite the fact that she'd calmed her fears Abby wished she dared clutch his hand. 'It's nothing,' she said hurriedly, though her eyes still searched the reeds that grew in such profusion along the waterway. 'I—' She had to say it. 'I thought I saw an alligator.' The lamplight revealed his wry expression as she added, with some embarrassment, 'But I'm sure it wasn't. And it's gone now, in any case.'

'So what do you think it was?' he asked, arching his dark brows enquiringly.

'I don't know.' She was sure he was making fun of her again, and she refused to let him see he had her spooked. 'A fox, maybe. Or a raccoon. You have them here, don't you? But it was in the water. I just saw its eyes watching me.'

Alejandro smiled. 'And you think it was admiring its supper before eating it, *bien*?' he mused softly, and she gave him an indignant look.

'I knew you wouldn't take it seriously,' she said, wrapping her arms about herself. 'Well, I'm not used to wild animals in my backyard.'

'Nor am I, *cara*,' he assured her softly. 'And I am sorry if you did not like my joke. But I doubt if it was an alligator, *mi amor*. Alligators do not usually scare my guests.'

'So what was it?'

Alejandro shrugged. 'A manatee, perhaps,' he replied consideringly. 'There used to be many of them about here. Regrettably the propellers of speedboats have made them an endangered species.'

'Oh.' Abby stared at him. 'That's awful!'

'It is also life,' said Alejandro drily. 'Or should I say death? You have a soft heart, *cara*. I like that.'

No, I'm just soft, thought Abby, not knowing how to answer him, and she was relieved when Alejandro changed the subject.

'Shall we go aboard?' he suggested, indicating the gangway he'd attached to the bow. He glanced at her feet. 'But perhaps you should take off your shoes, *no*? I would hate for you to lose your balance and fall into the creek with our uninvited guest.'

Abby glared at him. She hadn't had any option when it came to her choice of footwear, and she was perfectly well aware of how ridiculous her sandals must appear to him. He probably thought she'd worn them to impress him, she thought resentfully, and she kicked off her heels with some irritation.

'Much better,' he observed softly, and although he wasn't looking at them her toes curled just the same. He had a way of speaking to her that caused the fine hairs on the back of her neck to prickle in anticipation, and she was again reminded of the night they had spent together.

Brushing past him, she made for the gangway. She wanted the evening over, she told herself. And once he realised that he was wasting his time baiting her he'd surely get to the point of this meeting.

He followed her aboard and the boat rocked alarmingly on the swell. But, although she half expected him to take advantage of her momentary unsteadiness to touch her, he just moved ahead into the pilot's cabin and switched on the generator.

Almost immediately lights flowered all over the vessel and Abby caught her breath at the beauty of polished wood and shining brass. A steep stairway led down into the stateroom and Alejandro came out of the cabin to indicate that she should follow him.

She would have preferred to go ahead rather than follow him. It meant she had to expose herself to his enigmatic gaze. But he was already descending the steps with the ease of familiarity, and, dropping her sandals onto the deck, she grasped the handrail and started down.

Keeping her eyes firmly on her feet, and not on his dark upturned face, she looked about her. Below deck was just as impressive as above. A galley was situated to one side and a narrow companionway gave access to the main cabin. Beyond that, she guessed, were the sleeping quarters. But that was definitely something she didn't want to think about now.

There was the delicious scent of cooked food, but a brief glance into the galley convinced her that no one had been cooking there. As with Lauren and Edward's apartment, the kitchen looked untouched, and she was therefore unprepared for the sight that met her eyes when she stepped into the stateroom.

A long buffet table had been laid beneath the square windows, and the scents she had detected earlier evidently came from here. Everything was steaming hot, and she could only assume that while she and Alejandro had been having their drinks at the house a veritable army of servants had been working tirelessly. How long had it taken, she wondered, to set this up?

'I hope you like Cuban food,' murmured Alejandro half apologetically, and she shook her head in total disbelief.

'It—smells delicious,' she said hastily, realising that he might misinterpret that reaction. Then, because she couldn't remain angry with him when he'd obviously gone to so much trouble on her account, she added softly, 'You'll have to tell me what everything is. Apart from stone crabs, I don't think I've tried Cuban food before.'

'O—kay.' The word sounded strange coming from his lips, but his smile was genuine enough. 'Let me introduce you, hmm?'

He collected a fork from the display and invited her to join him beside the table. Then, dipping the fork into a concoction of saffron-flavoured rice and peas, he skewered an enormous shrimp and offered it to her.

It was delicious: fleshy and sweet, and dripping with a rich creamy sauce. '*Camarones,*' Alejandro said, indicating the shrimp. He watched her bite into it with obvious enjoyment. 'You like, *sí*?'

'*Sí.*'

Abby dabbed at her chin with a napkin, aware that she probably shouldn't be enjoying herself. But she was. Nevertheless, letting him take her to dinner was one thing. Letting him feed her from his own hand was something else.

The next thing he offered was a golden-brown roll that she'd assumed was made of potato but wasn't. Delicious curls of ham delighted her tastebuds as she bit into it. Mixed with shredded vegetables and fried to a consistency that was crisp on the outside and juicily soft within, it was both sweet and spicy. It reminded her of fritters she'd tasted at home.

'*Croquetas,*' he said, once again enjoying her pleasure. Then, with disturbing intimacy. 'Has anyone ever told you what a delight you are to please, *cara*? So many women would starve themselves before they would eat this food.'

Abby grimaced, wiping her mouth. 'What are you saying? That I'm a lost cause?' she asked. She was gazing longingly at the crisply roasted chicken he had chosen next, and Alejandro's brows drew together in confusion.

'*Que?*' he said. 'I do not know what you mean?'

'That I'm fat?' suggested Abby wryly, and he made an astonished sound.

'You are not fat, *cara*,' he said huskily. 'And I should know, *recuerda?* Remember?'

She remembered, but now was not the time to be thinking of that. Not when he was so near, when he was being so nice, and when she was definitely in danger of forgetting why she was here.

'Um—what's this?' she asked, moving away from him along the table, and to her relief he accepted her attempt to change the subject.

'That is *ropa vieja*,' he told her lightly. 'A shredded beef stew. And the spicy-smelling dish beside it is gumbo, which is not a Cuban speciality at all. It actually comes from the Cajun district of southern Louisiana, but I like it and I am hoping you will like it also.'

Abby was very much afraid that she liked everything—which wasn't very wise when the dishes she was being offered were all rich in carbohydrates and served in heavy sauces. She dreaded to think how many calories she was consuming. But the food didn't seem to have done Alejandro any harm, she reflected ruefully, and stopped worrying about her diet and just indulged herself.

As well as all the spicy dishes there were other things to tempt her. *Plátano*, which was deep-fried banana; crème caramel Hispanic-style, cooked in a crisply baked pastry shell; Florida's own key lime pie and fruits of every kind.

They eventually filled their plates and retired to the cushioned banquette that circled the bow. From here long windows gave an uninterrupted view of the creek, where the dancing lights of vessels out in the bay glinted in the darkness.

Alejandro put some Latino music on the hi-fi, and the exotic rhythms of salsa and merengue couldn't help but fire her blood. Sometimes the beat was fast, but at others it was slower and sensually appealing. It was music to dance to or make love to, and her senses wavered at the prospect of doing either of those things with Alejandro.

Even so, she was relaxing. Slowly, but surely she could feel the tension in her body slipping away. Alejandro had made no move towards her and she was half inclined to believe that her awareness of him was exaggerated. He was certainly doing his best to put her at her ease.

Nevertheless, she was aware that the wine might have something to do with it. Despite her misgivings, it would have been churlish to refuse. But it was certainly heady stuff, and she'd drunk several glasses. By the time the meal was over she was feeling decidedly muzzy.

But pleasantly so, she assured herself, unable at that moment to find the energy to worry about it. She was enjoying herself too much, and she didn't want to spoil it by thinking about anything else.

Edward!

Her brother's face swam before her eyes and she blinked determinedly. That was why she was here: to talk about Edward. Nothing else. She was letting herself be seduced by the night and the wine and the music—and the man, she thought impatiently. She should never forget the reasons that had brought her here.

Or the man who was to blame.

Alejandro.

She started when he got to his feet, but he only collected their plates and went aft to deposit them in the galley. Then he was back again, holding out his hand towards her, inviting her to get to her feet.

He expected her to dance with him, she realised, disbelievingly. Just as she was preparing herself to confront him, he was following his own agenda again. And this time there was no escape. Setting her wine glass aside, he pulled her up from the banquette. Before she knew what was happening, she was in his arms.

'We have to talk,' she protested, feeling the heat of his fingers through the thin fabric of her top. His thumb brushed the bare skin above the back of the halter and she shivered. 'Alejandro, I don't want to dance with you. That's not why I came.'

'No.' He conceded the point, but he didn't let her go. 'But that does not mean we cannot enjoy ourselves, *cara*. Trust me. We will get to what you want in good time.'

Trust him? Abby felt a hysterical desire to laugh. Yeah, right, she thought wildly. She could do that. She'd done it before and look where it had got her. She wouldn't be here at all if she hadn't made the mistake of trusting Alejandro before. How could he ask her to trust him when she didn't even trust herself?

Nevertheless, when he started to move in time to the music it was incredibly difficult to keep that in mind. The night, the hypnotic rhythm of the music, the lean strength of his body moving against hers, sent her senses reeling. His hand was in the small of her back, pressing her even closer. If she relaxed and leaned into him would she feel the hard length of his manhood against her stomach?

But that was madness. They were dancing, not indulging in some illicit foreplay to sex. Yet sex was in her mind; sex was all she could think of. Dear God, how much wine had he fed her? What had been in it to make her feel almost wild with desire?

She felt dizzy, disorientated. Being here with Alejandro seemed unbelievable, unreal. When she dared a glance up at him she glimpsed a matching anguish in his expression. But then it was gone, replaced by the mocking sensuality of his smile.

Watching her intently, he slid his fingers between hers and brought their hands close to his body. Now she could feel the sinuous movement of his leg as he moved against her, and he deliberately pressed her hand against his thigh.

'Do you want to feel what you do to me, *cara*?' he breathed against her ear before catching the gold hoop of her earring between his teeth and tugging gently on it. 'Or perhaps you are not ready to share that with me yet.'

'Alejandro—'

The word was choked. She wanted to tell him that she'd never be ready to share anything with him, but he only gave a soft laugh and swung her round.

The cabin spun wildly about her. She couldn't keep her balance, and she groped for his shoulder, needing something solid to hold on to. But his shirt was smooth and silky, and instead of grasping a handful of the cloth her fingers slid onto his neck.

She snatched her hand away at once, but not before she'd registered warm, slightly damp skin, and dark hair that curled about her fingers. And recognised the fact that he was as sensitive to her touch as she was to his.

'*Querida,*' he said huskily, pressing her free hand against his groin. Then, skimming both hands up her arms, he took possession of her shoulders. 'Do you have any idea what I am thinking at this moment? Do you know how often I have imagined this moment in my dreams?'

'Alejandro—'

'Even the way you say my name is different from anyone else,' he continued, his thumb massaging the curve of her jawline. 'Do you remember how it was with us? Do you remember that night as well as I do? We could not get enough of one another, *cara*. And you—you tasted so good—'

'Stop it!'

Abby almost choked on the word. This couldn't be happening. Was he completely shameless? Was she? She was an engaged woman, for heaven's sake. Didn't that mean anything to him? Didn't it mean anything to Edward either? she wondered desperately. She rather thought the answer had to be no, on both counts.

'You do not mean that, *cara*.'

He didn't believe her. She almost groaned. Why was she not surprised? Whatever Edward thought, she was not prepared for this. Nor was she prepared to—to prostitute herself because her brother thought it might give him some advantage. What was going on? Why was nobody telling her the truth?

She realised suddenly that Alejandro was nuzzling her neck. She felt his teeth against her skin and her own flesh betrayed her. When he bit her, when he sucked an inch of skin into his mouth and drew on it with hard, purposeful lips and tongue, she couldn't suppress the helpless moan that escaped her. God, it felt so good, and she felt the wet heat of her own arousal between her legs.

'*Esto te gusta?*' he asked her thickly. 'Do you like?' His hands were gripping her midriff and she realised that he was touching her bare flesh. The halter had separated from her shorts when he'd spun her around, and his fingers dipped into her waistband to probe the sensitive hollow at the base of her spine. '*Tu eres muy hermoso, cara.* You are very beautiful. But you know this. I have told you many times before.'

Yes, he had. And she'd believed him then. To her cost. She didn't believe him now. He was only playing with her. He was seeing how far she would go, how far she would let *him* go. And somehow—somehow, God help her!—she had to call a halt before it was too late.

'Please, Alejandro,' she begged, despising herself for pleading with him. 'You said—you said you would do what I wanted if—if I agreed to dance with you. Well, we're not dancing now.'

'You think not, *cara*?' His tone was softly sensual. 'But surely this is the oldest dance there is.'

'I don't understand you.' But she did. She understood him only too well.

'No?' Alejandro's eyes searched her face. 'You surprise me, *cara*. Well—let me show you how it is with me.'

He bent his head then, and although she turned her face aside his lips grazed the corner of her mouth. It was not a forceful kiss. His tongue barely touched her cheek. But she felt it deep down in the knotted core of her stomach, and, despite everything she'd been telling herself, she couldn't prevent the wave of longing that swept over her.

And he knew it, damn him. Knew that if he kissed her again, if he parted his legs and drew her close enough to feel the unmistakable stirring of his erection, she would not be able to resist him. The fight was an unequal one. She wasn't only fighting him, she was fighting herself.

He did kiss her again, his hand at the back of her head guiding her mouth to his. His tongue swept between her lips, exulting in her submission, and she could no longer pretend that she wasn't participating in her own seduction. She was drowning in sensation, and this time she couldn't blame the wine.

He kissed her over and over, slanting his mouth across hers as if he wanted to drag the very breath from her. Her lungs were labouring and she was dizzy from the lack of air. But hunger seemed to have taken the place of the anxiety she'd been suffering all evening. A hunger for him that was increasing with every sensual caress.

She wanted to meet his need, God help her. If she was totally honest she'd admit she wanted to give herself to him. She opened herself as she opened her mouth, letting his tongue tangle with hers and sweep all her doubts away.

Her knees were so weak that she was glad when his hands curved over her bottom. He caressed her boldly, his fingers invading the cleft between her cheeks. He was holding her tightly against him, and she felt his erection thrusting against her stomach.

The blood was now racing through her veins like liquid fire, the music playing in her ears like a plaintive song inside her head. Every nerve was acutely sensitive, feeding the needs he was inciting. She wanted him, she wanted his hands on her body. She wanted to be naked for him, she thought shamelessly. She wanted to feel his naked flesh against her skin.

When he bent lower and caught one taut nipple between his teeth, she almost went wild with longing. He sucked it strongly through the cloth, eliciting a moan of frustration from her lips. Looking down at his bent head, she couldn't prevent herself from touching him, feeling his sharp reaction under her palm.

Her free hand stroked his cheek, felt the faint roughness of his stubble beneath her touch. And when he released her breast she lifted his face to hers, initiating the kiss, cupping his face between her hands.

Her tongue darted to meet his and she heard his groan of pleasure. Then he took over, and she was helpless again beneath the eager, searching pressure of his mouth. Her head was spinning. She felt as if she was swimming in a rich dark sea of emotion. Yet she didn't—couldn't—think of drawing away.

The sensations that were governing her body were so delicious she couldn't deny them. Her breasts, her stomach, her abdomen, were sensitised to such an extent that she could do nothing but show him how she felt. She ached with feelings that compelled her to give in to him. She'd never experienced so much emotion in her life.

When he trailed hot kisses along her jawline to the quivering column of her throat she burrowed against him. They were still wearing their clothes and she wanted to be closer yet. She hardly hesitated before attempting to drag his shirt out of his pants. She wanted to feel his warm flesh beneath her hands.

But, as if that was the signal he had been waiting for, Alejandro stiffened. Expelling an uneven sigh, he lifted his head. His hands gripped her upper arms and he put her away from him. Holding her as she struggled to understand.

'I think not,' he said softly, as she swayed uncertainly before him. 'I think this is the moment when I say we have to talk.'

'To talk?' Abby tried to clear her head, but it wasn't easy. She blinked uncomprehendingly. 'I don't understand.'

'I think you do, *cara*,' he said, releasing her and moving across the cabin to pour himself more wine. 'I am only doing what you wanted. So talk to me, Abigail. Tell me why you think Edward is so keen for us to renew our—acquaintance.'

CHAPTER ELEVEN

ABBY shook her head, and then wished she hadn't. It just made her feel slightly sick and she prayed she wasn't about to throw up. That would be the last straw, she thought bitterly. The final humiliation. Somehow she had to deal with this with some dignity and pride.

But the rich food, the wine, dancing with Alejandro—especially dancing with Alejandro—had left her feeling dazed and vulnerable. And he knew it. That was why he was standing there, legs slightly apart, arms crossed over his midriff, the glass of red wine in his hand a scarlet stain against his white shirt. There was amusement in his face, too, she thought. A mocking acknowledgement of her weakness. Of how easy it had been to rob her of the veneer of indifference she'd attempted to display.

She wasn't displaying any indifference now. On the contrary, she knew she must look a total disaster. Her hair, unruly at the best of times, was wild about her shoulders, her shorts had been pushed low on her hips and her halter clung clammily to her breasts. She looked what she was: a woman who had been made mad, passionate love to. By a man who had deliberately robbed her of any self-respect...

She had to say something, she told herself urgently. She had to try and rescue the situation by showing him that she was above his petty sarcasm. It would be pointless to pretend that she hadn't been aroused by his lovemaking, but if she could convince him that she was no more ashamed of what had happened than he was, then she might stand a chance of saving face.

'I'm sorry,' she said at last, lifting both hands and sweeping her hair back from her face. She allowed her hands to rest at the back of her neck, even though she knew it drew attention to the swollen fullness of her breasts and the betraying darkness on the cloth that his lips and tongue had made. 'I'm afraid I'd forgotten all about Eddie. Isn't that awful?' She forced a smile. 'Forgive me. What was it you were saying? Something about Eddie wanting us to get together?'

He was surprised. She could see that. And there was a faint trace of admiration in his eyes. He indicated the wine bottle beside him, offering her refreshment, but she wanted nothing else to impair her judgment tonight.

She moved her wrist in a negative gesture. She had to keep her head now, even if she had already proved how difficult that could be. And, groping behind her, she found the banquette, sinking down onto it with some relief.

'So,' she went on, not giving him the chance to take the initiative, 'perhaps you should tell me why you think that is.'

Alejandro lifted his glass to his lips before replying, and she had to steel herself not to watch the powerful muscles moving in his throat. Perhaps he needed the wine to give him courage, she thought without conviction. But surely what had happened hadn't all been on her side? He had been aroused. She was sure of it. And there'd been times when he'd seemed as much at the mercy of his senses as she was herself.

'*Bravo,*' he said now, putting down his empty glass and seating himself on the banquette opposite. 'You turn my words back on me in the hope that I will forget who started this— conversation, *no*?'

'*Well, I didn't start it,*' muttered Abby under her breath, relieved that he hadn't taken the seat beside her. But it wasn't all good news. Now he could look at her without obstruction. She felt as if she was in a spotlight, his dark eyes on her, narrowed and intent.

She licked her lips and tried to speak casually. 'I—I hoped you would tell me why you think Eddie is afraid,' she said evenly. She paused, and when he didn't answer her, she continued, 'You act like you have all the answers, but you don't explain what you mean.'

'Did I say I had all the answers?'

His brows arched interrogatively and she knew she was going to get no real explanations from him. The most she'd hoped for was that he might betray some titbit of information she could use to get her brother to confide in her. But Alejandro was giving nothing away.

Changing the subject, she said abruptly, 'What about the break-in at Eddie's apartment? I know you denied knowing anything about it when I mentioned it to Mrs Esquival, but we both know that wasn't what you said to me.'

'Do we?'

Once again he was deliberately obtuse, and she turned her head away from his bland look of enquiry. She could hardly believe that only a few minutes before they had been locked in each other's arms. She might still feel the shame of his lovemaking in her throbbing breast and in the burning and—oh, Lord—the *visible* scar on her neck, but he looked as cool and composed as ever. She could almost believe she'd imagined the whole thing.

Her eyes filled with tears and she had to blink hard to drive them away. She must not—*must not*—let him see that he had hurt as well as humiliated her. She might despise herself, but she refused to let him see it.

'So?' She had been silent too long, and he was waiting for her to answer him. 'Perhaps you should tell me what you feel about the break-in, *cara*. Do you think it was, as they say, some addict searching for money for a fix? Or was it—perhaps—a warning? Does your brother have enemies we know nothing about?'

He had her whole attention now, and she swiped the heels of her hands over her eyes before turning to look at him again. 'What enemies?' she echoed blankly, remembering the laptop computer lying untouched on the shelf.

'Who knows?' Again he drew back from telling her anything positive. 'But maybe it is time that you asked him.'

Abby swallowed. 'I'm asking you.'

'I know. But I cannot answer you.'

Abby shook her head. 'Can't or won't?' She sniffed. 'Are you sure you're not enjoying this?'

'Enjoying what?'

'This. Confusing me. Saying the robbery might be a warning.' Despite her best efforts, a tremor had entered her voice. 'Why can't you be honest with me for a change?'

'As you were with me?' he queried bleakly, and she gazed at him blankly.

'As I was with you?' she echoed. 'What are you talking about?'

'It is of no matter,' he replied, not pursuing it. He glanced behind him. 'Can I offer you some more wine?'

'I don't want anything. Only the truth,' she retorted unsteadily. Then, with determination, 'All right, if you won't tell me what you know about the break-in, perhaps you can tell me why Eddie and Lauren are having personal problems if they don't involve you? Eddie seems convinced she is seeing someone. Do you know if she is involved with someone else?'

Alejandro blew out a breath. 'Truly, you are *increíble, cara*. Why would you suppose that I would know this?'

'You are—close to her,' insisted Abby doggedly. 'She seems to trust you. If anyone knows what she's doing, it's you.'

'You flatter me.' Alejandro rose negligently to his feet. 'And even if it was true—and I am admitting nothing, you understand?—then you must know that I would respect her confidence in the same way as I respect yours.'

'Mine?' Abby said the word contemptuously, stung into retaliation. 'You've never shown me any respect. On the contrary. All you've ever done for me is ensure that I can never have—'

She broke off abruptly. Dear heaven, she'd almost said it. A sense of horror engulfed her at the realisation that she'd been in danger of betraying her deepest secret to him. The frustration she'd been feeling had briefly robbed her of her usual caution, and all the promises she'd made to herself while she'd been lying in her hospital bed had taken second place to the desire to wipe the smug complacency from his face.

She fought for control, aware that he was looking at her curiously now. The expression that had crossed her face, or perhaps the anguished sincerity in her voice, had alerted him to the fact that she had been about to deliver some telling news. He was obviously waiting for her to go on, but it would never happen, she assured herself sickly. He was never— *never*—going to find out what he'd done to her.

Feeling incredibly weak, she got unsteadily to her feet and said, 'I'd like to leave now.' She held up her head. 'Perhaps I could call a cab?'

'That will not be necessary.' Alejandro's eyes were narrowed. 'Carlos will take you.' He paused. 'But are you sure you want to go? You did not finish what you started to say.'

'It was of no importance,' she lied, aware that he didn't believe her. 'Actually, I'm not feeling very well. I'm sure you wouldn't want your friends to think you'd upset me.'

'Even if I have?' he countered, his tone betraying more warmth, as if he was feeling sorry for her, which she couldn't bear. 'I am sorry if I have disappointed you, Abigail. That was not my intention. But we are all human. And you are—you always were—a disturbingly attractive woman. I am afraid I let things go too far.'

'And you were always full of—' She bit off the word. 'Excuse me, Señor Varga, but I think I'm going to be sick.'

Of course she wasn't sick, even if her stomach was decidedly wobbly as Carlos drove her back to the Esquivals' villa.

'You all right, ma'am?' Carlos asked as he paused at the gates of the estate, and Abby wondered if he knew what was going on. Because Alejandro had bid her a polite, but definitely cool farewell, perhaps? The chauffeur must have noticed that his employer's attitude had been vastly different from the way he'd greeted her on her arrival. But had he also sensed the hostility that simmered between them? The awareness that held both distrust and suspicion?

She told herself she didn't care, and, forcing a small smile, she said, 'I'm fine, thank you. Just a little tired, that's all. You know how it is with jet lag.'

Carlos nodded, but she had the feeling he was far more astute than she was giving him credit for. 'I know how it is,' he conceded, and she had the bitter thought that this probably wasn't the first time he'd driven some pathetic woman home after Alejandro had discarded them. Someone had to do it, and his employer wouldn't do it himself.

To her relief, there was no sign of her hosts when she entered the villa. She thought she could hear the sound of voices and laughter from the patio, but she didn't stop to investigate. She remembered that the Esquivals had been expecting visitors that evening, and she had no desire to meet anyone else. She just wanted to go to bed and escape her thoughts in oblivion.

Informing the maid who had let her in that she was going to her room, she ran quickly up the stairs, not stopping until the door was closed behind her. She was making a habit of this, she thought miserably. Running away from her problems. Hiding in her room. And she had still to cope with the guilt she was feeling over betraying Ross. That ought to have been her main misgiving, but she couldn't deal with that tonight.

She knew Ross would be expecting her to call him. But there was no way she could come from Alejandro's arms and speak to her fiancé normally. He would hear the hesitation in her voice. What she'd done was unforgivable. And she didn't feel she could contemplate it.

Shedding the hateful shorts and halter, she went into her bathroom and stood for several minutes under a cool shower. She was trying to wash away the memory of Alejandro's hands upon her, trying to rid herself of the feeling that his fingerprints must still be visible on her skin.

As his teeth marks were visible on her neck, she acknowledged anxiously, seeing her reflection in the mirror and touching the bruised flesh with reluctant fingers. Dear Lord, why had he done it? Why had he branded her? Was it some sick way of showing her how helpless she was with him? Or was this Edward's answer? That he shouldn't send a woman to do a man's job?

Whatever his motives, she would have to hide it before she went down to breakfast in the morning. She could imagine Dolores's revulsion if she saw the mark. Not to mention Lauren and her brother. She had some elastic plasters in her toilet bag. She would have to use one of them.

It was after eleven by the time she crawled into bed, but she wasn't sleepy. She was tired, yes, but her mind was too active to allow her to sleep. The events of the evening kept going round and round in her head. Whatever way she looked at it, she had to admit that she had been as much to blame for what had happened as Alejandro.

Oh, he had instigated it, no doubt, by inviting her to dance, but he hadn't been totally responsible for what had come after. She'd wanted to dance with him. She'd wanted him to hold her, to kiss her, to *make love* to her. She'd been wholly at the mercy of her senses, and it was galling to realise that if he hadn't called a halt to what was happening, what had happened two years ago would have happened all over again.

But why? *Why?* Her eyes filled with tears. Was she so lacking in moral fibre that any man's embrace would have achieved the same result? No! It was Alejandro. It had always been Alejandro. He was like a fever in her blood, and, damn him, she didn't seem capable of putting him out of her mind…

Abby met Alejandro Varga for the first time just three days before her brother's wedding.

She'd arrived from England the day before, weary and jet lagged. It was the first time she'd travelled so far, and she was still slightly overwhelmed by the richness and beauty of her surroundings when she went down to the pool the next morning for a swim.

Mrs Esquival—there was no question of calling her Dolores in those days—had assured her she was welcome to treat the place as her home for the duration of her stay. Abby couldn't wait for Edward to arrive before taking advantage of the deliciously cool water.

Her brother was still living in the apartment he shared with two of the other chefs from the restaurant where he worked. And, although he'd put in an appearance the night before, it had been obvious to his sister that his association with the Esquivals was still very much that of employer and employee.

But meeting Lauren had been reassuring. She was evidently very much in love with her English fiancé. She'd greeted Abby like the sister she'd never had, asking her lots of questions about Edward's childhood, showing sympathy for the fact that Abby had virtually had to bring her brother up on her own. She'd thanked her, too, for allowing Edward to come to Florida, teasing him by speculating who she might have been marrying if he hadn't come to work for her father.

They'd seemed extremely happy together, and Abby, who had had some misgivings about the wedding, had been completely won over by Lauren's warmth and sincerity. For the first time in her life she felt that Edward was standing on his own two feet, and she was able to relax.

The plan was that Edward would come around this morning and take Abby sightseeing. But the pool was irresistible, and she'd swum several lengths before she realised that someone was standing on the tiled surround, watching her.

She thought at first that it was Edward. She came up, sweeping her hair from her eyes, prepared to make some teasing comment about him sleeping in as usual. Then she saw that it wasn't her brother, after all. The watcher was too tall, too dark, too overwhelmingly masculine to be mistaken for the younger man. Despite the heat, he was dressed in a charcoal-grey suit that fairly screamed its designer label, and, with his hands tucked casually into his trouser pockets, he looked both broodingly thoughtful and sexy as hell.

Abby's breath caught in the back of her throat as she struggled to put a name to the visitor. She'd met various members of Lauren's family the night before, but she was sure if she'd seen this man she'd have remembered. Though perhaps not.

She had been tired and there had been so many unfamiliar faces.

Whatever, she was at a disadvantage in the pool, and, wishing her swimsuit was more stylish than practical, she swam to the side where she'd left a towel and scrambled out. Then, wrapping the towel sarong-wise about her, she offered the man a tentative smile.

'I—it's a beautiful morning,' she said, groaning to find herself speaking about the weather. He would think that was all English people ever spoke about. 'I suppose you're used to it.'

The man inclined his head. 'I suppose I am,' he agreed, with a small smile that caused a ripple of awareness to feather down her spine. He had a faint accent, just as the Esquivals did, and there was an indulgent note in his voice as he added softly, 'You must be Edward's sister. Abigail, is it not?'

Abby swallowed. 'That's right.' She wasn't sure whether he expected them to shake hands and she made an awkward little move towards him. 'Um—have we met?'

'Regrettably, not until this moment,' he replied, solving her problem by closing the distance between them and bending to bestow a kiss on each cheek in turn. '*Bienvenido a* Miami, Abigail. I am happy to meet you.'

Abby gazed up at him for a moment, totally incapable of saying anything. She could still feel the brush of his lips on her cheek, the warmth of his breath against her skin. His response had been so swift, so unexpected, so totally earth-shattering, that she found herself speechless. And she was uneasily aware of a vulnerability she'd never felt before.

But she had to say something, and, taking a step back from him, she managed breathlessly, 'And you are…?'

'*Ah, perdón, cara,*' he exclaimed, his dark eyes alight with self-recrimination. '*Me olivido.* I forget. We have not been introduced. *No importa.* I am the cousin of Dolores, *sí*? Alejandro Varga. I am most happy to meet you, Abigail. We must see that you enjoy your visit to Florida. So much so that you will want to come back, *no*?'

'No. I mean, yes.' Abby was flustered. She realised the towel was slipping and hastily gathered it more closely about her. 'That is—I hope so.'

Alejandro smiled again and Abby felt a pleasurable pain in the pit of her stomach. But her face was hot and she was sure she must look like a ripe tomato.

'Good,' he said, and to her relief—or was it to her disappointment?—he made no further attempt to detain her. Instead, he stepped aside, allowing her free access to the steps that led up to the patio. 'I am sure we will meet again very soon,' he added as she reached the top of the steps. 'Until then, *adios.*'

'*Adi*—um—goodbye,' she mumbled foolishly, hardly knowing what she was saying. With a nervous backward glance she hurried into the house.

Of course she despised herself afterwards. She was sure he must have been amused by her complete lack of sophistication. It had only been his innate courtesy that had saved what had been for her a totally embarrassing encounter.

But that didn't stop her from wondering what he'd thought of her, from fretting over the way she'd reacted to what had actually been a perfectly normal introduction. He'd probably thought she wasn't used to talking to men. Which, unfortunately, was only too true. He might even have felt sorry for her. No, scrub that. He had definitely felt sorry for her. That was why he'd gone out of his way to put her at her ease.

But, heavens, he was so different from anyone she had ever dealt with, and she'd been hopelessly overwhelmed when she'd emerged from the water to find him watching her. Why had he been watching her? What possible interest could she have for him?

Despite his promises to take her sightseeing, Edward seemed more concerned with the final arrangements for his honeymoon than in making sure his sister was entertained. The Esquivals, naturally, were busy with the preparations for the wedding. Consequently, Abby found time lying heavily on her hands, and not even the delights of being able to swim and

sunbathe if she wanted could entirely remove the suspicion
that she was in the way.

There was so much going on around her: the house was
rapidly filling with flowers, and marquee erectors and caterers
were constantly on hand, discussing guest numbers and menus
with Mrs Esquival. If Abby went down to the pool she had to
run the gamut of a dozen pairs of dark eyes, and exposing her
body to their evaluation became less and less appealing.

She had suggested that she might go out on her own, but
Lauren's father had been unenthusiastic.

'You are a stranger here, Abigail,' he said on her second
evening at dinner. 'You do not know your way about.' He
looked at her brother then. 'Edward will look after you. You
have some free time for your sister, *no*? You must make sure
you do not neglect her, eh?'

Of course Edward would have promised his future father-
in-law anything. But he had been absent for most of the day.
He had said he would come round the following morning. But
she was still waiting when Alejandro arrived.

The Cuban was dressed much less formally today, Abby
noticed. Even so, his black tee shirt and drawstring khaki pants
still looked expensive and elegant. But then, on him, anything
would look good, she thought enviously. It was something to
do with the almost graceful way he moved.

For once Dolores wasn't about, and he strolled onto the
terrace with a cool familiarity. He smiled at the sight of Abby
sitting on a lounge chair, an unopened book beside her. Her
jean-clad knees were drawn up to her chin, and her arms were
wrapped almost wistfully about them.

'All alone?' he remarked, startling her out of her reverie,
and she immediately straightened her legs and ran a nervous
hand over the curling halo of her hair.

'For now,' she agreed, glancing swiftly about her. 'Um—
Mrs Esquival is somewhere around. Would you like me to get
her for you?'

'No.' Alejandro raised his hand in a negative gesture when
she would have scrambled off the lounger and gone looking

for the other woman. 'I did not come here to interrupt Dolores. I am sure she has enough to do as it is. If I know my cousin, everything will have to adhere to her most exacting standards. The bride, the flowers, the service; even the cake must not be less than perfect, *no*?'

'No.' Abby felt a smile tilt the corners of her mouth. He was obviously amused, too, and he didn't hide it. His eyes glinted with a rueful humour that she could share.

'So, what have you planned for the rest of the day?' he enquired, seating himself on the side of the lounger nearest to her. He arched a dark brow. 'Your brother is taking you sight-seeing, perhaps?'

'I don't know what Eddie's doing,' she replied, unable to keep the disappointment out of her voice. 'I've hardly seen him since I arrived.'

'No?' Alejandro frowned. 'But surely yesterday—?'

'He arrived in time for dinner,' said Abby, and then, feeling slightly disloyal for talking about her brother in this way, she added quickly, 'He has a lot to do, too. He and Lauren are going to Bali for their honeymoon, as you probably know, and he wants to make sure everything goes smoothly. He wants no hang-ups over passports or accommodation, that sort of thing.'

Alejandro was silent for a moment, and then he said quietly, 'I would have thought such details could be safely left in the hands of his travel agent, but who knows? Edward may be like Dolores. I know she worries too much.'

Abby had the feeling that Edward was nothing like his future mother-in-law. He'd never worried about anything in his life. But she didn't say so. This man was a stranger to her, after all. Just because he was a cousin of Dolores that did not give her a reason to confide in him.

'*Bien.*' He seemed to come to a decision. 'Then perhaps you will permit me to give you a guided tour of the city, *no*? I do not promise to know everything about it. I was born in Havana, *por supuesto*. But I have lived here for over twenty years, and I have come to regard the city as my home.'

Abby's face flamed. 'Oh—but that's not necessary,' she began, sure now that he was feeling sorry for her. 'I mean—I can wait—'

'For Edward?' suggested Alejandro drily. 'Yes, you can. But I am here and I am more than willing to offer myself as your escort.' His dark eyes searched her face. 'What do you say?'

What could she say? What *should* she say? she asked herself a little breathlessly. She wanted to go. Of course she did. But should she? Would Edward approve?

Did she care?

'I—it's very kind of you,' she murmured. 'If Dolores doesn't need my help—'

'You will come?'

Abby took a breath. 'All right,' she said weakly. Then, glancing at her jeans, 'But I'll have to change first.'

'Very well.'

Alejandro inclined his head, getting to his feet as she did, and for a heart-stopping moment he was close enough for her to feel the heat of his muscled frame. His arm touched her breast as he turned away, and, hearing her sudden intake of air, he turned towards her.

'I am sorry,' he said softly. 'I am clumsy. Are you hurt?'

'No. No, not at all,' she assured him urgently, putting the width of the terrace between them. If she felt any discomfort it was not because of the disturbing brush of his hand. 'I—I'll get changed. I won't be long.'

CHAPTER TWELVE

ABBY took a few minutes to sluice her hot face with cold water, but it did no good. When she gazed at her reflection in the bathroom mirror her cheeks were still bright with colour. But what could she expect? It wasn't every day that she was invited to go sightseeing with an attractive man like Alejandro Varga. And, whether he felt sorry for her or not, she owed it to herself to enjoy the experience.

Fortunately, she'd brought some pretty outfits with her, imagining that Edward would be only too eager to show her where he lived and how familiar with the city he was. But then, she'd also expected to stay with him, not with his future in-laws, and she wasn't entirely sure that accepting Alejandro's invitation would meet with universal approval.

Dismissing such negative thoughts, she chose a simple cream dress with an embroidered hem. Its draped bodice exposed the dusky hollow of her cleavage and its short skirt complemented her long shapely legs.

No one could ever accuse her of being thin, she thought ruefully, turning sideways in front of the mirror. But she was slim in all the right places, and with her hair controlled by two narrow braids at each temple she had infinitely more confidence in herself. She was still flushed, of course, but she couldn't help that. At least the cream dress didn't clash with her fiery hair.

Slipping slingbacks that added an extra couple of inches to her height onto her feet, she left her room and went back downstairs. And knew, as soon as she saw Alejandro waiting in the marble entry, that he thought she had made the right choice.

'I have told Dolores you are going out,' he said at once,

forestalling her intention of going to speak to her hostess. His eyes assessed her appearance with evident approval. 'You look delightful, *cara*. Come. My car is just outside.'

'But what about Lauren?'

'I'm told that Lauren is having a final fitting at the dressmaker's,' Alejandro informed her smoothly, urging her towards the door. He cast a faintly impatient glance at the hovering maid. 'Tell your mistress the young lady will be back after lunch, *por favor*.'

'Oughtn't I to say goodbye to Dolores?' Abby persisted, and Alejandro gave a mocking smile.

'So long as you are aware that she may feel obligated to act as chaperon,' he remarked drily 'She probably thinks your brother is going with us. I have said nothing to disabuse her of the thought.'

'Well…' Abby murmured weakly, aware that she was probably taking an enormous risk by going out with him alone. 'All right.' She stepped out into the bright sunlight. 'What a beautiful morning! It is a shame to stay in the house.'

Alejandro inclined his head, going past her to swing open the nearside door of the sleek black limousine that was parked at the foot of the steps. Then, after helping her inside, where the feel of cool soft leather and the pleasurable aromas of expensive soap and clean male skin assaulted her senses, he walked round the bonnet and coiled his length beside her.

The look he gave her then mingled warm admiration with satisfaction, and she realised once again that he had probably known she'd give in all along. 'If you will forgive the presumption, I prefer there to be no extraneous distractions,' he remarked, starting the engine of the powerful vehicle. 'You will forgive me for wanting you to myself.'

Abby shook her head. She didn't really believe him, but she had the feeling it would be better if she didn't probe too deeply into his motivations. One way or another, she was committed to spending the morning with him. If Dolores didn't approve, she would get over it. She would just have to face the consequences when she got back.

They drove first to Miami Beach, crossing one of the many causeways that linked the long strip of land, famous for its many fabulous hotels, from the mainland. Abby found the trip along Collins Avenue a revelation. Each glass and steel monolith seemed to be trying to outdo its neighbour, with the art deco hotels of Ocean Drive monuments to its colourful history.

Alejandro parked the car and they walked past the bars and sidewalk cafés that spilled from hotel patios all along the boulevard. He explained that the area had undergone a complete renovation in recent years, and that it was very much a going place after dark. But he also showed her the mansion where a famous dress designer had been murdered on his own doorstep, and took her for coffee at the News Café, which was already packed with residents and tourists eager for the latest gossip.

Later, they drove into the city itself, and Abby was amazed to see what a mixture of styles and cultures it was. Skyscrapers stood cheek by jowl with tacky discount stores, and many of the shops catered to a mainly South American clientele.

Once again Alejandro parked the car in one of the secure lots, and, after assuring himself that she was happy to walk, he took her on a tour of some of Miami's more impressive tourist establishments. Flagler Street was home to two of southern Florida's more famous museums, one of which was an art museum which Abby loved. A visitors' gallery provided lots of ways to research the paintings being exhibited and she wished museums back home were more visitor-friendly like this.

Alejandro also showed her a part of Biscayne Boulevard that was more continental than anything she had seen so far. Then he took her for lunch at the top of one of the tallest buildings in the city. The view across the bay was stunning, blue skies and sunlit water providing a vista she thought she'd never forget.

Abby was so glad she hadn't allowed her innate cautiousness to deter her from spending this time with Alejandro. He had been a marvellous guide, both interesting and knowledgeable, and she was sure she'd learned more in the past few hours than she would ever have thought possible. She already felt more at home here and, although she had listened to his warning about taking safety for granted, she had been given an unforgettable taste of the real Miami.

Not surprisingly, Alejandro offered to choose what they had for lunch also. And, after dining on broiled shrimp and tangy cheese and fresh fruit salad, Abby was glad she'd taken his advice. She'd never eaten such tasty shellfish, or gorged on such juicy pineapple and melon. There was papaya, too, its orange flesh sweet and luscious, and slices of avocado, sharp with a lemon dressing.

Although they'd conducted a desultory conversation throughout the meal, it wasn't until rich dark coffee had been served that Alejandro asked her if she had enjoyed herself.

'Need you ask?' Abby was amazed that he should have any doubts. But, meeting his dark eyes across the suddenly narrow width of the table, she was immediately aware of the intimacy of his question. Yet, determined not to back down, she countered daringly, 'Have you?'

Alejandro's lips tilted. 'What was it you said?' he murmured. 'Need you ask?' His smile deepened. 'But, yes, I have enjoyed myself very much, *cara*. You are a—how shall I put it?—a delightful companion.'

'A naïve one,' said Abby ruefully, guessing he would never be anything but polite. 'But I am grateful to you for taking the time to—'

'No.' His sudden interjection caused her to break off in midsentence. 'Do not say it, *cara*. Your gratitude is not necessary. Not necessary at all. Spending the morning with you has been a pleasure. I am lucky to have been honoured with the experience.'

Abby smiled then. She couldn't help herself. He was so charming! He always said the right thing. But, while she appreciated his kindness, she couldn't help wishing she was the kind of woman who took his brand of flattery for granted.

'You're a nice man, Mr Varga,' she said, not knowing what

to say. She put down her coffee cup and linked her fingers on the table. 'But I'm sure you have more important things to do than take me sightseeing.'

Alejandro shrugged. 'And if I tell you that I do not? What then?'

A trace of colour invaded her cheeks. 'I'd say you were being polite—but not entirely truthful.'

'No?'

'No.' She sighed, spreading one hand expressively. 'You're Dolores's cousin, right?' And, at his nod, 'You arrived this morning—as you did yesterday morning,' she reminded him nervously, 'and found me on my own again. I'd say you felt sorry for me. That was why you asked me out.'

Alejandro lay back in his chair. 'Is that the impression I have given you?'

'No.' Abby had to be honest. 'But sightseeing can be boring. Particularly if you've seen it all before. Eddie hates looking round museums. I have to admit he's not much interested in the past.'

'So—I have saved your brother from a fate worse than death, hmm?' he remarked drily, and she had to smile again.

'I suppose,' she murmured ruefully. 'Whatever, I know he'll be grateful to you for looking after me as you have.'

'You think so?'

'I know so,' she assured him fervently, hoping Edward would agree. 'Um—do you know my brother well?'

'I have met him,' said Alejandro non-committally. 'I understand he works for Luis in one of his restaurants, *no*?'

'That's right.' Abby nodded. 'That was how he met Lauren. He came to work in America two years ago.'

'Ah.' Alejandro absorbed this. 'But you are the only member of his family coming for the wedding, *sí*?'

'Yes.' Abby loved the way he interspersed his sentences with Spanish words and phrases. 'Actually, apart from some distant cousins, there is no one else. Our father—died some years ago.'

'And your mother also?'

'Well—no.' Abby hesitated. 'Our mother left when Eddie and I were just children. We haven't seen her since.'

'*Lo entiendo.*' Alejandro saw her confusion and added swiftly, 'I understand.' He frowned. 'But you must have been devastated when your brother left England. Did you never consider accompanying him?'

'Oh, no.' Abby spoke without thinking. 'I wouldn't have wanted to cramp his style.'

'To cramp his style?' echoed Alejandro curiously, and Abby sighed.

'Well, yes,' she responded lamely. 'That is—Eddie had a job waiting for him and I—I didn't.'

She could hardly tell this man about Edward's infatuation with Selina Steward. Not when she was here to attend his wedding to someone else.

'I see.' Alejandro nodded, and although Abby knew he couldn't possibly know what she was thinking she had the uneasy feeling that he did. 'And do you work in the restaurant business also?'

'I'm a teacher,' said Abby at once, feeling on safer ground. 'An English teacher.' She pulled a wry face. 'Not half as glamorous, I'm afraid.'

'That depends on your point of view,' remarked her companion easily. 'Not everyone who works in the restaurant business is involved in the preparation of the food, *tu sabes.*'

'No.' Abby conceded his point. Then, deciding they had talked enough about her, she ventured, 'And you, Mr Varga? Are you involved in the restaurant business yourself?'

'Not directly,' he replied, his dark eyes disturbingly indulgent. 'I do many things, Abigail. Not all of them either glamorous or interesting.'

'I'm sure that's not true.' Abby's tongue circled her upper lip. 'But you weren't born here, you said?' she persisted. 'Does—er—does the rest of your family still live in Cuba?'

He was quiet for so long she thought at first he wasn't going to answer her. But then he shifted in his seat and said, 'I have relatives who still live in the old country, it is true. Aunts, uncles, cousins—many of whom would never dream of leaving their homeland. But I have relatives here, too. When my grandfather moved his family to the United States my father and mother came with him.'

'And your mother didn't mind?' Abby asked. 'Leaving her own family behind?'

'Ah, no.' Alejandro straightened, resting one elbow on the table. 'You do not understand, *cara*. My mother was an American.'

'Oh.' Abby supposed that explained why he possessed such an attractive mix of Spanish gallantry and American sophistication. She hesitated a moment, and then said a little daringly, 'So—how did they meet?'

'You mean, because of the hostilities that have existed between this country and Cuba for so many years?' he queried softly, and she nodded. '*Sí*, you might think it was an unlikely union, eh?'

'I was curious, that's all.' Abby felt embarrassed. 'But if you'd rather not talk about it—'

'Not at all.' He shrugged, his powerful shoulders moving easily beneath his silk jacket. 'My mother was a nurse. She had been working in Cuba prior to the revolution, and regrettably she was caught up in the civil war that devastated the country. She was given refuge by my father's family and she and my father fell in love. They were married in 1960, just as the US government declared an economic embargo. I was born the following year.'

Abby was intrigued. 'What a wonderful story.'

'You think?' Alejandro paused. 'Well, they loved one another, that is true. But because of land reform, and the fact that my grandfather was unable to sell his sugar cane to the United States, they were eventually forced to leave. We were virtually penniless when we arrived in Florida. But my grandfather was an enterprising man and he invested what little money he had in the leisure and tourism industry. By the time my father took over the business it was a much bigger concern, and I—' He pulled a wry face. 'I have been lucky.'

Abby doubted luck had much to do with it. Alejandro struck her as being a very astute individual himself. But she didn't want to press him, so instead she said, 'Are your grandparents still alive?'

'Regrettably, no.' Alejandro shook his head. 'My father is, *por supuesto*. But my mother died five years ago.'

Abby was sympathetic. 'Do you have brothers and sisters?'

'Two brothers, three sisters.' He smiled mockingly. 'Cubans usually have large families. But only my oldest sister still lives in Florida. The rest are married and scattered about the country.'

'But you see them often?' suggested Abby, thinking how nice it must be to have a large family. 'I hope Eddie and Lauren go ahead and have children. I can't wait to become an aunt myself.'

'Or a mother?' remarked Alejandro seductively. 'Surely you wish to have children of your own?'

'Well, of course I do,' Abby exclaimed, feeling her face heating again. 'But I'm not on the point of getting married. Eddie is.'

'You do not have to be married to have children,' pointed out Alejandro drily, and Abby quivered at the images his words created. A vision of herself pregnant with his child flashed before her eyes and she hurriedly addressed herself to her coffee again to avoid his knowing gaze.

'Well, as I'm not involved with anyone at the moment, the question doesn't arise,' she mumbled into her cup. 'Um—I think I ought to be getting back, don't you?'

Contrary to what Alejandro had told her, Mrs Esquival wasn't at all pleased to hear where Abby had been and who she had been with. Apparently Alejandro had given Dolores the impression that he'd arranged for her guest to join a sightseeing tour—which was probably why he'd balked Abby's efforts to speak to the other woman before they left. He'd said nothing about escorting her himself, and it was obvious that Lauren's mother thought Abby had taken advantage of his kindness.

Abby went from feeling guilty to harbouring a certain resentment towards the older woman. It wasn't as if Alejandro was complaining, and she certainly hadn't asked him to take her out. Consequently, when he rang her the following morning and offered to take her to dinner at a famous South Beach restaurant that evening, she didn't hesitate before accepting his invitation.

Why shouldn't she have some fun while she was here? she defended herself. It wasn't as if Edward was falling over himself to look after her. And, although the Esquivals were polite, she never felt anything but a guest in their home.

The evening was every bit as exciting as she'd anticipated. This time there was no avoiding Dolores's disapproval, but Alejandro seemed indifferent to his cousin's displeasure. When she suggested that perhaps Abby ought to be resting, in preparation for the following evening's festivities, he merely pulled a wry face and said, 'I am sure Abigail will have plenty of time to relax tomorrow, *querida*. And, as you appear to have everything under control, why should she not enjoy herself?'

'People will talk,' Dolores exclaimed tersely, but Alejandro's face only stiffened into a sardonic smile.

'Let them,' he remarked, ushering his companion towards the door. '*Adios*, Luis. I promise I will return your guest safely to you.'

They started the evening at a flashy bar on Ocean Drive, rubbing shoulders with several famous Hollywood faces who seemed to be enjoying their celebrity status. Abby was sure Alejandro had only taken her there to see the wide-eyed bemusement on her face, and she wasn't at all surprised when he took her somewhere much more exclusive for dinner.

The food had a West Indian bias this time, and Abby enjoyed the subtle blends of herbs and spices that flavoured the many exotic dishes she was offered. Afterwards, they strolled along the sidewalk, taking in the culture overload that was South Beach, and Abby caught her breath when he took her hand and linked his fingers with hers.

Although she'd sensed that he seemed to find her particularly attractive this evening, she was totally unprepared when
he backed her into a shadowy doorway between two hotels
and kissed her. The fire that leapt between them startled him,
too, she thought, and he repeated the kiss, this time parting
her lips with his tongue and thrusting his way into her mouth.

He whispered to her in his own language, low, husky sounds
that made her feel weak at the knees. Cupping her head in one
large hand, he angled her face so that he could go on kissing
her, drinking from her lips, reducing her to a trembling mass
of shivering anticipation.

She had never had such feelings before. She'd been kissed
before; of course she had. But the men she'd dated had never
made her feel like this, had never aroused the needs that were
now churning inside her.

Almost without thinking, she lifted her hands to his shoulders, gripping the satin lapels of his tuxedo, trying to anchor
herself in a world that was suddenly out of control. The
crowds about them disappeared, the sounds and the music fading into nothingness as she drowned in the sensuous ardour
of his touch. She felt his hands at her waist, felt them brush
too briefly over the rounded curve of her bottom, and arched
against him. And felt the unmistakable ridge of his arousal
hard between them.

'*Cara.*' His voice was thick with emotion, but although she
wanted to protest she sensed his withdrawal. '*No ahora,*' he
whispered ruefully. 'Not here. Not now.' His thumb brushed
across her soft mouth, parting her lips almost roughly. 'Tomorrow, hmm? We will continue this tomorrow. After the
wedding, *no*? We will go somewhere where we can be alone.'

Of course she told herself that nothing more would come
of it. The things he'd said had been spoken in the heat of the
moment, and once he had had time to think about it he'd
realise that they had nothing in common. Except a mutual
desire to tear one another's clothes off, she thought, quivering
as she lay in bed that night. And how sensible was that?

But she feared sense had little to do with it.

The wedding took place in the late afternoon. Lauren made a beautiful bride, and Abby had never been so proud of her brother as she was when he stood at his wife's side welcoming their guests.

As Alejandro had teased, Dolores had left nothing to chance, and every detail of the ceremony and the reception that followed it had been organised in every detail. A twenty-four-piece orchestra played while the guests dined on steak and shellfish, strawberries and champagne. A veritable swarm of waiters kept glasses filled and offered trays of seafood delicacies, chicken *vol-au-vents*, mounds of caviar. Ice sculptures melted in the early-evening heat, and jackets were shed as the bride and groom shared a romantic waltz before going to prepare for their departure.

After they had left for the airport Abby, who had felt very much the outsider for most of the afternoon, eased her feet out of her high heels and sought the comparative coolness of the loggia. She was glad everything had gone so well, but she was also glad it was over. The Esquivals' friends and relations were almost all of Cuban descent, and she had little in common with them.

All except Alejandro, she thought, finding a lounge chair and stretching her toes with some relief. But then, Lauren's mother had ensured that he had no time to waste on their annoying little English guest. Dolores had spent most of the reception hanging onto his arm and Alejandro had been too polite—or too relieved at having the initiative snatched away from him—to do anything about it.

'So this is where you are hiding yourself.'

His voice came out of the darkness. Although the rest of the garden was floodlit for the occasion, the servants had extinguished many of the lamps around the house. In consequence, Alejandro was in shadow. Until he moved closer and she could see his face.

'I—I was just resting my feet,' she said awkwardly, wondering if she could slip her shoes on without him noticing. 'It's been a long evening.'

'But a very successful one,' remarked Alejandro, moving her feet aside to sit on the end of her chair. His hands lingered on her instep, his fingers searching for and finding the aching pads beneath her toes. 'Your brother and his new wife looked suitably virginal, did you not think so? It is amazing what an occasion like this can do.'

Abby swallowed. 'It was a wonderful wedding,' she agreed. Then, with some embarrassment, 'You don't have to do that, you know.'

'But you are enjoying it, *sí*,' he murmured, his fingers miraculously massaging her aches and pains away. '*Lo importante*, you are enjoying it, *no*? I know you are. Your eyes betray you.'

'All the same…' Abby made a helpless gesture. 'Shouldn't you be with the other guests? The dancing has started. I'm sure Dolores will be looking for you.'

'I have done my duty, *cara*,' he told her softly. 'The bride and groom have departed and the rest of the evening is mine. *Ours*,' he corrected himself, his fingers circling her ankle possessively. 'Come, *cara*. I want to take you for a drive.'

Abby knew she should demur. She knew perfectly well that Dolores would not approve, and as she was leaving for home the next day she should be doing her packing. But her host and hostess were busy with their guests and no one noticed them leaving. Feeling like a thief, she allowed Alejandro to whisk her away in his convertible, the night air cooling her temples but making little impact on her blood.

They drove for a while along the coastal highway, and the breeze off the ocean made a tangle of her hair. She'd secured it in a French twist for the wedding, the formal style had seemed more suitable for the occasion, but now she gave up any hope of rescuing the fiery strands that blew about her face. Besides, she had the feeling that Alejandro preferred her hair loose, despite its wildness. His arm was along the back of her seat and his fingers caressed her nape, dislodging the few clips that still remained.

They eventually turned away from the water, threading their

way through wide streets with gabled houses that had given
this area of Miami its name. Street lamps illuminated pastel-
shaded houses and parks where fountains played. But the most
memorable thing of all was the lush vegetation, and the exciting scents of the flowers on display.

The house Alejandro took her to was on Old Okra Road,
an impressive Spanish-style dwelling, set behind towering
oaks and stucco walls. A servant admitted them and then, on
Alejandro's orders, left them to themselves, allowing him to
show her round his home.

The things Abby remembered afterwards were the huge fireplace that took up almost the whole of one wall in the drawing
room, decorated with Italian tile, and the massive oval swimming pool that was lit from below and gleamed with a turquoise beauty in the darkness. She also remembered the master
bedroom suite and the enormous square bed that adorned it.

Alejandro poured them both a glass of wine and then
opened the sliding doors onto the patio. They stepped outside
with their drinks and Abby expressed her delight at the sight
of the pool. 'You're so lucky,' she said. 'In this climate I
expect you can swim all the year round. Apart from the fact
that few people have pools back home, there are only a few
months in the year when it's warm enough to use them.'

Alejandro shrugged. 'We have our cold days, too,' he said
drily. 'And just occasionally a hurricane comes along to—how
do you say it?—to keep us on our toes, *no*?' He smiled. 'You
like to swim?'

Abby glanced up at him for a moment and then took a sip
of her wine. 'Very much,' she said, wondering if he was remembering how they had met.

'Then perhaps we should,' murmured Alejandro softly.
'What do you think? It is warm enough, *desde luego*. And I
can recommend it.'

Abby's jaw dropped. 'What? Now?'

'Why not?' His dark gaze seemed to caress her. 'Have you
never gone swimming after dark?'

'Only—only in a hotel pool,' she admitted after a moment.

'When a girlfriend and I went on holiday to France. But lots of people were in the pool at the time. It was a sort of evening pool-party-cum-barbecue, you see.'

'Ah.' Alejandro inclined his head. 'So—shall we?'

Abby shook her head. 'I don't have anything to wear.'

'Why wear anything?' asked Alejandro, his fingertips tracing the soft contours of her arm. 'In this country we call it skinny-dipping. It is much more fun to swim without clothes.'

Abby was sure it was. She was also sure he was probably experienced at it. But she wasn't. She'd never taken her clothes off in front of a man before. The very idea was daunting.

'I—don't think—' she was beginning, when he set down his glass and started to unfasten his dinner jacket. Depositing it on the nearby swing-seat, he tackled the buttons on his shirt, tossing his tie aside as he did so.

Beneath his shirt, his skin was darkly tanned and roughened by a mat of dark hair. The hair was thickest between his nipples and arrowed down to his navel. Abby dragged her eyes away when his hand moved to the buckle of his belt.

With his belt hanging loose and the waistband of his trousers unfastened he stood before her, and Abby's mouth dried at the realisation that he intended to go the whole way. 'Do not be afraid, *cara*,' he said softly. 'I will not hurt you. I just want you to enjoy yourself, to cast off these inhibitions that are stopping you from having fun.'

Abby shook her head. 'I can't,' she said, emptying her glass in one unladylike gulp and turning away. 'If you want to swim, go ahead. I—I'll wait for you in the house.'

'*Pobrecita,*' he whispered huskily, and when she would have put the width of the patio between them he caught her from behind, his arm strong about her waist. 'Such a *timido* little one,' he added, drawing her back against his powerful frame. 'Have I embarrassed you again? Would you not like to cool off in the water?'

Abby could think of nothing she'd like more—if she wasn't

so nervous about taking off her clothes. But it was no good. She couldn't do it. However tempting the prospect might be.

'I'm—I'm sure it would be delightful,' she said honestly. 'But we hardly know one another. I couldn't—'

'Okay.' Without another word he released her. And as Abby hovered uncertainly by the glass doors, not sure how—or even if—she should proceed, she heard a sudden splash behind her and realised Alejandro had dived into the pool.

She turned then, unable to prevent herself, and was just in time to see Alejandro's dark head appear above the water. He swept back his hair with a careless hand and then grinned in a way that sent a coil of heat into the pit of her stomach. *'Dios,'* he said ruefully, 'I am not in good shape. I must start taking regular exercise again.'

Abby thought that was something of an exaggeration. From what she'd seen, Alejandro was in very good shape indeed. All he was trying to do was make her feel better about herself. Perhaps he suspected that the real reason she hadn't accepted his invitation was because she was intensely conscious of being several pounds overweight.

'Is the water cold?' she asked, unable to force herself to leave him and go into the house.

'Try it,' he said, and she stepped forward and squatted down on the tiled surround. She dipped her hand into the water and found it wasn't cold at all, just soft and inviting. How she wished she had the guts to join him. This might be her only chance to swim in the nude.

But such thoughts seemed a betrayal of all she'd ever tried to teach her brother. Abby straightened, and Alejandro swam to the side to look up at her with an enquiring gaze. 'What are you afraid of, *cara*?' he asked. 'I promise I will keep my distance. I will even allow you to keep on your underwear, if that will satisfy your modest little soul.'

Abby expelled a breath, remembering that her underwear was barely worthy of the name. Her cream lace bra and matching panties had been designed with tantalisation in mind, not modesty. She had the feeling she'd feel more exposed in them than in her bare skin.

'You don't understand,' she said at last, her breasts rising and falling rapidly with the agitation she was feeling. 'I'm not like you, Alejandro. I'm not used to getting undressed in front of strangers.'

'And you think I am?' he queried gently. '*Querida,* I thought I was making it easier for you. Contrary to your suspicions, I do not make a habit of taking my clothes off in public. But we are alone here. There are no eyes watching us. No eyes watching *you*. Only mine.'

And that was what she was afraid of.

And yet…

What did she really have to lose? she asked herself. She wasn't a virgin. True, her only experience of sex had been in the back seat of a car, and that had ended almost as soon as it had begun. But she wasn't afraid. Only afraid of getting hurt—emotionally hurt, she acknowledged unhappily. Alejandro Varga was like no man she had ever known. And in a few short days he had unknowingly captured her heart.

CHAPTER THIRTEEN

As IF abandoning any further attempt to persuade her, Alejandro turned and swam leisurely away from her. The movement caused the water to ripple along the edge of the pool below her, fragmenting the underwater lighting like shards of glass. And exposing the paler shade of his buttocks, taut and firm beneath the surface.

Abby sucked in a breath and, unable to stop herself, she took one foot out of her shoe and tested the temperature of the water again. As before, it felt lukewarm, still retaining the heat from that day's sun. Without giving herself time to have second thoughts, she stepped out of her shoes and unbuttoned the ice-green jacket of her two-piece. Shedding it onto the tiled surround, she dropped her skirt, too, and quickly slipped into the water.

Despite its apparent warmth, that initial plunge almost took her breath away. But she didn't think about that. Didn't think about anything—particularly not Alejandro. Kicking away from the side, she swam smoothly across the pool.

She was aware that Alejandro must have felt the movement in the water, but she didn't allow herself to speculate on what might happen now. This was her last night in Miami; her last chance to do something reckless. Tomorrow she would be sane and sensible again. And what could be more sane and sensible than getting on the plane back home?

The pool was perhaps five feet in depth around the rim, but it swiftly sloped away to deeper water. It was long, too, easily seventy-five feet, surrounded at the far end by lush greenery, the petals of a magnolia floating like stars upon the water.

When Alejandro surfaced some six feet away from where she was standing she couldn't prevent one hand from spreading almost protectively across her chest. She was uneasily aware that her bra and panties were virtually transparent now that they were wet, and looked just as provocatively suggestive as she'd imagined.

'You changed your mind,' he said, not coming any closer, and she wondered if that was for her benefit or his. Beneath the surface his skin gleamed darkly, and she had to force herself not to speculate about what she couldn't see.

'I was hot,' she said, as if that was an answer. 'You don't mind, do you?' Which was a ridiculous question to ask.

'Why should I mind?' he queried, his lips tilting humorously. 'You are free to do what you like in my home.' But his eyes darkened as he looked at her, and she was suddenly aware of how impulsive she'd been in taking off her clothes.

'It's a big pool,' she said foolishly, desperate to say something, *anything*, to deflect the deepening awareness between them, and he shook his head, flicking droplets of water in all directions.

'Size is not everything,' he remarked drily. 'I believe that is what they say. Personally, I think it depends what you are talking about, *no*?'

Abby felt her face grow warm with colour. Although he wasn't touching her, his words brushed seductively across her skin. It was so easy for him to embarrass her. She'd never met anyone who played these verbal games so well.

'Well, I think it's a big pool,' she insisted, trying to ignore his amusement. 'It's bigger than the one at the Esquivals', anyway. And deeper, too, I should imagine. How deep is it, actually?'

Alejandro's mouth compressed for a moment, and then, to her dismay, he swam lazily across the space between them. 'The pool is twenty-five metres in length, and it is four metres at its deepest point,' he told her solemnly. His feet touched the tiles as he straightened. 'And I know what you are trying to do.'

Abby recoiled, but with the edge of the pool at her back she didn't have far to go. 'I'm trying to show an interest in my surroundings,' she replied defensively. 'You may be used to—to all this, but I'm not.'

Alejandro put one hand on the rim at either side of her, successfully imprisoning her within the circle of his arms. 'No,' he said softly, his eyes warm and invasive, 'you are trying to distract me. You think if you babble on about the pool and its size I will forget the reason why I brought you here.' His gaze dropped to the revealing cleavage of her bra, where her treacherous nipples strained against the lace. '*Ni hablar, cara*. No way. I am a man, and I would not be human if I did not want to make love to you.'

Abby tried to keep calm. 'I thought you invited me to swim in the pool,' she said, resisting the urge she had to try and cover herself. 'That's why I'm here, anyway.'

'*Ah, cara...*' His lips twisted. 'I did not know you could be such a liar.' One hand moved and curved knowingly about her nape, his thumb catching in the gold hoop she wore in her ear and tugging almost cruelly. 'Do you not know that your body is betraying you? That it is almost as eager as I to cast off these—' one finger slid the strap of her bra off her shoulder '—these unnecessary sops to your conscience, *no*?'

Abby's fingers moved to restore the strap to her shoulder, but Alejandro was quicker. With ruthless efficiency his hand dipped behind her back and unfastened the clasp, so that her breasts tumbled free of the confining lace.

That was too much. 'Don't!' she exclaimed in a panicked voice. 'You're wrong about me. I didn't come here to—to sleep with you. I—don't do things like that.'

'Who said anything about sleeping?' countered Alejandro, lowering his head and covering her anxious lips with his. The hair on his chest brushed provocatively against her nipples and her breath caught in her throat. '*Ah, querida, te deseo*. I want you. *Besame, cara*. Kiss me. *Quiero hacerte el amor*.'

Abby felt the weakness of her own defences. The reality of his nude body against hers was more sensual than she had ever dreamed. Around them, the water ebbed and flowed, sensitising her skin in ways she had never known before. Its coolness lapped like silk about her shoulders, moving as he was moving, letting her feel the heat that their bodies were creating. When he tossed her bra onto the side she was almost grateful for the freedom it gave her.

Then his lips were on hers again, his tongue slipping between her teeth and making its own possession. The kiss deepened, lengthened, robbed her of breath so that she could only cling to his arms for support. Hot and unashamedly sexual, his mouth plundered hers hungrily, his tongue invading and retreating in a dance as old as time.

Abby was incapable of resisting him. She felt his hands beneath the water, shaping the curve of her waist, caressing the rounded swell of her bottom. She was suddenly desperate to be free of the scrap of lace that prevented him from touching her there, and when Alejandro found the high leg of her panties and probed beneath she whimpered. The wet petals spread eagerly to admit his searching fingers and a pulse beat hotly between her legs.

'Oh, my God,' she groaned shakily, unable to prevent herself from crying out, and Alejandro's face filled with satisfaction as he pressed the offending garment down her legs.

'Better?' he asked huskily, the throbbing heat of his arousal nudging her mound. And when she could only nod her agreement, he tucked his hands beneath her bottom and lifted her against him.

Abby wound her legs about his waist, but although it pleased her to feel his erection touching her aching core, it was not what Alejandro wanted.

'Not here,' he said. 'Not like this, *cara*. I want to love you, Abigail. But I want to lay you on my bed, to look at you, to show how much I want you.'

At that moment Abby thought she would have been content if he'd pushed his way inside her there and then. She'd never felt this desire for a man before, and the needs he'd inspired inside her—had been inspiring inside her, actually, since they'd first met—demanded an immediate response.

When he lifted her onto the side of the pool she knew he

was tempted. For a moment he moved between her thighs, took her breasts in his hands. Then, as she trembled at his touch, he took one swollen nipple into his mouth, tugging on it with his lips and tongue until she was throbbing all over.

Each nipple received the same treatment, and by the time he sprang out of the pool and drew her to her feet she could barely stand. Her legs were weak and her senses felt as if they were as taut as violin strings. Seeing him, aroused and magnificent, was no turn-off. Springing proudly from its nest of hair, his manhood was as powerful as he was.

'Come,' he said, taking her hand and starting towards the house, and when she stumbled he turned back and swung her into his arms. '*Pobrecita,*' he whispered, his lips finding the vulnerable curve of her nape. 'Am I going too fast for you? I want this to be as good for you as it is for me.'

Alejandro carried her into the house and up the stairs, apparently uncaring that neither of them was wearing any clothes. Abby, who had admired the soaring ceiling of the reception area earlier, barely noticed it now. The exquisite crystal chandelier, whose lamps had been muted since their arrival, shone down on a scene more unreal than any she had ever imagined. But Abby's eyes were focused on Alejandro, on the lean, aristocratic lines of his dark face as he mounted the stairs without effort, taking them to the upper floor.

His bedroom was just as opulent. A huge square bed occupied a central position, with several chairs grouped beneath the wide windows. There were shaded lamps and concealed lighting up near the moulded ceiling, but Alejandro turned off the switch as he came through the door. Now only two or three bulbs provided a subtle illumination, highlighting the satin coverlet, creating shadows in the corners of the room.

When he laid her down, the coverlet clung to her shoulders. 'I'm wet,' she protested, but Alejandro's response was merely to stretch his length beside her on the bed.

'I know,' he said, one hand playing sensuously across her stomach and sliding briefly down between her thighs. 'I can feel it here.'

'That—that wasn't what I meant,' she got out breathlessly, and he smiled.

'I know,' he said again. 'But our skin will dry soon enough. Between us we will generate enough heat to drain the pool, *no*?'

Abby quivered. 'Alejandro—'

'Relax,' he told her softly, bending to bestow a line of kisses that followed the passage of his hand. With the utmost patience, he eased her shaking legs apart and licked her with obvious enjoyment. 'You are as delicious as you look,' he added, sliding back to share his explorations with her, and she could taste the spicy heat of her arousal on his tongue.

Her head swam as he continued to kiss her, but he seemed determined to prolong her delight. Every inch of her flesh— her limbs, her shoulders, her breasts—all received his sensual ministrations, and Abby reached for him mindlessly, eager to end this torment that was both a pleasure and a pain.

But Alejandro was in no hurry, and it was only when she captured him between her palms and caressed his silky length that he moaned in protest. *'Es inútil, cara,'* he whispered achingly. 'It is no good. I must have you.' And, easing her legs wider, he moved between her thighs.

And then swore.

Softly, but distinctly. The word he used was unfamiliar to her, but Abby knew it wasn't good. *'Caray,'* he added, less violently. 'I have left my wallet by the pool.'

Abby blinked, confused. 'Your wallet?' she echoed. 'But surely you can trust your—'

'That is not what I mean,' he said thickly. 'I have no protection here.' He raked back his hair with a savage hand. *'Mierda*, I will have to go downstairs.'

'Oh, no, please...' Abby thought she wouldn't be able to bear it if he left her now. 'It's all right,' she told him frantically. 'I—I can handle it. Just—just don't leave me, please.'

Now, two years later, lying chilled and sleepless in her bed, Abby acknowledged for the first time that Alejandro hadn't been totally to blame for what had happened next. How had she blotted that out of her mind? Oh, he hadn't been completely honest with her about the fact that he was still married, however unstable that marriage had been, or made any attempt to see her again after she'd gone back to England. But he had believed she was more experienced than she was. He'd probably imagined that she was taking the Pill.

Whatever, her words had evidently reassured him, because he hadn't hesitated any longer. He'd entered her in one swift thrust that had had her catching her breath. He'd been so big, so thick, he'd filled her completely. She'd been halfway to an orgasm before he'd started to move.

She hadn't known that then, of course. Her previous encounter had given her no reason to believe that there was more to sex than the excitement Alejandro had engendered this far. Even the undeveloped sensations she'd had when he'd pulled back, before surging into her again, had had her arching towards him more in need than expectation. The feelings that had been building inside her were tantalising but, she'd believed, unreachable. The incredible truth of her own sexuality had yet to dawn on her.

That it had, in such a fantastic fashion, had been all due to Alejandro, she admitted painfully. She recalled him kissing her and caressing her as he drove them both to the very peak of sensual fulfilment. He'd been sweating, she remembered, his eyes dark and passionate, gleaming as he'd shared her breathless climb. She'd cried out as she'd reached her climax, only seconds before he'd collapsed, shuddering, in her arms. And feeling his hot seed spilling inside her had renewed the feeling, sending her shattering into a million shards of light…

She shuddered now, the memories suddenly too painful to rekindle. Had she really been that frantic, that naïve, that desperate? She'd been like moulding clay in his hands, only far more responsive to his touch.

She expelled a long breath. Of course, at the time, she'd been too dazed to realise what had happened. Too pathetically grateful to him for showing her how incredible sex could be.

But then, he had been a master at the art of seduction, and she'd been a willing novice, eager to learn.

He'd made love to her again before he'd carried her into his shower and allowed the cool water to cleanse their sweating bodies. Then he'd collected their clothes from beside the pool, helped her to dress, and taken her back to the Esquivals. She'd known she should have told him she was leaving the next afternoon, but it would have sounded like begging. How could she pretend that what had happened had been the same for him as it had been for her?

It hadn't been until a few weeks after she'd got back to London that she'd discovered she was pregnant. By that time Edward and Lauren had come back from their honeymoon, and it had been a simpler thing to ask her brother who Alejandro really was. When Edward had told her he was married she'd been devastated. And when, a couple of weeks later, she'd miscarried the baby, she'd told herself it was all for the best.

Only it hadn't been.

Rolling onto her stomach, Abby let the hot tears seep into her pillow. Tragically, while she was in the hospital, she'd contracted an infection, and after spending several days flat on her back recovering from a haemorrhage she'd been told that it was unlikely that she'd ever conceive again.

Ross knew, of course. She'd had to tell him when he'd asked her to marry him. She hadn't told him how it had happened, of course, and she hadn't known whether to be glad or sorry when he'd confessed that he had no desire to have children anyway. Somehow she'd always imagined that one day she would be a mother, even if she had to adopt a child to satisfy the maternal instincts inside her.

And that was why she was so protective of her brother, she thought. Despite the considerable distance between them, she still felt responsible for him. It was the main bone of contention between her and Ross—or it had been. Now she wondered if she had any future with anyone, when it seemed obvious that she hadn't got over Alejandro as she'd thought...

CHAPTER FOURTEEN

ABBY had her chance to talk to Edward alone the next morning.

For once her brother was eager to talk to her. She knew it was because she'd had dinner with Alejandro the night before and Edward was eager to hear the outcome. But it hurt her that he could be so transparent. Didn't he care about her feelings at all?

Abby had already decided she was going home that evening. She'd rung the airport before going down to breakfast and had been both disappointed and relieved when she'd found she'd have no trouble getting on the flight. She was relieved because she wouldn't have to worry about seeing Alejandro again, but she was disappointed because her visit had solved nothing. Quite the opposite, in fact.

She knew it was cowardly to run away, but she couldn't help it. She couldn't bear to face Alejandro again, knowing what she knew now. Running away seemed the only answer; the only way she could hope to retain any dignity at all.

She was sitting on the patio, rehearsing what she was going to say to the Esquivals, when she heard Edward's uneven step behind her. His crutches rang against the tiles, heralding his approach, but she refused to acknowledge that she'd heard him. She wasn't sure what she was going to say to him, and knowing she was leaving that evening meant she couldn't be as frank as she'd have liked.

'Hey, you!' Edward exclaimed as he lowered himself onto the cushioned recliner beside her. 'Didn't you hear me coming?'

'I heard you.' Abby shrugged. 'Where's Lauren?'

'Lauren?' Edward blinked. 'I don't know. I think she's taking a shower. Does it matter?'

'It might.'

Abby was cool, and Edward seemed to realise that all was not as it should be. 'What's the matter?' he asked. 'Why are you giving me that dirty look? Am I in the doghouse?'

Abby hesitated before replying. Then she said quietly, 'You tell me.' She paused, and then went on, 'In fact, you might start by being honest with me for a change.'

Edward snorted. 'I beg your pardon. When haven't I been honest with you? I don't know what you're talking about.'

'Don't you?'

She arched her brows and Edward eyes narrowed, his expression changing in a flash. 'Oh, I get it,' he exclaimed. 'This has something to do with last night, doesn't it? Come on. Spit it out. What lies has Varga been telling about me now?'

Abby stared at him, suddenly realising what he was trying to do. Maybe, thanks to Alejandro, she was beginning to see her brother in a different light. Whatever, she suddenly knew that he was trying to make her feel defensive. He was hoping she'd feel threatened and blurt out everything Alejandro had said.

'Why should you think Alejandro would tell me anything about you?' she asked innocently now. 'I thought all I was supposed to do was persuade him to leave Lauren alone?'

'Well, it was, of course.' Edward scowled. 'But I know Varga better than you do. It would be just like him to try and turn you against me.'

Abby considered her words before replying. 'I don't understand,' she said. 'What could Alejandro possibly say to achieve such a thing?'

Edward's face showed a trace of colour, and he moved his shoulders impatiently. 'I don't know,' he muttered sulkily. 'He—well—he could have made a crack about the fact that I'm always broke.'

Abby felt the first twinges of apprehension. 'You're always broke?' she echoed blankly. 'What are you saying? That

Lauren's father doesn't pay you a living wage? I don't be-lieve it.'

'Why not?' Edward was defensive now. 'You don't know what these people are like, Abby. They want to know how you've spent every cent. God, I can't even play the odds with-out Luis breathing down my neck every minute I'm at the track!'

'You go to the track?' Abby's heart sank. She had hoped that moving to America would cure him of that obsession. 'You do mean the racetrack, don't you? Oh, Eddie, you prom-ised me you wouldn't—'

'Oh, for God's sake, get off my back, why don't you?' Edward was bitter. 'Don't you think I get enough nagging from my wife? I have to have some bloody entertainment. Being the Esquivals' son-in-law isn't all fun, I can tell you that.'

Abby drew a careful breath. 'And—Alejandro knows about this? About your gambling, I mean?'

'I thought he might.' Edward tried to sound offhand. 'Like he knows everything else.' He waited a beat, and then he added grimly, 'These people all stick together, Abbs. I bet the thugs at the track are friends of his.'

'What thugs at the track?'

But Edward was suddenly hooking his crutches beneath his arms, getting ready to leave her. 'It doesn't matter,' he said shortly. 'It's not your concern.'

'Do you owe Alejandro money?' she asked, dreading his answer, her hand on his arm preventing him from getting up 'Is that what this is really all about?'

Edward swore then, surprising her with his vehemence. 'No,' he muttered angrily. 'What do you think I am? If I owed Varga money don't you think the Esquivals would have heard of it?'

'I don't know.' Despite her own dealings with Alejandro— or perhaps because of them—she didn't think he would betray a confidence. 'So why are you afraid of him?' she persisted. 'It's not because of Lauren. I know that.'

'How do you know?' Edward wasn't prepared to back down so easily. 'You know nothing about us. About the problems we have. Did you know, for instance, that Lauren's desperate to have a baby? These people put a lot of store in having children. We've been trying for two years and I haven't been able to come up with the goods yet.'

Abby gazed at him. She remembered what Lauren had said on her arrival. About the fact that things had been difficult for them in recent months. She thought she knew what she meant now. And Alejandro had nothing to do with it.

'Maybe that's why she spends so much time with Varga,' Edward continued aggressively, and Abby's hand fell from his arm as his words gathered strength. 'How do I know he's not trying to give her a baby? She spends enough time with him, goodness knows.'

'Don't be ridiculous!'

But Abby pressed a hand to her stomach as she chided him. She was feeling sick suddenly, and it wasn't easy to hide her feelings either. Alejandro had assured her that it wasn't true, that he had no interest in the younger woman. But could she trust him when she couldn't even trust her own brother?

'Why is it ridiculous?' Edward demanded now, staring at her suspiciously. 'That joker hates me, doesn't he? My God, what did the bastard say? Here I was, thinking you'd be having a cosy session getting it together with lover boy, and all the time you were pulling yours truly apart.'

Abby cringed at his accusation. But she couldn't allow him to get away with it without making an attempt to stand up for herself. 'So that *was* what you wanted,' she said, unable to keep the distaste out of her voice. 'You really did expect me to go to bed with Alejandro. But not because you suspected he was involved with Lauren. How much do you owe him, Eddie? You might as well tell me. I'm going to find out anyway.'

'I've told you, I don't owe him a cent,' retorted her brother harshly. 'All right, I may have asked him for a loan. But he wouldn't do anything to help me.'

'And you thought if I—if we—' Abby couldn't finish the sentence. 'You thought he might loan me the money.' Her face mirrored her contempt and she found it hard to look at him. 'Don't you know a man like Alejandro doesn't have to pay for it? Besides, wasn't it you who told me he was married, just to stop me from having any ideas about him myself?'

'I thought I was doing you a favour.' Edward hunched his shoulders. 'Anyway, why bring that up now?'

'Because it's relevant,' said Abby coldly. 'You use people, Eddie. You didn't want me to get involved with Alejandro, so you told him some cock-and-bull story that I was engaged. That is true, isn't it?' She could tell from his face that it was. 'I've only just realised what Alejandro meant when he asked me about my engagement. You let him think I wasn't interested in him.'

'Well, you weren't.'

'How do you know that?' Abby felt cold inside now, cold and disillusioned. 'You didn't think about me at all, only what was best for you. What's the matter, Eddie? Were you afraid I'd be looking over your shoulder every time you strayed out of line?'

Edward grunted. 'It wasn't that simple. This was a new start for me. I didn't want—I didn't want—'

'Me screwing it up?' Abby felt hurt now, and angry. 'But now you need my help so you thought you'd take advantage of me again?'

'No—'

'Yes.' Abby couldn't bear to look at him. 'You disgust me, Eddie. You really do.' She hesitated, and then, deciding she had nothing to lose, she added painfully, 'I was pregnant when you told your pitiful little lies two years ago. When you decided to—mess up my life, I was expecting Alejandro's child!'

'No!'

The awed whisper came from somewhere behind them, and for an awful moment Abby thought Alejandro had come upon them, unobserved. But then the realisation that it had been a female voice brought her instantly to her feet.

'Lauren,' she said weakly, as the younger woman moved out of the shade of the awning. 'I—I didn't realise you were there.'

'Obviously not,' said Lauren evenly, but her eyes had turned to her husband in open enquiry.

'How long have you been there?' demanded Edward, struggling to his feet and casting a killing glance at his sister. 'I don't know what you think you've heard, but Abby was just letting off steam because she's got to go home.'

Lauren ignored him, her gaze returning to her sister-in-law now. 'You said you were expecting Alejandro's baby,' she prompted, causing Abby's heart to plummet. 'I did not know you knew my mother's cousin so well.'

'She didn't,' said Edward shortly, scowling at his sister. 'He must have—had sex with her the night of our wedding. That was all it was.'

Abby flinched at his callous dismissal of her relationship with Alejandro. Yet wasn't he right? Hadn't she been as easy as he accused her of being? She hadn't even had the sense to insist that Alejandro used protection. She'd been so frantic, so mindlessly eager, so afraid that he'd change his mind.

Lauren was waiting for her reply, and Abby took a steadying breath before saying flatly, 'It was a mistake.' It let her brother off the hook, but what the hell? She didn't want his broken relationship on her hands, too. 'It should never have happened. I lost the baby just a few weeks into term.'

Lauren pressed her hands to her mouth. 'Oh, Abby,' she said, her eyes filling with tears. 'I am so sorry. You must have been devastated.'

Abby couldn't let her think that. 'It wasn't so bad,' she lied. 'It would have been hard for me to bring a baby up on my own.'

'Of course.' Lauren nodded. 'Now I understand about your broken engagement. Edward told us what had happened, but didn't tell us why.'

'No.' Abby had to force herself not to look at her brother. She'd suspected what he'd done, but it wasn't the same as having it confirmed in this way. 'And now, if you'll excuse me, I'd like to go and pack. I'm leaving this afternoon. I have to get back to England, you see.'

'But what about Alejandro?' exclaimed Lauren, staring at Abby through lashes still wet with unshed tears. 'You must tell him what happened, Abigail. He deserves to know the truth—'

'No!'

'Dear God, no!'

Edward and Abby both spoke at once, and this time her brother had her full support. 'You must not mention a word of this to Varga,' he snarled. 'Are you out of your mind? He'd never forgive her for not telling him. Can't you see that?'

'I think you are afraid that he might blame you, Edward,' declared Lauren in her clear, slightly accusing, voice. 'I was coming to tell you, *cara*. They have found the men who trashed our apartment. Alejandro had his suspicions after learning that you owed money to some people at Hialeah Park, and with his help the police were able to arrest the guilty ones.'

CHAPTER FIFTEEN

ABBY took a taxi to her own tiny flat in Notting Hill when she got back to London. She argued with herself that it was early morning, that Ross wouldn't want to meet her and miss taking his first class of the day. But what she really meant was that she didn't want her fiancé turning up at the airport; didn't want to spend the best part of an hour making small talk on their journey into town.

In actual fact she'd been deliberately vague about her plans when she'd spoken to Ross before leaving Florida. She told herself it was because she hadn't decided what she was going to do yet, but that wasn't really true. She knew she was going to have to find a way to break her engagement. And that wasn't going to be easy when, as far as he was concerned, nothing had changed.

But things had changed for her. She'd changed, she acknowledged, after paying the driver and rummaging through her bag for her keys. It wasn't just the relief of knowing that Lauren knew about Edward's gambling, or that Alejandro had known what her brother was doing all along. It was the realisation that, long before Alejandro's behaviour had been justified, she'd realised that her feelings for him were not going to go away.

Which was stupid when it was obvious that he despised her. He thought the only reason she'd let him touch her was to save her brother's skin. And it was too late now to tell him that she hadn't been thinking about Edward when she'd kissed him—even if he wanted to hear it. Their whole relationship had been dogged with lies and half-truths, and although it wasn't all her fault he was never going to believe her now.

Endearingly, it had been Lauren who had begged her not to

leave without seeing him. Lauren who had so easily explained her own involvement with Alejandro when she'd admitted she was receiving treatment to help her conceive. Alejandro had been paying her medical bills. She was desperate for a baby, as Edward had said, and she hadn't wanted to tell her parents or worry her husband when she knew they were short of cash.

Of course her brother had maintained he'd known nothing about it. Whether he had nor not, Abby didn't know, but it was a relief to know that Lauren still loved him in spite of his faults. She was even going to ask her father to loan them the money to pay off Edward's debts. And, although Abby guessed her brother was going to have some difficult times ahead, perhaps that was the only way he was going to learn.

If only they could all have such a happy ending, she reflected ruefully, inserting her key in the lock and pushing open the door. Surprisingly, there was no pile of mail in the hallway, as she'd expected, and as she went into the living room she heard the radio playing in the kitchen annex next door.

She didn't have time to panic, however. She had barely registered that there was someone in the flat before Ross put his head round the door. 'Surprise, surprise,' he said, evidently expecting her to be delighted. 'I had a free first lesson, so old Banks said I could come in later on.'

Abby dropped her haversack onto the floor. She'd left her suitcase in the hall and she had the unpleasant feeling that she was a stranger in her own home. How had Ross got in? To her knowledge, he didn't have a key. All right, perhaps she should have given him one, but this had always been the place where she could escape from everyone. It had been her bolt-hole ever since the house she'd shared with Edward had had to be sold.

Ross had come fully into the room now, and was advancing on her with arms outstretched. 'Hey, what's wrong?' he asked, his brows drawing together. 'I thought you'd be pleased to see me. I've got a pot of coffee brewing, and there's toast and bacon under the grill.'

Abby could hardly hide her revulsion. She'd been offered

bacon and eggs on the plane and she hadn't been able to eat them then either. She felt sick, not just with the change in time zones, but with apprehension. She so much didn't want to face this confrontation now.

Ross's arms dropped when he saw her expression. 'Oh, hey!' he exclaimed. 'I've been thoughtless, haven't I? You're not feeling well. What was it? A rough trip? The gales across the Atlantic can be murder. I remember once, when I was coming back from New York, we had to have our seatbelts on the whole—'

Abby held up her hand to stop him. 'How did you get in, Ross?' she asked, cutting him off in full flow.

'How did I get in?' Ross blinked. 'With my key, of course.' He pulled a face. 'I didn't break in, if that's what you're thinking. After I'd spoken to your brother, I had the bright idea of staying the night here.'

'You've been here all night?' Abby was incredulous. 'And how did you have a key to this place? I've never given you one.'

'No, well, I guessed that was just an oversight, so I had one made weeks ago,' said Ross comfortably. 'Now, aren't you glad I did? It wouldn't have been much fun to come home to an empty flat.'

Abby thought it would have been heaven, but she couldn't say that, so she said faintly. 'You say you've spoken to Edward?'

'Last night,' agreed Ross calmly. 'I wanted to speak to you, of course, but he told me you'd already left for the airport. I did think about coming to meet you at Heathrow, but this seemed the better option. I know you don't much feel like talking when you've come off a long flight.'

Abby took a deep breath. 'You shouldn't have bothered,' she said, trying to hide her frustration. It wasn't his fault that she'd made such a mess of her life.

'Well, take off your jacket,' he said now, evidently deciding not to press his luck by being too affectionate. 'Like I say, I've got some coffee in the kitchen. I'm sure you'd like a cup.'

'Not right now,' said Abby, unbuttoning her jacket almost automatically. And then, remembering what she was doing, she added. 'As a matter of fact, it's probably just as well you're here. We have to talk.'

Ross looked doubtful. 'Oh, I don't think we have time to talk about your trip now,' he said, glancing at his wristwatch. 'By my reckoning we've just got time to have breakfast together and then I'll have to go. I know I told Banks I'd be late, but we don't want to offend him, do we? I mean, especially when he was so understanding about you taking time off—'

'Ross, please!' Abby wished he would just shut up and let her speak. Didn't he realise she was on edge? She had virtually accused him of trespassing, for God's sake. Yet he happily went on trampling over everything she said.

'I'll get the coffee—'

'No!'

'No?' He looked confused. And then he noticed she wasn't wearing her engagement ring. 'Oh, Abby,' he exclaimed, 'don't say you've lost your ring? That was a very expensive ring, you know. I expected you to be more careful—'

'I haven't lost it,' she cried, scrabbling in her bag and bringing out the offending item. She held it out to him. 'That's what I wanted to tell you. I'm sorry, Ross. I'd have liked to give you more warning, but—well, I think you should take this back.'

Ross made no attempt to take the ring. 'You're not serious,' he said disbelievingly. 'You're tired. You don't know what you're saying.'

'Oh, I do.' Abby had never been so sure of anything in her life. 'I've thought about it and thought about it, and my feelings aren't going to change. I wish I didn't have to say this, but I can't marry you, Ross. I'm sorry.'

Ross's face was tight. 'This is your brother's doing, isn't it?' he said angrily. 'I knew I shouldn't have let you go out there.'

'You couldn't have stopped me,' said Abby, disliking his

proprietorial attitude. 'I thought Edward was badly injured and I had to go and see for myself.'

'That he wasn't,' said Ross sarcastically. 'Apart from that emotional stress you made so much of. For Pete's sake, Abby, don't be such a fool! We've got so much going for us: similar backgrounds, similar interests, similar jobs.'

And how depressing that sounded suddenly. Maybe she was being foolish. Maybe she'd never find another man as patient as Ross. Or another man who'd want a woman who couldn't give him children, she reminded herself painfully. But that was her tragedy, not his.

Whatever happened, she didn't love Ross. She knew that now. She'd probably known it even before she'd got on the plane to Miami. That was why she'd felt so strange, seeing his ring on her finger. She'd never intended to let things go so far.

Nevertheless, seeing Alejandro again had altered everything. Until then she'd been able to fool herself into thinking that what she'd felt for him had died along with their child. Now she knew it wasn't true. She'd never stopped loving Alejandro. She had hated him sometimes, but her real feelings had never changed.

'I'm sorry,' she said again now, putting the diamond ring down on the coffee table that stood between them. 'I'd like to be able to blame Eddie, too, but it's not true, Ross. He had nothing to do with my decision. I thought I loved you, but I don't. I like you. I like you a lot. But that's not enough to base a marriage on.'

He looked mutinous, but she noticed that he bent and picked up the ring and slipped it into his trouser pocket before he spoke again. 'So what now?' he demanded. 'Are you going back to Florida? I suppose your brother has finally persuaded you to settle over there.'

As if!

'Of course I'm not going back to Florida,' Abby answered. Her lips twisted. She doubted if she'd ever go to Florida again. 'I'll be going back to work next week. I expect we'll see one another in the staffroom, as usual. I'm hoping we can still be friends.'

Ross's face brightened. 'You're coming back to school?' he exclaimed. 'Well—of course we can still be friends.'

'Good.'

Abby was relieved, but she had the feeling Ross hadn't given up hope of her changing her mind. He probably thought she was just testing the waters. Perhaps it would be best to look for another appointment after all.

After Ross had gone, Abby collected her suitcase from the hall and loaded the washer. Then, going into her bedroom, she quickly stripped the bed. It was childish, she knew, but she couldn't bear the thought that Ross had slept there. She needed to make a fresh start, and clean sheets and pillowcases were a beginning.

And during the days that followed she did try to pick up the pieces of her life. Going back to work helped, so long as she could avoid any *tête-à-têtes* with her ex-fiancé. The children she taught, the teachers she worked with, were all reassuringly familiar, and she was soon caught up in the day-to-day activities of the school.

Only in her quieter moments, and when she got to bed at night, did she succumb to her emotions. She found herself remembering how she'd felt when she'd been pregnant with Alejandro's child. Not unnaturally, now she found herself wishing she could have had the baby. At least she would have had some part of him to love.

As she'd suspected, Ross had apparently decided that all she needed was a breathing space. When she encountered him in the staffroom he insisted on behaving as if it was only a matter of time before she took back his ring. She didn't know what he'd told his colleagues. She'd made it perfectly clear to her friends that the engagement was over. But Ross's skin was thicker, and he couldn't seem to accept that she wasn't going to change her mind again.

Perhaps that was her fault, too, she reflected, when she left work late one afternoon at the end of April to find Ross waiting at the gates. He'd known she'd stayed back that day to meet the parents of one of her students. And, although it was only a short walk from the school to her flat, he'd evidently decided to wait and give her a lift.

It was a pleasant afternoon. The almond blossom was out on the trees and Abby had been looking forward to the walk through the park that adjoined her square. Besides, she had no intention of giving Ross false hope by accepting his invitation. It had been thoughtful of him to wait, but he had to realise he was wasting his time.

'Everything okay?' he asked as she came through the gate, almost as if his waiting for her was still the usual thing. 'Who was it you had to see?'

'It was Shelly Lawson's parents,' said Abby, wishing she could just walk past him. 'What are you doing here, Ross? Did you have a meeting, too?'

'As if you didn't know,' he said, indicating his car parked on the street. 'Come on. I'll buy you a cup of coffee and a Danish. You look as though you could do with a break.'

Abby expelled a sigh. 'Ross—'

'Look, I know what you're going to say. I'd got no right to assume that you'd be glad to see me. But, hell, Abby, how long is this going to go on? It's already been five weeks!'

Abby shook her head. 'Go home, Ross. That's where I'm going. I'll see you tomorrow—'

'No, you won't.' To her astonishment, Ross grabbed her arm and prevented her from moving away. 'Like I say, I've been patient, but you've got to stop all this nonsense. I'm not going to be turned away like an unwanted toy.'

Abby stared at him incredulously. 'Ross, what do you think you're doing? Let go of my arm. You're hurting me.'

'Well, that's par for the course,' he said angrily. 'When you hurt people you have to expect to be hurt in return. You've made a fool of me, Abby, and I'm not going to stand for it. You're coming home with me and we're going to sort this out.'

Abby gasped. 'No.'

'Yes.' Ross started propelling her across the pavement. 'It's not as if there's anyone else. You ought to be grateful to me for taking pity on you. Everyone knows what a sad life you've led since Edward moved to the States and married that Spik!'

Abby's jaw dropped in horror at his words, but before she could respond a long shadow fell across the path. As Ross had been wrestling her towards his car another vehicle had cruised to a halt behind it. A tall, dark-clad individual had thrust open the door and uncoiled his long length from behind the wheel.

'Is something wrong, Abigail?'

The dark, disturbing tones were unmistakable. Managing to wrench her arm free of Ross's grasp, she turned and saw the Cuban standing negligently beside his car. His elegant suit and the shadow of stubble on his jawline were in stark contrast to Ross's sports coat and bearded countenance. Yet, despite the hollows beneath his eyes, Alejandro had never looked better or more familiar.

'Who the hell is this?' demanded Ross, unwilling to lose the initiative, and Alejandro inclined his head towards the other man.

'I am the cousin of the—er—Spik who married Abigail's brother,' he replied, and Abby's heart sank at the knowledge that he had heard Ross's coarse indictment. 'And you must be—'

'Abby's fiancé,' Ross put in aggressively, the colour in his cheeks the only indication he felt any shame.

'Her ex-fiancé,' she corrected him tersely. Then, managing to recover her composure, she turned to Alejandro, 'I must apologise for Ross's rudeness. He's not usually so crass. I'm afraid he's had a trying day.'

Alejandro's eyes were disturbingly intent as they appraised her. 'And you, *cara*,' he said softly. 'Have you had a trying day, too?'

'A long one,' she said. Then, nervously, 'What are you doing here, Alejandro? Did Eddie ask you to come and see me?' She paled a little at this thought. 'Nothing's wrong, is there?'

'With your brother, no,' Alejandro assured her smoothly. 'He is able to walk again and he is hoping to return to work in a few weeks.' He glanced thoughtfully at Ross before adding, 'I went to your flat, but it was unoccupied. Your neighbour directed me here.'

'You went to her flat?' echoed Ross, his face darkening ominously. 'I don't know who you are, friend, but you've got no right to turn up uninvited at Abby's door.'

'First, I am no friend of yours,' said Alejandro, his mouth twisting distastefully. 'And, as Ms Leighton was trying to get away from you when I arrived, perhaps you are no friend of hers either. In any event, if I understand her correctly, you are no longer her fiancé. I suggest you do as she says and go home.'

Ross snorted, stiffening his spine and squaring up to the other man. 'And if I don't?' he said challengingly, evidently spoiling for a fight. 'What are you going to do about it?'

Abby stifled a groan. 'Please, Ross,' she said desperately. 'Do as he says. I'll—I'll speak to you tomorrow. Alejandro's an old friend. I'll be perfectly all right with him.'

Ross's brows drew together. 'How old a friend?' he asked suspiciously. 'How long have you known him? Why haven't I heard about him before? Did you meet him when you went to Edward's wedding? Is that what he means when he says he's related to Edward's wife?'

Abby sighed. 'Well—yes. If you must know.' She cast a glance towards Alejandro, hoping he wasn't listening to this. She lowered her voice. 'Ross, please, this is not your business.' She took a breath. 'Just go home.'

But Ross seemed indifferent to her pleading. 'How well do you know him?' he demanded. 'Am I allowed to ask that?'

'I think you have asked enough,' broke in Alejandro, and Abby knew he'd been listening all along. 'How well Abigail and I know one another is our business. As she says, it is no concern of yours.'

'It is if you know the bastard who got her pregnant and abandoned her,' retorted Ross outrageously, his words chilling

Abby to the bone. 'I guess you didn't know about that,' he added, as Alejandro rocked back on his heels as if someone had struck him. 'Yeah, Abby thinks people here don't know what happened, but she's wrong. She'd just come back from her brother's wedding, and you don't spend over a week in the gynaecological ward of the hospital without people talking. I guess she lost the kid, but I'm not supposed to know. All she told me was that she couldn't have children, and that suited me. I get enough of them at school every day. I never wanted any of my own.'

ABBY didn't wait to hear any more. She wanted to die, she thought sickly. She could think of nothing she wanted more than for the earth to open up and swallow her. She didn't want to live. She'd didn't want to see the shock and horror on Alejandro's face. Nor did she want to have to defend herself to him. He hadn't known, he wasn't meant to know, and that was how she'd wanted it to stay.

Turning on her heel, she almost ran across the road, uncaring of the traffic, which fortunately was light. She could hear Ross calling her name, but she didn't answer. Right now she couldn't bear to look at him. How could she have ever contemplated spending her life with him?

She reached the park unharmed and set off swiftly along the path. She expected one or both of them would follow her, but if she could get into her flat she needn't open the door to anyone. All right, Ross had a key, but there were bolts at the top and bottom of the door. Surely one of them would respect her privacy. What had happened was her loss, no one else's.

As for Alejandro, she couldn't imagine what he must be thinking. He would probably consider the fact that she had been expecting his child without telling him a betrayal of the highest order. Yes, he'd been married, but Edward's story now was that he and his wife had been virtually separated. Would she have told him in those circumstances if she hadn't lost the child?

The answer was probably no, she conceded. After all, as far as she'd been concerned Alejandro hadn't wanted to see her again. They had had a one-night-stand, the kind of thing she would never have dreamed she was capable of. And, because of that, she'd spent the last two years trying to come to terms with it.

She'd thought she'd succeeded. She'd really thought that her relationship with Ross was all she wanted out of life. Or perhaps all that she deserved, she concluded sadly. She'd thought she was depriving him of the chance to become a father, before realizing it suited him far better than her.

But what had he hoped to gain, blurting it out like that? Did he suspect Alejandro was the man involved? And was it true that everyone at the school knew she'd had a miscarriage? My God, had Ross discussed her with the other teachers? Had they all speculated about who might be to blame?

Abby was feeling more and more desperate. It was a nightmare, she thought. How could she ever face her colleagues again? And Alejandro... Well, she couldn't even bear to think about how Alejandro might be feeling. Was he angry? Did he hate her? Or was he just full of contempt for the way she'd behaved?

To her surprise—and to her relief—she reached her flat without incident. There was no sign of Ross's car in the square; no sleek black Mercedes like the one Alejandro had apparently hired. Perhaps they'd both decided she wasn't worth bothering about, she thought painfully. It wouldn't be the first time she'd been on her own.

She was making herself a cup of tea with shaking hands when she heard a key rattling in the lock. But she'd bolted the door behind her, and now she was glad she had.

'Abby!' shouted Ross, evidently putting his mouth close to the letterbox. 'Open the door, Abby. I want you to see what that bastard has done to me.'

Abby groaned. What now? she wondered wearily. Didn't Ross realise he'd said enough? Besides, as far as Alejandro resorting to physical violence was concerned, she didn't believe it. He was far too laid-back to get into a fight over a woman he hardly knew.

'Go away, Ross,' she called, going out into the hall so he

could hear her. 'I don't want to speak to you now. In fact, I don't know if I'll ever want to speak to you again.'

'Oh, come on, Abby.' Ross was harsh. 'We both know you need me. Just because Varga's given me a black eye doesn't mean he's going to be hanging about.'

Abby's fingers trembled as she tore back the bolts and wrenched open the door. But when Ross would have stepped inside, she blocked him, her eyes turning incredulously to his face.

He was right. He did have the makings of a black eye. The skin around his eye looked puffed and sore, his eyelid swelling ominously over the pupil.

Her lips parted. 'Alejandro did this?' she breathed incredulously, and Ross took a belligerent stance.

'You needn't look so pleased about it,' he snapped. 'Now, are you going to let me in? I think you owe me an explanation. Who is this man Varga, for God's sake? Don't tell me he was the father of your child?'

Abby's mouth closed. 'I'm not going to tell you anything, Ross,' she said quietly. 'And as far as owing you an explanation is concerned, you can't be serious. You shamed me. You embarrassed me and humiliated me. And don't pretend you were doing it for my own good. I've never felt so awful in my life.'

Ross's jaw jutted. 'Well, you had to know sooner or later. People aren't fools, Abby. Women particularly gossip about stuff like that. I mean, they know something happened to prevent you from having children. What other explanation could there be?'

Abby stiffened. 'How do they know I can't have children?' she demanded.

Ross sighed. 'Well—I may have said something,' he muttered unwillingly, and Abby sagged against the door.

Then, straightening, she said, 'I meant what I said before. Go away, Ross. Go away, and don't ever come near me again.'

She slammed the door then, leaning back against it as hot tears flooded her eyes. My God, and she'd thought she could trust him. He was just like Edward. He said whatever was necessary to get his own way.

She had papers to mark, but she dumped them all on the table in the living room, too distressed to attempt any kind of work. Instead, she rescued her tea and curled up on the couch, trying not to think about the future. Her whole world seemed to be tumbling about her and she didn't know what she was going to do.

She supposed she ought to feel something about Alejandro's treatment of her ex-fiancé. Some gratitude, perhaps, that he had felt compelled to act in her defence. But she couldn't help wondering if he hadn't acted as he had because he'd been so furious about what Ross had told him. Alejandro was a proud man, and he probably thought she'd made him look like a fool.

Whatever, she thought wearily, there was nothing she could do about it now. The only thing she could hope for was that rumours didn't start flying about the school. If anyone had seen the fracas—and there had still been students about, she remembered—it would soon reach the ears of the head teacher.

She must have been sitting there for over an hour when someone knocked at her door. Ross, she thought tiredly. When was he going to realise their relationship was over? But then she remembered she hadn't bolted the door again after he'd left earlier. Surely if it had been Ross he'd have used his key first and argued later.

Getting to her feet, she went to the hall door and called, 'Who is it?' It was almost dark, the bright day giving way to an overcast sky. She seldom opened the door at this time of the evening without identifying her caller. It wasn't wise to take any chances, however unlikely danger might be.

'Abigail?'

Alejandro's voice was low and unmistakably weary. As soon as she heard it she knew she'd been half hoping that he might come. But why? she asked herself. Whatever had brought him to London, Ross's words had destroyed any empathy between them. And besides, after the way he'd behaved on his boat, she was foolish if she thought he was here because of her.

But she couldn't ignore him. Not when he had taken the trouble to come to the flat. So, abandoning any hope of disguising the tears she'd shed earlier, she rubbed brisk hands over her cheeks and opened the door.

She didn't know what she'd anticipated. Maybe some evidence of the fight he'd had with Ross. Perhaps she'd half expected him to be sporting a black eye, too. But apart from his drawn expression, which had not been there earlier, he looked much the same as he'd looked before.

Alejandro had been propped against the wall beside the door, but now he straightened. 'Do you want me to come in?' he asked, and she realised he wasn't angry with her.

'I—of course,' she said, stepping back so that he could move past her. She closed the door and followed him into the living room. 'So—this is a surprise.'

Alejandro turned in the middle of the living room floor, his size immediately dwarfing the apartment. 'But not a pleasant one,' he said, and she knew he'd noticed her swollen eyes. 'Is Kenyon here? I would like to apologise to him.'

Abby gasped. She couldn't help it. 'No, Ross isn't here,' she said, her heart sinking at the realisation that she'd been completely wrong about his visit. She swallowed. 'What made you think he was?'

'I saw him come here,' said Alejandro simply, his dark eyes shadowed. 'I waited for him to come out again, but his car is still downstairs.'

'His car is still downstairs?' Abby blinked. 'I didn't know that.' She licked her lips. 'He left here over an hour ago. Perhaps the car wouldn't start. That happens sometimes.'

'Ah.' Alejandro sounded thoughtful, but she could tell from his expression he wasn't convinced. 'Or perhaps he thought I would not come here if I thought he was still with you,' he remarked consideringly. 'Your fiancé is a determined man, *cara*. He does not give up.'

'He's not my fiancé,' insisted Abby tersely. But she suspected that was exactly what Ross might have done. He would never expect Alejandro might feel the need to apologise to him. Nevertheless, leaving his car outside was such a childish thing to do.

Alejandro shrugged, his shoulders moving freely beneath the fine wool of his jacket, and Abby couldn't help remembering that evening on his yacht. When he'd held her in his arms. When he'd danced with her and pretended he was going to seduce her. She wished he had. But, like Ross with his car, he'd only been playing a game.

'He's not here,' she repeated, when it seemed obvious something more was expected of her. She hesitated. 'I'm sorry if what he said upset you. You weren't ever supposed to find out.' She wrapped her arms about her midriff, unknowingly protective. 'I know I should have told you when it happened, but—well, I thought you were a happily married man.'

'And this would be because Edward told you?' suggested Alejandro harshly, his expression hardening as he spoke of her brother's involvement in the affair. He swore softly. 'I hope you know now that he was lying to you, Abigail. As he lied to me when I told him I wanted to see you again.'

Abby looked dazed. 'You wanted to see me again?'

'What else?' But Alejandro did not sound as if the knowledge pleased him. 'And I am not talking about today, this week, this month, even this year. *Por l'amor de Dios*, Abigail, I would have come to you after our first meeting. Edward knew that. I told him. I said I wanted to see you again, and he—' His lips twisted. 'He laughed in my face.'

Abby stared at him. 'He laughed?' She couldn't believe it.

'As good as,' said Alejandro dismissively. 'He told me you would not want to see me again. That you already had a fiancé. That you were planning to get married. That you would not welcome me turning up to complicate your life.'

Abby was aghast. 'I didn't know you wanted to see me again,' she got out at last, unable to cope with the implications of Edward's treachery right now. 'Besides, you were married,' she said again. She hesitated a moment, and then added, 'Eddie didn't lie about that.'

'What is that expression? He was economical with the truth.' Alejandro made an impatient gesture. 'I gather he did not tell you that I had already filed for divorce? Maria and I— that was my wife's name—we had separated some weeks before your brother's wedding. Lauren and her parents knew this. I find it hard to believe that Edward did not know this, too.'

'Perhaps he did.' Abby put an unsteady hand to her head. 'I had no idea that he had even spoken to you. When I asked him about you, all he said was that you already had a wife.'

Alejandro swore. 'I believe you,' he said harshly, and Abby noticed how pale he'd suddenly become. 'So—when I was imagining that your behaviour had been unforgivable, you were obviously thinking the same of me?'

'Something like that,' murmured Abby, hardly able to take it all in. Then, noticing that he was swaying on his feet, she indicated the sofa behind him. 'Won't you sit down?'

'*Gracias.*' Alejandro needed no second bidding. With a gesture of apology he sank down onto the sofa and expelled a long sigh. 'Forgive me,' he said. 'It was a long flight and I am tired. I fear the consequences of not sleeping for more than twenty-four hours are catching up with me.'

Abby glanced towards the kitchen. 'Are you thirsty?' she asked anxiously. 'Can I get you something to drink?'

'Sitting down will do it,' Alejandro assured her, loosening the buttons of his jacket. He looked up at her with a brave attempt at a smile. '*Sí*, I am feeling much better already.'

Abby doubted he was. Now that he was below her eye level she could see the shadows of weariness in his face. Dear God, what had Edward said? she wondered. How had he dismissed her behaviour at the wedding? Had Alejandro really thought that she had just been playing a game?

'Are you not going to join me?' he asked now, shifting along so that she could sit beside him. But Abby didn't trust herself to be so near to him when her emotions were in such a chaotic state. Despite what he'd implied, she wasn't sure what he expected of her now.

Instead, she perched on the arm of the chair opposite as she tried to make sense of all he'd said. It seemed apparent that he had come all this way just to see her, but was it to clear the air between them or because he wanted something more?

Before she could say anything, however, Alejandro spoke again. 'I do not blame you for being wary of me,' he observed bitterly. 'What did you think I was doing two years ago, I wonder? You must have believed I had only been amusing myself at your expense. Did you think I seduced you for fun? That I took you to my father's house and made love to you to satisfy some perverted need to prove I could?' His expression mirrored his disgust. 'It was not like that, Abigail. I am not like that, whatever you may have heard.'

'I know that now,' she murmured helplessly. 'And Ross is the first man I have been engaged to. There was no one else.'

'*Cristo!*' Alejandro swore violently. 'No wonder you hated me, *cara*.' His lips twisted. 'Perhaps you hate me still.'

'No.' Abby pushed herself up from the chair, unable to sit still under the accusation burning in his eyes. 'And I don't think you really believe that.'

He arched his dark brows. 'Why not?'

'Well…' Abby struggled to find the right words. 'That night on the yacht—'

'Ah, *sí*.' Alejandro's eyes darkened. 'Let us talk about that night on the yacht. Let us get all the—what do you call it?—the baggage out of the way first. Then we can talk about what is really important, hmm?'

Abby swallowed. 'If you like.' She glanced towards the kitchen once more. 'But, if you don't mind, I think I will make another pot of tea. I—I—' *Need it!* 'I'm thirsty.'

'*Bien.*'

He rose to his feet then, and she was taken aback to find him towering over her again. 'No—I mean, you can stay here,' she said hurriedly. 'Rest. Relax. I won't be long.'

'Do not ask me to wait here like a spurned lover,' he exclaimed huskily. 'Let me come with you. I promise I will not get in the way.'

Abby quivered. His entreating words stirred every nerve in her body, and it was all she could do not to ask him to explain himself there and then. But she had to keep her head, she reminded herself. Just because Alejandro was here that did not mean all her troubles were over.

He was waiting for her answer, and with a little shrug she said, 'Well, all right. But, I warn you, it's nothing like the kitchens you're used to.'

'Do you think I care?' His voice was suddenly thick with emotion, and he put out his hand to tuck a strand of her hair behind her ear. Then he trailed his fingers across her cheek with evident concern. 'You are not going to cry again, are you? I know that man—Ross—must have hurt you, but in his defence I have to say I think he does care about you very much.'

Abby found it difficult to speak, but, steeling herself against the tears that were still pressing, she said, 'I hurt him, too. He's not a bad person. He just—well, I'd rather not talk about it right now.'

'I understand.'

But Alejandro's mouth had tightened a little and his hand dropped to his side. Abby told herself she was glad. She couldn't bear for there to be any more mistakes. And if he had come to England to see her, what had taken him so long?

He stood at the entrance to the tiny kitchen as she plugged in the kettle and prepared a tray. At his nod she added an extra cup, and then waited nervously for the kettle to boil.

'You have lived here long?' he asked politely after a moment, and she explained that she had moved here when Edward went to live in the United States. She didn't add that it had always been her bolthole when the world had seemed an unfriendly place—like when she'd come back from Edward's wedding, for example—or that she would never be able to stand in her kitchen again without seeing him propped against the counter as he was now.

'And Ross?' he probed. 'Did he live here, too?'

'No!' Abby was very definite about that. 'Ross has his own place. A house not far from here.'

Alejandro absorbed this, the lines at either side of his mouth deepening as he continued, 'And do you still care about him? Despite the fact that you are no longer together—?'

'We're no longer together because I don't love Ross,' said Abby tensely, glad that the kettle boiled at that moment, giving her something to do to avoid his eyes. She hesitated. 'Do you—do you take sugar in your tea?'

'I will take it however you want to give it to me,' replied Alejandro roughly. Then, as if he couldn't stand to wait any longer, he said, 'You do know why I was so—so angry that night. The night on the yacht,' he elaborated shortly. 'I really thought you were only there because Edward had asked you to intercede on his behalf.'

Abby's hand shook a little as she placed the teapot on the tray. 'That was why I accepted your invitation,' she admitted unsteadily. 'But then, you know that. That was why you decided to—to teach me a lesson.'

Alejandro uttered an exclamation. 'Is that what you think?'

'I don't blame you,' said Abby hurriedly. 'Until then I'd only had a suspicion that Eddie wasn't telling me the truth. But I got it out of him later. Too late, sadly, to tell you.'

Alejandro's brows drew together. 'But you left the next day,' he exclaimed in protest. 'I had a business meeting in Tallahassee that I couldn't avoid, and by the time I got back you had gone. Your brother took great pleasure in telling me that, whatever I had told you, he didn't need me any more. Luis—proud fool that he is—had agreed to cover your brother's debts. For Lauren's sake, you understand? She still loves him—and the child which is even now growing inside her.'

Abby caught her breath. 'Lauren's pregnant?'

'With God and the IVF clinic's help,' agreed Alejandro drily. 'She is so happy that I do not think my friend could have forbidden her anything. Including his help for that un-grateful son-in-law of his.'

Abby trembled. 'I'm so happy for her,' she said. 'For them both.' She paused. 'When did they find out?'

Alejandro shrugged. 'Lauren had suspected for some time, I think, but she wanted to wait until she was sure before break-ing the news to her husband and her parents.'

'I see.'

'In any case, that is not why I came,' he said shortly. Then, moving forward, 'I will take the tray.'

'No.' Abby put herself between him and the counter. 'I can manage. Please. Just go and sit down.'

'And if I do not?' His eyes were on her deliberately averted face. *'Cara.'* His voice deepened. 'This is not going to work. How long do you think you can keep me at arm's length? I came to see you. Only you. To see if there was any chance that you might give me another chance.'

'Another chance?' The tray forgotten, Abby turned to him. She shook her head. 'But why did you wait so long?'

Alejandro shook his head. 'Why do you think?'

Abby blinked. 'Edward?' Though she couldn't see how her brother could have had anything to do with it.

'Of course Edward,' said Alejandro heavily. 'You have to know that I assumed you were still engaged to this man Ross. *Por Dios,* you were wearing his ring. I had no doubt this time that he did exist.'

Abby stared at him. 'So how did you—?'

'Find out your engagement was ended?' he finished harshly. His lips twisted. 'For reasons best known to himself, but I suspect because Lauren asked him to, Edward admitted that you had broken up with your boyfriend. But that was not until yesterday, you understand? Until then I believed what you had told me. *En realidad*, I thought you probably hated me.'

'I never hated you,' she said huskily. 'Oh, Alejandro, I don't know what to say.'

'Me, either,' he said, straightening and running the knuckles

of one hand down her flushed cheek. 'Can you ever forgive me?'

'Forgive you?'

'For not being there when you needed me,' he said, and she
expelled a sigh.

'But you didn't know.'

'And you think that is a good enough excuse? You do not
think I should have tried to see you again?'

'In the circumstances, probably not,' she conceded tremu-
lously. 'You have to remember, I had just learned that you
were married.'

'*Dios!*' Alejandro's eyes were dark with emotion. 'Such a
tangled web!'

'And mostly of Eddie's making,' said Abby unhappily. 'He
was so desperate to make it on his own. Since our parents died
I've been more like a mother than a sister to him, and he
resents it.'

'You know him too well, *cara*,' said Alejandro softly. 'You
know his faults and his weaknesses whereas I do not. And
because of that I assumed you were just like him. When you
returned to Florida, all I could think about was finding some
way of hurting you as you had hurt me.' He groaned. 'What
a stupid, arrogant fool I was.'

'Alejandro—'

'No, listen to me, *cara*. You have to know how it was.' He
blew out a breath. 'You see, this was not the first time your
brother had found himself in financial difficulties since he
came to the States. A year ago—the details are not important
now—I agreed to help him, mainly because Lauren asked me
to. But on this occasion—' He made a negative gesture. 'I
refused.'

Abby turned horrified eyes towards him. 'Did he return the
money?'

Alejandro sighed. 'That is not important, as I have said.'

'But did he?'

Alejandro hesitated. 'Some,' he admitted at last. 'The

money was not an issue, *cara*. Edward needed to realise he was living beyond his means.'

Abby shivered. 'You knew about those men at the track, didn't you? The ones who broke into their apartment?'

'When you told me what had happened, I suspected,' he agreed. 'And your arrival had been so convenient.'

'I thought Eddie had been badly hurt,' protested Abby weakly. 'I had no idea—'

'No.' Alejandro had moved a little nearer as she was speaking, and now his fingers linked caressingly around her wrist. 'You were worried about him. I know that now. At a guess, I'd say he let you think he was badly injured because he knew how you would feel. If I did not know for a fact that the other driver had been drinking, I would have to wonder if Edward had not caused the accident himself.'

Abby looked down at his fingers, brown against her paler flesh. 'If only I had told you about the baby,' she said huskily, unable to think of anything else when he was touching her. Besides he deserved to hear the story from her lips, not the garbled version Ross had vented on him. 'I wanted to tell you, but—well, you know what I thought. And then, when I miscarried—' She broke off, her voice wobbling revealingly. 'It was as if it was never meant to be.'

'And I knew nothing about it,' said Alejandro grimly. 'Edward should have told me.'

'He didn't know.' Abby was glad she could tell him that, at least. 'No one knew. That is, I thought they didn't. If what Ross said is true, I've been fooling myself for almost two years.'

'But you told him?' Alejandro ventured, his breath warm against her temple.

Abby shook her head. 'Not about you, no.' She paused. 'Just that I couldn't have children. I had no idea he suspected the truth.'

'*Sí.*' Alejandro said the word heavily. 'I knew you were upset when you ran away.' He waited a beat and then went on, 'But I should not have taken my frustration out on him. He was the catalyst, but not the offender. That was my role.'

'No!' Abby lifted her head to stare up at him with tear-washed green eyes. 'It wasn't your fault. It wasn't anybody's fault. Not even Edward's. If I'd been honest with him perhaps he'd have been honest with you. Who knows?'

'You are a very forgiving woman,' said Alejandro, gazing down at her. He lifted his hands to rub them almost possessively up and down her arms. 'Do I dare to hope that you might forgive me also?'

'There's nothing to forgive.' Abby was intensely conscious that there were only inches between them now, and her heart was beating faster every minute. 'Besides,' she added softly, 'Now that you know the truth, you must also realise that there is no future for us.'

'Que?' His reaction was violent. His hands gripped her upper arms with unwarranted strength and there was no mistaking the angry confusion in his eyes. 'What do you mean?' he demanded, practically shaking her in his desire to make her see sense. 'I thought— Surely I cannot have been wrong all along? I thought you cared for me—at least half as much as I care for you.'

'I do—'

'Then—'

'Wait.' Abby's lungs felt as if they were labouring. 'Alejandro, my feelings are not the most important thing here.'

'No?' He looked both puzzled and frustrated now. 'You cannot doubt that I care about you. I love you, Abigail. I have loved you ever since that morning you scrambled out of the Esquivals' swimming pool at my feet.'

Abby closed her eyes against his dark enchantment. It would be so easy to give in, so easy to delude herself that love would be enough. It wasn't. He had proved that by waiting over an hour before coming to see her tonight. He had been stunned by Ross's revelations. He had needed time to come to terms with what the other man had said.

'You forget,' she said with difficulty, 'I can't have another baby. I love you, but I know you want children of your own. For heaven's sake, you're your father's eldest son. When Ross told you—what he told you—you were shattered. I was there, Alejandro. I saw it in your face.'

'What did you see?' Alejandro wouldn't let her go when she tried to pull away from him. 'Did you see distress? Disappointment? Or did you see my pain at your devastation? Can you honestly say what you saw in my eyes?'

Abby was uncertain. 'You can't deny you took a long time to come to the flat.'

'You think it did not hurt me, too?' he demanded. 'You think I can hear that the woman I love has lost my child without feeling totally devastated myself? *Cara*, I needed time to come to terms with it. I admit it. But not because I had any doubts about how I felt.'

Abby shook her head. 'I don't know if I can believe you.'

'Why not?' He gathered her into his arms, pressing his forehead to hers. '*Por Dios*, Abigail, I cannot live without you now. You are my life, my future. You are all I care about. What use would there be for me to marry another woman when the only woman I want has admitted she loves me?'

Some time later, Abby stirred in the rather cramped surroundings of her bed to find Alejandro sound asleep beside her. He had been exhausted, she thought, stretching out a hand to push a lock of silky dark hair back from his temple. But not too exhausted to show her that he meant what he said. He loved her. The unbelievable was true. He loved her. And he didn't care that she was unable to give him another child. They could adopt, he'd told her gently, when she'd persisted in labouring the point. If that was what she wanted. For himself, she would be his wife. She was all he needed.

'What are you thinking?'

Unbeknownst to her, Alejandro's eyes had opened and now he was watching her with a sleepy amorous gaze. She was immediately conscious of the fact that the sheet had fallen

away to reveal the rounded swell of her breasts, but although
she blushed a little she didn't attempt to hide herself.

'I was thinking how much I love you,' she told him honestly. 'And I was also thinking that this bed isn't really big
enough for you.'

'This bed is perfect,' Alejandro contradicted her softly, rolling nearer to bury his face between her warm breasts. 'I hope
you are not suggesting that I should return to my hotel? Apart
from anything else, it is—' he screwed up his eyes to look at
the clock on her bedside table '—two o'clock in the morning.
And I am so comfortable here.'

Abby's lips tilted. 'You don't really think I want you to go,
do you?' she asked, as he lifted his head to nuzzle the curve
of her neck. She wound her arms about his neck. 'I'm just
finding it very hard to believe, that's all.'

'Believe it,' he told her fiercely. 'We are going to spend
every night together from now on.' He grimaced. 'Whatever
your brother has to say about it.'

Abby pulled a rueful face. 'I think he'll be surprised.'

'I do, too, though not perhaps as surprised as you, *cara*. He
knew it was in his best interests to be honest with me. Perhaps
he has realised that I can be of more use to him as a brother-
in-law than an enemy.'

'Oh, Alejandro!'

'"Oh, Alejandro,"' he teased her, mimicking her outrage.
Then his lips found hers with sudden ardour, his leg straddling
her thigh so that she was left in no doubt as to his arousal.
'Te amo, querida,' he murmured, whispering to her in his own
language. 'Do you know how much I love you? How much I
need you? You are my soul. The very meaning of my exis-
tence.'

His tongue slipped between her teeth then, finding the vulnerable contours of her mouth with hungry passion. One hand
slid into her hair, the other cupping her bottom, holding her
close against him.

'Tell me,' he said, his voice thick with emotion. 'Tell me
you love me also. Then perhaps I will let you get some sleep.'

EPILOGUE

ABBY and Lauren were cooling off in the spa bath when Alejandro arrived home.

'Your husband is early,' observed Abby's sister-in-law uneasily, hearing the car, and Abby didn't correct her. But the truth was Alejandro was usually home early. He'd told her he resented every minute he spent away from her.

'I hope I am not interrupting anything,' he remarked a few minutes later, strolling out onto the deck that was steaming after the recent rainstorm. He had shed his tie, but he was still dressed in the suit he'd worn to his office. Although Abby was sure he must feel the heat, he looked as cool and dangerously attractive as ever.

He smiled at his cousin, but it was Abby who held his attention. Circling the tub, he bent and bestowed a lingering kiss on her mouth. Lauren shifted a little awkwardly, but Alejandro had no inhibitions. *'Hola, cara,'* he said, one hand straying sensuously across his wife's bare shoulder. 'Do you mind if I join you?'

Abby, who was used to her husband's outrageous behaviour, hid a smile, but Lauren had been born of more modest genes. 'I must be going,' she said hastily, reaching for the towel she had placed strategically beside her. She gave Alejandro a nervous look. 'Katie will have woken from her nap by now, and you know she doesn't like it if I'm not there to give her her juice.'

Abby reserved judgement. Catriona—Katie—was Edward and Lauren's small daughter. At eighteen months old, she was as pretty and feminine as her mother. Unfortunately, she was also spoiled, by both her parents and her grandparents, and she was becoming quite a tyrant.

'Oh, por favor!' Alejandro pretended to be devastated. 'Do not let me drive you away, *pequeña.*' He glanced down at his wife as he spoke, however, and she saw the wicked humour glinting in his eyes. 'Surely there is room in the tub for three?'

Lauren's lips tightened, and for a moment she looked disagreeably like her mother. 'I am sorry,' she said stiffly, clearly waiting for him to leave so that she could get out and wrap herself in the enveloping folds of the towel. 'I am sure you and your wife would prefer to be alone.'

Alejandro would have continued to tease her, but a look from his wife deterred him. 'You may be right,' he murmured, brushing his lips across Abby's head before heading for the sliding doors. 'If you will excuse me, I will go and get changed.'

However, as he entered the building another sound invaded the heat-laden air. A baby's cry, swiftly hushed, had him casting a wry backward glance at his wife.

'No,' he said imploringly, but Abby was already getting to her feet, climbing out of the pool, wrapping a towel about her nakedness with an innocent disregard for Lauren's feelings.

'Yes,' she said, catching up with her husband in a few barefoot strides. 'It is his teatime.' She had fastened the towel sarong-wise under her arms, and now she caught Alejandro's arm in a possessive grasp. 'It serves you right,' she added in an undertone, pressing against him. 'You were teasing Lauren mercilessly. You know how she feels about bathing in the nude.'

'She did not have to worry,' Alejandro assured her drily as they entered the spacious living room. 'She should know by now that I am not interested in looking at her naked body. I merely thought it would have been fun for us all to enjoy the tub together.'

'No, you didn't,' Abby contradicted him, but then he turned the tables on her by loosening the towel and gathering her into his arms.

'Tell me you are not going to spend the next hour feeding

our son,' he demanded pleadingly, burying his face in the damp hollow of her neck. 'I want you all to myself.'

'Hardly an hour,' murmured Abby, a catch in her voice. 'Darling, I'm going to lose the towel completely if you don't let me go.'

'I do not want to let you go,' he informed her thickly. *'Ah, cara, quiero hacerte el amor!'*

'And I want to make love with you, too,' responded Abby, who had learned quite a bit of Spanish in the past couple of years. 'But Antonio is hungry and my breasts are aching.'

Alejandro closed his eyes. 'Lucky Antonio,' he muttered, and then, opening them again, he helped her adjust the towel once more. 'I hope he realises what I am sacrificing for his sake.'

Abby dimpled. 'I am sure he does,' she murmured. Then, more soberly, 'And we are so lucky to have him.'

'Hmm.' Alejandro pulled a wry face. 'I know. Although I sometimes think that if you had not been so sure you would not conceive again we might have taken more care than we did. I never intended us to have a baby just eighteen months after we were married.'

Abby smiled. 'But you're glad we have him, aren't you?'

'Our son?' Alejandro cupped her face between his hands. *'Querida*, you have no idea how proud I felt when you told me you were carrying our child. And watching him grow inside you...' He pressed a kiss to the corner of her mouth. 'That was—indescribable.'

The baby's cry could be heard again, and although the nursemaid was doing her best Abby knew that he would not settle until she had fed him.

'I won't be long,' she promised, escaping from her husband's arms with real regret. 'And afterwards—'

'Afterwards I will make up for lost time,' Alejandro assured her huskily. He stepped nearer. 'I suckled at your breasts long before he did,' he added, his hands straying irresistibly to the fullness outlined beneath the towelling. Then, restraining himself, 'Now I will see our cousin off the premises before she dies of embarrassment.'

Abby's laugh was soft and intimate. 'Don't be long,' she said. 'Oh, and by the way, she told me that Edward has finally finished paying off his debts. Whatever you say about Luis, he is not as soft as he appears. I think he and Edward are going to be good for one another.'

'Let us hope so.' Alejandro cupped her cheek. 'But I have to tell you, right now it does not interest me greatly.' Antonio's cry was becoming a little more urgent and he scowled. 'I have other matters to contend with,' he observed, glancing into the hall, where the stairs rose to the upper floor. 'Go and feed our son, *cara*. He sounds almost as impatient as I am.'

Abby started towards the door, but his voice caused her to glance round once more. 'I love you,' he said simply, and Abby's heart turned over.

'I love you, too,' she whispered. '*Te quiero, Alejandro. Tu eres mi vida.* You are my life.'

LET'S TALK

Romance

For exclusive extracts, competitions
and special offers, find us online:

☑ facebook.com/millsandboon

🐦 @MillsandBoon

📷 @MillsandBoonUK

Get in touch on 01413 063232

For all the latest titles coming soon, visit
millsandboon.co.uk/nextmonth